DAWN SKY RISING
H A WALKER

CONTENTS

CONTENT WARNINGS

Dawn Sky Rising is a new adult fantasy novel that contains the following:

Animal cruelty and death

Explicit sex scenes

Mild torture, grievous injury, blood and imprisonment

Death of a parent/family member and themes of grief/depression.

Attempted suicide (on page but very brief and not in the character's POV.) Prevention of suicide (on page, several lines from character's POV.)

Birth trauma (off page) Child loss (off page)

This tale contains scenes of violence from the outset. Tread with care through the Boreals and, as always, keep an eye on the skies.

For Brydee, our little fighter.

And for you, dear reader, the dawn will always break through the
darkness.

Tarrain Sea

Petowin

Colladon

River Niem

The Searp

Lake Somaro

Lake Sakora

Doradar

Mount Ghel

Lake Rovesi

Lake Rovan

Mount Serebo

Moray Castle

Lake Wylda

Glentay Forest

Mount Bronzo

The Stone Cabin

Reckforton Castle

Aarine

The Moorlands

River Breccan

Harracombe Moor

Selmon Moor

Saltfen

Ilrair

Oroton

The Roost

Pineris

The Adacus residence

Orman

Cape of Kitrinos

SHROUDED strait

OMIARRE

Alsida Archipelago

OMICHAR

The Boreals

PROLOGUE

CALLIOPE

There was a face under the night-washed ice.

From my vantage point on a snow-covered branch of birch, the Nokken was of no threat to me. Only to the humans that were running through the forest, rushing closer and closer to the semi-frozen lake.

In my owl form, I could hear their frantic, muffled footsteps and racking breaths. Four adults and ... and a child. Behind them, gaining ground at sickening speed, came ten horsemen.

I had no business in the fates of the humans, none whatsoever. That had not changed since I'd inherited my shifter magic, passed down from mother to daughter, on my eleventh birthday, and I had taken to the remote northern forests to protect myself.

These may have been the first people I'd seen in years, but I was not about to step in to save them. No. Not the adults ... or the child. I would watch and preserve their passage through the forest in my mind for as long as I drew breath. But I would not save them. Not from the Nokken or the horsemen who harried them.

Ice cracked close to the shore of the lake, as the Nokken swam up to the surface, its equine eyes glowing pale green in the darkness. My snow-white, gold-tipped feathers rustled, and my talons gripped the birch branch with iron strength.

Galloping hooves thundered over the ferns and bracken, and the family of five finally broke free of the undergrowth. Even at this distance, I could see the beads of sweat on their flushed faces and the threads of fabric that had been torn apart from their clothes.

Golden eyes piercing the dark, I gazed at the child being carried by one of the two women running. A small boy, no older than five, clung to his mother's neck, wide-eyed and pale. It took all my strength not to take flight, despite sorrow gripping and slicing through my heart.

I could not intervene. Would *not* intervene, for my own safety. I couldn't risk it.

The family raced for the frozen water's edge, oblivious to the danger that lurked beneath the ice. There would be no safe place for them in this forest. A horse's whinny sounded loudly in the chilled air as the small unit of soldiers crashed through the darkness of the tree line and onto the moonlit lake shore.

The family shuddered to a halt at the very edge of the water, turning to face the unit who urged their horses onward. Their mounts tossed their bridled heads, nostrils flaring as they tread forward onto the snow-topped sand. The lone bright blue banner they held, a polar bear holding a spear in its center, fluttered on a silent breeze. The royal sigil of Colladon.

The oldest man of the family dropped to his knees. The mother and child cowered behind him.

Something delicate and dark, crumpled in my chest. To reveal myself here, now, would create my own death sentence. But the child ... the *child*. The little boy turned his head, burying his face into his mother's sweat-soaked neck, and he clung to her tightly.

White wings arching, I hissed. Instinct tugged at my blood, my bones. I didn't know why this family was being hunted, but from their golden hair and sea green eyes, I knew they weren't from the north.

Yet in a time I had tried to forget, I was in that mother's shoes. Helpless, trapped, and-and …

My hiss turned into a guttural screech.

The ice coating the lake cracked and forked like lightning.

"Please," cried the elder, his hands splayed wide before him. He wore a noble's clothes, but they were torn and bloodied. "*Please.*"

The Commander of the unit broke rank, his gray horse pawing at the snow. "You shouldn't have run, Ambassador. This could have been painless for you and your family."

"The King promised us safe passage back to Ilrair. I had no knowledge of Jaryn's—"

The Commander, a bearded man in his late forties, dismounted and unsheathed his sword, moonlight glinting off the blade.

Green light bloomed underneath the ice, growing brighter and brighter.

"Please, *please,*" begged the ambassador.

My mind reeled back to that place intime where it had been me screaming those words, over and over, my throat ravaged, and my heart broken.

I hunkered low on the branch, every muscle in my body trembling.

The mother cradled her little boy, clutching him to her. Silver flashed as the Commander raised his sword high above his head.

Ice exploded in every direction as the eel-like body of the Nokken burst from water, its rows of dagger in the dark. The horses screamed in fright, and their riders fought to stay aboard as they bucked and shied.

I held no fear in my heart, as I dove from the birch tree, wings spread wide, talons outstretched, and aimed for those horrendous glowing green eyes. Mother and son scrambled on the snow, and the Nokken released a scream of pain, as my black talons found their mark.

Its equine head thrashed back and forth, but I swept upward and struck again, until black blood sprayed over the white ground. The Nokken yowled in fury, and it twisted on a large expanse of intact ice, before diving back into the murky depths of its watery home.

Wings pummeling the air, I shot skyward, then dove again, straight for the unit Commander.

One of the hunters wrenched on his horse's reins, just as he yelled out, "Commander! Her wings, her fucking *wings*."

The men hollered back and forth, scrambling to find a net, and I only hoped I could be quicker than them. I had to be. I allowed myself all of one glance at the mother and son, to see them sprinting back into the trees, before I struck at the Commander's face.

I was three times the size of a snowy owl, and the downdraft of my gold-tipped wings launched the Colladonian soldier flat on his back. He lunged blindly upward with his sword, but I skittered backward, pummeling the snow around me. Landing haphazardly on the shoreline, I hunkered my head low and arched my wings.

My screech echoed over the lake and trees. The Colladonian unit halted. A beat of silence washed over me, and I felt no regret as realization hit the soldiers.

A little boy would live tonight, safe in his mother's arms.

The Commander staggered to his feet, his face aghast as he appraised me.

One of his men behind him whispered fervently, "A Truth Keeper."

My heart pounded in my chest as I held their gazes. They were enraptured, like sailors to a siren. I had to hold them here just long enough for the family to escape. No doubt the Nokken would be back, and I would need to be airborne again.

"The rumors are true," whispered the Commander. The bright blue of his cloak fluttered behind him.

I hunkered lower over the snow, the moonlight glancing off my feathers.

My movement seemed to break their trance, as one of the archers leveled his recurve bow at my outstretched wings. Not my chest, or my head. I would be of no use to them dead. One breath passed, two.

The Commander drew himself to his full height and raised his right arm.

I shot to the sky, talons and wings raking the freezing night, just as that right hand came down. I saw the arrow take flight a fraction of a second before I heard it. Wheeling harshly in the air, I banked to the east, racing for the cover of the trees. The arrow hurtled past the apex of my right wing.

"Bring her *down*," yelled the Commander.

"The Ambassador!"

"Fuck him, *she* is our prize now."

Two more arrows shot past me as I flew, faster and faster, my heartbeat thundering in my chest. The fir and birch trees beckoned, and I dove for them. Then I heard the string of the longbow draw back, the only weapon that could reach me now.

Wings folding to my sides, I dove. Wind whipped at the white disc of my face as the snow-topped boughs drew closer, closer, *closer*.

The upper branches embraced me just as pain cleaved through my right shoulder. My cry rolled over the forest, and I lost control of my flight. I fell, crashing through the frozen canopy. Wings flailing uselessly, branches broke and whipped against me as I tumbled down. What had been my sanctuary became my cage, as gnarled tree limbs lashed my body. The white ground rose up to meet me, and I hit the forest floor with a sickening crack that echoed loudly in my head.

I choked on blood from the fall, as my lungs tried in vain to gasp down a breath. My body shook violently, the pain making me lose control of my owl form. A searing, golden flash illuminated the broken ferns and snapped tree branches around me. Red stained wings became tanned, honed arms, the arrow still puncturing my right shoulder. Blinking desperately, the world a vortex of snow and stars, I rolled onto my left side. By some spirits forsaken fucking miracle, my legs weren't broken.

The earth rumbled beneath my body with the galloping of horses.

I had to move. I had to *run*, but my shoulder, fuck, my *shoulder*.

Rolling onto all fours, I spat a mouthful of blood onto the snow and fought to get my battered body under control. My golden eyes had lost their owl sight, but my hearing remained elevated enough to mark where the unit was within the forest. They would have to skirt around the lake to find me.

Gritting my teeth, I hauled myself to my feet and prepared to run. My natural woman form with its wide-flared hips, broad shoulders, and snow-white hair felt alien and utterly useless. I had been twenty-two when I last used it, four years ago.

The muscles in my legs trembled, as I took one step, then two, the leather boots on my feet feeling like leaden blocks. My left hand reached up to brace my right shoulder, blood smearing on my fingertips.

Breath sawing from my chest, I half limped, half ran from where I had crash landed beneath a giant fir tree.

PART ONE

The Shadows

CHAPTER ONE

DESTRY

I would not yield to him. I would not yield to any of them. My fight with Rekorious atop Serebo felt like a lifetime ago, but only a week had passed. I had been foolhardy to cross swords with him, but I had been so furious. I still was. The one cut I had managed to get across his chest had taken him by surprise, but he had easily sidestepped and parried the rest. He had used my own fury and frustration against me, smiling all the while.

Craning my neck, I peered through the tiny crack in the stone wall of my room. There were no windows in this part of the keep. It had been carved along a granite, mountainous ridgeline, where it was difficult to tell where rock ended and military defenses began. If I pressed my hand hard enough against the exterior wall of my room, I could almost feel the thrum of the mountain itself. The small crack in the granite only boasted a dim, gloomy view of the empty room next to mine.

Kathkar had been stripped from me again. I kept my mouth shut, but I let them, let *him*, see my rage, my wildness that would not be broken. I would not bend to him. The Petish warlord only noted my fury with small, undeterred smiles.

A detachment of Royants had found Rekorious and me, the pair of us bloodied and half-frozen, about halfway down Serebo's flanks.

The warlord now sported an ugly scar that ran along his collarbone, courtesy of *Kathkar*, the only real blow I had landed on him.

"Wedding gift from your bride, Commander?" snickered one of the Royants when they had found us at sunrise, the morning after the spirits had been freed. Rekorious had told him to fuck off and had proceeded to bind me and unceremoniously throw me onto the back of Kalana.

Ebrel had been nowhere in sight.

My fear for the semi-wild Pegasus kept me awake at night. Had the Royants captured her and kept her away from me? I prayed she had found refuge with the last Mountain Horse within Glentay instead. And a desperate, fragile part of me prayed she knew where I was and would fly to free me.

A foolhardy dream.

I slunk down against the granite-slabbed wall of the sparse room and sat on the floor, tucking my knees to my chin, my hands penned uselessly against my abdomen. My wrists were no longer bound, but they still bore the red welts from when they had been.

A faint rustling sounded beside me, and a small, slender creature, probably a rat, loped up from a crack on the floor, squeaked once at me, then dove under the locked bedroom door and into the hall beyond.

The hours ticked by in this old, unknown keep. Drawing closer and closer to a wedding I did not consent to. If the Night Pegasus heard my prayers, he didn't answer them. He had said he'd find me, no matter where they had me locked away. Yet since I had freed the spirits, I hadn't felt the tiniest flicker of him. Even the lambent stone that I wore around my neck felt heavy, like an anchor. It did not flicker with power.

Maybe I had just been his insurance policy all this time. I was just a fragile, vulnerable thing to be held together until the time was right, then ripped apart for his own use. What was left of my light, just small, dark violet strands, twined through my numb fingertips. I wasn't sure why the light had shifted from its usual sage green to purple, but I had come to like the darker shade. Clenching my fists, the light trailed around my wrists like shimmering gauntlets. Tucking my knees tighter to me, I curved into the wall, bracing the side of my body against it, letting the chill of the mountain sink deep into my soul. Once it coiled within the rockbed of my heart, I felt it brush against colder, more ancient magic. A small gift from Serebo and Varranar for freeing the spirits, a little taper of ice. The same power that had been imbued into *Kathkar*. The taper sat dormant and quiet deep within me, like a frosted pane of twisted glass. Waiting. I closed a mental fist around it, chilled tendrils sliding down my spine in response.

Closing my eyes, I thought of the only thing that might warm me. The Golden Warrior. Yet that was just another foolish dream. He wasn't coming to save me.

No one was.

I had a plan, a reckless one, one that heralded ancient texts and extinct mythical creatures. I just had to get Rekorious, and his people, *my* people, to believe me.

CHAPTER TWO

ASHER

They didn't know it was a trap, one that had been effortless to make. Pherox keened softly on the dusken air, the noise traveling to me easily through the southern Colladonian forest.

I was darkness, a spell of deception and killing instinct. Weaving past the giant fir trunks, I reached the granite cliff face, so similar to ones I climbed as a young boy. It took little effort to climb onto the snow-dusted ledge ten meters up and wait.

The Colladonian unit had tailed me for the entirety of yesterday, and I had led them on a merry dance, just like a Nijinx male would have done to protect wha was his. The Nijinx kin swarm females were safely hidden well away from here, and now, the unit would realize just exactly what and who they were fucking with.

The ten horsemen broke free from the shelter of the trees and rode through the snow toward the cliff face. Their Commander spotted me first, his blue cloak wrapped tightly around him. He froze in the saddle, his horse unsettled beneath him.

I locked my gaze with his and gave him a wild, savage smile. "Looking for something, Commander?"

Anger flitted across the Commander's face, yet it soon melted to panic, as five Nijinx males, Pherox in the center, stalked through the trees behind the horsemen, blocking off any escape.

Their horses squealed and half reared, whipping their bodies around to stare the predators down with white-rimmed eyes. The soldiers were torn between controlling their mounts and deciding on who to turn their backs against. Me or the Njinxes.

The soldiers wisely kept their horses pointed toward the Nijinxes but turned in their saddles to look up at me.

I slung my legs to dangle over the ledge. One bowman reached for his quiver full of arrows, but I slowly shook my head at him. His hand froze, then he moved back to hold the reins.

A small curling shadow twined around my right ear, and I looked back at the Commander.

"Want to tell me why you've been a pain in my ass for the past twenty-four hours?" I asked darkly. "What do you want?"

The Colladonian swallowed loudly. "My name is Aron Isark. I'm a Commander in the King's Guard. We're looking for someone."

"No shit," I snarled.

Aron's lips pursed in annoyance. "We ... we heard you were now roaming these forests and with the wild ward now dead, we thought you might be able to help us. You were her huntsman, yes?"

I stiffened, but kept the growl locked in my throat. Yes, I had been her huntsman, but not by choice. The spirit of darkness, Iltavorn, now claimed me, and I had sought refuge with the Nijinxes since the wild ward's death a week ago. The kin swarm had fled Aarine and the Ilrairian soldiers riddling it, to find sanctuary in the wilds beyond Serebo. Orrin, now the undisputed King of the Forest, had granted us safe passage through his lands, as long as the Nijinxes promised not to kill any of his subjects.

The Mountain Horse and I would never be friends, I wasn't even sure I could call him an ally, after killing his father, but the Mountie made sure no humans from Aarine would follow us. And he had kept his word.

We had reached Colladon's border two days ago, meaning to head northwest toward the Scarp, the miles-long ridgeline of cliffs and spires that separated Petowin from Colladon, yet these soldiers had changed our plans.

They smelled of frozen seas and steel. My father and uncle's countrymen. Sadness and guilt punched me in the gut. I hadn't returned to the valley where I had burned their bodies. Not yet. Without the wild ward's magic riddling me, I could remember everything. Their screams as they died, more than anything.

I braced my honed forearms on my thighs, my worn leathers and fur cloak rustling. "Why do you want to know?"

"We have need of your services."

An elegant shadow reared up and peered over my right shoulder. I exhaled slowly, and the darkness retreated to rest alongside my throat. "I'm not for hire."

The Commander's jaw clenched, his gaze flicking to Pherox, then back to me, weighing up who was the greater threat.

Pherox flashed his fangs. Our blood was free from the wild ward magic, but as both Nijinxes and I were scions to Iltavorn, it had kept an open channel of communication in our minds. I would be forever grateful to the spirit of darkness because of it. Pherox was my friend, my counsel, and my brother in battle. Vesperum's mate huffed, his ears snapping back to lie flat against his skull. His patience was wearing thin. As was mine.

"You would be compensated, of course. My King would set you up for life."

I would never take my newly found freedom for granted, and for that of the Nijinxes. My future was hazy. Beyond getting the Nijinxes to the Scarp, I had no plans, and I was content with that for now. The thought of being under someone else's command, so soon after the wild ward, grated on me. I was Iltavorn's scion, but beyond claiming me as his own, the spirit had never forced his will onto me.

"What is it you're searching for?"

Hesitation warred on Aron's face.

I quirked a dark eyebrow.

"A Truth Keeper." The Commander's northern accent was low, like the words had been wrenched from him unwillingly.

I huffed a scratchy laugh. They were rare northern folklore, just like Unicorns. Olwen had disappeared in a dawn mist after the wild ward was slain, and I hadn't come across her scent during our trek northward. The only pure, clandestine part of me that existed was where the memory of that Unicorn resided. My gaze raked over the horsemen. "You're not serious?"

All the men looked at me then, like *I* was the one that had lost my damn mind. I surveyed them in turn, noting every single one of them, the weapons they bore. "You hoped to find a Truth Keeper with ten men? No wonder you haven't found anything. You're making an absolute fucking racket in this forest."

Aron rested his hands on the pommel of his saddle, the figure of ease, yet his shoulders were tight beneath his cloak. "She wasn't our initial target. We ... we were tracking criminals when she crossed our path."

"She willingly showed herself to you?" I couldn't keep the surprise out of my voice. "In her owl form?"

The soldier who had reached for his quiver nodded. "Aye, she took one of my arrows to her shoulder. She's wounded and grounded, likely shifted into her human form by now."

Shadows curled over my tight fists, and my nostrils flared, the muscle in my jaw ticking away. They had shot to hinder and maim, but not to kill. She would be suffering. It went against everything a hunter was taught. My father had instilled in me that we shoot to kill, instantly, the creatures we targeted barely registering the fact they had been slain before they died.

I shuddered, thinking back to Raiden, the Pegasus I had meant to shoot as an apprentice. The young stallion had known something was stalking him, that his life was at stake.

Distantly, the image of a burning white feather flashed across my mind. Nausea rolled on my stomach, and I took a deep, freezing cold breath.

The Commander noted the fury on my face with a flash of alarm. "My King needs her alive."

"The blood loss won't kill her, but infection might, you stupid *fucks*," I snarled, the sound laced with a dark, haunting promise. It was a slow, horrible way to die. I would hunt her down just to end her suffering if I had to.

Pherox let out a low, rumbling warning. and the cavalry horses skittered backward. *"Let us end them and be done with this."*

"Then help us find her." Aron smiled cunningly then, and I hissed in return. "The sooner we find her, the sooner we can treat her."

I rose into a crouch and waved a casual hand. "Say I find her, what happens then? She submits to a lifetime of questioning from your King?"

"She will want for nothing."

"Only her *freedom*," I spat, a notion I was all too familiar with.

With a tutting sigh, the Commander leaned forward and dismounted from his horse. Tucking the reins behind a stirrup leather, he walked closer to the cliff, the weak winter sun tarnishing his pale face and dark hair. Like he had no sense of self-preservation, or maybe he was just desperate, the Commander held out his right hand.

"As I said, my King would set you up for life. You can dwell where you see fit, live out your days in peace, with ... with your companions. Colladon would forever be indebted to you if you do this."

I leaped. Aron shifted backward as I slammed to the snow, my fist bracing me against the ground as my knees bent with the impact. Then I drew myself up to my full height, noting, with a small sense of satisfaction, I had twice the brawn on him.

One final hunt. One final hunt, then I could whisper away into the wilds in peace.

"I want the Scarp for the Nijinxes."

Aron gasped, disgruntled. "I beg your *pardon*?"

"You heard what I said. Don't make me repeat myself."

Aron went slack-jawed. "But we have *gold*."

I bared my teeth. "I don't give a fuck about your King's gold. I want the Scarp to be officially made Nijinx territory, so they can live and hunt there in peace."

"You surprise me yet again, huntsman," murmured Pherox, his voice laced with gratitude.

The Commander shook his head, and he looked back at the bow-man, who gave him a bemused, unbelieving shrug. Aron's mouth flattened into a grim line, *not helpful,* he seemed to say.

Aron straightened, glanced down at his muddied boots, then back up at me. Quickly, not giving himself the time to think about it, he proffered his right hand again. "Deal."

I smirked and sensed Pherox's hum of approval against my bones. "Pleasure to be of service, Commander Isark." I tugged the Commander closer. "If you do not deliver your end of the bargain, I will take the Scarp by force, and spirits help any creature that disturbs me or my companions up there."

CHAPTER THREE

EBREL

I dreamed of the wildflower meadow, the one that held those special blue flowers close to the cropped spring grass. My dam walked beside me, her brown, pink specked wing arching, offering warmth and shelter next to her flank. I tucked in close, my nose pressing against her elbow.

"Why are we different?" my younger self asked.

She clucked and turned her head to nuzzle my cheek. I leaned into the touch, breathing in her scent. *"We were too far north when the Trinitors were cursed all those years ago. It didn't take hold of our family like it did with all the others. Yes, it ripped us of our magic and speed ... but it did not press that savagery into our blood."*

Folding her wing again, my dam turned and nosed me closer to her chest.

"But nobody wants us now."

"You are wanted and cherished and loved," she huffed, her sweet, warm breath brushing over my forelock. *"Yet loneliness is not always a curse. It can lead you to depths of strength you didn't know existed."*

My breath turned rasping, heartache lancing through the dreamscape. *"It hurts."*

"Be brave, my love." Her voice was fading. *"Those who love you are with you, always, even if you can't see them."*

I reached out with my muzzle, but she was backing away. *"No."*

"You will find her, my darling." Her wings swept downward, and she was gone.

My mind clung to the meadow, but the worry in my heart grew stronger, stripping away the little blue wildflowers and sweet grass. The warm spring wind was torn away, replaced by a crushing cold.

The meadow vanished entirely. It was dark here and freezing. I rolled from my side onto my stomach, my legs curled beneath me on a patch of bare dirt I had found under a cluster of close-growing birch trees. Brown eyes peering skyward, I took in the clear, star-washed night. The northern sky called my name, a clear, ice-hewn song, the frigid wind sifting through my mane. Heaving myself to a standstill, I peered from my little shelter and inhaled deeply.

Her scent was barely there, a frail filament of alpine flowers, but it wove through the wind like a desperate taunt. Destry had been in this northern Serebo valley, and she had been afraid.

Anger made my tail lash my roan-flecked flanks. I knew what it was like to be helpless and alone. I would not abandon her. I could taste Aalto's betrayal in the air, a sour note on my muzzle and tongue.

My wings arched, sure and strong, and with my dam's words a balm in my mind, I launched my body into the night. To find my fated rider.

CHAPTER FOUR

DESTRY

The following morning, the door of my room unlocked loudly with a screech of metal, then slowly swung open. I wrenched myself to my feet, my back braced against the far wall, as Rekorious walked calmly into the room, bearing a plate of steaming soup and hot buttered bread.

Instantly, the room seemed to warp and shrink, the sheer presence of him dominating the small space. Kicking the door closed behind him with a booted foot, he placed the wooden tray on the small bed, the only furniture in here other than the latrine pot, and then he eased into a quiet stillness.

Looking at me.

My jaw ached with how hard I was clenching it, the air clawing into my lungs with silent, hurried breaths. He moved with an easy grace, which hid just how ruthless he really was. The northern territory agreed with him, he looked utterly in control, a true commander.

Releasing a heavy sigh, the warlord leaned back against the door, hands in his pockets, his ankles crossed. The thick wool of his gray shirt clung to his chest, the V of the neckline revealing a long slice of freshly scabbed skin. The scar I had given him. Dark bronze eyes appraised me fully, from head to toe, taking in my creased, bloodied riding skirt and sweater, and unwashed, barely braided hair. I desperately needed a bath and clean clothes.

I could almost taste my fury in the room, it permeated every sense I had.

His gaze paused on my face. Full lips pursing, he cocked his head. "You're not sleeping, are you?"

"Not for want of trying," I replied, my voice hoarse. Spirits, when had we last spoken? Two days ago? Aside from the silent maid who brought me food and emptied the latrine pot, and what I was sure was a stoat scampering across my room, not a rat, no one had visited me.

I couldn't keep my hands from trembling, so I hid them behind my back.

Aalto—*fuck*, Rekorious, shook his head, a small strand of auburn hair falling over his brow. "This could all be so easy."

My gaze locked onto his, full of challenge. He met it, not disturbed in the slightest. "I won't do it."

He looked up at the rafted ceiling, took a deep breath, then pushed himself away from the door. I wrenched myself back fully against the wall, keeping wholly still as he stalked forward. My breath snatched away from my throat, as he paused a hair's breadth before me, his left arm lifting to lay a palm on the wall beside my head. His warm breath skittered over the bare skin of my neck.

And where I had once felt allure, now I felt only anger tainted with fear. That despite his coaxing words, he would still go through with his plan. I'd be his wife whether I wanted it or not. He'd made it known to his followers that the light wielder of Petowin, the beloved *Koskivarri*, was to be his bride.

I was ensnared in his net, and he knew it.

"I'm ... I'm not like Narve, Destry." His murmur was silken, and it caressed the curve of my ear.

I looked down at the floor, at the worn flagstones beneath our boots. Closing my eyes, I inhaled deeply, as the memory of that night in the cave with Narve coiled around my heart and squeezed. Releasing a shuddering breath, I looked back up into those bronze-flecked eyes.

Rekorious waited, the muscle in his jaw jumping.

"No," I murmured. His face softened a fraction. My light twined up my arms and coiled around my throat. The ice in my heart cracked and thrummed. "You're a different kind of monster."

I flinched, as his hand curled into a fist next to my head, and he shoved himself away from me. Panting harshly, I watched on helplessly, as Rekorious wrenched open the door and slammed it shut behind him.

The sound of the lock clicking home scraped down my spine, and I let out a jagged breath. Thoughts of Narve threatened to overwhelm me, panic leaching through my blood as sweat slicked my palms. *Not here* ... my mind bleated. *Narve isn't here.* I tried to picture *Kathkar* cleaving that cretin's hands from his body, but I could still feel the ghost of his touch trailing up, up my torso.

My breath heaved in galloping pants, and my light flickered like a candle that couldn't withstand a gust of wind, the violet straining against the shadows of my room. Ice snapped in my chest, frosting over the terror that slicked inside my frantic heart. I sank back down to the floor before my legs could give out and placed my head between my knees, forcing deep lungfuls of air down my throat, begging my blood to calm.

He can't hurt you here.

He can't. He can't.

You cut off that bastard's hands. He can't touch anyone like that ever again.

The slender taper of ice cracked, forking with fresh, white tendrils.

A brisk knock on the door sounded, and my head snapped up. Blinking wildly, I gripped my knees to hide my shaking as the Petish maid who tended to me, a woman in her early thirties, dressed in a simple, yet warm gown of dark green wool, entered my room. Her gray, full-length apron was creased and well worn, yet her hair, which was as dark as my own, was coiled tightly atop her head. A simple amethyst and silver necklace hung just below her collarbone, and the dark, rough-cut crystal emitted a faint glow in the corridor torchlight.

I eased myself back to my feet, smoothing down the wide panels of my riding skirt as I cleared my throat, adrenaline still careening through my body. The maid simply waited, hands clasped in front of her. Her eyebrows pinched together as she ran a critical gaze over me, then she took in the light that dimly wreathed my trembling fingers.

"Lord Niemi has requested you be prepared for the council meeting tomorrow morning. If you'd like to follow me to the bathing chambers? We have a new set of clothing waiting for you." Her accent was like a balm to me, fully Petish and lilting, some of the vowels drawn out like a tender song. She gestured to the open door with an elegant hand and guarded smile. "This way."

I gingerly followed her out of my room, eyes wide as I mentally mapped every corridor and exit. A small pool of rectangular daylight shone on an interior gray stone wall, and I halted as we passed one of the few slit-like windows. Snow crusted around the lower lip of the freezing paned glass, yielding a view of a seemingly sparse, snow-covered landscape that basked in the soft pink of a winter sunset. To the left, a distant forest of birch trees sheltered a small herd of grazing reindeer and near the watercolor horizon, the low sun reflected over a sliver of ice-clad river.

My heart stuttered as I drank the scene in, like a woman parched of water, desperate to observe and memorize as much as I could. I had been hooded when Kalana had made the final descent through snow clouds to this low-lying mountain range, yet I could feel the land beyond that portion of frozen river calling to my soul. Home lay beyond that golden horizon.

The maid cleared her throat, and my right hand that had been drifting upward to touch the glass, lowered back to my side.

"This way, *Koskivarri*," she murmured.

Tearing my dejected gaze from the window, the maid guided me deeper into the sublevels of the keep, our footsteps muffled against stone scuffed and scraped by countless boots and weapon strikes. This place had known war, yet the air did not feel heavy with grief of a bloody past. That despite its winding corridors, flickering torchlight and battered, ancient shields hanging from the walls, it felt more homely than Reckforton Castle ever did.

We passed nobody else, not a single servant or soldier. Yet from the faint shouts and whinnies that echoed distantly to us, I know there are plenty of other inhabitants of this keep. The maid paused before a solid pine door studded with iron and yanked it open. Warm steam played with the dirtied tendrils of hair that framed my face, and I'm suddenly transported to a different castle, a different thermal pool, a different woman at my side.

My heart ached at the thought of Amadea, the water-wielding Queen who had become my friend. Did she feel as lost and trapped as I did?

"I'll be waiting out here when you're finished. The other door is locked, so don't bother trying to use it." Again, she cast a critical gaze at my clothes, lingering on the blood under my fingernails. Niemi's blood, I noted with a small kick of warm satisfaction, carved from his forearms when he'd tried to pin me against Serebo's snow. The fucker. "Take as much time as you need."

I ignored her arched eyebrow and the words she didn't need to say. *Take as much time as you need, because, by the spirits, you need it.*

The lock clanked into place behind me as I stepped into the bathing chamber. Unlike the large, subterranean square pool in the Adacus Residence, eight rectangular baths, each about two meters long and a meter wide, had been carved into the stone floor. Steam curled from each one, the flaming sconces bracketed high along the walls, reflecting off the surface of the stippled water. Across the long, low-ceilinged room, atop a simple carved granite bench, sat a large copper bowl. Wafting from it came the twirling scents of pine needles, raspberries, and something like caramel.

This place had the same womb-like temple reverence that I had felt in the Adacus Residence, yet here, I was utterly alone. Hot, humid air sweeping into my lungs, I padded on silent feet to the farthest stone bath on my right. Half surrounded by fat, guttering candles, a stack of white towels awaited me, alongside a neatly folded pile of clean clothes and fawn-colored soap.

My breath and the sound of trickling water orbited around me, as I stripped off my bloodied and dirt-ridden clothes, not caring if someone else walked in. The almost too hot water created light tan rivulets over my bare, grimy skin, sluicing away the events of the past week. Sinking up to my chin, I untangled the last stubborn knots from my hair, and it fanned out like a dark web around me.

A distant, faint squeaking threaded its way through the steam, and the small mammal that had scampered across my room and into the hall the night before, bounded over the slick slabs of the floor toward me. Definitely not a rat, I realized with several relieved blinks, but something much smaller, swifter, its spine convex as it drew closer. As white as the cotton towels it drew up alongside, a pair of black button eyes checked me over inquisitively, its tiny whiskers twitching.

"Hello, little stoat," I whispered with a half-smile.

The dainty predator rose up on its small hind legs, sniffed once, then proceeded to steal my spare small washcloth. A low, rasping laugh escaped my lips, as the stoat galloped the way it had come, the washcloth held firmly between its razor-sharp teeth.

"Go make your den cozy and warm," I said faintly after it, as the stoat disappeared like a ghost through the stone wall. The laugh I had emitted died in my chest as I looked down at the water's surface.

I was to be brought before the council meeting in the morning. *What council?* I had been raised almost utterly devoid of knowledge of Petish culture and governance. Being in this keep, despite being a prisoner within its walls, was the closest I had been to my homeland in twenty-three years. I assumed Niemi could not plot and plan without this council's say-so, which meant they must have an overriding voice when it came to my future, a future that I would fight tooth and nail to defend.

Picking up a small, soft cloth and a bar of juniper scented soap, I scrubbed every inch of myself, tenderly moving around the scar Lonan had given me on my left bicep that had never quite healed right from Narve's nightmare-inducing poison. Taking a settling breath, I let that memory siphon away like the steam around me, letting it evaporate in the pine rafters of the ceiling.

I had lost a piece of myself that night, a fragile slice of my soul that I would never be able to get back. I would need to find the strength to forge something else in the brazier of my being, making it sharper, deadlier, toward anyone who dared try to hurt me like that again. The taper of twisting ice in my chest cracked and groaned in response, like a beast waiting for an awakening after a long hibernation. My light bannered dimly over the water in response, but the lambent stone hanging around my neck did not flicker in reply. It did nothing but rise and fall with the beat of my breath, its power dormant ... forgotten.

In the half hour that followed, the ice popped and groaned in my mind in an eerie half-frozen song, expanding with tiny filaments of power.

Instinct told me that night had fallen. The rooms and corridors beyond my own grew quiet, I couldn't even hear the wind tear at the exterior of the walls. I had no candles in my bedroom. A lone torch in the hallway illuminated the cramped space through an iron grill in the door.

I finished coiling my still-damp hair into a low knot, freshly dressed in perfectly fitting, fur-lined leather leggings and a dark blue, long-sleeved knitted tunic made of the softest wool. The high collar was snug against my throat, a simple bronze clasp resting over my collarbone. Thankfully, there were no Niemi River fish sigils in sight on any of my clothing.

I flinched, recognizing the candor of his footsteps in the hallway. Hastily, I backed away from the bed, as Rekorious unlocked my door and entered the room.

His demeanor seemed different from before. Defeat clung to the tightness in his shoulders, and his face was grim and just … tired. He paid me no heed at all, as he slung himself onto my mussed bed and tucked his hands behind his head. He was so spirits damned tall, his lower legs dangled off the edge of it. Like earlier, he bore no weapons, just his boots, woolen trousers, and buttery soft, gray shirt. His dark hair was loose now, the strands tangling through the long fingers tucked behind his head.

From his mouth came a deep, exhausted sigh.

Blinking, unsure what to make of this, I took a hesitant step forward. My voice was soft and uncertain. Maybe my words from earlier had struck a chord on his immoral heart. "Niemi?"

His name hung between us in the delicate darkness, but he just stared up at the rafted ceiling. Tanned throat bobbing, the deep timber of his voice was low and laced with longing. "I could never love you, Destry."

Perplexed, unable to hide the surprise on my face, I cocked my head and took another small step toward him. My light wreathed the space between us, casting a violet glow on the walls.

"If this is some kind of trick—"

"I wish it was, Destry."

I ... I had never heard him so utterly defeated. His chest expanded as he breathed slowly through his nose, keeping quiet, letting me decide on the next move. Gingerly, I crept forward and sat at the very end of the bed, finding space between the edge of the coarse mattress and his long legs. I kept a hand braced on the footboard, ready to bolt if needed.

The ice power in my chest splintered and cracked.

His gaze met mine as I looked down at him. He truly was beautiful, in a savage and searing way, and I didn't blame myself for becoming entranced in the spell of him. It seemed like the weight of the world pressed down on his broad chest, and for a few moments, silence wove an intricate beat around us, twining with the violet light in the room.

He swallowed again and moved his right hand from behind his head. Moving slowly, so as not to startle me, I realized with a jolt, he reached out and gently clasped the hand that rested on my lap. My chest was tight, my mind racketing between panic and confusion, as he nestled my palm within his. Gently, he squeezed my fingers.

"Tell me," I whispered, as I searched his face. His touch felt utterly unexpected, but it was ... strangely comforting. A small, fragile bridge of connection. My fear of him abated a fraction. "Tell me *why*?"

The bronze in his eyes darkened to something primal. "Amadea."

"*What*?" I breathed, shock spearing through my chest.

"She ... I ... I love her, with my entire being, but I can't be with her. For her own safety."

Grief lanced every single one of his words, as if he were being struck with a dozen swords. My light lowered over him in an unconscious effort to soothe. A memory, as clear as a spring day, pounded through my head. Gently, I ran a thumb over the broad width of his hand. "She told me there was someone in Saltfen who she trusted completely, who she wanted to train me. That was you, wasn't it?"

His full lips quirked upward at my words, then he gave the tiniest nod of his head.

"What happened?" I asked softly, almost afraid to probe too far. Even if I had an inkling as to what had happened. King Jaryn Adacus of Ilrair, Amadea's husband, was ruthless.

He cleared his throat and looked back up at the ceiling, but his thumb traced small, faint circles on the back of my hand. Likely re-assuring himself more than me. The scar I had given him gleamed in the low light.

"I was the commanding officer that brought De over from Omivarra. It was a six-week voyage. Jaryn didn't want to use Pegasi, and she was terrified about what awaited her. She had only met Jaryn once, but, naturally, he had made enough of an impression that she was scared out of her wits. I ..." He released a long, slow breath, and it felt utterly natural to squeeze his hand in support. "I can't explain it, the need to protect her. I wanted to shield her from everything that Jaryn had lying in wait, and by doing so, I threw her straight into the viper's pit. Every plan I devised on that ship to get her to safety was foiled. We ran out of options." His gaze met mine then. "Coen knew. He knew as soon we walked off the ship ... what we'd done. I tried to reassure him that we would be fine, that Amadea would be safe, that Jaryn would never know."

The silence twisted, becoming taut. My jaw clenched, my entire body bracing as I anticipated his next words.

"How wrong I was," he whispered.

"What did Jaryn do?" Amadea, beautiful, strong, unwavering Amadea. It felt like my heart was breaking all over again. I had left her there with Jaryn, and I was an utter wretch because of it.

"He discovered she'd been sleeping with someone during the voyage but never found out who. I was in the clear, but he ..." Rekorious' rage was like a second skin, clinging to the marrow of his bones. "Two days after her arrival in Ilrair, he had her flayed in a private ceremony for just him and his closest advisors. To *cleanse* her."

A horrified gasp escaped my mouth. I was going to be sick. Holy *fuck*. I gripped Rekorious' hand tighter, and he held me just as fiercely, as if he were trying to anchor himself to the here and now. The ice in my chest radiated outward, chilling the very blood in my veins. *He speaks the truth.* I welcomed it. *Jaryn.* For a brief moment, my light flickered to a vibrant red, then filtered back to purple.

He ran his right hand through his tousled hair, his jaw tight. "Coen walked in on it, the *ceremony*. He got Jaryn to stop, and he managed to pull her out of there and take her to the medics. He got word to me about what had happened, and warned me to stay far, far away. Jaryn threatened to slaughter her entire family if it happened again."

Slowly, gently, Rekorious withdrew his hand from mine and sat up. Placing his feet on the floor, he braced his forearms over his strong thighs and interlaced his fingers. I watched him warily, acutely aware of the rage and tension that rippled from him. My light swirled around our boots, arching like a cat against us.

"Does she know? About who you really are?" I whispered, twisting to face him. This man loved Amadea, yet he was hundreds of miles away from her and wanted to marry me instead? It made no fucking sense.

He looked across at me from under his thick, dark hair. "Yes."

"Go get her, Rekorious, don't marry me. Go get *her*."

"After I abandoned her to that *snake*? She would never have me, Destry. This"—he waved at the small, fraught space between us—"our marriage is purely for convenience, there's no point in lying to you now. It's either kill you and take your title or marry you and claim it."

I froze at the threat, my lips pulling back from my teeth in a silent snarl. Rekorious searched my face, his gaze unflinching.

"What if there was a third option?" My voice was glacial, my free hand clenching the iron foot rail.

His lips pursed, and his nostrils flared. "And what would that be?"

Releasing a taut breath, I whispered, "Let me relinquish the claim to the Petish throne to you. Let me be your blood rider, your knight, instead."

Rekorious blinked, then heaved himself off the bed. Raking a hand through his hair again, he started to pace the worn floor beside the bed. "You would do such a thing?"

My family may turn in their graves because of it, but I had no experience in ruling, in garnering support from strangers. I would lose the ability to govern Petowin, but I would gain freedoms I otherwise wouldn't have. My one goal that I had hoped to achieve by marrying

Narve, was to rid the country of Nijinxes and help its people return and live there in peace. Rekorious, however, had successfully led a dissension of Ilrairian soldiers to the Petish cause, and despite his lies and deceit toward me, was clearly an established leader and well respected by those that followed him.

"I would. I saved your life three times in the mountains. Three spirits damned times, Rekorious. You wouldn't be breathing if it weren't for me. Let me be your blood rider, not your bride."

Rekorious halted before me, his hands resting on his hips. Lost in thought, he chewed his full bottom lip. "It could work."

I sat tall on the bed, taking in the commanding presence of him. "Let me do this, Rekorious. Let me have a *choice*," I pleaded, my gaze raking along the long scar on his chest. An eternal reminder that I had fought him, and he hadn't come out unscathed. My offer was brash, I knew that. I was only in the beginning stages of learning to wield *Kathkar*. But, if I could unite with Ebrel, and Rekorious held out on his promise to train me, I could be a *knight*. With the magic in my veins, I would even dare to take on Jaryn and kill that sadistic bastard, Narve, too. Even Lonan, wherever that cruel craven was hiding.

Deftly, the Royant Commander crouched on the slabs in front of me, his large hands dangling between his knees.

I cocked an eyebrow and gave him a small, hesitant smile. "What do you think of my offer?"

"We'll need to discuss it with my council in the morning. Nothing is done without their approval. By becoming my blood rider, Destry, you will need to swear to fight at my side when I need you. To protect Petowin from all who may harm her. In return, I will keep my promise and train you. You may reside where you wish and marry whoever you want." He reached forward and clasped my right hand in his again. "If

Ebrel does not return, we will find another mount for you, one of our Lake Horses that the ground cavalry use, perhaps."

Hope swirled in my chest, the ice magic that lingered there rumbling in agreement. I could do this. I *wanted* to do this. I wanted to protect my people from monsters like Narve and Jaryn.

A small sigh escaped Rekorious' mouth, and I eyed him warily. "What is it?"

"Coen's not coming, Destry."

My back went rigid at his words, and my voice was hushed. "You don't know that."

"He is tied too tightly to Jaryn. My spies at Aarine reported he rescued Jaryn from the spirit magic and hauled his heartless ass back to Ilrair. Coen saved his *life*, Destry. That monster is still living and breathing because Coen intervened."

My lips twisted in a grim line as exhaustion and hurt clawed at me. The hope I had built in my chest shattered once more.

Rekorious squeezed my hand. "I'm sorry, Destry."

I hastily dashed tears from my eyes before they had a chance to fall. I had left Coen there in Saltfen, he had no reason to come after me. And yet ... *and yet* ... a tiny part of me still thought he would. That he would fly here on his golden Pegasus, wrap me up in his arms like he had the night when I was nearly murdered in Ilrair, and sweep me away to freedom.

A fool. I was a fool, wishing and hoping on falling stars for something that would never be. I looked the Commander in the eye, his gaze soft and earnest. "You told me once that you didn't want to be the kind of man who wakes up at dawn and does not see the beauty in it."

"It's the truth."

"Then go get Amadea. Coen might not come for me, but that doesn't mean you can't free her from her cage."

"She's so heavily guarded. Since the day she was flayed, I have thought of every possible way to get her out of there, but Jaryn would rather kill her and her family than see her be freed. I can't risk that." The Commander rose then, tucking his hands into his trouser pockets. "You should rest. I'll come fetch you for the meeting with council in the morning."

"I'm no longer your prisoner?" I asked quietly, bracing a palm on the rumpled blankets.

"We'll find out tomorrow," was his only reply, before seeing himself out and locking the door behind him.

Slumping onto the bed, I stared up at the ceiling as he had done and tried to gather the incinerated pieces of dashed hope in my chest.

CHAPTER FIVE

ASHER

"I guess this is goodbye," I murmured, as I ran my roughened palm down the middle of Pherox's silken head.

The giant Nijinx male nudged my fussing away, but gently pressed his nose to my chest. I pressed my forehead to his, something we had done so many times before, and lingered there for a moment. My respect for this creature was depthless, and he owed me nothing.

"This is not our final farewell, huntsman. Tread with caution."

"Don't get caught between the cliff faces and the forest up there. Make sure you only travel at night."

Pherox sighed, his fangs flashing, and stepped backward. A deep, rumbling clicking resounded in his chest. I could feel him survey me, noting every scar, both visible and hidden on my body and soul. *"Take care, hunter."*

I stepped up beside him and patted his broad, muscled shoulder. He nudged my arm in return, then walked away to join Vesperum and the rest of the kin swarm. They would travel north to the Scarp and wait for me there. I would stay here, in these craggy, wild Colladonian forests to track down the wounded Truth Keeper.

The kin swarm released a series of clicks, a goodbye, I realized, and then the Nijinxes melted into the darkness beneath the tree canopy. Pherox was the last to leave, his mighty frame dappled with moonlight under the trees. *"You are not the monster you believe yourself to be, Asher."*

I cleared my throat, not ready for the flood of emotion that hauled its way through my heart as the Nijinx male turned and followed the kin swarm into the skies, leaving me with just my shadows and the bitter cold. Nightfall was settling around me, the stars slowly appearing in the sky above.

The unit of Colladonian soldiers had left, with instructions to bring the Truth Keeper to Fort Garobear once I'd found her. The fort was a good five-day trek from here. Shrugging my pack of supplies across my muscle-hewn back, including a medic kit and extra weapons, I trudged through the snow and oncoming night. I felt Iltavorn press against my senses a few moments later, the spirit of darkness no longer surprising me with his fleeting appearances.

"Good hunting," the archaic voice rumbled in my mind.

My shadows wreathed my hands, which they did whenever the spirit visited, the power in me multiplying whenever Iltavorn was near. "You know what I'm searching for?"

"I do, huntsman. Something broken and bleeding. She is adrift."

My jaw clenched. "Care to tell me where she is?"

That dark power uttered a low laugh. *"Trust your shadows, huntsman. They will not misguide you."*

The shadows peeled away to probe the night before me, and I followed them.

"But be warned, Asher. She could still cleave your heart from your chest. An injured creature can still attack when cornered."

I muttered my thanks for the warning, and Iltavorn laughed again, the sound ancient yet ageless. Then he was gone, no more than a breath of winter wind. Shadows twined on a deer trail up ahead, wending around a standing of small birch trees. Taking a settling breath, I walked onward. For the Nijinxes' freedom, I would do this. For their peace and happiness, I would put this creature out of her misery. Even if it meant damning my soul even further.

I walked for hours, traversing the forests and small lakes with little effort. The wild creatures steered clear of me, sensing the darkness that prowled in my veins. Different to the wild ward magic that had once possessed me, but still lethal nonetheless. My shadows weaved back and forth like a snake ahead of me, pulling me ever onward, and I followed them trustingly through the night.

We had just skirted a large lake, its center glowing a faint green hue, when the shadows halted. They dipped and rose, like a wave. *Here,* they seemed to say, *look here.*

I looked up, taking in the broken branches of the fir tree and the trampled ground at its base. Then, there, amongst the pine needles and snow drifts. Dried blood. A fucking great deal of it. My shadows retreated back to me, hovering around my shoulders. I knelt upon the frozen ground, fist clenched atop the snow, and I inhaled deeply. The scent of terror still clung to the foliage. Terror ... and pain.

Slowly, I stood, my long wool-lined, leather coat shifting over me. I wouldn't need my shadows now. Instinct took over, and I treaded silently forward, following the scent of fear and blood still thick in the air.

Memories of my father and uncle hounded me, but I shook my head, trying to ignore the guilt that pursued me in turn. My daggers were a reassuring weight on either side of my hips, as I followed the intermittent blood trail. How the fuck she had managed to *run* after her fall and taking an arrow was beyond me. Yet she had for a good mile and a half. The blood was sparse now, only the odd drop and smear here and there, where she had braced herself against a tree trunk for support.

She had used a small creek to hide her scent, *clever creature,* but I picked up a gray thread from her dress against a fern soon after. I felt an energy drawing me onward, and finally, the shadows slithered away from my neck, and they sifted through the night air like smoke.

I slammed to a stop, the movement jarring my bones. Inhaling deeply, I caught her fresh scent, and it struck me like a fist to the chest. It was haunting and delicate, with hints of moss and golden sunlight. Lured forward by her scent alone, I walked on silent feet to where she had made her sanctuary. The shadows whipped back and forth now between me and a small stone rise.

She had somehow managed to drag fallen tree branches over the opening of a cave, doing everything she could to avoid detection. Yet she had never anticipated a predator like me. Straining my neck in the darkness, I listened for her. Over the gossamer sigh of the midnight breeze and rustle of leaves, I picked up her sharp, haggard breaths.

Silently withdrawing my left dagger, I stalked forward and pulled back the dead branches with a leather gloved hand. Iltavorn's warning rang like a bell in the back of my head, as my eyes adjusted to the pitch-black gloom beyond.

An owl-like hiss sounded from the back of the cave, echoing over me like a riptide. Blinking, my sight finally took in what huddled there in the dark. Hair so blonde it was white, cascaded raggedly over the tanned, snarling face of a young woman. Her face was utterly beautiful but pinched with rage and pain. The air in my lungs halted, as I drank her in.

The cave stank of sweat. It clung to her brow and elegant neck, the gray wool of her dress hanging limply from her body and legs.

A large patch of blood soaked her right shoulder. Rage at what the soldiers had done to her made me clench my dagger harder. In her quivering left hand, she held the tip of the arrow that had brought her down. With an arm that shook with adrenaline and fever, she pointed that metal arrowhead at my chest.

Gingerly, I dropped to one knee at the cave's mouth, resting my right forearm across my thigh. "Easy there, owling, *easy*."

She emitted another hiss from her pale lips, the sound full of desperate challenge. Yet her breath was still labored, her golden-eyed gaze glassy and barely coherent. A long tendril of shadow curled beside her collarbone and over her hammering heart.

Wild-eyed, she glanced at the cave mouth to me, then to where she sat. Painstakingly slowly, she twisted the arrowhead in her hand and jutted it toward her chest.

Holy shit. She was willing to end her life, to end her pain and suffering, rather than face me. Launching myself forward, I grabbed ahold of her hand, my grip firm yet gentle, stopping the arrowhead just as it punctured the wool of her dress.

Undiluted wrath washed over her face as she bared her teeth at me again, yet her pupils widened in terror.

"The world would be a far darker place without you in it," I murmured softly.

With a clench of my right hand, the shadow that clung to her shoulder darted forward and ripped the weapon away before it could pierce her skin. The metal rang sharply as it clattered to the stone floor, and I pocketed it before she could harm herself further. I paused for a moment, my hand still gripping her wrist and breathing deeply, my gaze cataloged every piece of her, admiring her fierceness in the face of utter despair.

"Please." Her voice was hoarse, and pain pierced my own chest at her agony. "Please, don't take me to them."

This woman had run nearly two miles while injured, had taken every precaution to hide herself away, and tried to end her own life, rather than face a fate filled with servitude. Clarity slammed into me then. I had been faced with something similar, and the choice to say no had been ripped from my very soul, a soul that was now dark, hurting, and full of guilt. Yet I had been promised the Scarp in exchange for her. I was doing this for the Nijinxes, for Pherox and Vesperum.

A shadow swept over the back of my neck, a calming, settling gesture. I had been *her*, in what felt like another lifetime, I had been locked into a life where I had become a monster.

I looked her over once more, my brown gaze meeting hers. Her golden eyes were like a summer dawn. Dropping to both knees, I sheathed my dagger and slowly released her wrist. She snatched it back to her chest, her entire body trembling.

"Your wound is starting to become infected, but I think you already know that," I said, my voice low and deep. The tightening of her jaw was my only confirmation. "I have a medic kit with me. Let me heal you. You won't survive tomorrow if you leave it untreated."

"Maybe," she panted. "That would be better."

I gave a slow shake of my head, my now longer brown hair falling over my brow. "I'm not going to be letting you die anytime soon, owling. So, you either let me take care of you willingly, or you can sit here and suffer in this dark pit."

She scowled, the expression so human for something born of legend. Her gaze roved over the shadows that curled around my neck and shoulders. Her golden eyes started to glow, and I stiffened. "Darkness is your master, huntsman."

Power crackled from her broken body despite her injuries, and I could taste the truth magic that rolled off her, like frigid, ancient ice. All Truth Keepers were blessed yet cursed with an untold amount of Varranar's magic. The ability to untangle lies and speak only the truth. None had been seen since the fall of the Trinitors, and now here I was, arguing with one. Just like the Mountain Horses, they were believed to have been hunted and captured to extinction. Yet here she was. Broken. Bleeding. Adrift in fever and despair, just like Iltavorn had said.

"He is," I answered gutturally.

The glow of her irises flickered, her power waning with her lack of strength. Her dark blonde lashes blinked, and her magic vanished. I released a taut, panting breath, and she slumped against the wall of the cave.

"Let me heal you." It was a request, yet I let her see the determination on my face. "I won't hurt you."

She swallowed, the pulse on her neck beating wildly. Her gaze burned into mine, stripping me bare. "You ..." Her shoulders began to slump, and I inched closer, guessing what was coming. "You would be the first."

Moving lithely, I wrapped my right arm around her upper back as she passed out, the fever wholly claiming her. My breath sawed out of me, as I gently laid her down on the dry floor of the cave, careful not to touch her injured shoulder. A twist of pale white hair fell over her face, and I swept it back across the sharp plane of her cheekbone. Even with my gloves on, I could feel the heat of her skin pressing into me.

I had a Truth Keeper in my arms, and while she was there, nothing and no one was going to harm her.

Once the campfire was holding steadily, I dragged over my leather pack and retrieved the medical kit Isark had given me. Colladonian medics were some of the finest in the continent, both men and women studied for several years to learn the craft, working closely with local village healers and midwives. The kit contained everything I'd need to retrieve the rest of the wooden arrow shaft that I suspected was still lodged in the Truth Keeper's shoulder.

Unbuckling the roll of worn, black leather, I pulled out a pair of long, dark metal tongs, bandages, and a jar of honey. Setting them down on a folded piece of clean linen, I withdrew my right dagger and crouched over where the owling slept fitfully. I had laid her face down on my bedroll, with my leather coat wrapped around her lower body. She was shivering hard, and her closed eyes darted endlessly.

Shadows circled the crown of her head, and I gave myself a small, encouraging nod as I reached for her right shoulder. My dagger cut through the woolen fabric of her dress like it was butter, despite the crusted blood soaking it. As gently as I could, I peeled back the fabric, revealing the wound that lay beneath.

I blinked in surprise at her toned and muscled back, yet given her animal form, it would make sense for her to be so strong. My lips pressed together tightly, as I smoothed her long hair away and coiled it at the nape of her neck. Her breaths were shallow, her lips wan, yet she slept on.

It felt wrong to be doing this while she was unconscious, but if I didn't help her, she would die. And I would not let that happen. I sent a small prayer to Iltavorn that my shadows would keep her asleep until this was finished. Having scrubbed my hands clean and dousing them with alcohol, I gently palpated the arrow wound. It had entered above her scapula, the metal head puncturing cleanly. Yet she had snapped the shaft in trying to retrieve it, leaving a piece of ash wood behind. The blood was clotted, but it would soon bleed again when I tried to get the bastard thing out.

"I'm so sorry," I whispered, as my right forefinger felt the entry wound. Almost instantly, I brushed against something hard yet splintered. Praying it wasn't too long of a piece, I reached for the tongs and held them over the fire's flames.

Field medicine and surgery had been drilled into me since I went into the wilds with my father and uncle, and I had them to thank for being able to use the kit I had been loaned from Isark. I ignored the pain fisting over my heart at the thought of my family, and the guilt that threatened to devour me from the inside out. Slowly, I brought the tongs to the owling's shoulder.

My mind reached out to my shadows, and they hovered closer to her brow, primed to send her back to sleep should this wake her. Delicately, I opened the black metal tongs and grasped the end of the broken shaft, the scent of burning skin filling my nose. Thanking the spirits she hadn't woken, I pulled back, and the rest of the arrow followed suit.

Thank fuck. Panting, I placed the tongs down and picked up an alcohol-soaked compress, pressing it to the wound. She flinched, and

I tensed, but darkness still held her under. My gaze shifted from her shoulder to her upturned face.

She truly was beautiful, a sun-kissed energy rippling from her even as she slept. No wonder kings and lords had hunted her kind down. Not just for their power, but for their sheer radiance and grace. Truth Keepers weren't immortal, they stuck to a human life span, and she looked no older than I was. The King of Colladon wanted this creature to be trapped within his court, to be used during the day as an interrogation tactic, and likely at night for his own pleasure.

The thought brought a deep, rumbling snarl from my chest, and the muscles across my back tightened. This exchange would bring the Nijinxes peace. I had to stick to my plan. Shaking my head, I wiped away the remaining splatters of blood from her golden skin, the freckles scattered across it like dune sand. I ignored the temptation to trace those freckles with my calloused palm and instead reached for the honey. The sweet scent permeated the small cave as I applied it to the wound, then finally wrapped her entire shoulder with wide, coarse bandages.

The wound would need to be treated and re-bandaged again over the next coming days, but for now, there was nothing more I could do. The fire crackled steadily, and I sat cross-legged with a heavy sigh beside it. The night wore on while I kept guard, monitoring the forest outside and the owling's breath. Just before dawn broke, I heard her stir, and I looked over my shoulder at her. She curled her arms under her chest, her hands folded beside her neck, bringing the collar of my coat up to her chin.

Seeing her wrapped up in my coat twisted my heart in a way I hadn't felt in a long time. She had stopped shivering now and was likely feeling cold with the fever's passing. Ignoring the small voice in the back of my head that was calling me a fool, I shucked off my thick brown gambeson.

A deep sigh escaped her mouth, as I wrapped it around her torso over my coat. My chest ached again as I crouched beside her, hands dangling between my knees. I ran my gaze over her tanned face. One way or another, this woman was going to be my undoing. She could either lead me to salvation or lure me into utter, complete damnation, and I wondered, with the power slumbering in her veins, if she knew it too.

CHAPTER SIX

EBREL

The stallion blessed by fire was following me. I had managed to lose him beyond Mount Ghel's lower flanks, but by the following midday, he was tailing me again, easily keeping pace no matter how swiftly I flew, clearly unencumbered by the brawn of his rider.

Ears snapping to my skull, the wind tossing my reddish mane, I dove for a frozen valley floor. Like golden lightning, the stallion and rider tracked me down, down, down, the arctic breeze roaring around us.

With the late winter sun barely breaching the horizon, I landed hastily atop a snow-covered clearing and whipped my scarred body around to face the pair. The palomino stallion made a show of landing slowly, his foot placement perfect despite his larger size, as he elegantly lowered himself to the earth.

"I think only a peregrine is faster than you, roan one," noted the stallion with a toss of his bridled head.

My brown tail lashed my freckled flanks, and my nostrils flared. *"Flattery will not work on me."*

The palomino simply arched his muscled neck at the challenge and angled his powerful body to reveal the male rider on his back.

He bore no uniform now. Only a wool-lined, long leather coat, warm breeches and scuffed leather boots. A thick burgundy scarf was wrapped around his head and neck, offsetting the golden blonde of his hair and deep green of his eyes.

I pawed at the snow, ears flicking uneasily as the soldier dismounted and looped the reins over the palomino's head. Wisely, the pair didn't approach me.

"Ebrel," breathed Coen, his deep voice laced with wonder as he looked me over. "You're looking for Destry?"

Standing tall before the pair, I bobbed my head in a gesture Kalana had taught me meant "yes" to humans. The palomino, I think his name was Hestian, pricked his ears in surprise.

Coen took a slow, steady step forward, and I watched him warily. His face was filled with steely determination and longing. "I'm looking for her too."

I flashed my teeth, but Hestian bared his in return. *"You shall not harm him, roan one."*

"You wouldn't be quick enough to stop me," I retorted.

Hestian rolled his eyes in a gesture that clearly meant "stubborn females," but I ignored him, my attention fixed on the soldier who took another cautious step forward. Slowly, he extended his gloved right palm. Nostrils flaring, my breath clouding us both, I extended my neck and probed his hand with my muzzle.

My body twitched with tension, and Hestian watched me closely, his head cocked with interest, as I took in the faint scent that clung to the Commander. Destry's scent. I blinked, then inhaled again. It was definitely there, laced with Coen's.

Gently, Coen stroked two long fingers down my nose. His voice was a sheltered whisper. "I know where she is. Fly with us, help me free her."

CHAPTER SEVEN

DESTRY

The pale pink of the morning sun cast a faint glow through the reindeer antler-framed windows of the keep's council room. Dark-stained pine beams flowed around huge granite stones of the hexagon-shaped room. Long tapered candles sat snugly within bough-like chandeliers, held by short iron chains from the domed, wooden ceiling. The largest chandelier hung over a huge, horse-shoe-shaped table carved from pale birch and sat around it in rough-sawn spindle-back chairs, were the six men and four women about to seal my fate.

Standing in a pen-like pulpit at the back of the room, my fists clenched the pine rail in front of me, as I silently appraised the strangers who talked quietly amongst themselves. Cream papers, pens, and steaming wooden cups of warm blueberry juice were scattered across the table. Yet singing a half-frozen song to me from the center of the table, held aloft delicately by two sets of iron prongs sunk into the birch wood, was *Kathkar*. The lambent stones in the hilt flickered faintly, the sheen of the steel blade glowing the palest blue.

A hush had descended upon the room when I had been brought in at Niemi's side and placed in the pulpit. A few Royant Platoon members, including Niemi's second-in-command, Shepherd Sherwood and what had to be a dozen nobles known as Hearas and Hearans, occupied the long, Norwickan fleece-draped benches lining the walls of the room.

Heart thundering in my chest, my light a barely there dim glow around my white-knuckled hands, I tore my gaze from an anxious -looking Shep to Rekorious. He sat directly opposite me at the center of the horseshoe. Draped over a powerful shoulder was his family's sage green cloak, a sterling silver fish brooch clasping it tightly over his broad chest. He cleared his throat, and silence descended heavily upon the room. My breath caught in my chest as every head turned to me, then back to their leader.

"*Tarva*, I hereby call this meeting to order." Niemi's voice rang low yet clear, the perfect fit for a commander used to directing his followers. The council members around the table straightened. "This council has been called to discuss two matters. My betrothal to Destry Kivisto *Koskivarri* and her pledge to relinquish her title to the Petish throne."

A collective gasp echoed. One councilman outright paled as he twisted in his seat to look back at me. I stared right at him, unflinching, immovable, unconquerable.

"No one is that foolish," muttered a Petish councilwoman on the right-hand curve of the table. White strands streaked through her coiled, dark hair, and her brown eyes pierced into me. Dressed in a navy high-collared tunic similar to my own, she shuffled the papers before her, a quiet *hurrmph* on her breath.

A younger man on her left, barrel-chested, bearded, and cloaked in dark green, rolled his eyes and grumbled, "Stubborn, Kivisto."

"We shall hear her reasoning shortly, Heara Helmi," placated Rekorious, as he rested a tight fist on the pale table top. "Destry is wholly opposed to the betrothal, and ... as our custom dictates, this means I would have to kill her to claim the throne that is rightfully hers by blood."

Shep shook his head and ran an exasperated hand through his wild, dark blonde curls. Rekorious met my gaze over the heads of the council members, and my mouth set into a mutinous line. He damn well could try and kill me, and I'd give him more scars to add to his budding collection. "Destry has proposed to me that upon relinquishing her throne, she would swear oaths to become my blood rider instead."

A councilman in his late forties, his skin darker than my own, with thick brows and tan-colored eyes, shifted in his seat. His body was thickset and wrapped in a dark red cloak held by a simple birch clasp. "There has not been a blood rider since the fall of the Trinitors." His Petish accent was the strongest I'd ever heard. "Does she have the skillset that warrants such a title?"

Rekorious inhaled deeply, his eyes softening as he appraised me again. "You speak true, Hearan Lael. I believe Destry would have the skills required, in time."

"In time?" piped Heara Helmi, as she arched an eyebrow over her papers. "Time is something we do not have, my lord. Colladon has called its banners to war with Jaryn. Meanwhile, Ilrair encroaches further and further north, both by land and by sea. Your soldiers merely reported to us three days ago that the settlement at Saltfen was now a fully fledged fort. She should accept the betrothal and be done with it."

Anger spiked in my veins, and I ground my teeth as Helmi sat primly in her chair. Yet the news that Jaryn's forces were creeping further north past Aarine, the province now crumbled ruins and ash thanks to his cavalry and the wild ward, left an oily, cold slick down my spine.

A woman of similar age to me, with hair so dark it was near black, scowled at Helmi from her place on the left-hand side of the table. She wore her charcoal-colored cloak twisted over her chest and muscled shoulders, leaving her leather gauntleted arms to move freely as she clenched her pen like a dagger.

"I understand your reservations, Heara Helmi, but Destry is already well established in the basics of swordplay and riding. With the light in her veins, she would be a worthy opponent on the battlefields to come," Niemi ground out.

"She cannot be a blood rider without a mount," said Hearan Lael. "Where is her Pegasus?"

"Ebrel has not returned since saving Kalana." My voice echoed over the room and was met by incredulous silence. "But … I believe that she will."

Lael turned to face me fully then, and I squared my shoulders. "You have a bond with this creature?"

"I do. I believe the Night Pegasus had a hand in our meeting. I doubt that she would let such a bond grow cold." At least, I prayed that she wouldn't.

Helmi rolled her eyes. "No Pegasus, no battle experience. I'm not overly versed in the ancient ways of blood riders, my lord, but I do find Destry foolhardy in thinking she can simply be one"—the Heara snapped her fingers—"just like that."

I had called myself a fool several times this week. I knew there would be a slim chance of avoiding the future that awaited me, but Helmi's words still struck me like a slap in the face. Yet anger warred fiercely with the disappointment that crackled in my chest, and I wouldn't lose this fight lying down.

"How dare you sit there and judge my future, using *my* sword like some spirits damned midwinter decoration?" I snapped harshly, frost and pale purple light coating my nails and the tips of my fingers. *Kathkar* glowed a shade of brighter blue as my anger, that I had tried so hard to leash, cracked to the surface. "I am willingly giving Rekorious the powers he needs to govern this land as *Crevatarn* peacefully, with no blood shed, while also pledging my loyalty to him and maintaining some of my freedoms?"

A *Crevatarn*, a king.

"*I* think," murmured the young woman in the dark gray cloak on my left, as she effortlessly twirled her pen over her fingers. "You should show a little more respect to the woman who freed the spirits, Heara Helmi."

"And *I* think, Minna Turunin, you should only speak when called upon, since you are only seated at this table as a *courtesy* to your military rank," Helmi muttered in reply.

The two women eyeballed each other over the table, Minna choosing to stab the papers before her with her pen. It seemed I had an ally at the table after all.

A young councilman on Rekorious' right, dressed in the same sage green of the Niemi clan, raised a dark tan hand that glinted with two wide, silver rings. He watched me warily over the table, and I looked between him and Rekorious, noting the same brown hair and rugged features, but he was angular and lean compared to the brawn of the Commander. Brothers maybe, or even a cousin? "What freedoms were you hoping to maintain?"

I eased a jagged breath from my lungs, the shards of hope I'd collected like precious gems now tucked deep within my heart, nicked and scratched at my blood and bone. "To dwell where I wish and to marry who I wish. That's hardly unreasonable."

"The *Koskivarri* bloodline is not something to be given away so wistfully," murmured an aged councilman sitting next to Minna, a fawn-colored cloak draped over his withered shoulders. "You are the last of your family. You, my dear, are as precious as winter sunshine."

"Judge my future partner however you wish," I reply, my tone soft yet laced with steel. "But I am *done* bargaining and dealing for my own future. I've had this with the Duke of Aarine, the Heir Lord of Moray, with the King of Ilrair. I will *not* tolerate it from my own people. My *countrymen*. I am offering my service to Petowin in a way that will do her justice. Give me back my sword and my cloak, and I will show you how a Kivisto fights. With grit and light and ice, to my very last *breath*." I waved a shaking hand around the room and threw a daggered look at Helmi, my teeth bared. "Your lord would not be alive right now if it weren't for me. He would be a frozen corpse on the slopes of Serebo."

Helmi released a hiss of outrage, but Lael, Minna, and Shep nodded in affirmation.

Rekorious dragged a hand over his bearded jaw. "It's the truth. Destry saved my life more than once on Serebo. I owe her a debt." He gazed down at his fist that he clenched and unfurled. "Several."

"We vote," croaked the elder next to Minna. "All those in favor of Destry's pledge and the dissolvement of the betrothal, raise your hand."

I tensed, letting go of the pine rail and stepping back. The taste of hoarfrost coated my tongue, and my light twirled from my hands, around my body, pooling in ripples at my feet.

"I propose a caveat, before we vote," said Helmi. *Of course you do,* I hissed in my mind. "A council meeting must be held to deem Destry's future partner as worthy, when her heart has decided that is. Yet how she'll best Lord Niemi, I'll never know. If the council meeting is a hung vote, then a *morean* must be declared, and *not* a ceremonial one. A proper *morean*, like our ancestors once did."

Everyone in the room tensed and surprised glances were thrown around the hexagon space. What on earth was a *morean?* Some kind of ritual? My mind grasped and filtered through the little Petish I knew, but I came up with nothing for the new word.

Rekorious' throat bobbed, the muscle in his jaw jumping as he cast me a glance that was near impossible to read. "Caveat accepted."

Disappointment cracked down the nodules of my spine, and I swallowed, my mouth paper dry.

"Then let's vote," murmured Lael.

Eight hands rose into the air. Three did not. I counted Lael, Minna, the elder, and Rekorious' family member amongst those in favor, even Helmi and the young woman at her side, I noted with a flicker of suspicion. Two men, both in their late fifties and so similar they had to be brothers, wearing identical jade-green cloaks, had not been in favor. A woman with pale white hair and sun-wrinkled skin next to them, had kept her arms crossed over her rose-pink cloak the entire time, refusing to meet my gaze as I looked her over.

I had won the vote, a massive victory, and the weight of the betrothal melted away from my shoulders like late spring snow. Yet digging its claws into my mind with viscous intent, was Helmi's *little caveat* and the havoc-wreaking consequences it could bring. I'd drag Rekorious to one side and get him to explain what the hell a *morean* was, and why everyone looked so bloody worried about it.

"What of the blood rider oaths, my lord?" asked the elder, as he reached for his cup of blueberry juice with a shaking and sun-speckled hand. Minna picked it up for him and helped gently clasp his hand around it.

Rekorious looked down and across at him with a warm smile. I blinked, it was the most tender expression I had seen him make. "At the end of the month, on the full moon, I should think. If tradition should be upheld then—"

The council room door banged open, and all heads twisted toward the wind-whipped Royant messenger, snowmelt still clinging to his shoulders and felt hat, as he raced toward his Commander.

I stepped around the side of the pulpit, noting Shep rising slowly from his bench as the messenger darted to Rekorious' side and whispered fervently in his ear. The Commander shoved to his feet a moment later, sending his papers flying, his breath coming in sharp pants. He stared down at the messenger with such laser focus that my spine locked.

"You're sure?" Rekorious asked harshly.

The messenger nodded. "Arnar's unit confirmed it at dawn this morning."

Rounding on his family member, Rekorious clasped a hand on the wiry young man's shoulder who had sat beside him and hauled him to his feet.

"What did my unit confirm?" asked Arnar, shrugging Rekorious hand off him and crossing his arms.

"Everyone is excused, the meeting is over," ordered Rekorious. "Royants and Minna, to me."

Murmuring amongst themselves, the council members and nobles shuffled quietly from the room, the air now fraught with the tension and urgency that rolled off the Commander. Five other Royant soldiers, including Shep, circled around Rekorious. Seemingly forgotten about and surely no longer a prisoner, I stepped silently from the pulpit to stand beside the table, a healthy distance behind Shep. At such close proximity to *Kathkar*, the blade's arctic song trilled in my head, coaxing me to lift it from where it lay, waiting.

My fingers itched with the urge to don my sword, but I kept my attention on the messenger and the stranglehold he seemed to have on Rekorious with his words.

The messenger cleared his throat, his gaze darting between all of us. "Amadea's at Fort Erskine with a small detachment from Knock Platoon. Jaryn, however, is still in Ilrair."

"Holy shit," whispered a Royant soldier, a female lance corporal.

Minna threw the messenger a wary glance, her arms crossed over the woven leather of her breastplate. "This can't be true."

"A trap surely?" said Shep. "Rek, this *has* to be. Jaryn has never left her so unguarded before, or so far north."

Arnar looked cooly across at Shep. "It could also be the perfect opportunity we've been waiting for."

My gaze snapped to Arnar, as tendrils of ice curled away from the central taper in my mind. A flutter of unease roiled in my stomach.

"It's a chance I'm not willing to let pass," ground out Rekorious. "If this is our one attempt to free her, I'll take it. Assemble the full platoon, we fly out as soon as we're ready."

I stepped forward, pushing in to stand between Shep and Minna. "Let me come with you."

Rekorious bared his teeth. "I'm not risking it. You're not going anywhere near that fort."

I stiffened. "The hell I am."

Shep shrugged, casting his Commander a wary glance. "We can use every person we can get. I wouldn't be surprised if Commander Halle hasn't already called for reinforcements to fly north. She's a ruthless piece of shit."

Rekorious dragged a palm over his trimmed beard, then rested his hands on his hips. "They'll see us flying in from a mile away, there's no cover out there. We could try using the cliff face to our advantage.

We have some of our best bowmen with us. Shoot as many as we can, then we dive down."

"Amadea is my friend," I pleaded. "Let me go in. Surely this Knock Platoon Commander has orders to capture us. Let me go in, blind them, then you attack. Use the dawn sun tomorrow to shield your approach."

"Do you have enough power to blind a whole platoon?" Rekorious' voice was the harshest, most lethal I'd ever heard it, even when he'd been captured by Narve. Barely leashed aggression rippled off him.

"Yes." *No*, but for Amadea I would risk it. Ice dragged a primordial touch over my skin and I leaned into it, brushing against it with my purple-tinted light. "Let me try."

"We risk losing you and Amadea to Jaryn, if this doesn't work," said Rekorious, leveling a stare that had me clenching my fists. I ground down on the part of me that quaked at the mention of the King's name.

I inched forward, lifted my chin and stared the Commander down. Something cracked and groaned in my veins, whispering against my skin with every pounding beat of my heart. My light shuddered against it, welcoming it. The Night Pegasus might have forsaken me, but the mountain spirits and Varranar had given me a gift for freeing them. One that ached to be used. "Let me try."

CHAPTER EIGHT

ASHER

Another guttural hiss greeted me as I returned to the cave with two skinfuls of freshwater. Straight white teeth flashed in the brighter gloom, and I gave the owling a crooked grin.

"Good morning to you too," I muttered, as I held out one of the water skins to her.

The owling scowled, her back braced against the cave wall, knees tucked tight to her chest. My gambeson sat folded beside her, but she had kept my coat wrapped around her. Color had returned to the sharp planes of her face, and she no longer looked like she was on death's door. I patted my right trouser pocket, checking the arrowhead was tucked safely away.

Hesitantly, she reached out with her uninjured left arm and plucked the waterskin from my grasp. She had nearly drunk the whole thing dry, before passing it back to me.

"Hungry?" My eyebrows lifted, glancing between her and the strips of rabbit meat I had roasted after sunrise.

That got her interest. She sniffed eagerly. "Yes."

Sitting down a healthy distance away, I passed her a thin slab of rock with the cooked meat atop it, along with a slice of slightly crushed bread.

"Eat them slowly," I ordered, eyeing the ravenous look on her face. "Or you'll be sick."

A curt nod was her only reply, before she dove into her meal. I ate silently beside her, mentally tallying the supplies we had. We'd have enough to get us to Fort Garobear, plus a little extra if I supplemented it with hunting.

I threw a quick sidelong glance at the Truth Keeper. She watched the fire while she ate, slowly, like I'd told her. I doubted she would be able to fly if she shifted, which would make stopping her from escaping a little easier. Without Pherox, there would be no way I could keep up with her should she fly away.

Even with my shadows tailing her, she'd quickly gain the miles and simply vanish. I had to get her to Fort Garobear before she could fly again. It would make the exchange easier if she stayed in her human form. I ignored the pang of unease in my gut as I ate. I'd deal with the consequences of trading her later and refused to acknowledge the fact I was being no better than the wild ward right now.

The owling finished her meal and placed her stone down, tucking her knees to her chest again.

"How does your shoulder feel?" I asked quietly, noting that she hadn't bled through her bandages. The fabric of her thick woolen, shin-length dress hung haphazardly around her collarbone, but it kept her covered after I'd cut it last night.

She eyed me silently, her features warring between gratitude and anger. "It throbs, but nothing like it did." She held my gaze then, and my breath hitched. "I feel like I should thank you, but I won't."

Stiffening, I jutted my chin upward. "Couldn't have you dying on me."

A scowl flitted across her ethereal face. "Tell me what the deal is."

"By giving you to the King of Colladon, the Scarp becomes Nijinx territory." I twined my long fingers in my lap and didn't back down from her.

Her irises glowed in confirmation at my words, and I didn't miss her sharp swallow. She searched my face, and I refused to let myself fidget under her golden gaze.

"You're doing this ... to help the Nijinxes?" She quirked a dark blonde eyebrow in genuine confusion.

"Yes," I muttered. A good deed to try and balance out the horrors I had inflicted on my family, on Orrin, on innocents of Saltfen. My fingers curled into fists on my lap. I looked down, then up, and we held each other's stare for what felt like a lifetime, becoming lost in a tide of scorching dawn light and seething darkness. My heart hammered in my chest as she drank me in. "Tell me your name."

She blinked at the request, her white hair shifting over her toned shoulders. "My name?"

The sudden need to know it, to hear it, overwhelmed me. "Please."

Biting her full lower lip, she gazed down at her knees, her hair cascading around her like a shroud. It took all my willpower to stay still, not to reach forward and sweep back that pale mane to see her face. Her voice was hushed, as if spoken in a willful prayer. "My name is Calliope."

Her words washed over me, the knowledge she had shared, settling deep within my core. My shadows sifted over it, anchoring it to my soul. I would never forget it. Just like Pherox and Vesperum's. My body would age, my mind would fray, but I would remember those names until they were the last things my conscious clung to.

I dipped my head so that she would meet my gaze again. She settled her chin on her knees and looked across at me. Wariness clung to every part of her taut body. My left hand reached out, and she flinched. My heart twisted again, yet I held steady, waiting.

"My name is Asher. Asher Fields."

Gingerly, she placed her left hand in mine, and my palm dwarfed hers, yet I could sense the iron-strong power in her bones. Her grip was firm despite the scent of her fear. Gently, almost reluctantly, I let go, and her hand retreated to the folds of my coat.

"You gain nothing from this deal," she whispered, tucking my coat tighter around herself. "The Nijinxes will have the Scarp, the King ... will have me, but what about you? What do you get?"

I ran a hand over the week's worth of stubble that covered my jaw. "A reprieve."

Those golden eyes seared into the very depths of my soul, and I would be lying if I said it didn't frighten me. Just a little.

"A reprieve from what?" she whispered.

"The guilt." It was all I was willing to offer her. This conversation was over. I stood, picked up my gambeson and pulled it on.

I glanced down at her face that seemed to glow with the light of a pre-dawn sky. Her eyebrows pinched together, her lips parted like she would ask more. It was the first time she had looked at me without fear gleaming in those unearthly eyes.

"Can you walk?" I asked, my voice rough. With a booted foot, I knocked the campfire apart, snow hissing where the ashes touched it.

Her face tightened, but she hauled herself to her feet, awkwardly draping my coat over her shoulders. I blinked in surprise. I was tall, but she easily came up to my shoulder. My shadows lingered around her, orbiting her like meteors. Rolling my eyes, I huffed, and the shadows dispersed, albeit slowly.

Calliope tracked them suspiciously. "They are sentient? Your shadows?"

I heaved on my pack and checked my daggers. "They certainly have a mind of their own."

A tiny shadow curled around my ear, and I brushed it away. They were incessant today, like hungry cats.

"They bother you?"

"Not usually," I muttered, throwing a long, tapering shadow that lingered behind Calliope a glare. The shadow curled inward and vanished. I trusted my shadows wholeheartedly, but I could do without their busybodyness today.

They could rip the air from someone's lungs, could turn the mind, so that all you could see was darkness and could gather information if I needed it. Getting used to them had been as easy as breathing, easier still when the wild ward had been killed. Yet it still surprised me that even though I controlled them, could wield them as easily as any weapon, they could think and act of their own accord when they felt like it.

Which now that Calliope was up and walking, was a little fucking unnerving.

Calliope's left hand reached out tentatively, and a shadow twined gently through her tanned fingers. I watched closely, my body frozen in place. My nostrils flared, and the shadow pulled away, but I could feel its reluctance to leave her embrace.

The Truth Keeper dropped her hand slowly, an unspoken question on her face. I ignored it. "Let's go. It's a five-day trek where we're headed, and I don't want to waste any more daylight."

"And what makes you think I'm going anywhere with *you*, huntsman?"

I turned to face her slowly, my shoulders thrown back. Her words sliced into me like knives, yet I ground down on that part of me that had been in her shoes. My hands were tense fists at my sides, and I took a deep, settling breath. "I'm here to do a job, to get you from this hellhole to the King. In return, my friends get to live in the peace they deserve."

She seemed to grow another inch, as she lifted her chin and somehow managed to stare *down* at me. "And do I not deserve peace?"

"Do you?" I snarled, running a hand through my hair.

Calliope recoiled like I'd struck her, and I immediately regretted my words.

"You know what awaits me, you know the kind of life you're dragging me to."

"I don't care." If she heard the thrum of warning in my voice, she didn't heed it.

Her hands curled into fists then, and they shook with rage. "*Liar.*"

Fucking Truth Keepers. I pointed at the cave's entrance, my expression murderous as I angled my body to let her clearly see the daggers strapped to my waist. Calliope arched an elegant eyebrow, like she *knew* I would never use them on her, despite my threat. "Get. Moving."

"Where will the exchange take place?"

"Fort Garobear," I gritted out.

I had never seen a ghost, but I imagined my face would look like hers if I did. Calliope's eyes widened, and her golden face paled to a sickly white. Her voice was an unearthly, low rasp. "*No.*"

"I wasn't asking."

"You *cannot* take me back there."

I cocked my head, intrigued that this wild creature had ever seen the fort. "You've been there before?"

Her entire body was shaking now. "I vowed to never step foot in that place again."

My nonchalant shrug was utterly feigned. "Sounds like you'll be no stranger to the place. Care to show me the way?"

Calliope revealed to me then, the true wild nature that roiled beneath her skin. Her chapped lips fully pulled back from her teeth, and the hiss she emitted was the most hostile sound I'd ever heard. Her long fingers curled into tense claws that probably ached to tear me apart limb from limb. I was tempted to let her try.

Forcing a sigh from my throat, I palmed a dagger free and pointed it at her panting chest. "Start walking, owling."

CHAPTER NINE

EBREL

"*He dreams of the fire,*" murmured Hestian. The stallion stood over his sleeping rider, steadfastly keeping watch through the long, dark hours. Coen's body was curled beside the small campfire, a thick woolen blanket tucked tightly around him. Yet the soldier's body twitched with tension, and a low, pain-filled hiss escaped his mouth as he slept.

I stepped closer to the golden stallion, grateful for the body heat he emitted. "*What fire?*"

Hestian exhaled and gazed down at Coen. "*We Ilrairian Pegasi must undergo a bonding process when it's time for us to be broken in and paired with a rider. We don't get to choose who that person will be, and the bonding process is different for every pairing.*"

"*What happened to you? To Coen?*" I asked softly.

"*Soldier and Pegasus are locked in a stone tower. About halfway up, the walls are too slick for a human to climb. There is a latch that opens a huge door to open sky and freedom beyond. Only a Pegasus can reach the door, but only a human can operate the latch to open it.*"

"*So, you have to work together to get out?*"

"*There's that.*" Hestian's body tensed, and I brushed his shoulder with my wing in comfort. "*Then there's the smoke too.*" He tossed his head at the small, flickering campfire. "*It is not natural woodsmoke, in truth, I'm not sure if it's even smoke at all, but it's what we, the Pegasi that survived, call it."*

"Some of you die *during this? This bonding process?"*

"Those in high command keep it contained, but yes, Ebrel, some Pegasi don't survive. Especially those from bloodlines that hark back to the more powerful Trinitors." I watched Hestian closely, as the stallion seemed to lose himself in the flames that danced over the snapping birch logs and stag moss. *"The smoke, it's hallucinogenic. Some say it's freezing to the touch, but for Silvano and I ... the smoke burned. To breathe it in felt like it was scorching your lungs, disintegrating them. Yet I think, had it been cold, we wouldn't have survived. We spent a full day lost to the visions the smoke induces. I dreamed that I flew so high I was caught between the light banners of the Night Pegasus and the heat of our sun. No matter how hard I tried, I couldn't break through back to Earth. I was utterly alone up there, penned between the scorching flames of Tavaris and the banners of the Night Pegasus. No matter how quickly I flew, the Night Pegasus flew faster, keeping me trapped up there."*

"How did you wake up?"

Hestian flinched and lowered his muzzle to breathe softly over Coen's tousled, night-washed hair. *"I stopped flying and let myself free fall. The moment I stopped fighting, the Night Pegasus vanished, and I was able to get beneath the clouds of our Earth, then I woke up. But those moments of free falling, of giving up ..."* He looked up and met my gaze. *"I never want to feel that helpless again. I came to first and hauled Silvano onto my back and flew to the ledge that holds the latch, out of the reach of the smoke. I figured he would be enduring something similar to what I had just experienced, and I would want someone to wake me up."*

Our sweet, grass-scented breaths mingled in the frozen air as Hestian fell into a poignant silence beside me. I took in the noble carriage of his head, the blonde tendrils of his forelock that fell over his tawny eyes, then I looked down at the male who slept fitfully at our hooves.

Hestian followed my gaze. *"Silvano told me once what he saw. That he would touch those he loved and they would burn, rendered to nothing but ashes."*

Coen's face contorted in pain, and his fist clenched against the dark gray wool of the blanket. Did the visions still haunt him? The warrior hissed once more, his jaw tight, and my muzzle lowered to wake him from his nightmare, but Hestian blocked me with a gentle, velveteen touch.

"Don't wake him, roan one. The dream will just start afresh when he falls asleep again. Let it come to an end. Then he can truly rest."

"That will work?"

Hestian released a long breath, snowflakes twirling with the exhale. *"It works for me."*

Coen doused his small campfire and wrapped his thick, burgundy scarf around his head again. The wind caressed the strong, tanned planes of his face, and even I had to admit that the wilds agreed with him. Away from the strict rules of the Ilrair cavalry and that snake Jaryn, Coen appeared ... adept ... *alive*. Like whatever had been holding him back was finally freed. My ears twitched back and forth as my earth-brown eyes surveyed him.

Destry had felt something for this man, likely still did. I felt how torn she had been at Saltfen, when Aalto Thorra had urged her to flee. She had wanted to stay, to go to the Commander flying beside me. I had sensed his longing for her too. It was what had me traveling with him now. That deep, desperate longing that did not bargain with reason or doubt.

Yet he was Ilrairian, would always be Ilrairian, and those roots ran deep. If he so much as looked at Destry wrong, I would cave in his chest. I'd hurt Thorra too. I'd scented Destry's fear and hurt mixed with the Royant Commander's scent. Thorra had caused that.

Coen mounted his golden stallion and nodded to me. "Follow Hestian, Ebrel. We can't be too far now. I-I can *feel* it."

I whickered in response, the freezing wind ruffling the dusky brown of my feathers as I extended them. The sky called my name like a siren's song, and I leaned into it, desperate to take to the air.

Clouds plumed and whipped across the peaks surrounding us, each tainted a pale lavender as the sun rose. This far north, the days were short in winter, the sun never quite fully breaching the horizon. The eternal dawn, humans and animals alike called it. It made whatever daylight there was very precious and valuable. Not something to be wasted.

Coen urged Hestian to take flight, and the palomino surged effortlessly into the ice-hewn air. I followed a breath behind them, our shadows flitting over the snow-covered ground below. Urgency rolled off Coen even as he rode, his body sure and strong in the saddle. He had likely ridden a horse before he could even walk as a child, and it showed.

"I can't tell, roan one, if it's me or my rider you keep watching," chided Hestian, his powerful white wings beating the air with ease. The heaviness of last night seemed to have left him this morning, and he wanted to distract himself.

The stallion made a show of arching his neck, and I huffed. *"I don't trust either of you, despite Coen's best intentions."*

Hestian snorted and banked to the east under Coen's expert guidance. *"His intentions are pure. He only wants Destry to be safe, just as you do."*

"Only he can prove that, Hestian. Jaryn holds his reins, just as Coen holds yours."

Smaller peaks darted by, hiding us in long, gnarled shadows once more. It felt right to be flying so far north, like the land and sky had been calling me home all this time. We rose to surge over a granite saddleback between two rounded, boulder-strewn mountains, then dropped to stay sheltered between the steep valley sides long-lost glaciers had created.

Hestian's gold and dark tan eyes roved over me once more as I drew up alongside him, our hooves shearing the tiny ice particles that hung suspended through the sky. They skittered in our wake in a swirl of freezing air.

"Jaryn no longer holds his reins, roan one."

"Again, only Coen can prove that. As prettily as you talk, Hestian, I don't trust one word that leaves that charming muzzle of yours."

Hestian tucked his forelimbs to his deep chest and rose in the air, a haughty expression in the angle of his golden head. *"You find me charming?"*

I rolled my eyes, and my nostrils flared. *"Stallions."*

The tips of his gleaming white feathers brushed against my pink speckled ones. *"That wasn't a no."*

Slowly, I banked away from him, creating a larger distance between us. I had been close to Orrin after Fintan's death, but that had been a familial relationship rooted in survival and respect. This was different. Just the thought of Fintan made my chest tighten. Orrin's older brother had loved me deeply, the Mountain Horse had been as strong and as powerful as Hestian, yet he had still been killed. Murdered for loving a branded loner like me.

I dipped my nose to the right to peer back at the brand that still tarnished my haunch. It no longer burned in the vicinity of other northern Pegasi, with the wild ward dead, her magic was null and void. But the large scar shaped as a cross remained, seared into my skin for the rest of my life.

Hestian, sensing my sadness, whickered softly in his throat, the sound swiftly snatched away by the speed in which we flew. I ignored him and let the gloom of my past seep into every corner of my soul. My dam had been a loner, only seeking the shelter of small herds when it suited her. I had come to love the lifestyle also, the freedom, until the wild ward had taken Fintan and cursed me into a solitude I couldn't escape without her death. Finding Destry had been a solace, a balm over my shattered soul, and I still thanked the Night Pegasus for guiding me to her.

I wouldn't leave Destry to some unknown, cruel fate.

CHAPTER TEN

DESTRY

B eing on the back of the Pegasus again felt like coming home. I just wished it had been Ebrel and not Kalana. The mare flew as if she wasn't hindered by the two riders on her back. She flew so swiftly, it brought tears to my eyes, despite being sheltered from most of the wind by Rekorious' warrior body. We had raced from the keep with a full detachment of Royants to find Amadea. Despite being freed from my betrothal, Rekorious had been firm in not allowing me to don *Kathkar*. To risk wielding it now, before I had the true expertise to use it like an extension of my own body, would also risk losing it.

A low-lying winter sun had dimly lit our flight from the eastern Petish border into the Andun Mountain Range. Amadea's life and freedom wobbled on a knife's edge. Jaryn would not let such a prize go so easily, yet despite Rek's certainty, Shep's warning of a trap made my blood run cold. Jaryn made every move with cold, cruel precision, and placing Amadea at such close vicinity to us made no sense.

As soon as we passed into the Anduns, I felt that well of ice magic in my chest rumble awake. It cracked and splintered, veins of it growing and spreading outward. A clear, star-filled night beckoned. I glanced up at the dusk-readied sky with a mix of longing and anger. Maybe I was of no use to the Night Pegasus now, with most of my light gone, yet what little remained simmered and spat like a wildfire. It was upset. *I* was upset.

The spirits were free, and I felt those belonging to the mountains brush up against my consciousness as we flew past. Ghel, the northernmost mountain, Serebo's younger sister, felt like hoarfrost and stag moss in my mind, twined with a sighing, thankful breath. It brought me a small dose of pride and comfort that I was remembered by these lands, by thoughts and memories passed between crevasses and snowmelt-filled rivers.

Ghel whispered away from me, and the ice in my veins thundered in reply, as we descended in pink and violet skies. Rekorious squeezed my arm that was wrapped around his solid torso, a warning to the swift plunge of Kalana, as the unit of Royants plummeted for a valley far below.

The soldiers and their Pegasi landed swiftly. Shep dismounted his sorrel-colored mare and walked over to a wiry young man and a middle-aged woman with short black hair, who stood before a flickering campfire. Cautiously, I slipped off Kalana, my feet frozen in their boots, and walked stiffly after Rekorious and his second-in-command.

My gaze bounced between the pair we approached. They wore Niemi-green cloaks over their thick woolen gambesons, and I recognized the woman from the stone cabin, where the Royants had fled after deserting Saltfen, but the young man was a stranger. A similar age and build to Arnar, but with cropped, jet-black hair, he noted me warily over the flames, a sword strapped down his spine.

Rekorious stalked toward them both and pulled each of them into a hug. "Grier, Elias, tell me everything."

Shep stepped back into the gathering shadows beside me, his face fully chilled and windswept. He kept his voice low. "Grier is Rek's ghost spy, Elias is her apprentice, a wisp spy. He's Rek's youngest cousin and Arnar's younger brother."

I nodded, my light twining around our boots, casting the snow a deep purple color. Despite abandoning their posts as Ilrairian soldiers, it seemed they had kept their ranks and formation after deserting. They were wholly Rekorious' warriors now, and they probably always had been.

Shep removed his felt hat and ran a gloved hand through his mop of tight blonde curls. Cunningly, he glanced between me and the warlord. "He's not a monster, you know."

"He told me the same thing," I said softly. I knew deep in my bones, he was not the same as Narve, that there was kindness in the warlord, alongside his ruthlessness.

"He's bound by duty to Petowin, his family, and to us. Everything he's done has been to create a better future for Petowin."

I glanced sidelong at the sergeant, noting the earnest honesty on his golden face. "That's all I want for Petowin too, Shep. I just wish ..." I looked across from him to Rekorious, whose serious face nodded along to the report Grier was hastily giving him. "I'm done being a pawn, Shep. He knows that. Now the council knows it too."

The sergeant chuffed and crossed his arms over his chest. "I should hope so. It's a hell of a scar you've given him." He glanced down at his boots, taking in my swirling light. "I-I was on the ship, when Amadea sailed for Ilrair. The love they shared ... I hope we can get her out. Rekorious has never been the same without her."

Yet hope was a delicate thing in my chest, twining with the ice that cracked there. Being here, so close to the mountains and the ice spirit that had gifted it, made the power feel heightened. I sucked down a steadying breath, urging it to settle and calm. Inwardly, my light brushed against it. *Soon*, it whispered. *Soon*.

Rekorious squeezed Elias' shoulder then walked back toward us, a plan already forming on his handsome face. Arnar fell into step beside him. "We'll case Fort Erskine tonight and get into position for a dawn attack tomorrow. Elias confirmed it's a small detachment, twenty-five soldiers at the very most. The rest of the platoon is readying Fort Ankory after it was abandoned."

"Ankory is a good thirty miles away to the west," explained Shep for my benefit. "Seems like they're looking to bring all the old forts up and running again. If they go for Fort Vervelli and Fort Hound too, that'll give them footholds across the width of the Boreals."

"We can't risk that," murmured Arnar.

"Once we get Amadea out, we'll have the remaining forts manned," ordered Rekorious. "We can't let those bastards get any further north."

The soldiers rested, fed and watered the Pegasi, then we took to the skies again. It was somewhere past midnight, a crescent moon hanging low in the sky. An urgent, determined energy rolled off Rekorious as I sat tucked behind him on Kalana's back. I had no choice but to hang on tight to the leather of his long riding coat, as the gray Pegasus mare swept low over snow-draped granite cliffs and frozen creeks. This close to the mountainous foothills, there wasn't much in the way of trees, just low-lying shrubs, caves, and sheer cliff faces. Unicorn territory. Rekorious and I had become well acquainted with this kind of terrain on our trek to Serebo with the Kottin Mirror.

A low, punching feeling hit my gut, as something akin to mourning for Aalto washed over me. The man in front of me, a gifted rider and fighter, was still all those things I had found alluring and admirable, but now he had an edge to him, as sharp of the two short swords strapped to his back.

The scabbards of *Vorna* and *Vayla* pressed into the leather breastplate strapped over my chest as Kalana dropped lower in the sky. Spirits, if Jaryn or one of his wretched dogs like Narve or Lonan, decided to punish Amadea if our rescue attempt failed ... I knew all too well the kind of terror they liked to inflict. Yet under *Kathkar's* glowing blade, I had made sure Narve never touched a woman like that again. It made the hollow, distant torment of what he did to me a little easier to bear, yet there had been nights this week when nightmares had cleaved me from what little sleep I had found. Nightmares filled with his face and the feeling of his cold lips pressing to mine.

Hastily, I swallowed the bile that rose in my throat.

As the night drew on, I felt Rekorious' body grow more tense in front of me.

"We'll find her," I said over the chill wind.

The Commander swallowed, his shoulders tight under his coat. "We have to."

Up ahead, the faint wooden towers of Fort Erskine came into view, and we lowered in altitude even further. The alpine fort's northern wall was braced up against a towering cliff face, the rest of its palisades lurched against the banks of a now frozen river. It was nearly impenetrable, but no banners flew from its flag posts and no smoke drifted from its smithy and chimneys.

My light tugged against my chest, flickering over my collarbone. Ripping my gaze from the distant fort, I looked down at a snow-covered boulder field.

I froze. Rekorious twisted his head to look back at me, then down to where I stared and stared.

Kalana plummeted with her rider's grip on the reins, and we dropped from the pre-dawn sky. The Royants followed us, as we landed urgently amongst the rock-strewn meadow, snow vortexing upward with the downdraft of Pegasi wings. I dismounted and took a wary step forward, the hair on the back of my neck rising, Rekorious standing shoulder to shoulder with me.

There, lying beside a behemoth of a boulder, his neck and wings broken, was Amadea's gray Pegasus gelding.

Shep moved slowly to Rekorious' other side, his features awash with dread. Our gazes followed the blood trail that spattered over the snow like a morbid taunt, to the road that led straight to the fort.

The snarl that ripped from Rekorious was lethal, and he stalked forward. Shep and I moved in unison, wrenching against his iron-strong arms. It was like trying to stop an avalanche.

"It *is* a trap," warned Shep. "They *are* waiting for us. *Look*."

The sergeant pointed at the tallest wooden watchtower, where on a flurrying wind, a forest green banner was being hoisted. Embroidered with two crossed golden lances, it snapped as it was fully hoisted. I flinched. The royal emblem of Ilrair. Beneath it came a second banner. A hammer on a navy field. Knock Platoon.

"*Fuck*," snapped Shep. "They would only slaughter her Pegasus if she had tried to escape."

"She's in there." Rekorious trembled with rage. "They have her in there."

"Seems like Jaryn has a new pet platoon," growled Arnar as he stalked to Shep's side. "Who's been patrolling here? Are they sure it was just a detachment? The killing of her Pegasus is surely a taunt? They knew we were coming for her."

A horn blew in the gray air around us, three short blasts. The Ilrairian's knew we were here.

Rekorious clenched and unclenched his fists. "Elias patrols here."

My gaze danced from Rekorious to Shep, and I noted the doubt and anger that lay there. "Would your brother betray his cousin, Arnar?"

Arnar's face contorted with rage. "He would *never*."

Shep shook his head. "Grier wouldn't condemn Amadea like this."

"What's that supposed to mean, Sherwood?" spat Arnar. "My brother is innocent."

Rekorious' furious gaze whipped to me, but I didn't flinch from it. The ice magic under my skin moaned and shuddered. I was on to something. *Truth* ... it rumbled. *Truth*. But there was only one way to be certain. "Family can betray you, Niemi."

"He's young, but he's not that fucking *stupid*." Rekorious dragged a hand through his hair.

Shep shook his head. "Elias is the one who's been patrolling this territory, Rek. You have to consider the possibility."

"I'll kill him if he has," the Commander snarled. That was fear shining in his bronze eyes, not for himself, but for Amadea.

"How dare you accuse him of such treachery," hissed Arnar.

"I might be able to help you confirm it," I whispered. "But I'll need *Kathkar*."

Rekorious dipped his chin, he knew the power that Varranar had imbued into my family's sword. He had been there when the ice spirit had gifted it. He just didn't know that it pounded in my blood too, and I wasn't about to show him, not yet.

"Get a rider to Grier now. I want Elias secured. Don't tell him *anything*." He turned from Shep and a seething Arnar, to me. "He'll have a trial once we get Amadea out, you can use *Kathkar* then." He twisted, gazing up at the distant fort with barely checked rage. "They expect us to attack them openly. I say we surprise them."

Fear was a heady song in my bones, and I let it wash over me. My hands trembled as I walked up the worn, rutted road to the fort's main gates. I was utterly exposed out here. If one of the Knock Platoon archers fancied spearing an arrow through my chest, they could.

I shook that thought away as the long shadows of the eastern palisade doused me in gloom. High above the jutting walls, the sky was awash with amethyst. I quickly glanced to my right, where the wind-smoothed cliff face reached up and up, towering over the fort nestled beside it.

My heart stuttered in my chest as my boots crunched upon the snow. I paused, as the battered and worn double gates heaved inward with a long, rusted groan. A bitter breeze swept strands of my knotted hair off my face, and my shoulders were thrown back in wild defiance.

Yet my resolve cracked when I looked upon the warrior who awaited me in the vast courtyard. Not the formidable female Commander of Knock Platoon. Not Jaryn or Narve.

The bald-headed man, clothed in his typical black leather, threw me a wicked smile, as he clasped his hands in front of his towering body.

My nostrils flared, panic leaching into my blood. Oh, *fuck*. Memories assaulted me, and it took all my strength not to bolt. I dug the soles of my boots into the snow and breathed deeply through my nose. The sound of a cymbal being struck followed by a faint popping, resounded in my head, as ice magic surged through my body alongside pounding adrenaline.

"Hoping to find someone again, are we?" taunted Lonan Donaghue.

Beyond him, the courtyard was deserted, the cavalry soldiers of Knock Platoon nowhere in sight. Shimmering violet threads pulsed across my vision and twined around my clenched fists. Yet the last time we fought, my light had no effect on the warrior. I took a step forward and Lonan arched a dark brow.

"Where is she?" I hissed.

Lonan smiled. "You won't be finding her anytime soon, wild one."

Baring my teeth, I treaded forward over the threshold of the gate, and with another echoing screech, they slowly closed behind me. Caging me in here with this monster. I really wished I had *Kathkar*. Yet until I could wield that formidable sword with the same ease as taking a breath, I would not risk yielding it to my enemies. Even if Niemi had given me no bloody choice in the matter. Yet Shep had snuck three daggers into my coat while his Commander's back was turned. One in each deep pocket, the third tucked snugly beside the ankle of my right boot.

I glanced down at the trampled snow, strewn with blood, noting the countless recent hoof and footprints. A slim, speckled trail wove across the vast courtyard and toward an open door in the far corner. They had likely moved Amadea, but it was my only clue so far. Where the fuck was Knock Platoon? The mess hall and stables were utterly silent.

Lonan noted my gaze and stepped forward. He had an array of weapons on him, the most fearsome being his new sword, which was strapped down his spine, the ruby-red hilt glowing faintly over his shoulder. He was strong and heavily armed, but I was leaner, quicker. I wouldn't lure him into a fight unless I absolutely had to. I wouldn't make that mistake twice.

"Narve sends his regards." Lonan's words struck me like a fist.

I couldn't hide my flinch. "I'm surprised he didn't ask you to kill him."

The warrior huffed and inched closer. "He's holed up in his father's lands, plotting your demise."

I rolled my eyes. "How original, if you see him again, tell him I'll happily cut off more of his body parts."

"Watch your mouth, winny."

I sneered, coaxing the rage that flickered across Lonan's face. "Does Jaryn know that you're a coward? That you *fled* instead of protecting Narve?" His stubbled jaw clenched. *Good*. "Does this platoon know that you will work for the highest bidder, and leave them high and dry if a better offer crawls into your lap?"

Slowly, his hands unfurled to claws at his sides. "Shut your goddamn mouth, *whore*."

Another step closer. "Or better still, that as soon as a real threat comes along, you'll hightail it out of here like the craven you are," I hissed.

Something dark snapped in Lonan, and he roared, his gloved right fist swinging wide, striking for my face. I ran, ducking his arm, my heart galloping in my chest, and I pelted for the open doorway.

Lonan swore, twisting on the snow and raced after me, but I was quicker. Boots unsteady on the slick ground, I closed the distance to the open door. Lonan's pounding feet echoed behind me as he snarled, hand outstretched to snare my neck.

I dove to one knee, skidding through the doorway in a spray of snow and slush. With a booted foot, I kicked the door closed and shoved my hand against the lock. Ice speared from my fingertips, melding the iron shut. A breath later, Lonan's body slammed into the wood, sending a shower of splinters over my face and neck.

"I will hunt you down, you little *rat*," snarled Lonan.

Panting harshly, I hauled myself back to my feet and gazed down at my trembling right hand. Power surged through my body, like a glacier tearing its way through stone and earth. Blood and frigid ice particles roared in my head. On panting, steadying breaths, I clenched and unfurled my fingers, desperately urging the ice to calm. The magic hummed and crackled in response.

It was dark in the paneled corridor, and I sent a plume of violet light out ahead of me with my left hand. Droplets shone on the worn cobblestones. Amadea's blood, it had to be. I walked quickly down the silent hallway, one hand braced on the wall, as I followed the blood trail. Where the hell was Knock Platoon hiding? Dust plumed in the beams of my light, striating and pulsing around me, as I rounded the corner slowly.

Three ceiling-height iron grates awaited me. My light fanned and skittered outward, like limbs of a tree, probing the darkened corners of each jail cell. Nothing. No one. Not a damn dratted soul.

"*Fuck*," I whispered. Looking back at the corridor, I retraced the blood trail again. The flecks stopped at the entryway to the cells. Beyond that, nothing. I peered down harder at the cobblestone floor. Delicately, I rocked my bodyweight back and forth, then I heard it. The unmistakable creak of wood. Dropping to one knee, I rapped my knuckles against the false, wooden cobblestones. Hollow.

My heart galloped in my chest as I desperately felt the seams of the hidden doorway. Gritting my teeth, I placed my flattened palm over the floor and pressed my full weight behind it. Ice speared from my fingers and enameled the wood, forming a large rectangle the width of the corridor. Large enough to fit a Pegasus through. I huffed and pressed down harder. The ice hummed in response as it penetrated deeper into the false floor. Wood creaked and groaned as my magic forced it to warp and buckle beneath my hand.

Carved cobblestones splintered and cracked, as the ice forced it to shrink and become brittle and weak under my touch. I rose slowly, purpose wreathing my bones as the door warped in on itself, then sheared into jagged shards before falling away into darkness. Picking up two long slivers of serrated oak wood, I tucked them into the woven fabric of my belt. A packed earth floor and frozen updraft greeted me, as I stepped into Fort Erskine's secret tunnels.

I reeled my light back, my eyes slowly adjusting to the utter darkness. Numb fingers softly following the contours of the wall, I kept my breath to silent, controlled sips, despite how much my heart pounded against my ribs. The faintest gray glow waited ahead, and I kept tucked beside the wall as I treaded on quiet feet closer and closer to it.

The coppery tang of blood hung in the damp air, and I swallowed harshly. Rage made my fingers shake. They would die for what they'd done to Amadea and her Pegasus.

Short, barked orders echoed from beyond the tunnel's mouth, and I shuddered to a stop, slinking to brace my back against the wall. Slowly, I palmed a dagger free from my pocket. Clamping my lips tightly together to stop my breath from clouding, I inched forward, closer. Closer.

My eyes adjusted to the weak pre-dawn reflecting off deep snow beyond the shadows of the tunnel. Ice clicked in my head as I counted the members of the cavalry unit that were preparing to take flight. Twenty Knock Platoon soldiers and their Pegasi, not the full platoon, but enough to be a big problem for me. At the center of where they congregated was a tall, pale blonde woman, her hair tightly coiled into a low bun at the nape of her neck. Her Ilrairian uniform hugged the angular planes of her honed body, and her muscled right arm and hand firmly held Amadea's throat in a viselike grip.

The Queen of Ilrair clawed at the woman's hand, but Commander Halle simply smiled and lowered her arm, forcing Amadea's legs to buckle on the snow as she gasped for air. Rage simmered under my skin, and a low snarl rumbled from my chest. Amadea's winter clothing, a thick woolen light gray coat, skirt, and sweater were smeared in blood from the cuts to her beautiful face. Dark curls swayed, matted and blood-crusted, over the deep brown of her skin.

"Fly with us or die, Amadea," crooned Commander Halle.

"Fuck. *You*," Amadea choked out as she struggled to get her legs underneath her in the deep snow. Her right arm swung wildly to try and punch the Commander, but Halle loosed a soft laugh and her grip tightened around the Queen's neck.

There were a dozen frozen rivers near here. Why wasn't Amadea using her power? She could drown Halle with ease, just like she had done to my attackers.

I whipped my head back to face the darkness of the tunnel as hurried footsteps echoed over the stone. *Lonan*. Panic roared in my blood as I inched closer to the meek dawn light and looked skyward. The Royants were about to attack an empty fortress when, in reality, the enemy was nowhere near them. From the thick pine forest beyond the Knock Platoon soldiers, I guessed we were a good half mile from the fort.

Steel scraped along stone behind me as Lonan's ruby-hilted sword made contact with the tunnel wall. My time had run out. Teeth gritted, I bolted into the clearing, arced my left arm back, and punched the air above my head. Violet light speared upward from my palm and burst into a thousand sparks high above everyone's heads. A flare. A plea.

I stood, panting, hemmed between the soldiers of Knock Platoon who closed rank around Amadea and their Commander, and Lonan who snarled before the tunnel entrance.

Halle released her choke hold on Amadea, who collapsed to the ground, and stepped past her soldiers to face me. "Well, if it isn't the Petish whore."

I dug my boots firmly into the snow, power rumbling through my bones. The tendrils of light I had left weaved through my trembling fingers, but the ice crackling in my blood flowed under my skin and leached into the ground around me. It fractured and broke off, hidden under the snow.

"Give me Amadea," I hissed. "And I'll let you all live."

Laughter burst from Halle's pretty mouth, her gaze flicking to Lonan behind me. "Seems Jaryn will have two prizes after all."

"No ... Destry," wheezed Amadea, from where she half lay crumpled on the ground. "Not for me."

"Shut your goddamn mouth, water witch," snapped Halle.

Lonan released a low chuckle behind me as he inched closer. "Destry's all talk, she doesn't have the spine or the talent to take a life. Do you, my sweet?"

Halle laughed again, her soldiers joining her.

I let the roar of the distant rivers, the unyielding chill of winter, and the snapping hunger of Varranar's ice clear my head. I shifted my gaze to Amadea, her golden eyes filled with utter pain. She gave the tiniest shake of her head. *Don't do this.*

She didn't think she warranted saving. I had thought the same thing about myself once. That I was unworthy. She was wrong. For her, I would do this, even if it barred me from the gates of blessed eternity after my own death, I would do this.

They had hurt her.

Lonan's blade tip pierced the leather of my rider's coat and nipped at the skin of my lower back. "On your knees, whore, and drop the dagger."

Fanned out under the snow like a giant intricate membrane, ice magic pulsed with readiness. I swallowed, my throat paper dry. The air in the clearing stilled, as if it detected what was about to be unleashed. The soldiers' Pegasi shifted uneasily, ears flicking back and forth, some half reared and arched their wings.

"Get on your knees," snarled Lonan.

"Fuck you," I spat over my shoulder.

Spears of ice erupted from the snow into Halle's lower legs, puncturing through flesh and bone. The soldiers cried out and flung themselves backward out of the way. Bloodlust roared in my head, and the lack of remorse scared me just a little, but I didn't dare dwell on that as I ducked and rolled from the strike of Lonan's sword. I had meant for the ice to impale him too, but it hadn't worked.

I rolled away again, as Lonan's sword came bearing down. "Your ice magic doesn't work on me, sweetling."

And why the hell was that? I thought, as panic thrummed in my veins. Glancing up at the warrior's looming torso, my gaze settled on the lead torc nestled around his thick neck. My head whipped to Amadea, noting the twin lead bands around her wrists. Lead blocked magic, like a shield. With my mind racing, memories hurled toward me of standing beside the old throne room in Ilrair, with the Trinitor King carved into the door. It had been sealed in lead, keeping whatever curse had cleaved a species apart, contained.

Lead made using magic impossible, and it was about to be the death of me.

Spinning onto my knees, I staggered onto my feet, desperate to create distance between me and Lonan, as he flipped his sword and brought the blade hiltfirst toward my side.

Commander Halle was snarling and bent over her ice-lanced calves, her breath coming in whinnying heaves. Amadea tried to get to her feet, but a Knock sergeant barreled into her, pinning her against the snow. I darted toward her, but Lonan was there, his brawn and the flat side of his sword knocking all the air from my lungs and slamming me into the ground.

"Alive," hissed Halle. "Jaryn wants ... her ... alive."

I kicked and scratched, my half-frozen hands reaching for a dagger, but Lonan snatched both my wrists and yanked them above my head. My ice rallied, I could feel it finding any way, any possible inlet, into the torc around Lonan's rotten throat. It coated the metal like a white marbled veneer, but Lonan simply laughed into my face.

"The King won't mind her a bit bloodied," he proclaimed, and with his spare hand, he released his sword and unsheathed his dagger. I froze beneath him, my vision tunneling, as he drove the dagger into my left thigh.

I couldn't contain the scream that burst from my mouth, pain erupting over me.

"*No!*" Amadea yelled.

"We can have our games before I have to let you go," whispered Lonan, his weight an immovable force pressing me deeper into the snow.

My entire being zeroed in where the dagger cut deeper, shearing off every rational thought and plan. Dread curled around my heart. The membrane of ice that lay in wait under the snow hurtled back to me like an avalanche, barreling into my blood.

The torc around Lonan's throat turned solid white.

"I'll kill you," I panted, blood and ice coating my tongue.

He dragged his nose down my neck, his stubbled jaw scratching against my skin. "No, you won't, sweetness. You can try and break this torc, but you'll kill yourself in the process. Amadea did the same thing, trying to break the lead on her wrists. It won't work."

Hands clenched into white-knuckled fists, I silently ordered the ice to do one thing, no matter what happened to me. Icicles speared away from the central taper in my chest, and cold like I had never felt, seeped into my body. Violet light cavorted and thrashed over my head, arms, and throat, yet Lonan simply twisted his dagger in response.

I whimpered, but the cold was slowly pushing the pain away. My fingers went numb, then the entirety of my hands.

"Do you feel your blood slowing down?" panted Lonan, the weight of his body and his weapons slowly crushing me. The blade of his dagger dug deeper into the flesh of my thigh, and I barely leashed my scream. We were both shivering hard now, but it's me that can no longer feel my upper torso, as ice magic leached from my body and carved its way deeper into the lead torc around Lonan's throat. "You'll be dead before you break the lead, sweetling."

His hot, clouding breath billowed over my face, and I didn't even have the energy or focus to spit at him, as I ground every ounce of strength I had left into cleaving the ice through the lead. My heartbeat was sluggish in my head, despite my roaring adrenaline and panic. The sound of ice cracking and spearing apart echoed against my eardrums, and I could no longer feel my legs. At least the pain from the dagger was dulled a fraction further.

Lonan pressed in closer, his lips brushing my right ear. "I could just stay here until your poor heart gives out. You're mine to do whatever I like with."

I tuned him out and shifted my head to look past him, taking in the watercolor sky above us. If I was going to die trying this, I didn't want his pitiful face to be the last thing I saw.

The sun was barely breaching the horizon, but what little rays there were glanced off something hurtling through the heavens. A golden falling star.

I blinked slowly, my vision speckling with tiny flashes of ice. The final layer of lead lay just within my grasp, if I could just reach a little further. Lonan twisted his dagger again, my muscle and sinew tearing with it. I couldn't hold back my brittle scream this time, and Lonan smiled gleefully as if he was devouring the sound.

The falling star fractured in two, one piece dark, the other a blinding gold, and the fragments hurtled for the clearing.

With the ever-patient might of a glacier, my gifted power slowly disintegrated the final shards of lead, and the dark torc erupted in a maelstrom of tiny metallic slivers. I barely closed my eyes in time, as the shower of lead sprayed over me and the churned, bloodied snow around us. The dagger jutted deeper, but I looked up at that hateful face and forced a smile to my shivering lips that were now a dangerous shade of pale blue.

"Got you," I hissed.

It felt like my bones were cracking apart, but I wrenched my hands free and wrapped my gnarled, pale fingers around his weathered throat. Lonan jerked backward, yanking the dagger free, as I bore a final torrent of my power at his carotid arteries.

Shoving upward with my hips, unleashing a screech of agony, I rolled Lonan's convulsing body off me and straddled him.

"*Lonan*," yelled Commander Halle.

My breaths were haggard and jerky, as my numb right hand fumbled for Lonan's dagger and wrenched it from him.

I could sense his blood slowly freezing over, at a faster rate than mine was, with the protection of the lead gone. My fingers arced into claws around his throat, forcing his head deeper into the snow.

"I have the spine," I whispered harshly to his rotten face. "And the talent."

I expected more resistance, as I plunged Lonan's own dagger into his chest. His gasp washed over me, and I blinked at the hilt protruding from the dark leather. It was so easy. In reality, killing took no talent at all. It was the fight before the death that mattered the most. As quickly as I could, I cut that torrent of ice power, like a scythe through summer grass, urging the ice to calm before it overtook me completely, and I ended up as frozen as Lonan's corpse. No steam rose from him, and ice crusted his lips.

My hands shook as his blood trailed down my fingers and wrist, yet I didn't feel even a whisper of regret.

For the second time, I reached down and plucked Lonan's sword from the snow. This ruby-hilted blade was heavier than *Kathkar*, and I gripped it with two trembling hands as I turned to face Halle and her soldiers.

Feet like wooden blocks, I half dragged, half carried the sword closer to the trapped Commander, the steel tip carving a deep gouge into the snow.

"You half killed yourself ... in the process," spat Halle.

Ignoring her taunt, my entire body shivered so hard I thought my bones might snap, I pointed the sword at the cavalryman who held Amadea.

"Let her go," I croaked.

"Was that supposed to be intimidating?" laughed the sergeant, as Amadea cursed beneath him.

Sensing my weakness, the other soldiers inched forward, although they eyed their trapped Commander warily.

"Her power is spent. Seize her," ordered Halle.

The platoon bolted for me, and I raised my second stolen sword across my torso, the ruby flashing a brilliant red as my light snaked down the dark steel of the blade. I had never been so cold, as numbness swept over my entire body, snatching my breath away as I tried to force down quick, shallow pants. Swaying on my feet, I braced for the impact of the first soldier's sword against mine.

A thunderclap rolled over the clearing, as those falling stars finally rammed into the snow, sending a tidal wave of white over us. I welcomed it, embracing that final layer of numbing cold, as a male soldier shoved me to my knees, knocking one of my hands free from the sword's hilt.

Snowflakes landed on my dark lashes, and I blinked, my heart pounding a lethargic beat against my ribs. My power had retreated, slowly melting away, but the damage was done. Amongst the whiteout of flurrying snow, a man screamed, then another. A Pegasus stallion's battle cry filled with fury, echoed over me as my right hand, still trying to hold onto Lonan's sword, slumped to the snow.

The earth beneath me trembled with the pounding of hooves and downdraft of wings. Daggers bared, the sergeant, who had been holding Amadea, ran for me through the falling snow, blood smattering his broken nose.

I had nothing left, *nothing*. Varranar's gift had also been my curse. My light, striating from a deep purple to vibrant green, bannered over my head, my hair lifting with it, and I looked upward to face those oncoming daggers. The soldier froze mid-stride, and I blinked again, but my ice power was quiet now, residing in the shadowed corners of my soul.

My vision ebbed then focused again on the curved silver blade protruding from the sergeant's chest. With a swift downward strike, the sword was yanked free, and the sergeant crumpled to the snow.

I was dying a slow, cold death, for the Golden Warrior to be standing there like a conquering, vengeful god. The blood on his sword matched the red of the hood covering his dark blonde hair. At least I had seen him one last time, and I could commit that devastating face to memory. Darkness streaked over the clearing, and I fought to stay conscious for as long as possible, to just look at him a moment longer.

Sheathing his sword, he ran for me and fell to his knees by my side. Then he was pulling me against his torso and into his solid, warm embrace.

"I've got you." His voice was a low, urgent plea over my hair. "I've got you."

The warmth of his body leached into me, and a low, pain-filled groan escaped my lips. Teeth clattering, I whispered, "*Silvano.*"

Death, noting the incremental warmth radiating into my bones, halted its dark embrace.

Pegasi landed and took flight around us, the ground thundering in response, as Silvano gently cradled my head. Those emerald eyes glinted with flecks of gold as I looked up at him. He looked ravaged, desperation clinging to the sculpted planes of his face.

He emitted a high-pitched whistle, then he lifted me, anchoring me against his chest as he waded through the shin-deep snow. A bellowing whinny replied, and I half thought I was dreaming, as Ebrel and Hestian bounded over the powder to us.

Then the Pegasi froze, ears snapping to their skulls, and as one, they brandished their wings. Silvano halted and turned on his heel, his shoulders thrown back in wild defiance.

"Let her go, Coen," ordered Rekorious, his twin swords brandished, the Royant Platoon triumphant behind him. Amadea stood shaking beside Shep and Arnar, her arms looped weakly over their shoulders.

I swallowed harshly at the slain Knock soldiers strewn at their feet. Halle was a slumped corpse over the ice pillars cleaved through her legs. Lonan a dark, frozen shadow on the ground not far from her.

My right hand rose to numbly grip the thick woolen lapel of Coen's riding coat, and the Bromtide Commander's arms tightened around me.

Rekorious simply noticed the motion with a snarl. "I said ... let her go."

The deep timber of Coen's voice rumbled through my chest as he replied, "Never again."

My light swirled around Coen's planted feet, his body braced for a fight despite effortlessly holding onto me.

Rekorious stepped forward. "She belongs with us."

Several Royant soldiers skirted around us, inching their way toward Ebrel and Hestian. Coen's golden stallion squealed a challenge at their approach.

"I think Destry can decide her own fate," snarled Coen. "But right now, she needs to see medics urgently, but I'll be fucking damned if you think I'm leaving her side."

Sheathing his swords in a well-practiced motion across his back, Rekorious' gaze snapped from Silvano, to me, and he noted the blood smeared over my left hip. "You'll be our prisoner, Coen, if you come with us. I won't have some southern snake slithering through my halls unguarded."

Silvano gave him a wicked grin that held as much warmth as a blizzard. "I expected nothing less, *Niemi*." The tanned lines of Silvano's throat bobbed as he turned his head to glare at the approaching Royant soldiers. "Lay a hand on mine or Destry's Pegasus, and you'll lose that hand."

"Do not threaten my men, Coen," snarled Rekorious.

"You may take me prisoner, but you won't entrap Hestian and Ebrel for you to use as leverage."

Rekorious' jaw clenched as he strode closer, his gaze analytical as he took in my pale hands and face. "I've sent a messenger to have my medics waiting for our arrival. We fly *now*, before Knock reinforcements arrive."

Denying the warlord a reply, Silvano turned for Hestian, and he gently set me onto the stallion's back. Ebrel nosed my blood-streaked left knee a moment later, her breath sending a balm of warmth over my frigid skin. She was *here*. Silvano was *here*. It had to be a dream. Shivering hard, I entangled my frozen, stiff fingers into the white strands of Hestian's mane. Silvano leaped up a moment later, his muscle-hewn arms wrapping tightly around me as he settled into the saddle. Gathering up the reins, he looked down at Rekorious.

The warlord glared up at us. "Follow me and Shep, you'll fly in the middle of our formation."

"I don't need you, Niemi. Farrow told me exactly where the keep is." Silvano's calves pressed against Hestian's sides, and with a defiant roar, the stallion leaped into the dawn sky.

CHAPTER ELEVEN

ASHER

My plans for a five-day trek were soon wrecked when I realized just how slow of a walker Calliope was. Her strength depleted from her injuries, she dragged behind me for the rest of the day. Constantly, my shadows weaved between us, urging me to slow down for her.

After an arduous creek crossing, I halted and waited for her to catch up. She walked with as much grace as a reveler leaving a tavern. Spirits, I could use a warm cider right now. Several of them.

Crossing my arms over my chest, I leaned against a half-fallen fir tree and monitored her every step. She judged the terrain before her like it might rise and bite her. How this woman had managed to run nearly two miles and not break a fucking leg was a spirits forsaken miracle.

She looked up and saw that I was waiting for her. Gritting her teeth, she heaved herself over a snow-covered log and trudged closer to me. Nursing her right arm with her left, she finally closed the distance between us.

I waved a casual hand at her. "Don't think I have to worry about you running away now, do I, owling?"

Calliope bared her teeth and came to a halt, her panting breath clouding between us. "I've not used my legs properly in years," she hissed. Then her tone grew softer, and she glanced up at the cloud-covered sky with piercing longing. "I'm used to flying."

I didn't think I could carry any more guilt in my body, but it turned out that I could, as another sliver of it punched into my heart. "It'll be sundown in an hour. We'll camp here. I need to change the dressing on your shoulder."

She jerked upright and ran her golden gaze up and down my body. "What?"

Spirits fucking spare me. I really wish I had brought some cider out here. There were no caves around, but there was plenty of snow and evergreen trees. Yanking open my pack, I pulled out my folded saw and got to work on the low-lying branches of a spruce tree.

"I'll need to check the wound and rebandage it. Now, you can either be awake for that, or, if you rather—" I started sawing and piling up branches of the bushy evergreen. "I can have my shadows send you to sleep." I refolded my saw and turned to face her, hands on my hips. "What will it be?"

She lifted her chin. "Awake."

"Fine."

"Fine," she muttered. With her injured arm, she couldn't help me dig out the pit in the snow, so, letting out a small sigh, I shucked off my gambeson, then my sweater.

"What are you doing?" she asked, taking a hasty step backward as I removed my shirt, the bare skin of my tanned torso stippling with the brutal cold.

I dropped to my knees in the snow and started to dig out the drifts by the trunk of the tree. "If I start sweating while I'm digging, it'll make me even colder. I'm not stripping for your benefit," I chided, arching an eyebrow at her as I created a large space under the low-hanging branches.

Calliope rolled her eyes, but her cheeks were flushed. Then she chewed her bottom lip. "Can I do anything to help?"

"See if you can find any dry tinder under those trees." I jerked my head to a close grouping of birch and fir trees, surprised that she would even want to help. "We'll need to start a fire soon."

Silently, she did as she was bid, awkwardly bundling small sticks and birch bark under her right arm. After another few moments of digging, I eventually made it to the pine needle-covered earth beneath the snow, and I widened the space until two people could curl up comfortably. With the snow walls around us and the tree above, it would be a tight fit, but we'd be out of the cold and wind.

Yanking my layers back on, I heaved myself out of the little shelter to find a neat pile of dry wood by the lip of snow. Calliope, however, was nowhere to be found.

Oh, for fuck's sake.

Instantly, my shadows ricocheted from me, yet I silently cursed them for not telling me she had tried to flee. For whatever reason, they had decided to torment me today. It took a matter of seconds to find her stumbling tracks in the snow and follow her. She had woven through the birch trees and tried to run. I broke into an easy jog, quickly spotting her mane of white hair whipping out behind her as she struggled through the snow, which was knee-deep in places.

Cursing ever coming across her, and noting the meek pink sky of dusk approaching, I quickened my pace and gained ground on her. My shadows flared outward, snaring her uninjured left arm. She let out a pissed off snarl, as those shadows whipped her around to face me.

"Let me go," she wheezed.

I noted the sweat on her brow and cursed inwardly. Barely winded, I bade my power to release her, and she yanked her forearm back to herself.

"Go where, owling? Back to preening and hiding? If I don't tend to that wound on your shoulder, it will get infected, and you'll end up rotting in a cave again."

"I can reach it."

I glared at her. "No. You can't. You need to get to the shelter and get warmed up before all the sweat on you makes you freeze out here."

Her lips set into a grim, mutinous line, but she hugged her elbows and trudged dejectedly past me. Shoving my hands into the pockets of my gambeson, I followed her slow steps back to the pit I had dug out.

Holding back a branch of the tree, I gestured at the shelter. "Just get inside the damn shelter, sweetheart." I shrugged off my gambeson again and handed it to her. "I'll get a fire going and cook us some dinner."

She eyed me for a moment, my clothing held lightly between her hands. I weathered her gaze as she searched my face, and it felt like I was bare before her again. Then her eyes dipped to my right hand and the long scar that ran across my palm, from where the wild ward had struck me with her brindled stone and claimed me with her power. The scar was a stark red line against my tanned skin and calluses.

I tensed as she looked up at me again. Did the magic in her veins detect what caused it? I couldn't read her mind, but I could guess what she was thinking. *Once upon a time, I wasn't given a choice, and now, neither was she.*

It felt like my heart was trying to claw its way out my chest, as the Truth Keeper hesitantly reached for my right hand and flipped it over to expose my palm. The fact I had let her do such a thing at all confused me even more. Her gentle touch seared me like a brand, as she ran a delicate forefinger over the gnarled, harsh skin.

My breathing hitched as I felt a chilled tendril of her power trace over my hand.

A shadow swirled around the base of my neck, and I was half tempted to let it shred me apart, as Calliope finally dropped my hand and turned away, lowering herself down under the tree. Silently, I started the fire. Pherox didn't think I was a monster, but as I roasted more rabbit meat and my shadows refused to twine around me, choosing to guard the tree shelter instead, I started to think that maybe, I truly was.

The Night Pegasus was cavorting above my head when I finally decided to stop putting off the inevitable and lowered myself into the shelter beside Calliope. I brought a burning torch with me and shoved it into the wall of snow above our heads, illuminating the cramped space.

As snug as it may be, it was certainly a lot warmer down here. The Truth Keeper sat cross-legged, her back braced against the trunk of the tree in the center of the shelter. I pulled out the medic kit and began plucking out my supplies. Calliope eyed me with suspicion.

"Will it hurt?" she whispered.

I looked up at her, noting the circles under her eyes. "A little."

She gave a small nod, her gaze meeting mine for a second, then she turned, shucking off my coat. Gingerly, she pulled the fabric of her dress away to reveal the golden skin of her shoulder and the coarse bandages.

Swallowing harshly, I knelt behind her, and goose bumps flickered over her skin. Softly, I heard her breath catch, as I gently unwound the bandages. Her jaw was clenched tight, and she kept her gaze locked onto the wall of snow in front of her.

I coiled up the roll of linen and appraised her injury once more. It didn't smell infected, but that didn't mean the risk of it wasn't there, lingering in the deeper tissues where the arrow had been lodged.

I picked up the small vial of strong alcohol, internally wincing at what I had to do. "This part will hurt the most."

She nodded swiftly and inhaled sharply as I cleaned the wound, her entire back quaking under my hands. Working quickly, I patted the torn skin dry, then applied fresh honey.

"The worst is over now," I murmured softly over her shoulder.

She turned her head, her gold-infused eyes watching me closely. I cleared my throat and started applying a new bandage, going up and over her upper arm.

"You're ... you know what you're doing ... with this sort of thing." Her voice was barely a whisper as she searched my face.

Guilt clenched my heart like a vise. I gave her bandage a final, soft tug. "I was taught well."

Her left hand rose to brush the fresh linen bound over her shoulder. My own hands retreated slowly, my shadows lingering in the roughened corners of the shelter, content to wreathe and watch. My back slumped against the packed snow wall.

Calliope pulled the sleeve of her torn dress back up, and she twisted to face me. The torch above our heads cast long shadows over her pale hair. "Who taught you?"

The words became lodged in my throat, yet I was able to rip them out. "My father and uncle."

Her gaze dipped to my clenched right hand that I rested on a bent knee, then back to my face. "Is it for them that the guilt clings to you?"

A low snarl rumbled in my chest. "Careful, owling."

"Is it?"

"Why did you vow not to return to Fort Garobear?"

It was her turn to snarl then, and she pulled her lower legs away from me, tucking them under the folds of her crumpled skirt. Silence lay heavy over us, above the faint crackling of the torchlight. I moved to lie on my side, content that she wouldn't reply, but she laced her hands together and gazed down at them in her lap.

"I lost something very precious to me, at the fort."

Her breathing hitched, those ethereal eyes met mine, and I had never seen a creature filled with such utter, desperate longing and hopelessness. What was left of my heart felt like it was breaking for her. For the hundredth time, my resolve wavered. A shadow draped over my torso, and I let it embrace me.

My voice was hoarse as I said, "You should get some sleep, we leave here at dawn."

Calliope looked down at her hands again, her hair pooling over her shoulders, then she turned her back to me and lay down on her side, curling her knees to her chest.

Through her shuddering breaths, I knew she fought hard to keep her tears locked within her, but as the torch finally sputtered and darkness swallowed us whole, the sound of her soft crying lanced through my soul.

CHAPTER TWELVE

EBREL

Snow was falling heavily by the time we reached the low-lying mountain range that was home to Niemi's keep. Night had fallen not long ago, as Hestian and I circled a torchlight-ringed courtyard. Wary of any threat, we landed slowly in the fetlock-deep fresh snow, our breaths quick with how swiftly we had flown here.

The Royant Platoon weren't far behind us.

A Petish-born warrior in his forties, with dark tan skin and wrapped in a deep red cloak that matched Silvano's scarf and hood, hurried into the courtyard, then jarred to a halt as he appraised who had landed. I lashed my tail at the sight of him, while Silvano dismounted and gently scooped Destry's half-frozen body into his arms once more. Her light was dim, a faint violet strand orbiting around her head like a hovering crown. She had lost consciousness during our descent through the snow clouds, and I yearned to tuck her under my wing to warm her.

Silvano turned to the stranger. "Where's your medic quarter?"

The warrior blinked and took a hesitant step forward. "Why does an Ilrairian carry our *Koskivarri* like his life depends on it?"

Distant wingbeats carried over the soft sound of falling snow, and Silvano walked determinedly up to the Petish stranger. "I said, *where is your medic quarter?*"

Blinking up at the darkened sky, then back to Silvano, the warrior swallowed, and with a broad, scarred hand, he gestured to an arched door behind him. "This way, Ilrairian."

Silvano half turned back to us, and my ears pricked. He gave two short whistles, and Hestian flinched beside me. The stallion took a step forward and whickered.

"Hestian," I murmured slowly, wings arching.

Again, Silvano repeated the whistles, but the Commander's face was pained.

Hestian arched his neck and bobbed his noble head. Swiftly, he lowered his head and began rubbing his leather bridle against his right foreleg.

"Hestian," I asked again, stepping closer to him, my gaze dancing between Destry and the stallion.

"We need to get out of here. Silvano's worried we'll be trapped if we stay."

"We can't just leave *them,"* I protested.

Hestian swung his head, and the bridle flew free over his ears and jaw, landing in a silent heap in the snow. *"Help me with the saddle, I can't reach the girth straps on my own."*

Throwing us one last anguished glance over his shoulder, Silvano strode through the doorway after the Petish warrior.

"Ebrel, help me, please, the Royants will be here soon, and we need to go before they get here." Hestian's voice held a harsh, stallion's bite of dominance that I hadn't heard before.

Flinching into action, I nosed the ornate saddle flap and knee roll upward and out of the way, then grasped the leather girth straps between my teeth. Pulling at them slowly, the metal buckle prongs slid free, and the girth swung out from under Hestian's sweat-soaked chest.

"And the crupper, I can get the rest off myself," asked Hestian, more gently this time, and he swept his wing over my back in reassurance as I reached over his lower back to grasp the last buckle. Giving it a short, sharp yank, the buckle snapped, and I stepped back. Hestian lowered his head and bucked, the breastplate and saddle sliding over his neck and head. Another quick shake of his body, and the quilted, maroon saddle pad fell to the ground.

Sweat and snow had turned his once-golden pelt a dark brown as he flexed his wings and looked skyward. I turned my head to look at the arched doorway.

"Silvano won't let any harm come to her again, Ebrel," said Hestian softly, his nose gently touching my lower neck. *"We need to fly, the Royants are here."*

Pegasi began to land all around us, and Kalana whinnied in greeting as Rekorious slipped from her back. He helped Amadea down next, but then his gaze found Hestian and me, the discarded saddle at our hooves.

"Rope them! Rope them now," yelled the warlord.

Hestian bared his teeth, a rumbling challenge sounding deep in his chest. *"Fly! Fly, Ebrel!"*

Kalana whinnied after us again as we launched ourselves into the night, seemingly abandoning our riders to an unknown fate. Our wings pounded the snow-laden air, a chilled wind cutting across our sweat-soaked bodies as we fought to break through the cloud cover.

Vertically we climbed, until the torchlights of the courtyard were mere specks of light, then they vanished entirely. Breaching the final swathe of cloud, we leveled out our flight, breathing hard. Hestian banked to fly close to my right flank, but the stallion's gaze was fixed to the heavens.

The Night Pegasus danced and leaped all around us, bannering from horizon to horizon. Following my lead through the night sky, Hestian stayed close as I cautiously flew further north, only dipping through the cloud when I felt like we had put as much distance between the Royant soldiers and us as we could in one night. Which wasn't far, given how exhausted we both were. Tired and hungry, I scoured the mountainous ridgeline, hoping to find a meadow amongst the stands of trees that hugged the rocks and valley sides. Lowering in altitude, my wings quivering to keep me airborne, I circled to land in a half-acre clearing beside a tiny, frozen stream.

I landed heavily, breath sawing from my chest, my forelimbs half staggering as I stumbled into the near knee-deep snow, Hestian a breath behind me. Pitched into deep darkness, with no moon or stars to light our way, we warily cast our heads about, listening for any dangers beyond the deep gloom of the trees.

"Follow me." Trudging through the snow, dreading having to dig through it for grass, I led Hestian down the shallow bank to the small stream. Stamping my forehooves, I cracked through the ice and rushing cold water frothed to the surface. Stepping back, I let Hestian drink first, then he warily looked for predators while I drank my fill. The ice-cold water was like a punch to the stomach, but it was all we had access to. Droplets freezing instantly to our muzzles and whiskers, we made our way slowly back to the clearing, our wings almost dragging along the snow drifts. Our pelts glittered as the sweat dried and froze over our backs and ribs.

I had barely started digging for the grass, showing Hestian how to shovel his muzzle deep to reach it, when a bright green light lashed into the meadow, swirling in a violent, sparking wheel suspended in the air. Hestian leaped in front of me, wings fully brandished despite his exhaustion, blocking me from the creature that stepped down from the sky.

Hestian's ears snapped to his skull, and he appeared to grow in height, neck arched in silent challenge. He looked back for a heartbeat, checking I was safe behind him, before focusing his entire being on the threat in front of him.

Only the creature wasn't a threat. I had met him before, when I had been broken and bleeding, near the brink of death on the edge of Harracombe Moor. I touched Hestian's neck with my muzzle in an attempt to reassure him. *"It's okay, Hestian, he won't hurt us."*

The palomino stallion relaxed a fraction, but still kept me behind him. I peered over his ghostly white wing to appraise the Night Pegasus as he stood silently several meters away. The light he had stepped down from vortexed outward to reconnect with the edges of his wings, morphing to ripple in waves over the snow. It was his sage and emerald green fire that outlined him against the darkness, revealing a tall, muscular body of a black Pegasus stallion. His gold-rimmed eyes glowed as he appraised us, his gaze noting every twitch of Hestian's body.

Frozen air crackled and whispered around the meadow, emerald sparks of his fire drifting with the wind to swirl between us. Folding his wings along his body, he stepped forward, his long ebony mane and tail shifting with the movement. Hestian lowered his head, the faintest rumble of a warning sounded in his throat.

The Fire Prince halted and cocked his head. *"Interesting,"* he murmured, his voice as deep and gravelly as I remembered. Then his gaze flicked to me. *"Ebrel is more than capable of defending herself."*

"Oh, I know," replied Hestian smoothly. *"It's you I don't trust."*

"Hmmm, is that so?" The great stallion stepped closer, ethereal light dancing in his wake, the entire meadow lit with a faint green glow from his presence. *"You're exhausted and hungry, you wouldn't last long in*

a fight against me. What you felt during the bonding process is not a true reflection of what I am to you. Besides, I know you better than you think."

Hestian bared his teeth. *"No, you don't."*

The Fire Prince exhaled, his muzzle twitching with amusement to a secret only he was privy to. I could understand why Hestian felt threatened by him. I had too, the first time I had encountered him. It was our bodies' natural reaction to the immortal and powerful energy that silently rippled from him.

Brushing my wing along Hestian's back in reassurance, I stepped around him to stand between the two stallions, one of shining gold, the other archaic night. The Fire Prince was right, he would win every battle. Even if Hestian was at the peak of his strength, the mighty beast would trample him to the ground with half a thought. I bowed my head in respect to the spirit of the aurora, then met that steadfast ochre and gilded gaze. We could trust him, he had saved my life, ensuring the Royant Platoon had found me before I bled to death, after Spearian had chased me from Glentay and sent me plummeting to the earth.

"Why have you stepped down from the skies?" I whispered.

He silently appraised me for a moment, his gaze searching for something that I had no idea how to give him. *"You have delivered the Ilrairian and my Koskivarri to where they are meant to be, now, you must find the answers that help them stay together."*

"They're in danger?" asked Hestian, stepping up beside me.

"We all are, the wild ward was the southern King's puppet. With her death, the spirits have regained our full strength, but ..." He sighed, his voice full of longing and remorse. *"We cannot face him alone."*

"Tear him apart like you did with the wild ward. Merevis and Serebo ended her easily enough," said Hestian.

"Some fates cannot be interfered with. Jaryn's death does not belong to the spirits."

"Then who does it belong to?" The Fire Prince fell silent and flicked me a pointed glance. *"Destry?"*

"Sending her into the palace will sign her own death warrant, Silvano's too. It cannot be infiltrated." Hestian shifted his weight over his hooves, the muscles of his back twitching.

Those otherworldly eyes slid to the palomino stallion, pinning him in place. *"It can, with help."*

Hestian blinked, realization making his entire body tense. *"The Ilrairian Pegasi cannot help them, the curse is too strong, any attempt to remove Jaryn or his kin from power, will see the Pegasi forfeit their lives. The curse is directly woven to protect the Adacus bloodline."*

"If Destry were to break the curse and restore the Trinitors, would they rise up? Become warriors in their own right, like they once were, long ago?"

I stared and stared at the Fire Prince. *"The curse can be broken?"*

Distant galaxies swirled in those eyes. *"Yes, Ebrel, it can. With the power of fire and ice, light and shadow, magic that if used in perfect union, will be strong enough to demolish the curse."*

"Fire," breathed Hestian. He turned his beautiful, noble head to look at me. *"Silvano's nightmares."*

The Fire Prince's jaw clenched. *"Go to the caves littering Serebo, they will give you the answers that you need."*

"And you can't?" I murmured as I took a small step forward.

He shook his head, his muzzle tight with an emotion I couldn't read in his Pegasus form. *"I am bound by rules not of your mortal world, Ebrel. Rest here for tonight, then go to Serebo, she's waiting for you both."* He reared, his wings arching higher and higher. Light flooded the meadow, the power of it lifting our manes upward, our feathers rustling and on edge in response. Tossing his head, he beat his ebony wings once, the light jackknifing from him, lifting the layers of snow from the grass at our hooves.

His forelimbs reconnected with the ground that was now clear of snow, then he propelled himself into the biting cold sky, raw energy whipping around us. Hestian tossed his neck over mine, half covering me with his left wing, as the light in the clearing gathered itself into a rapidly turning sphere. The Fire Prince flew straight for it, and the light parted for him in undulating curtains. A breath later and he was gone, his power with him, leaving Hestian and me gasping and shuddering in the dark.

CHAPTER THIRTEEN

DESTRY

A solid warmth encased my hands that lay clasped over my abdomen, a soft rhythmic motion brushing back and forth over the knuckles of my right hand. My extremities tingled, like blood was slowly returning to my feet and ears. Blinking, taking in a darkness speckled with torchlight, I looked to my right and saw the face that I thought I had dreamed of. But no, it was his hand holding mine, his thumb a gentle, reassuring caress over my skin. It was his eyes, emerald-flecked gold, looking down at me with a mix of concern and relief.

He looked wilder than I had seen him last, after our fraught goodbye in Saltfen. His dark blonde hair was windswept and tousled, strands of it loose from the leather tie he had tried to knot it in. A week's worth of stubble graced his strong jaw, the wild northern snow and wind weathering his golden skin. A dark red swathe of wool was wrapped around his shoulders, over a quilted black tunic, replacing his usual Ilrair cavalry uniform. In fact, he bore no Ilrair sigils at all.

Silvano Coen. He was *here*.

Wherever the hell here was.

His large, calloused hand squeezed mine gently, and I couldn't tear my gaze away from him. In a voice that was low and rumbling that made my heart tighten, he said, "Hello, wild one."

Words lodged in my throat as I struggled to form some kind of coherent greeting and failed. I could only drink him in, enraptured, anchored to the here and now by the feeling of his hand on mine. For the second time, this man had saved me from death's door. He had come for me, even after I had abandoned him.

I glanced down at our joined hands, unable to voice the truth to his face. "You came to Erskine."

I could feel his gaze burning into me, silently willing me to turn and face him again. Slowly, I peeked across at him from under my mess of hair. His expression was open, earnest, a warmth in his gaze that I had never seen before.

"I did."

"Why?" I asked softly.

"Destry." Spirits, my name on his lips, spoken like some whispered prayer, would be my undoing. He leaned forward, bracing his forearms over his powerful thighs. "I have thought of nothing else, of no one else, since the night you left Saltfen."

Shame sluiced over me, and I looked down once more. "I'm sorry."

He gently swept my dark mane back over my shoulder, his touch whisper soft. "Don't be sorry. You thought it was your one chance at freedom. I would have done the same had I been in your shoes. It's me that should be sorry, for not coming for you sooner, for not stopping what Niemi had planned."

"How did you find out?"

His voice was guttural as he ground out, "Farrow. Turns out he's been Niemi's spy in my platoon all these years. He came crawling back after the spirits were freed and told me everything. Even where this place was, tucked away in the north." His jaw clenched, and he curled and unfurled his fists.

"We're back at Niemi's keep?" I asked hoarsely from where I lay, on some medic pallet, swathed in thick woolen blankets. Six other empty pallets lined the low-ceiling room, and a large hearth roared at the end of the row of beds. Quickly, I took stock of the state of my battered body. I wore a soft, light gray undershift, and my left thigh throbbed viciously, the thick, coarse bandages covering the stab wound a stark contrast to the tan of my skin.

Lonan. I had killed Lonan Donaghue. I had killed a man in cold blood. I braced for it, the whip of remorse and shock, but it didn't come, and instead, fear at that brutal recognition constricted around my heart. I had killed him, and I wasn't one bit sorry about it.

Fingers stiff and aching, I traced my left hand over my chest, the high-necked shift bunching with the movement. The ice magic that had nearly killed me, but had allowed me to kill Lonan, was a frozen, slumbering beast in my mind once more, the taper a shimmering, quiet force in the dark.

Silvano tore his gaze away from me then, cautiously taking in the room around us. "We are. Tell me, has Niemi hurt you? Has he forced this marriage on you?"

I swallowed, my throat paper dry at the barely sheathed rage in his voice. "The betrothal has been dissolved, his council voted on it yesterday."

"That answers one part of my question, wild one."

"We ... we fought atop Serebo once he told me the truth, but that's all. I was a prisoner here for just over a week before the council meeting yesterday. He hasn't hurt me." My eyes flared wide, and I fought to sit upright, shoving the blankets back. "But you can't be here, Silvano, if Rekorious finds out he'll—"

"Oh, Niemi knows." He released my hand to reach forward and sweep a tangled piece of hair off my face. I stilled at the contact, my heart hammering in my chest. "Shep is currently guarding that door. I'm technically Niemi's prisoner."

"His *what*?" I seethed, surprised by the anger that speared through me. "If he hurt *you*—"

Silvano sat back with a deep chuckle resounding in his chest. "He hasn't laid a hand on me, Destry, and he won't get close enough to try."

"Amadea? Is she alright?" The last time I had seen her, she'd barely been able to stand, her face awash with shock and pain, horrid twin lead cuffs on her wrists.

"She's been tended to, they managed to get the lead off her using a medic's bone saw, but it took hours. I believe they've taken her to a private room now, to rest."

Thank the spirits.

My fingers, chilled without his touch, tangled together atop the blankets in my lap. I was about to tell him about Narve and what that psychopath had done, how he still plagued me with nightmares, but the heavy wooden door to the medic quarter swung open and Rekorious strode into the room, shadowed by Shep, Minna, and Hearan Lael.

Silvano and I both straightened as the walls seemed to push in around us.

"Good to see you awake, Destry," said Rekorious quietly, giving me a brief, cursory nod.

Shep and Minna stepped around their Commander to take up seats on the unoccupied pallets across from us. Minna, her body lithe and powerful under her leather armor and cloak, looked at Silvano with guarded caution, but her face was full of warmth as she turned to face me, a leg resting over a knee, her hands laced before her. Lael looked tempted to follow suit but remained standing. Rekorious closed the door behind them and leaned back against it, leveling Silvano a cold, distrustful look.

"We need to discuss the next steps, about what to do with you, Coen." Rekorious crossed his arms over his chest. He still wore his worn, bloodied woven leather armor and sage green cloak. His swords, thankfully, were nowhere to be seen.

None of them bore any weapons, even Silvano, who leaned back gracefully in his chair, hands clasped over his abdomen and crossed a boot foot over a shin. "And what do you propose, *Lord* Niemi?"

Shep threw a pleading look up at the ceiling and ran a hand through his hair.

Lael stepped forward from a corner of shadows. "You have to return to Ilrair, Bromtide Commander. Your presence here threatens all of us."

I stared across at Silvano, desperately trying to read the expression on his handsome face. He tilted his head, meeting my gaze, then he looked back at Lael, gesturing to his black tunic. "I'm not sure if you can tell, but I'm not here under orders. I left. I'm no longer a commander."

Shock lanced through my heart. He had dissented too? Jaryn would have his head. My head swam at the thought, holy spirits, the repercussions of this if what he said was true. It was one thing for the Royants to have fled, but for one of Jaryn's closest friends and commander of his most powerful platoon? And he had abandoned it all ... for me?

"Bullshit," snarled Rekorious. "You would never surrender that title or abandon your post. Let alone that you're Jaryn's closest friend for fuck's sake."

Silvano's gaze darkened, his jaw tightening. "Keep telling yourself that, Niemi, but here I am."

"You could be a spy for Jaryn, simply using Destry as an entry point into our stronghold and to learn of our plans," muttered Lael darkly.

An anxious knot tightened in my chest, as I turned my head to look at Silvano. Would he do such a thing? Use me like that? He had saved Jaryn from the wild ward, yes, but had also left him and traveled all the way here, risking his life to save me once more. With Hestian's help, they had found Ebrel, and we had been reunited, however briefly. If Silvano hadn't arrived at Erskine when he did, I would be a frozen corpse in that clearing.

I have thought of nothing else, of no one else.

Silvano angled his head in a cool, predatory manner that made Lael take a step back. "I'm no spy." He cut Rekorious a scathing glare. "But I know how much *you* favor them."

The warlord's jaw clenched, his arms tightening around his chest. "What happened to Farrow?"

"Oh, he's still alive for now, don't worry. He's doing what he's been trained to do, keeping an eye on Saltfen and Jaryn's movements in Ilrair. Although I did warn him." Silvano's voice lowered a fraction further, laced with deadly intent. "If he breathes a word about me, about any of us up here, I'll leave his dead body in some forgotten bog with no one to mourn over him."

Minna straightened as she silently assessed the former Commander at my side, as if she finally realized the threat he posed. Her dark hair shone ebony in the firelight, the tight braid down her back heightening the angular planes of her face and uptilted eyes. Her long, dark tan fingers absentmindedly played with the edge of her charcoal cloak. "I never liked Farrow, or what you had him do, Rekorious."

The warlord released a tight breath through his nose, his entire body tense.

Shep leaned forward, his face grave. "What does Jaryn know? What does Bromtide think happened? We know you dumped Jaryn's sadistic ass back in Saltfen after the spirits were freed."

"Everyone thinks I'm hunting down dissenters around Aarine." Silvano looked back at me, an apology in those stalwart green eyes. "There was no formal resignation, it would have taken too long."

"Hunting down dissenters?" hissed Rekorious.

"The lie had to be believable," said Silvano softly. "I made my case that I would move more quickly and be less noticeable on my own." The Ilrairian leaned forward again, his laser focus pinned on Rekorious. "I'm not the only one who threatens your safety up here though. Am I, Niemi? Jaryn laid out a trap for you, with the perfect bait, and you flew straight into it."

The warlord released a guttural snarl that echoed over the room. Silvano subtly shifted closer to me in response, his entire body taut with the readiness to fight.

"Refer to Amadea as bait again, and I will have your head upon my palisades, Silvano," growled Rekorious.

"Did you consider the risk to her life? To her family's? Jaryn has likely slaughtered them all in retaliation."

"Everyone in this room knows what I would risk to free Amadea." Sitting across from me, Shep nodded solemnly.

"Jaryn will come for her," whispered Silvano.

Rekorious bared his teeth, then threw me a glance filled with warning. *Jaryn will come for both of you.* "He'll be dead before he can get the chance."

"And then who do you replace him with, another sadistic monster?" I murmured.

Silvano flinched as he clasped his hands between his knees.

Lael cleared his throat. "We push to have power transferred to the senate alone. Give the city back to the Ilrairian people. The framework for which was put in place prior to the Royant Platoon's dissension."

Silvano blinked, the only surprise he showed, before it was replaced with a wary calculation. "You certainly have been busy."

Lael grumbled quietly from the corner of the room, his expression full of mistrust. Minna's gaze bounced between Silvano and me, as if she was trying to read the invisible, woven threads between us. I silently wished her luck, even I couldn't begin to decipher them.

Clearing my throat, I looked at each of them in turn. "Did you secure Elias?"

"He's fled. Grier reported that he didn't return from his patrol after we had left for Erskine," said Shep.

"It would seem your cousin is a traitor, Rekorious." I leveled him with a cool expression. "Is he working with anyone else?"

"Not that I'm aware of," the warlord bit out. "I have Grier and her unit hunting him down." He shifted from the door and looped his thumbs through his sword belt. "You're officially our prisoner until my council weighs up the threat you pose, Silvano. We'll hold a meeting in the morning. If it were up to me alone, I'd exile you right here and now."

A tiny dip of his chin was the only affirmation Silvano gave in reply. I opened my mouth to speak, but the words refused to come out. I wanted to vouch for him, he had saved my life today, but he did pose a threat to everyone in this keep. If, no, *when* Jaryn discovered that Silvano had abandoned him, he'd likely use every resource available to track the Commander down and make an example of him. Alongside retrieving Amadea, it would give the King of Ilrair an even greater incentive to keep pushing north.

"We'll escort you down to your cell now, Coen." Lael stepped closer and pulled a set of iron cuffs and chains from his belt. "Don't act a fool, and I won't put these on you."

Silvano stood slowly, the northerners tensing in response. The Il-rairian ignored them all wholly, as he half turned and swept a gentle caress over my cheek with the palm of his hand, the coarseness of his calluses scraping along my chilled skin. He held my gaze for what felt like an eternity, a silent goodbye passing gently between us, then he was moving, striding to where Rekorious stood by the door.

The muscle in the warlord's jaw twitched, as he yanked the door open and led the group of men out of the room. Fraught tension whispered away with their fading footsteps, leaving me alone with Minna.

The warrior rose and unclasped the twisted iron pin from her right shoulder, allowing her dark cloak to slip free. Tenderly, she gathered up the warm, butter-soft fabric in her arms and walked over to me, where she unfurled it again, gently draping it over my shoulders.

"Come now, *Koskivarri*, let's get you to your new room." With no effort at all, she looped her right arm under my left and hoisted me out of the pallet and onto my felt-slippered feet. My thigh throbbed with the movement, and I released a hiss through gritted teeth.

Minna's leather armor pressed against my arm, as we took a tentative step forward. "That's it, Destry, you can do it, the walk isn't far, I promise. Your room is next to mine now."

I felt awful for bracing my weight and height against her. I had a good three inches on her, but she didn't utter a word or sound of protest, as she eased me from the medic quarter and into the quiet, shadowed hall beyond.

Needing a distraction from the pain that rippled out from my wound with every limping step, I ground out. "You work for Rekorious?"

Minna nodded, keeping her dark gaze fixed on the hall ahead of us, only sparse torchlight marking our passing. "I command his northern land cavalry, have done for about four years now."

I blinked in awe. She had to be the same age as me, and she was a Commander? "Land cavalry?"

"We use Lake Horses, sturdy beasts that are native to this region. They're not the quickest, but they make up for it with stamina and courage. I'll show you mine sometime and the stables, it's lovely down there." She hummed to herself, and her full lips quirked upward. "I prefer sleeping in the hay platform over the stables than in the keep itself, less likely to run into Hearans and Hearas there. The grooms know to leave my makeshift bed alone now."

Remembering the times when I had slept in Ebrel's stable, waking to find my hair full of straw, I could relate.

"You're not a noble?" I panted, as Minna helped ease me up a short flight of steps.

"I'm not, which some people like to remind me of."

We drew to a stop before a pale birch door, a carving of two Boreal stoats spanning its length. The small mammals circled each other, nose to tail, one in its winter white coloring, the opposite a dark, summer brown. Minna fished out a brass key from her black riding skirt. She patted the carved white stoat fondly.

"I selected this room for you, figured it would be fitting."

I quirked an eyebrow. "Stoats?"

"Didn't you know?" She threw a sidelong glance at me, a ghost of a smile playing on her lips. "They're symbols of transformation, we see them as messengers of the spirits. That, and they're well known for taking on creatures three times their size. I'm pretty sure we have a few who roam the keep. If you have any socks go missing, don't worry, it's usually these little culprits that are to blame."

She unlocked the door, and using a booted foot, pushed it open and ushered me inside.

My eyes widened as I took in the small but cozy space. A pine sleigh bed with traditional Petish woven blankets made with cream and gray Norwickan fleece, sat tucked against the right-hand wall. A matching dresser stood against the opposite wall, two tapering candles atop it in small brass holders illuminated the space, the stone slabbed floor between the furniture warmed by two white reindeer hides. Set into the foot-thick wall directly across from the door was an iron-cased window, the snow-powdered glass overlooking a quaint courtyard. A small ewer and basin were tucked behind the arc of the door, but it was what hung in an iron bracket on the wall beside the footboard that drew my attention.

Clad in its black leather, moon phase scabbard, the lambent stone in *Kathkar's* pommel shone faintly in the candlelight.

"There's no hearth, but don't worry, the water from the hot springs runs through the floor, so the rooms stay warm all winter," explained Minna.

The bedroom was far from opulent, which suited me just fine. It was warm, comfortable, and the bed practically sang my name. Minna lowered me down onto the plush covers and freed her cloak from my shoulders, draping it over her left arm.

"Thank you," I murmured, hugging my elbows.

Minna smiled warmly in return. "Not a problem at all. If you need me, I'm just next door on the right. There's a crescent moon carving on the door." She set about lighting another candle held in a metal bracket on the wall beside the headboard, casting the lofty pillows in a soft, flickering glow. "I'll come and help you get ready for the council meeting in the morning. It'll be different this time, with Coen in the pulpit, you'll be sat next to me."

I looked up at her and gave her a half grin, imagining, in time, that between us we could cause a riot for people like Heara Helmi.

"I'll leave you to rest. Try and get some sleep. There's a tonic for the pain in that wooden cup on the dresser, if you need it." She threw me a warm smile, before leaving the brass room key beside the cup and slipping silently out of the door.

I slumped against the beautifully carved headboard, my head reeling from the dull ache in my thigh, to the fact Coen was in this keep, and had apparently traded everything to be here. Even his freedom. Would Niemi throw him in a jail cell or in a room similar to what I had been locked in? Did he regret it, coming to rescue me? Thoughts gnawed at my mind, and I ricocheted between bewilderment, relief, and guilt.

Wincing, I eased back the downy soft coverlet and slid in between the cool sheets. A faint rustling came a moment later, and I arched an eyebrow in amusement, as the stoat popped its head under the door.

"Oh, hello?" I whispered with a chuckle. "What are you stealing from me this time?"

It wriggled the rest of its slender, practically contortionist body under the door and scampered over to where the ewer sat on a small, three-legged stool.

"You better not knock that over."

The stoat squeaked, its coal button eyes peering at me, then it jumped onto the stool and snatched another small washcloth into its mouth. It rose on its back legs to look at me over the footboard, whiskers twitching this way and that, then it leaped back onto the floor, its small black-tipped tail thrashing with delight at its prize.

"I'd love to see your den, with how many socks and cloths you steal. I bet it's really cozy," I teased, as a flicker of joy at the small creature's antics resonated in my chest.

Squeaking once more, the stoat wriggled under the door and disappeared into the night.

CHAPTER
FOURTEEN

ASHER

I awoke before she did, her back still turned to me. The long strands of her knotted hair spread out behind her like a pale tapestry, her exquisite scent hitting me head on. Absent-mindedly, my right hand rubbed a blonde strand between my fingers. I blinked, catching myself. What the hell was I doing?

A shadow curled over my hand, and I swatted it away, inhaling deeply. Spirits, this woman. Tucked away from the world down here, I could easily forget about the bargain I had struck and could just set her free.

Calliope shifted under my coat and rolled over, facing me in the cramped space. She slowly blinked the drowsiness from her eyes, clarity hitting her at just how close we were. Steadily, so I wouldn't spook her, I propped myself onto an elbow and gazed down at her in the meek gray light.

The circles under her eyes were less pronounced today, yet wariness still clung heavily to her. That was my doing, but I deserved it, though a part of me longed for her to look at me with anything other than loathing.

"Why did you reveal yourself to the Colladonians?" My voice was rough and low.

Stiffly, she sat up and tilted her head back to rest against the wall of snow. "I wanted to help protect something ... something that I wasn't able to when I was at the fort."

"Was it worth it?"

Her left hand brushed her injured shoulder. "I don't regret what I did." She dipped her chin and looked at me, cataloging every part of my body. Heat hurtled over me, and my jaw clenched under her unwavering gaze. "And I never will."

Not for the first time, I missed Pherox. I missed his confidence and advice, but most of all, I missed climbing onto his back and whispering into the night. Just me and him. Certainly not with a Truth Keeper in tow, who I was beginning to think was setting such a slow pace deliberately.

"There's nothing wrong with your legs," I muttered, as I stretched out a hand to Calliope and helped her over a frozen creek.

She ignored me, content to walk in silence, although I caught her watching my dancing shadows more than once. Snow fell softly around us, spring and its greenery a distant, near-forgotten thing this far north. With no wind to blind and rake at us, the snow muffled the sounds of our footsteps, covering every inch of clothing, before it melted away. It felt like being trapped under a gray dome, with just the forest and the sounds of Calliope's measured breath for company.

As we approached midday, I halted, swept a snowdrift from a fallen, dead tree, and set down my pack. "We'll rest here for a moment."

Sheltered by three close-growing spruces, we were mostly protected from the weather. Calliope watched on silently, hugging her elbows, while I set out some dried meat and bread. Then she turned her head, her eyebrows flitting upward for a moment, before she schooled her devastating features into a mask of wariness once more.

Moving slowly, she walked away from me to a cluster of low-lying shrubs, her gaze analytical as she ran a hand over a thorny branch. Tiny, sparse clusters of burgundy fruit weighed down each tendril of the plant. Wicken berry bushes. I never bothered to harvest them as they took long to prepare to warrant eating, but they were handy in an emergency.

I didn't protest, as Calliope plucked several bunches of berries from the plants, tucking them safely away in the pockets of her dress. A shadow nudged my left ear, but I ignored it, content to let her forage. If she wanted wicken berry tea or stew, she could make it herself later over a fire.

Leaning against the fallen tree, we ate and drank in silence, the fingertips of Calliope's left hand stained a blood red from the berries. The sight of it, like she had just cleaved a man's heart from his chest, unnerved me. Settling my pack over a shoulder once more, I gestured to the never-ending forest, eager to get moving.

Calliope's jaw tightened, her gaze meeting mine for a moment. I tensed, expecting defiance from the way her eyes shone with a raw, golden fire. Then her shoulders slumped, and she trudged onward, cradling her right arm once more.

I took a single step after her, then froze in place, eyes widening. "Wait."

The Truth Keeper halted mid-stride, half turning to look over her shoulder at me, eyebrows furrowed.

Her lips parted to speak, but I was already moving. Wrapping a hand over her uninjured left arm, I spun her around so her back was flush against my torso. My right hand flew upward to cover her mouth, stifling her yelp. She wrenched against my hold, but I held her firmly in place.

My mouth lowered to her right ear, my breath caressing the smooth plane of her neck, and I gently whispered, "Look, beyond that stand of birch trees."

She stilled against me, and my throat worked, as my body realized just how close we were pressed together. Swallowing hard, I followed her line of sight to the trees. Guessing that she would stay quiet now, I slowly lowered the hand covering her mouth, but a deep, protective part of me kept holding her close.

The equine form beyond the tree line shifted with instinctual grace, moving slowly through pocked shadows and dove-gray light. My shadows had frozen in place at the sight of it, but now they spread like a delicate web between us and those trees.

I didn't think the Truth Keeper was breathing, as the otherworldly creature, just as rare and as precious as Calliope, stepped out from the trees. A small, sheltered part of me, untouched by savagery and shame, trembled with a sudden awareness at the sight of Olwen.

"Spirits above," whispered Calliope in awed reverence, her body relaxing against mine a fraction. My shadows undulated in response, curling over the snow like smoke.

Olwen walked closer, her ears pricked toward us, her crystalline blue eyes relaxed. She showed no signs of fear toward my shadows, and she treaded confidently through them, sending tendrils curling in her wake. Her breath was deep, and she appeared utterly at ease, her ice-colored body free from any tension or worry. My gaze drifted from her piercing blue eyes to the twisting, pale horn atop her head.

Her voice was silent to me, just as it had been that night in Aarine, when the wild ward had nearly slaughtered her. Even if I could converse with her, I doubted the Unicorn would speak to me. An aura of complex magic and mystery shrouded Olwen, as if her arctic glare held not just Mount Serebo's secrets but ones that mere humans could not even begin to comprehend. Olwen was a keeper of mountains, a language of glaciers and depthless crevasses, that defied time itself.

The young mare angled her head, her gaze drifting from me to take in Calliope. The Truth Keeper went utterly still in my arms, but intention hit me clear in the chest, an invisible request that had me releasing her and stepping back.

"Her name is Olwen," I murmured gently. "She won't hurt you."

As if pulled by some invisible force, Calliope walked slowly forward. Olwen stood silently, waiting, her only movement the rise and fall of her ribs, her nostrils flaring slightly with each breath.

I edged slowly to my right to get a better view of the pair, my gaze flitting between them, before resting on Calliope's beautiful, wonder-struck face. Darkness shivered down my spine a moment later, and I silently acknowledged Iltavorn's presence around me. The ancient spirit said nothing, however, merely observed, while Calliope extended her left palm toward the Unicorn.

Her breathing hitched, eyes widening, as Olwen gently pressed her gray muzzle into her waiting hand. Seconds passed between them, their breathing becoming in sync, and the tightness in Calliope's shoulders slowly melted away.

Chest constricting, my shadows wove their way back to me, pooling at my feet. A deep, settling sigh rushed from Calliope, and she leaned closer to Olwen, until her forehead pressed against the Unicorn's, just below that lethal horn.

My shadows sensed that Olwen still had magic remaining in her body, yet only the spirits knew if the mare would cast it before her death.

"Care to tell me what this means?" I asked Iltavorn in my mind. *"Olwen is a long way from the protection of Serebo."*

The spirit of darkness was silent for several heartbeats, until I thought he wouldn't reply at all. Then came that archaic voice that imbued both safety and violence, beginnings and enduring death. *"Look upon them, huntsman, what do you see?"*

"A scion of Serebo and a woman blessed with truth magic?"

"And to think, this moment might never have existed if the wild ward had come to power."

A shadow drifted upward to curl against my throat. *"But Orrin, Ebrel, and Olwen, I freed—"* It felt like the spirit had punched me in the gut as realization struck me, striking deep, disturbing the very rockbed of my soul. Grinding my teeth, I swallowed harshly. *"I made a deal to protect the Nijinxes."*

"The Nijinxes are equipped to protect themselves, and where they fail ... well, that is where you and I step in. But what makes you think the fickle heart of humans will honor their part of the deal? The Colladonians will never surrender the Scarp to them."

"And you didn't care to warn me of this before I accepted the hunt?" Anger at the spirit of darkness roiled in my veins, but Iltavorn's voice was unperturbed.

"Look again, hunter. No man on this Earth, be they king, commander, or commoner, will let such a creature of beauty and power walk free. She will be doomed to a life of servitude, and I think that you know what that feels like more than anyone."

Crossing my arms over my chest, my gaze rose from my whirling shadows to take in Calliope once more. Her eyes were closed, and her left hand had risen to gently stroke Olwen's cheek.

"If I don't secure the Scarp, the Nijinxes will be hunted down out of fear and retribution."

"There are many reasons why I chose you as my scion, Asher Turunin Fields. You save those who cannot save themselves."

I uttered a clipped, dark laugh. The sound had both Unicorn and Truth Keeper pulling apart to fix me with their gazes, one timeless ice, the other a burning gold.

Iltavorn ignored my laughter, the spirit's tone turning deeper and harsher. I stiffened as his parting words vibrated against my ribs. *"And in turn, it will take a rare creature to save you from yourself."*

With that, the spirit drifted away on a phantom wind, my shadows vortexing in his wake. I took a deep breath and looked up at Calliope once more. She resolutely met my gaze, and my skin stippled in response. I knew she hadn't heard Iltavorn's words, but what had passed between the spirit and me made my fists clench.

The space between the Truth Keeper and me pulled taut, neither one of us willing to break and look away first. Heart quickening in my chest, I searched her devastating face. What horrors had she seen, in both her human and owl form? Absentmindedly, Calliope ran her red-stained left hand down Olwen's head, and it felt like she was looking through me, to the very depths of my tarnished soul and the dark deeds I had attempted to bury and suffocate there.

A muscle in my jaw ticked as the air between us pulsed with tension. That small, pure part of me desperately wanted to walk over to her, gently hold her face between my palms, and whisper that she was free. That she could leave this clearing with Olwen and filter into the trees like the ethereal creature she was.

Arms aching with the restraint I was wielding, my throat bobbed. Calliope tracked the movement, her lips parting slightly.

Without the Nijinxes, I would be utterly lost, no more than a rabid killer without mercy or hope. I wanted them to be safe, for Pherox and Vesperum to live with their kin swarm and prosper, memories of the wild ward left to wither and crumble to dust. The thought of anything, or anyone harming them, made my bones lock with rage. Aron had sworn the Scarp would become sanctioned Nijinx territory, and I would hold him to it.

And yet, as Calliope took a shuddering breath, her gaze flitting to my eyes, to my mouth, then lower, the thought of someone hurting *her*, of wanting to control something so wild and defiant, left my body trembling with unspent power.

I shook my head, breaking away to stare at my shadows, my breath coming in heaving sips. But the thought of someone harming her didn't leave, and I knew in my bones that if anyone tried, I would annihilate them.

At the sound of hoofbeats through the snow, I looked back up. Olwen had left Calliope and walked slowly over to me. Placing my hands in the pockets of my gambeson, I let the Unicorn approach until the mare was less than a foot in front of me. Gently, her warm breath caressing my face, Olwen nosed my jaw.

A faint, soft nicker sounded in her throat. I desperately wanted to thread my fingers through her glowing mane and marvel at the creature that so few humans ever saw. Yet I kept my hands where they were. I was not worthy to touch something so legendary.

Olwen stepped back, her ears twitching back and forth, but her gaze remained fixed on me. An unspoken question hung between us, and I gave the tiniest shake of my head. Olwen released a long breath, and I found myself doing the same.

I had read that equines were mirrors, that they reflected your own emotions back to you. An angry man could tame a horse and break him to submission, but that horse would never be his friend. Olwen and I couldn't talk with one another, but we could still have a conversation, a mutual understanding.

Steadily, my heart filled with remorse, I took a hesitant step back. Olwen turned her head to look back at Calliope, who stood in the center of the clearing, chin held high. A gentle winter wind blew the tendrils of her hair back from her proud face, and my heart stuttered in response.

With a final nudge of my shoulder with her gray muzzle, Olwen swung her body away from me, whispering into the trees like a ghost.

Leaving me alone with the Truth Keeper.

Calliope's left hand rose to clasp my coat tighter around her shoulders. Where I had looked away, surrendering, she had not, and that golden gaze continued to lance through the very fibres of my being. The wind grew stronger, playing with the skirt of her dress and bannering her hair behind her.

My body grew taut, and I ground my teeth. Indecision gripped my bones with a sudden viciousness. I could feel the pull of my shadows toward her, my future suddenly feeling like it was balanced on a precipice between salvation and despair.

My fingers ran over the scarred flesh of my right palm.

Rolling my shoulders, I walked forward, my shadows parting as I stalked toward Calliope, my gaze trained on her face. I refused to look away this time. I didn't stop until I was a hand's-breadth in front of her.

Resolutely, she looked up at me, a calm, steely determination in her golden eyes, yet I noticed how her breathing quickened.

"What will it be?" she whispered.

I wondered then, if just because Olwen had been silent to me, didn't mean she couldn't talk to Calliope. They were both creatures of ice and mountain, crafted from related spirits.

My voice was rasping. "We keep walking."

The Truth Keeper pressed closer, and it took all my self-control not to touch that beautiful face.

Her eyes silently implored me. "And?"

I swallowed, my eyes closing for a heartbeat. "We continue to Fort Garobear in the morning."

She stiffened, the only tell she let show, before giving the slightest dip of her chin. "So be it, huntsman."

CHAPTER FIFTEEN

EBREL

We had grazed until the early hours of the morning, before the pair of us had curled up on the ground side by side, Hestian's neck over mine once more, and we had shared each other's body heat while we had fitfully slept. It felt right to be tucked close to his powerful body, feathers intertwining as the sun rose, piercing light through the undergrowth of the trees.

I stirred before he did, taking in the clear, freezing sky above us. Hestian exhaled deeply, gently shifting to follow my gaze that was fixed on the heavens.

"Do you hear it?" I whispered. *"The song of the sky?"*

His gaze dropped to look at me, those gold and brown eyes softening. *"It's faint, probably due to the curse, but it's there, calling to me. I couldn't hear it at all in Ilrair. I think if we did, the stables would be empty."*

"We belong up here. Ilrair, Glentay… it was never our true home. The mountains, the glens, and the skies above them," I inhaled, eyes closing. *"It's where we're meant to be. The Mounties chose Glentay because it was the only place that offered them protection, but the Unicorns must feel it too. Serebo practically touches the sky."* I shifted and stiffly unfolded my limbs to stand, shaking free from the light layer of snow that had fallen in the night. I glanced down at Hestian to find him watching me. *"We were truly warriors once?"*

Hestian heaved himself to his hooves and stretched out his wings. *"There was never any mention of it in Ilrair, but that doesn't mean it's not true. The Adacus family would have done everything they could have to bury any Trinitor knowledge, shaping the narrative to suit them."*

I ground my teeth in frustration. *"What do you think we'll find in the caves?"*

"Likely the only remaining evidence that Trinitors even existed," he mused. *"Lowlanders used to live in the Serebo foothill caves."*

"Only one way to find out," I murmured.

"Or we could find hibernating bears and ravenous lynx, in that case, I'll let you explore them first, being the brave, wild Pegasus that you are." He winked.

I shook my head. *"You're insufferable."*

Hestian angled his head at me, ears pricked. *"And you're easy to rile. Consider it my favorite form of entertainment."*

"Hmmm, and do you know what my favorite form of entertainment is?" I purred, inching closer to him.

"Sneaking glances at me when you think I won't notice?" he countered.

"Leaving you in the snow," I said sweetly, then I propelled myself into the sky.

Flying wide around to avoid detection from the Royant Platoon, we headed south, retracing our wing beats. We flew high, the land a quilt of snow-capped forest, rivers, and high mountain plains below us. The air was thin and freezing, but we were well suited to it, our lungs expanding to their limit, enabling us to inhale the oxygen we needed. Just after midmorning, we put several miles between us and Fort Erskine, then descended. Hestian nosed my shoulder, and I pulled back, letting him take the lead as we dropped beneath the valley peaks.

"The other platoons know what I look like," he said over the rush of the wind. *"I'm the only male palomino in the cavalry. They may already be looking for Silvano, and if they see me without him, flying with you, Destry's Pegasus, they'll shoot first and ask questions later."*

I shuddered, nudging closer to his side, as sheer cliff walls flicked by us.

"At lower altitudes like this, we need to stick to as much cover as possible, vary your flight path as you descend, don't be predictable. Once you find a landing site, don't just dive straight for it. Be quick but be agile. Luckily for you, you're a natural at that style of flying."

"Style of flying?" I asked.

His gaze was serious but sincere. *"Like your life depends on it."* He quickly looked at my brand, then away, and I tensed in response. *"I'm sorry that happened to you, that I couldn't help stop it."*

"I hate it," I whispered, my chest tight. *"It reminds me of when I failed."*

His wing brushed mine, snow white against earth brown. *"But it's a part of you, Ebrel, therefore, it's beautiful. Your scars, your speed, the fairy knots in your mane, the way your feathers turn rose pink in a sunset, all of it is beautiful, roan one. Your brand shows everyone that you survived the fight."*

I quirked my head at him, my wings pummeling the air as I overtook him slightly. *"You think I'm beautiful?"*

"It's like how you find me charming, remember?"

A laugh echoed over my mind, my feather rustling in response. We darted down beside a small birch forest, where patches of snowmelt had revealed early spring grass. Eating quickly, twitching at every sound that echoed around the valleys that surrounded us, we rested for as briefly as our bodies would allow, then took flight once more. In the far-off distance to the west, another fort loomed, faint horn blows from within barely reaching us.

Hestian listened intently, ears flicking back and forth to catch the sounds distorted by the wind. *"Bromtide Platoon,"* he said quietly, throwing me a worried glance. *"That's Fort Vervelli."*

"They have a new commander already?"

He swallowed. *"It would seem so, they wouldn't push north without one. Silvano gave them orders to stay put in Aarine, it seems like he's been overruled."*

"They know he's dissented?"

"Hard to say, we can't risk flying there to check, even if we wanted to warn Silvano and Destry, we don't have time."

We climbed higher, constantly searching for cavalry scouting parties and nomadic Pegasus herds. As the sun inched past mid-afternoon, Mount Ghel loomed in the distance, Mount Serebo a faint gray and white sentinel behind her. Cautiously, we lowered, scouring the landscape for somewhere to rest before we continued once darkness had fallen.

Dipping between two jagged peaks, we were doused into chilling shadows as the valley floor rose to meet us. Our hooves had barely connected with the packed snow, when I heard the faint strain of a bowstring being drawn back.

Squealing a warning, I barreled into Hestian, nearly knocking him over, as a dark wood arrow flew between us. Dark brown eyes scanning the nearby fir trees and underlying brush, I locked onto the sound of the bow being drawn again.

"Get airborne, now," ordered Hestian.

"They'll be expecting that." Anger like I'd never felt, surged in my blood, and I didn't give myself a second to hesitate, before I launched toward the undergrowth, leaping left then right. Another arrow flitted past my right shoulder, and then there were sudden movements in the bushes, like someone was scrambling backward.

I careened through the frozen ferns, wings brandished and leaped, pinning the lone huntsman between my forehooves. He was young, wiry, his hair a mess of thick, black curls. Dark shadows stood out under his brown eyes, his tattered green cloak pulled tight over his torso and back. It was his scent that had me baring my teeth.

The Petish man flinched, eyes wide with shock, his fists frozen still on either side of his head. He quivered against the frozen ground, his breath clouding with my own. I inhaled deeply, confirming what I knew to be true.

"He's related to Rekorious," I snarled. My muzzle twitched. *"A cousin, I'm sure of it."*

Hestian treaded quietly forward to stand at my side, hostility thrumming from every inch of him. The young man trapped beneath me cowered at the sight of the stallion.

"P-please," he begged, his voice hoarse. "Don't kill me. I know you can understand me. Please. I'm under orders."

I lifted a forehoof, angling it so the very tip pressed against his heaving sternum. I could crush his ribcage with half a thought, but for now, the threat of it would suffice. My dark gaze bore into the human's, and I conveyed every ounce of intention I could at him.

One question. If he was quiet enough, he'd hear it. If he was humble enough, he'd hear it. *"Who gave you your orders?"*

But he was panicked, too far gone to understand me, or even try to decipher what I wanted. "I didn't mean to shoot, I swear. If it were up to me, I would have never fired the arrows I—" I placed a fraction more weight onto my hoof on his chest. *"Please."*

"He has the scent of Ilrairian Pegasi on him," said Hestian, his voice so low and harsh that it sent a shiver up my spine. *"He's a spy, a traitor."*

Another fraction of weight had him whimpering on the ground. *"You're sure?"*

The stallion nodded, not taking his eyes off the human. Hestian inhaled deeply, then rolled his top lip upward to analyze the scent more closely. A deep rumble of anger echoed up his throat as he looked down again. *"There's another scent there I can't place. It's not one I've encountered before. It reminds me of cold oceans."*

"I can't place it either. So, what do we do with him? If he's under orders, he'll shoot us as soon as we're airborne again. And if he doesn't shoot, he'll report back to whoever holds his leash that he's seen us."

Hestian glanced at me, his white forelock covering a golden eye. *"It leaves us with only one option, roan one."*

I stared at the young man beneath my hoof. The stranger panted, his terrified gaze glancing between the stallion and me. Any anger I had felt shuddered from my body, leaving it torn at the impossible thought. Could I end this stranger's life? He had tried to kill me and Hestian, but could I retaliate like that? I didn't hold the all-consuming hatred for him like I had with the wild ward or Spearian. This man was young and scared out of his wits.

Hestian pressed his nose to my cheek. *"Go back to the clearing, Ebrel. It's alright."*

"We can't risk letting him live," I whispered.

"I know, roan one, but I won't let you carry this death." His voice was heartbreakingly tender, and I let myself lean into his touch. *"Go back to the clearing. Leave him to me."*

"We break his arm. It'll leave him unable to shoot and take him long enough to get back to his master that we'll be well away from here." Shifting my hoof off the stranger's chest, I stepped back, trying to shut out his deep, human inhales of relief. Closing my eyes, I backed up slowly, wings tucked tight and trembling to my body. I blinked at the stranger's wail, and Hestian stepped forward to take my place, the promise of death in the carriage of his head and neck.

"If we break his arm, he'll only suffer out here. He won't survive, and the pain will be unbearable." Hestian turned to look at me. *"It'll be a horrible way to die. I'll make this quick, he'll be gone before he feels any pain."* The stranger whimpered as the stallion looked down at him once more. Hestian didn't look away as he murmured gently, *"Go wait for me in the clearing, Ebrel."*

I nodded, words beyond me, then I turned on my haunches and fled. *Coward.* I was a wretched coward. Bursting back onto the darkening meadow, I tried in vain to block out the sound, shaking my head from left to right, but nothing could stop me from hearing it. My senses were too attuned to every sight, smell, and sound around me. I sensed Hestian rear, heard the stranger's scream of fear that was cut horrifyingly short by the crunch of hooves through bone and flesh.

Jerking my head away, I tucked my nose under the curve of my right wing, unable to stop my shaking. I didn't object when Hestian walked quietly over to me, extended his glossy white wing over my quivering back, and tucked me close to his side. His steady breath and heat washed over me.

"I'm sorry," I whispered, my eyes closed.

"Don't, Ebrel," he murmured, his voice void of judgement. *"His life wasn't yours to take, let me shield you from darkness like that."*

"I fled like a coward, Hestian."

"You are not a coward, Ebrel, you've faced horrors I would never have survived." His warm, sweet breath trickled over my pelt. *"Doing what needs to be done doesn't always make it feel right. He's not the first traitor I've ended. Silvano and I have dispatched numerous monsters together over the years, but it doesn't make it easier. I carry every death with me."* He nuzzled my cheek with his gray nose. *"But it's a stallion's duty to protect, and if I can spare you from something like that, I will."*

Warmth radiated through my bones, and for the first time in my life, I let a Pegasus stallion embrace me, hold me in the only way he could, with his neck and wing over me, until my heart slowed and eventide rippled over the meadow.

CHAPTER SIXTEEN

DESTRY

I awoke before dawn and quickly lit the candles, the ache in my thigh a constant, dull thrum, as I washed and knotted my hair at the base of my neck. The flagstones were a warm balm against my bare feet, as I peered into the dresser drawers. The first held underwear, socks, mittens, scarves, and woolen shirts and leggings, basic necessities for living in a place where the cold was constant all year round. In the second drawer, I found multiple long riding skirts and tunics, and in the third, a pair of fur-lined, supple leather boots, a sword belt, and a set of twin daggers.

Picking out one of everything bar the mittens and a scarf, I dressed slowly, my leg stiff as I pulled on and buckled up the deep navy riding skirt, tucking a dove-gray tunic into it, the soft wool brushing against my throat. Next came the sword belt, and almost reverently, I plucked *Kathkar* from its holder. The metal sent a thrum of power down my arm as I twisted the hilt in my grasp, relishing the weight and feel of the sword again. I wondered what had become of Lonan's second sword, and if any of the Royants had picked it up from the snows in the carnage of Erskine.

The image of Lonan's frozen corpse flashed through my mind, and my fingers stilled in buckling *Kathkar* to my belt. I killed a man yesterday. My body braced for the wave of remorse to hit me, but there was only chilling, endless silence. Swallowing harshly, I finished securing *Kathkar* and jumped when a soft *tap-tap* sounded against the door.

Unlatching it, I opened the door slowly, to reveal Minna fully ready for the day, a short sword strapped across her back over her black cloak. She smiled as my eyes widened, taking in the pale blue bundle in her grasp.

"It's tradition to wear your family's cloak to all council meetings. I thought it was time to reunite you with yours."

Nodding, I stepped back, letting her breeze in. Minna set the Kivisto family cloak down on the rumpled bedcovers, then fished in her tunic pocket for something. Pinched between a forefinger and thumb, she lifted her hand across to me. A stitch cutter.

"For the Niemi River fish Marte sewed on," she said with a sly wink.

I choked on a hoarse laugh, as I stepped forward and gently took the silver stitch cutter from her. Unfolding the cloak, I peered down at the twin, curving fish sewn in glittering thread on either side of the collar.

Watching on while I carefully removed the Niemi sigil, Minna said softly, "How are you feeling?"

"Sore but functioning. What will happen ... to Silvano today?"

The cavalry Commander swallowed. She wore her hair in a tight crown braid today and a pair of tiny amethyst ear studs with a matching silver-chained necklace, the only small flicker of color she wore, the gemstones standing out against the black of her tunic and skirt. "It's likely most councilors will vote for exile, as they'll want to throw support behind Rekorious and a few of them, especially the older ones, have a deep mistrust of Ilrairians."

Finishing the last stitch, I unfurled the cloak fully and wrapped it around my shoulders, its familiar lavender and woodsmoke scent clouding around me. "And what will you vote for?"

Intelligence beyond her years danced in Minna's dark brown eyes, and her full lips quirked upward. "Well, *Koskivarri*, that depends on you and how much you want to fight for the man who saved your life yesterday."

My palms were clammy as I sat on the end of the horseshoe-shaped council table. Minna, a solid, confident presence on my right. Helmi scowled at me from where she sat, her nose wrinkling in distaste. I ignored her, my attention fixed on the doors. Thudding footsteps sounded and the council room fell quiet, as the double set of thick, iron-plated doors swung outward and Rekorious stalked in the room, a hand clasped around Silvano's left bicep. Arnar a step behind them.

The men were rigid with tension, like Silvano was barely tolerating the warlord's touch and wanted rid of him as soon as possible. His own hands were chained together, his curved sword nowhere in sight. His gaze swept the room but halted when he finally found me. A riot of relief, followed by blazing heat, flooded through my body at the sight of him, and Rekorious led him to the pulpit. Silvano stood like I had done, his fists braced against the handrail. His deep green eyes gave nothing away as he searched my face.

Spirits, if they exiled him today, or worse, what on earth would I do? Where would he go? The threat of Jaryn setting his claws into him had my jaw clenching.

Shep walked in next, followed by Amadea. I nearly bolted from my chair at the sight of her, but Minna gave a small shake of her head. She looked a great deal brighter than she had yesterday, her black curls a wild halo about her dark face yet her eyes were hallowed ... haunted. Dressed in a simple, high-necked navy gown, she watched the table warily, as she silently followed Shep to a back bench behind my chair.

I twisted in my seat, desperate for her to look at me. She hadn't realized I was there. A heartbeat later, as the Queen of Ilrair scanned the room, her golden gaze fell on me, and as if pulled on a phantom wind, she broke off from Shep and stalked toward where I sat. I was on my feet a heartbeat later, my chair screeching against the floor, as I heaved Amadea into my arms, and I into hers.

Neither of us spoke as we held each other tightly, the kind of embrace that was soul-binding, threaded with relief and warmth. Amadea pulled back an inch, her calloused palm rising to cup my cheek.

"We'll talk later," she whispered, and I nodded in reply, fighting back tears. Smiling softly, her gaze flicked to Silvano, then back to me. "He made the right choice."

Giving my hands a final squeeze, she stepped back, gathered the skirt of her gown, and went to sit beside Shep. Swallowing harshly, my throat burning with the tears that battled to fall, I pulled my chair back up and sat, suddenly noting every pair of eyes watching me with a mix of awe and suspicion. I was friends with King Jaryn's wife and his top, albeit former, Commander. I was one of them, Petish, yet the company I seemed to keep was questionable at the very least. Even Minna looked bewildered by what had just occurred.

Only Rekorious and Silvano looked at me like they understood. They knew the kind of torture Jaryn liked to dole out, and the bonds that could form under such treatment. The fact that Amadea was here at all was a testament to that.

I looked across at Silvano to find his expression contented, a faint, almost sad smile on his lips. My heart thundered as I drank him in, happy to do so for as long as I could, especially after yesterday, when I had thought I would never see it again, and it had all been some frozen dream.

Rekorious cleared his throat, standing slowly, and I snapped back to the present, my fingers a tight knot in my lap. "I call this trial to order."

Trial? I jolted, and Minna tensed beside me. Not a council meeting, but a fucking trial. Panic leached the color from my face as I glared at Rekorious. This wasn't what was discussed in the medic quarter last night.

"Silvano Coen, you are accused of spying for the Ilrairian crown, torturing Taneli Farrow for information and using our *Koskivarri* to gain entry into our stronghold." Rekorious refused to look at me as I seethed in my chair. Amadea gasped behind me.

Silvano simply rolled his eyes at the words, not giving the warlord the satisfaction of a reply.

"He saved my life yesterday," I snarled.

"How convenient for him," muttered Helmi.

"How do you plead?" Rekorious stared Silvano down, who raised his chin in defiance.

"Not guilty, Lord Niemi. Although, I find the tale you and your counterparts have woven to be quite fanciful. As I told you yesterday, with three of your advisors present, I have abandoned my position as Bromtide Commander. Taneli Farrow, being the coward he is, came crawling to me in order to try and gain favor and told me your plot to ensnare Destry into a betrothal she did not want. And when you wouldn't take no for an answer, she left you a little reminder about when a woman says no, *she fucking means it*." Silvano angled his head to gesture toward the small section of red scar across Rekorious' collarbone.

Air heaved from my lungs, my heart thundering in my chest at the fury that flashed across the warlord's face, but Silvano spoke the truth.

"I flew north to make sure that she was free and not thrown from Jaryn's cage and straight into *yours*." Silvano's voice was practically a snarl that mirrored my own. "You should all be ashamed, you, her countrymen, in going along with Niemi's plans, in trying to yank a woman who is free in her own right, into something she never wanted."

The councilors sat in stunned, blinking silence, cowed by the fury and fire of the bound warrior in the pulpit. I had never had someone fight so viciously for me, with intelligence and pride, and spirits be damned, I was sure as hell going to do the same for him. He had risked his career, his political standing, even making an enemy of his oldest friend and King, to stand in this room today.

Hearan Lael cleared his throat, his wary yet flustered gaze flitting between his lord, Silvano, and me. "The betrothal has been dissolved."

"It shouldn't have needed your dissolvement in the first place. You should have respected her wishes from the start. She freed your beloved spirits almost single-handedly, and that was how you repaid her? With lies and force?" Silvano paused, and Rekorious looked ready to rip into him with his bare hands, but the ex-Commander wasn't finished. "And as for yesterday, do your councilors know that the *Koskivarri* almost died trying to free Amadea? That you led the Royants into an obvious trap, endangering your cavalry riders in the process?"

Lael turned slowly in his chair. "Is this true, lord?"

Rekorious clenched and unclenched his fists. "It's true, yet with Destry's new gift, I figured we had a chance of getting Amadea out alive."

"New gift?" One of the twin brothers sat beside Helmi, arching a thick eyebrow, his face deadly serious.

The wooden handrail of the pulpit groaned with the force that Silvano placed on it. I looked coolly across at the councilor, letting the ice in my chest spread a fraction. "One I killed a man with."

The councilor rolled his eyes while Helmi scoffed beside him. "Just the one? That's hardly a victory."

Rage at their utter indignation flared down my bones, and I slammed my right palm down against the pale wood of the table top. Ice and hoarfrost speared from my fingertips, weaving and twisting over the table like an intricate latticework, until it stopped dead in a glittering spear point in front of the councilor's hooked nose. A breath later, my light twirled around the woven ice strands, casting every council member in a deep green glow tainted with red.

Silence rippled through the room, as wide, aghast eyes took in my power that still sent a ripple through the suddenly chilled air. The councilor I had targeted, swallowed loudly and leaned back in his chair, a shaking hand braced on the table before him.

Slowly, I returned my hand to my lap, content to let the aftershocks at what I'd shown them finish peeling away. My gaze snagged on Arnar, who sat on Rekorious' right again. He stared at me with such open, wanton need on his face that I bared my teeth in reply, *Kathkar* sending a pulse of power against my hip in warning. After yesterday, I didn't trust him as far as I could throw him. I hadn't heard what had become of Elias, and if he had truly betrayed Rekorious by giving away our location yesterday, but judging how smugly Arnar sat in his chair, fingers drumming the table top, I wondered if Elias had merely been a puppet.

I peeked across at Silvano, who gave me a wry smile and a pride-filled nod. Feeling like we were a pair of conspirators, I dared a small smile of my own in return. Then Silvano slid his gaze to Arnar with a predator's deadly focus.

Lael, somewhat slowly, rose from his chair, and Rekorious sat down, his expression hard and cold as he took in my ice on the table. Shifting his bloodred cloak over his shoulder, Lael turned to face Silvano fully.

"You saved the *Koskivarri's* life, for which we shall be forever thankful. However, I'm afraid proving your worth to us will take much more than that. The company you kept in Ilrair cannot be ignored."

Helmi leaned forward, trailing a finger down a strand of curved ice. "I have a proposal, if Destry is willing to vouch for him?"

I assessed the Heara with cold, calculating warning, a sliver of unease slicking down my spine at her words.

Lael looked across to her, brow furrowed. "And that is?"

Under the table, Minna reached across and clasped my left hand, her rough yet warm fingers squeezing tightly. A warning.

It was Rekorious who muttered darkly from where he sat, his gaze never leaving Silvano. "She wishes to use the caveat of the betrothal dissolvement."

"The *morean*?" sputtered Lael.

Helmi straightened, triumphant. "Yes, the *morean*. If Commander Coen's character is as pure as he and Destry pledges, then I'm sure she'll have no qualms at consenting to it. It'll prove his worth as a warrior to us. And if he refuses." The councilwoman shrugged. "Then it will be exile or death. Whichever Lord Niemi chooses."

"I can't consent to it if I have no idea what a *morean* is," I hissed.

Lael turned to face me then, his face grave. "It's one of our oldest Petish traditions. Nowadays, it is purely ceremonial, with no risk to life, *spirits*, most couples make a party out of it."

"Get to the point, Lael," muttered Rekorious.

The older warrior stiffened, but his words were steady, calm. "*Morean* translates to 'bride trial.' The bride's intended partner must battle however many opponents are selected, usually three or four men or women of a similar age and standing. If the intended successfully defeats them all, he is deemed worthy of his bride, and the wedding ceremony is conducted shortly afterward."

The councilor leaned forward again, a smirk on his tanned face. "And I'm sure my fellow councilor's are in agreement, that a wedding should indeed follow the *morean*. It would bind the accused to our cause."

Holy spirits, holy fucking spirits. Heart thundering, I whipped my head to Silvano. This or exile? A gauntlet of fights and a marriage to me? Again, Silvano searched my face, and he gave me another small nod. It was up to me. He would leave his fate in my hands. I felt sick. If I said no to this, and he was exiled, would I join him in the wilds, ensuring he survived out there?

"What say you, my lord?" asked Helmi, her gaze never leaving my anguished face.

Rekorious rose slowly, a hand braced on the table. He looked down at me now, and I craned my neck to face him, desperately trying to read the expression on his rugged face. "I declare a *morean*. Six challengers, steel weapons, no kill strikes. If Coen fails in the *morean*, he will be exiled. If he refuses to participate, he will be exiled. If the binds of exile are ignored and he steps foot into Petowin again, he will be killed on sight."

My chest heaved for a breath that battled to flow into my lungs.

Rekorious' gaze darkened. "And if Coen is victorious, he and Destry with be handfasted that same day. He will be granted amnesty, free to travel, work, and live within these borders unthreatened. He will be welcomed as a brother-in-arms by me and by my people. Do you accept the caveat of your betrothal dissolvement, Destry? Do you consent to the *morean*?"

Minna gave me a subtle nudge of her elbow, and I rose on shaking legs to a standstill. Purple light flickered at my fingertips, and frost coated my nails. I looked across to Silvano one final time, praying he could read the desperate earnestness on my face. I wanted him here, with me. Spirits, I wanted him, had longed for him during every night away from Saltfen, had prayed for him under Narve's torture. Yet to consent to this would bind him to me. Where was his consent? Where was his choice in all of this?

I knew there was something between us and that it had been there since before I was nearly killed in Ilrair, when we had been hissing and snarling at each other for days. Yet I was about to plunge headfirst into marriage, if spirits forbid he even survived the bride trial.

Silvano's gaze softened, and he gave me a reassuring smile. He was steadfast, a solid presence of confidence in himself. In *us*, I realized with a wave of shuddering relief. Throwing back my shoulders, I turned to face Rekorious, defiance rolling from every pore in my body.

"I accept the *morean*."

CHAPTER
SEVENTEEN

ASHER

M y campfire was holding steadily, the smoke filtering into the violet evening sky above us. The snow cloud had cleared, leaving a thousand glittering stars in its wake. I had managed to find an arrowhead-shaped cave at the base of a granite rise, and I had set up the fire just in front of it.

The cave was a narrow but deep space, and fairly dry despite the risk of ice and snowmelt. I had expected Calliope to curl up on herself in the farthest reaches of it, but she hadn't. Instead, she sat across the fire from me, knees tucked tight to her chest, while she stirred wicken berry juice into a small cast-iron pot of boiling water.

My shadows wreathed the trees, shielding us from the deeper forest beyond like dark, undulating sentinels. The air was laden with everything I wanted to say to Calliope, all my reasonings and fears, but the words remained locked in my throat, content to torture me from the inside out.

I had felt her withdrawing deeper and deeper into herself, like the final throes of a doomed star. Keeping busy by carving up strips of dried reindeer meat and tending the fire, I tried to ignore the sense of foreboding that the dawn would bring.

Calliope cleared her throat, and I looked up to find a small steaming earthenware cup in her hand. Another sat precariously by her right foot.

I arched an eyebrow, the scent of the fruit filtering past me. "You don't mind?"

"You're sharing all your supplies with me." She gave a small half-shrug. "It's only fair that I do the same."

She pressed the cup closer to me, and I noted her shaking hand. "Do you need my gambeson too? It'll be below freezing tonight."

"No, I'm fine, honestly. Your coat is more than enough."

"Okay," I whispered, not entirely convinced. Reaching forward, I clasped the cup in my hand, my fingers brushing hers. Calliope stilled at the contact, and my own breath caught, heat rolling over my body. Then she blinked and pulled away, staring hard at the bare ground, like it might yield all the answers she needed.

I didn't look away from her as I raised the cup to my lips and drank. The taste of the steaming hot, cinnamon-flavored tea was a welcome relief from the melted snow we had been consuming in lieu of water. Letting the steam trickle over my face, I took another sip, then placed the cup down beside me. Carving up a final slice of meat, I passed it to her.

Calliope looked up at me then. She swallowed hard and balanced the sheaf of birch bark bearing her meal on her knees. I dove into my food, but she picked silently at hers.

The questions of *what's wrong?* and *are you okay?* nearly rolled off my tongue, but I cursed myself as an idiot. I was her captor, taking her to a fate worse than a clean death. *I* was the wrong thing, a dark, horrid creature who was not deserving to even be in her presence.

Tiny, dark specks flitted over my vision, and I blinked. Glancing over at my shadows, I ran a critical gaze over where they waited quietly, content to watch me in my emotional torment. Setting my birch bark down, I blinked again, but the dark specks didn't disappear. They intensified.

I felt a shadow rise then, like a cat spotting prey.

A wave of dizziness barreled through me, and I released a sharp gasp.

My gaze ripped from Calliope's untouched cup to her face. Her eyes were soft, an apology written in every line of her body.

"*No*," I ground out. My unsteady hands splayed on the ground at my side. I tried reaching out for my shadows. They were there, awaiting a command, but I couldn't form the thought. Then realization dealt me a crushing blow, they wouldn't harm Calliope in retribution. And, I knew in my heart, I wouldn't want them to.

I collapsed onto an elbow, my breath coming in uneven pants. The forest and cave rose and dipped around me, but Calliope remained constant, an anchor. Then she was moving. Edging around the fire, she knelt by my head and smoothed my hair off my sweat-slicked forehead.

"What ... did you give me?" I asked, the words ripped out of me felt like serrated thorns in my throat.

She caught me then, as my arm gave way, and my torso rested in her lap. I stared up at her ethereal face, one that now morphed rhythmically from that of a human, to the solemn, moon-white disk of an owl, and back again.

Her long fingers swept down the plane of my jaw, and I groaned, unbidden, at her touch. Her searing golden gaze roved over every part of my face. "The berries are harmless," she whispered. "But the bark is hallucinogenic."

The sheer rock wall above us cracked, splintered, then reformed behind Calliope, and I could feel myself losing my grip on where I was in relation to the earth and sky. It was I who was adrift now, darkness spearing across my vision like meteors.

My eyes rolled as she trailed a finger from my chin and down the length of my throat. Spirits, I wanted her, wanted that touch everywhere, my body yearning for more. It was the feeling of her hand brushing against my collarbone that kept me moored to my body, her eyes blazing like beacons in the dark.

"I will find you," I rasped.

Calliope gave me a small, crooked smile, and I screamed at my body to move, to touch her, hold her, but I couldn't. I was completely at her mercy, even before I drank the wicken berry tea.

"I will be long gone by the time you wake up, huntsman." Her hand drifted back up to cradle my head. My shadows reared upward behind her, appearing like dark, phantasmal wings.

I could feel myself being pulled under. "I ... will ... find ... you."

She leaned forward, her lips hovering over mine, our breaths intertwined. I desperately wanted to thread my hand through her hair, clasp the back of her head, and draw her closer, the promise of a kiss so tantalizingly close. My body trembled with the need to move, but it felt like my spine had rooted to the earth.

Her melodic voice whispered softly in my ear. "When I said that darkness was your master, it wasn't Iltavorn I was referring to."

Then she was pulling away, and I hissed through gritted teeth at her absence. Tenderly, she laid a spare blanket over me, placed another log onto the simmering fire, then she began to fade, like a goddess called to a higher realm.

The stars began to wink out, the earth rising like a wave, then it plunged to devour me whole.

PART TWO

The Sanctuary

CHAPTER
EIGHTEEN

SILVANO

The possibility that I could die tomorrow visited me briefly in my cell, like a draft of cold, unwanted air. I briskly waved it aside, acknowledging it but deciding not to dwell on it. Dawn was still several hours away, the chill of the jail cell stark against my tunic and cloak. The cell wasn't your typical square-cut stone. It was a natural cave within the bedrock, an iron door retrofitted to cover the opening. The jagged, rough-hewn walls jabbed into my spine, and with every nick of pain, the shuddering sense of déjà vu washed over me, but I wasn't afraid.

I had total faith in my body, in my training, in my sword.

I had total faith in my purpose too.

Swords would clash, sweat would pour, snow would spray, but I would do it a hundred times over, to prove to her, to her people, that I was worth it. That *we* were worth it. When I had flown north with Hestian, abandoning my rank and southern life, I had done it purely to mark Destry as safe and in control of her own future. Guilt at not having acted sooner chased me the entire way, like a relentless pack of snarling wolves. It was out of pure selfishness, the need to be close to her, to hold her, that I had stayed.

The memory of Farrow carrying Destry's unconscious body over the moorlands was forever seared in my mind. I had been content to abandon her to the wilderness and bitter, biting cold and let her die in that no-man's-land. Hatred and grief over what I thought her family had done, had fueled me then, such dark loathing hatred that the memory of who that man had been scared me. A man so content to let an innocent woman die, over an atrocity that her clan hadn't even committed. History and Ilrairan royal plotting had twisted and warped the truth about what had happened at Lake Wylda. I had believed for nearly all my life that my father had been slaughtered alongside his soldiers by Petish, blood-crazed warriors, when, in stark reality, Destry's father had tried to save mine.

Before Amadea had carved Destry's memory from the water in Ilrair, I had begun to soften towards the wild, fierce young woman. Her absolute determination in the face of conquest and the otherworldly light in her brown eyes had enraptured me.

Then those bastard guards had tried to kill her, and rage like I had never felt before, steered my body with lethal precision. I wish they had died more slowly under my blade, taking my time to make them pay for the pain they had inflicted upon her.

I didn't begrudge the Petish people's resentment and mistrust toward me. I had treated them just as poorly until recently, just like my forefathers had. Yet times had changed, *I* had changed, and I would fight with my bare fists if needed to right the wrongs between our peoples.

The look on Destry's face at Erskine, when she had been on her knees in the snow, haunted me. I had seen her kill Lonan, and after that, after she had conquered one of her greatest foes, she looked content to die, to whisper away from this world. Safe in the knowledge that one less monster prowled the wilds. Her face, resigned to death, stalked my nightmares alongside steadfast flames.

CHAPTER NINETEEN

DESTRY

I tossed and turned in bed, sleep utterly out of reach. Dawn was still hours away, and I sat up, shoving the suddenly suffocating blankets off me, and stood in the center of my room. My breath was hurried, anxiety a tangle of thorns in my chest as I paced the warm stone floor.

Rekorious had ordered no kill strikes today, but a slip on the ice, a misjudgment, a deadly vendetta, could see Coen's soul slip from this world. I desperately wanted to see him, but we were forbidden to talk to each other before the bride trial. Dragging a hand through my hair, I gritted my teeth in frustration.

A faint scuffle had me turning mid-stride, and my gaze fell to the bottom of my bedroom door. The little stoat wriggled through the gap under the knotted and gnarled wood, a long piece of metal clamped between its sharp teeth. Squeaking happily, it bounded over to my bare feet and dropped the rod of metal with a dull clang.

Stunned, I knelt stiffly on my right leg and picked up what the stoat had delivered. It cavorted on its short legs, black-tipped tail whipping back and forth in excitement as I held the piece of black iron. A key. My gaze flicked between it and the stoat.

"Is this for what I think it is?" I whispered hoarsely in amazement.

The stoat bounded forward, placing a tiny white paw on the large toe of my right foot, then it galloped to the door and back to me.

Nudging my toe with its cold, black nose, it raced for the door once more and scuttled under it. A second later, its pointed head shoved back through with a determined squeak.

"What in the spirit's name is happening?" I rose, heaved on a thick knitted shawl over my sleep shift, and, clutching the key in my right hand, I snuck out of my room as silently as I could after the tiny mammal.

Tail whipping, it bounced around me once, then it took off down the hallway like a little white sprite. I didn't hesitate and limped hurriedly after it, ignoring the pulsing throb down my left leg. Heart pounding in my chest, I sipped urgent pants of air as we traveled down the silent, torchlit corridors. The stoat didn't pause to check on me or give me a rest, as it led me past the bathing chamber and into a lower level of the keep, the air growing sharper, colder, until my breath clouded in front of me. I prayed I would remember the way back if the stoat decided to disappear back to its den.

Reaching a crossroad in the wide stone hallway, it paused and sniffed delicately, whiskers twitching, then it galloped down the dim, right-hand corridor. Pausing before a grated metal door, the stoat rose on its back legs and braced its front paws against the bottom lip.

"This one?" I whispered.

A short, sharp squeak was its only answer.

Breathing harshly, I lifted the key into the lock and slowly twisted it, the satisfying clicks of metal sounding a heartbeat later. Seemingly happy its job was done, the stoat nudged my bare lower calf, its tiny sharp claws making faint indentations into my skin, before it ran the way we came, disappearing into the dark.

Leaving me with an unlocked jail cell.

Gingerly, I pushed the metal door inward, a frigid breeze and pitch-black darkness greeting me a moment later. A sense of déjà vu gripped my bones for a moment, and I swayed on my feet, distant past and present suddenly roaring through my head. Blinking, it took a second for my eyes to adjust to the gloom, but sitting beside the right-hand wall, his hands resting between his bent knees, was Silvano Coen.

His eyes widened as he registered me, backlit amongst the corridor's torchlight. He made to stand, but I slowly shook my head, carefully and quietly shutting the cell door behind me. It felt so right to walk silently toward him, his dark gaze holding mine as I limped closer.

My light washed over the ancient stone floor as a gentle, amethyst wave. As it breached against Silvano, it crested into sparks of sage green. I halted, eyes widening, as the lambent stone that rested against my clavicle thrummed with power.

Silvano gazed up at me, the smooth planes of his tanned throat exposed. "Destry."

I had never heard his voice so quiet and gentle, like I might disappear if he spoke my name too loudly. Stiffly, I knelt before him, my legs quaking with the effort. Silvano shifted to mirror me, each movement lithe and deliberate, our knees almost touching.

Holding my gaze, he gently reached forward and clasped my chilled fingers in his own. My breathing hitched at the contact, followed by a shudder of relief, like my soul had been reminded that he truly was there. Time slowed, the cold air of the cell shifting with an ancient energy weaving around the stone walls like vines. It was incredibly old, this part of the keep, the walls of the cell carved from the very rockbed, a coarse bookmark amidst the fabric and pace of our world, where one could pause and reflect, be at peace.

Silvano swallowed, his voice whisper quiet. "I didn't take you for a jail breaker, wild one."

Again, that brush of his thumb over my knuckles. I huffed out a breath, a ghost of a smile on my lips. "I had help, albeit, not from something I expected."

He went wholly still, then his right hand rose to brush along my cheekbone. "When tomorrow is over, I can't wait to see you smile again."

"If you get hurt, I—"

"They won't get close enough to try." His hand shifted to gently cup the back of my neck, and his gaze silently implored me. "I believe ... that every battle I have ever fought, every training session, every bare-knuckle fight, was to prepare me for this, for what tomorrow holds."

A gold fire burned in those emerald eyes, and it stoked embers of purpose in my soul. He could do this, *we* could do this. A fight for survival. I didn't know why fate had tossed me into Silvano's path or why we kept owing each other a life's debt, but despite it all, despite everything I had endured, I was glad it had.

"You've left everything you've ever known, everything you've worked so hard for ... to find me?" I felt petty, small, to want that reassurance from him.

"And I would risk it all again in a heartbeat for you."

I gave the tiniest shake of my head. "You'll lose everything, Silvano."

"The things I have lost are those worth losing, Destry. My place in a poisoned court, a friend gone beyond the voice of reason or mercy, a career that stoked fear and entrapped a sentient creature to my side? Compared to what I could have, what I could dream of, a life free from tyranny. A life lived beyond twisted lies and games ... a life ..." His gaze silently searched my face, saying everything he didn't need to.

I clutched his hand in mine and leaned forward, until our foreheads touched, our breaths intermingling and clouding in the cold air of the cell. My body sang with the need to be closer to him, to feel the thrum of power in his body against mine, but for now, for tonight, sharing breath with him felt more intimate than anything my imagination could possibly conjure.

Silvano's eyes were closed as he whispered, "I came here to find you, to make sure you hadn't been thrown from one trap to another. And Destry, I refuse to be that next cage for you." He leaned back and surveyed me, his wild, wind-tossed hair falling over his brow. "You deserve to be free, to mark your own path in this world. Your worth is more than whoever walks by your side."

Words failed me again, my lips parting, but what I could say just tangled in an unspoken mess within my chest. This all felt like some feverish dream that could be ripped apart at any moment.

"If you wish it, after we are handfasted tomorrow, you are not beholden to me, do you understand? We ... we can live separately, if that is what you want. Hell." He cleared his throat, his words rasping. "We can have an annulment the very next day."

"No," I whispered. My right hand rose slowly, then after a breath of hesitation, I swept the hair back from his brow. Silvano went utterly still at my touch, his eyes flickering shut for a moment as he breathed deeply through his nose. Entranced, I repeated the motion, exulting in the feeling of running my fingers gently through his thick hair. "I wouldn't want an annulment. I left Saltfen to find my freedom, but Niemi was just another trap ... and yet the spirits were freed ... and I think, in some ways, you were cut free too."

His eyes flickered open slowly, as my touch drifted away. I held my uptilted palm between us and let my light weave between my fingertips. The shades of undulating green were growing stronger, interwoven with striated veins of lavender.

"I can't imagine what pain you have been through, wild one. Share it with me, so I can help you bear it, heal from it." I shuddered, as a memory of Narve sliced over my heart. Silvano tilted his head, registering my sharp intake of breath. "I said in Ilrair that I understand if you never forgive me for how I treated you then. Hate and prejudice have walked beside me for many years, Destry, and I—" He swallowed, and his hand clasped my own once more. I blinked, noting just how much his hands engulfed mine. "I am so incredibly sorry. I'm sorry for not coming for you sooner. I should have followed you as soon as you fled Saltfen."

"Will you regret it ... becoming my husband?"

"Destry, I have many regrets in this life, but this, us, will never be one of them."

"When Jaryn discovers you've betrayed him—"

Silvano tensed then, and he slowly shook his head. "I won't lie to you and say that he won't find out what I've done, it's just a matter of time. But when he does, just know that I will fight until my last breath for you, for what I've tried to make right in this lifetime."

"Train me and let me fight beside you."

Silvano quirked an eyebrow and revealed a roguish smile that made my heart thunder in my chest. "I promise."

"Don't want to resort to stabbing someone with a piece of pottery."

I lost all coherent thought, as Silvano winked. "Your resourcefulness is part of your charm, Destry."

My light sparked around my hands, as I choked on a laugh. "Why, thank you."

The lambent stone necklace thrummed with a pulse of power at my laughter, and I glanced down to where it lay against my chest. "The Night Pegasus once said that I had met a man that was worthy of me, it was after I had fled Saltfen. He ... might have abandoned me now, but a part of me lies within this lambent stone." Slowly, I lifted the leather cord up and over my head, my hand clasped over the small fragment of glinting stone tucked safely against the skin of my palm. "I won't be able to fight alongside you tomorrow, but I'll be with you, for every step, every sword strike."

On a halted breath, I gently looped the necklace over Silvano's head, my fingers brushing the tanned nape of his neck as it settled into place. Slowly, feeling a dash of bravery and sense of utter completeness, I swept my right palm from his neck, along his jaw to brush my thumb over his cheekbone.

Silvano's silent breath washed over me, his eyes closed, as he leaned into my whisper of touch. The eternal flames of the Night Pegasus may have forgotten me, but I hoped, by some distant miracle and throe of ancient magic, that the power in my veins could protect Silvano.

He shifted, moving from the wall to sit beside me. It felt perfectly natural to rest my head against his shoulder, as he wrapped an arm around me, tucking me in close to his side. I felt his deep inhale against my hair a moment later.

In the ancient, cave-like quiet of the keep, we held each other, dreading the hour when we had to let go.

CHAPTER TWENTY

ASHER

I knew this clearing, this frozen valley and birch trees. Yet the wind did not stir, and the cold did not burn my skin. Time. It did not exist here. The edges of my vision were blurred like an ice-webbed vignette, as I turned in place, my legs stuck in shin-deep snow.

Whipping my head around, I looked for someone, anyone, my shadows. Nothing. Turning back to the wide-open space, I froze, as not someone, but *something*, stood several meters away.

I'd blinked and he had appeared, exactly as he had been before his death, wings arched, nostrils flaring, eyes wide and white rimmed in panic.

Raiden.

The wicken berry tea. I swallowed, battling nausea as the colt stared at me. I was having a vision. Desperately, I glanced down at my hands and sagged with relief. There was no crossbow in sight.

I peered across the clearing to where my father—

"No!" I roared, heaving my legs through the snowdrifts. "*Don't.*"

Staggering, my leg catching on a hidden root, I half fell into the snow. I gasped, heart racing, and looked back up. The colt was gone. Gracien now stood in his place.

My body went utterly still, air locked in my chest as the once King of the Forest turned his gaze at me, his dulcet eyes unafraid. I sank to my knees in the snow. Gracien crossed the clearing to stand before me, his blonde mane cascading down his neck that rippled with power.

"*Asher.*" His voice, coarse and guttural, cleaved my soul apart, and I released a shuddering breath. He inhaled, scenting me.

"Gracien, I—I—" What could I say to the creature I had slain in cold blood? It was my crossbow bolt that had speared through his heart.

The stallion angled his head, his forelock falling to the side to conceal his left eye. "*My son lives because of you, huntsman.*"

"And he roams his forest without you, because of *me*." I looked up at that fearsome and noble head.

Gracien reared, forehooves tucked tight to his muscled chest. I closed my eyes, grateful for this fate, but the blow did not fall. Eyelids flickering open, I looked on, aghast, as the scene before me began to drift away like pieces of blackened ash on a heaving wind. Utter darkness filtered into its place, until I knelt, suspended in a void.

Faintly, above and below and as far as the eye could see, starlight began to flicker. The air crackled and hummed, causing a ceaseless vibration against the marrow of my bones. My body was not meant to be here. This was the realm of spirits and those long past. Where entire planets had conquered one another. The territory of the Night Pegasus.

Like my thoughts had conjured him, he appeared from a swathe of unending darkness. His pelt was so black, it reflected the starlight that shone softly upon him. Hoofbeats making no sound, he halted several meters away, forelimbs planted close to one another, neck arched. He was taller than Gracien and leaner in build. A mane like ebony silk flowed down a muscled shoulder, where it brushed against his wing.

Holy spirits. His wings.

He held them close to his body, the small, downy feathers as black as he was, but as my gaze drifted, they shimmered, undulating green light cascading from them like a waterfall. Where that light brushed up against the inky depths of the night sky, it diluted to a faint mist, coloring the ends of his long tail that pooled beside his hind hooves. His shoulders shifted, and a small flutter of purple flickered over his gigantic primary feathers.

Instinct kept me on my knees, sheer awe had me bowing my head. Yet I tilted my gaze up slightly, in order to look at his eyes, glowing amber pupils encircled by ochre.

"Huntsman."

His voice spoke of cunning and knee-bending power. I raised my head fully then, knowing all too well that he could hear my heart hammering in my chest. Could he scent my fear in this eerily quiet vastness, where only my breath and the faint roaring of distant stars could be heard?

I swallowed, my throat feeling like sandpaper. Every lungful of air felt heavy and arduous. "I shouldn't be here."

"Every decision you have ever made has led you to this moment."

"Why? As punishment for the lives I have taken?"

The Night Pegasus fixed me with his piercing gaze. *"The guilt that grinds down on your bones is more than enough punishment, compared to anything I could torment you with."* The mighty stallion sidestepped, his every movement precise and elegant. *"That is not the reason you were called up here, mortal. I need you."*

"The wild ward is dead," I ground out. "The spirits are free, what else do you want from me?"

"My human form is destined to die, and I need you to be there when it does."

"The *Koskivarri* will die?"

The great beast shook his head. *"No, not my scion, not if I can help it. If she is harmed, there is no cosmos that will be safe from me, no extent of our realm that will not feel my wrath."*

I heaved in another breath. "Then who is it?"

"Your Truth Keeper will answer that question, if you and your shadows can locate her."

"*My* Truth Keeper?"

"Do you not feel her calling to you, even now? While your body is helpless and your mind is trapped here, with me?" He stepped closer, ears pricked forward. *"Sometimes, our hardest choices yield our greatest gifts. Those choices you will carry with you to your last breath, but it is up to you whether you let them consume every ounce of joy you may possibly feel."*

"The Nijinxes—"

"Will come to no harm with Ilravorn and yourself protecting them. The Scarp is vast. The Truth Keeper on the other hand ..."

"What about her?" My voice was low in warning.

"The protectiveness you feel toward her is justified. She is at risk, a treasure to be cradled and revered, just like my Koskivarri. So, you will understand, hunter, how I feel at the thought of her being harmed."

"Tell me what you need me to do."

"Do what you do best, take life. Yet now, you will take it where it is warranted, where it helps rid this continent of its greatest threat, the mortal King who wishes to destroy and conquer all that I hold dear."

"You are an all-powerful spirit, why can't you intervene?"

"My time will come, trust me." His wings half arched, the motion causing the light cascading from them to turn from a swirling mist to pulsing stations that lashed out into the sky, rippling away from us like a wave at sea.

"How can you be both human and immortal?" My lungs constricted, every breath harder and harder to suck down.

"Time is nothing here. The legends of our ancient past and the horrors of our present are not linear for us spirits."

"But the future?"

The Night Pegasus turned his neck to look back over his muscled shoulder and wing. In the distance to my right, an opalescent figure was coming toward us, appearing like a falling star in the darkness, silver and pearl shards of light scintillating in its wake. The aurora spirit was quiet for several heartbeats, as that star arced through the heavens.

"Some fates are blind to us, yet we do what we can to steer them in the right direction." He shifted his wings and looked at me once more, nostrils flaring. *"Find your Truth Keeper, huntsman, protect her, honor her, as a Nijinx male would care for his mate. None of this can be done without her. My scion and I—neither can be saved without your darkness and her truth."* One by one, the stars around us began to wink out, and the Night Pegasus fully extended his glorious wings. Sage green light lashed around into the sky, hurtling toward the falling star and far, far beyond. *"Wake up, huntsman, she needs you."*

My lungs took in a shuddering breath, the thrumming against my bones becoming almost unbearable, as the Night Pegasus launched himself into all-consuming darkness.

CHAPTER
TWENTY-ONE

DESTRY

The *morean* was held in a literal gauntlet. A long ditch with high stone walls had been carved from the earth and cleared of most of the snow, leaving slush and patches of black ice in its wake. Positioned at the base of the keep's western wall, anyone standing on the balconies would have a clear view of the contenders who fought in the five-meter-wide ditch. Opposite the keep, on what would be a glade in summer, wooden tiered seating had been erected, like this was all some great spectacle and not something that would decide a man's fate, and mine.

Standing on the balcony closest to the gauntlet, I peered over. Amadea was a tense, quiet presence wrapped in a thick woolen cloak on my right. Standing on my left, armed to the teeth, her solemn face pinched, was Minna. All three of us took in the six contenders placed at ten-meter intervals along the gauntlet.

Silvano would face off against Shep Sherwood first, the Royant Platoon sergeant having drawn the shortest straw that morning. Next was Minna's second-in-command, Salo, a lean but strong thirty-year-old man who I'd been told was lethal with his own curved sword. The hook-nosed councilman who I'd nearly speared with ice, Koski, was third. A broad-chested warrior named Virtanen, a sergeant in Rekorious' western land cavalry, casually twirled twin short swords in his hands as he threw Minna a bored look.

I swallowed a knot of disgust, dread slowly thickening in my blood, as I took in the fifth contender. Arnar, armed with an axe and short sword, came next. Rekorious' cousin kept throwing me smirking grins as he went through his warm-ups, like he had already won.

The sixth and final contender was Rekorious himself. He was utterly silent at the end of the gauntlet, ignoring everyone assembled on the balconies, as he warmed up with his own twin swords, *Vorna* and *Vayla* flashing brightly in the early morning sun.

With every contender, Silvano would tire, his fighting style on display for the fights to come, leaving him at a weaker position with every battle. By the time he got to Virtanen, then Arner, they would have noted his every move, what his weaknesses were, and the tactics he favored.

"If Silvano loses to one of them," I said in a hushed whisper. "Do I have to marry the man he yields to?"

Minna shook her head. "They earn the right to propose to you, but you can turn them down."

"Thank the spirits," I muttered.

An array of councilors, nobles, and the staff of the keep took their seats within the glade, while our balcony suddenly grew more crowded. Lael strode up to the balustrade, taking up a free space beside Amadea. People had been giving the Ilrairian Queen a wide berth, utterly unsure of what to make of her.

A true *morean* hadn't been held in over a century, I had been told. Heart thundering, I leaned further over the edge, as Silvano was led out to the start of the gauntlet. He looked calm and focused, like he had mentally descended into himself, stoking the endurance and strength he'd need to survive this.

The thorns in my chest expanded with every ragged breath I took. Spirits, if he was wounded today, if he failed and was exiled.

I'd risk it all again in a heartbeat for you.

Share your pain with me, wild one, so I can help you bear it, heal from it.

I should be fighting down there with him, not stuck up here.

Silvano cast his gaze over the fighters who stopped their warm-ups and turned to face him. The Ilrairian was silent as he surveyed them, then, in one slow motion, he withdrew his curved blade from his side and twirled it once, twice. A guard who had escorted him out offered him a small round shield.

Minna made a small noise at the back of her throat, as Silvano refused it. My fingers turned to claws against the frigid stone wall, cracking two nails. Amadea reached out her mittened left hand and gently rested it atop my right.

From the stand in the glade came the short, piercing sound of a horn.

Onlookers pressed in closer, eyes wide with anticipation. The ice in my chest cracked, then splintered, the air around us seeming to pause and take notice.

Silvano took several deep, settling breaths, like a diver preparing for an unforgiving sea, his blade a whirl of silver across his torso, as he began to spin it, faster and faster.

The Golden Warrior launched himself into the gauntlet. Speed and deadly, ruthless efficiency, that was how the Commander fought, just like when we had sparred in Ilrair. Within two heartbeats, Shep was face down in the slush, his short sword plucked from him and held firmly in Silvano's left hand.

He didn't give Salo a chance to comprehend the now dual-wielding Ilrairian, as Silvano whirled on him. The two curved swords clashed in a thunderclap of metal, the sheer edges screeching a banshee's song while the two men fought for purchase against one another. Just as

Salo thrust the last of his weight behind his sword, Silvano was gone, a whiplash of motion that left the Petish warrior stumbling to regain his balance.

Spinning nimbly on the black ice, Silvano flipped his stolen short sword, bringing it hilt-first against Salo's lower back. Minna gaped in silent awe, as Silvano didn't even look back to see Salo fall to the snow like Shep had.

Koski launched himself backward against the wall of the gauntlet, pressing his spine firmly against it, a short sword and round shield raised. Wise of him to use the wall to protect his back, but Silvano charged regardless, using the coarse rock of the wall as a springboard to leap higher than the round shield's reach.

The Heara thrust blindly upward with his sword, only to find vacant air. Silvano arced over him, using the flat edge of his curved blade to ram Koski's sword arm, down, down, down. Koski roared at the strain in his right shoulder, just as Silvano reconnected with the ice-slicked earth, knees bending and twisting, effortlessly wrenching Koski's sword from his grip.

"Tavaris, spare us all," whispered Lael at my side, his awed face a mirror of Minna's.

Breath sawing from my lungs, I leaned further forward, the rock balustrade stabbing me in the abdomen as I desperately tracked Silvano below.

Virtanen hunkered low over his braced knees, his blades shining in his huge hands. The warrior had twice the brawn of Silvano, like he had been plucked from one of Serebo's boulder fields. Muscle-hewn, the sergeant threw Silvano an impressed but knowing smile, then attacked. The Ilrairian darted to the side, feinting with his curved blade. Virtanen grinned again and blocked the true strike that Silvano aimed at the warrior's chest.

Everyone on the balcony tensed, as we realized that now, the true test was starting. Silvano leaped backward, inching closer to a tense and waiting Arnar, who catalogued the soldier's moves with deadly focus. Virtanen came for him, twin blades slicing the frozen air, but Silvano was ready, his breath barely winded as he rained strike after strike toward the Petish warrior's chest and abdomen.

Virtanen blinked and inched backward from the onslaught, finally bringing up his twin swords in a cross over his chest, locking Silvano's curved blade between them. The second his sword was trapped, Silvano released the hilt, clenched his fist, and swung for Virtanen's unprotected face.

Lael gasped as the warrior ricocheted backward from the force of Silvano's punch and crumbled to the snow. Silvano retrieved his sword from the frozen ground and turned slowly on his heel to throw Arnar a silent snarl.

Rekorious' cousin bared his teeth in response, then he looked up at me with a glance filled with utter entitlement. The feeling of nausea rolled in my stomach at that look, one I had seen on Narve's and Jaryn's faces many times. My heart took on the thundering beat of a horse's gallop, and I sucked down deep lungfuls of air, my ears ringing a whistling, high-pitched note.

Those monsters weren't here. But Arnar ... instinct told me he was a snake like the others, but whether he would unleash venom, cutting deep like Narve had, or a crushing, deadly power akin to Jaryn, only fate would decide.

Silvano tracked the gaze Arnar had thrown my way and snarled again as he slowly prowled forward. Arnar was lithe, a finer build than any of the other warriors in the gauntlet, and the Petish soldier took full advantage of it. Wrenching his gaze away from me, he charged, feinting left then right with his sword and axe, forcing Silvano to match his breakneck speed.

Silvano blocked every strike, his curved blade flashing like lightning in the gloom of the ditch. Again and again, the two men attacked and blocked, their weapons a pure extension of themselves, reacting with skill and instinct to where each blow might land.

My shoulders and back throbbed with tension, and my breath snatched from my throat, as a backhanded strike from the shaft of Arnar's axe smacked into Silvano's side. Arnar laughed darkly, while Silvano backed away, his left arm curled protectively over his ribs. Blood trickled from a deep cut on his full lower lip.

Panic seized me. Had he broken a rib? A wave of possessiveness, the need to protect and defend, rattled through my core at the thought of Silvano being hurt, and my mind reeled in response. But this wasn't the lake at Saltfen. I couldn't dive into the gauntlet and save him this time, and a deep, primal part of me roared in frustration.

Salo, Koski, and Shep heaved up a haggard and bleeding Virtanen between them and closed rank, blocking any escape from the southern end of the gauntlet.

Chin held high, Arnar raised his weapons in the air, and the crowds gathered on the balconies cheered. Sword and axe crossed high above his head, Arnar turned his back on Silvano to receive the cries of praise from those seated in the snow-covered glade, a smug-filled smile on his face.

"Big mistake," whispered Minna, with a small shake of her head.

Sheathing his sword in one swift motion, Silvano sprang forward, slamming into Arnar's unprotected back and tackling him to the ground. Arnar cried out as Silvano twisted the axe from his grasp, sending it flying and clattering meters away. Grinding his right knee into Arnar's lower back, Silvano snatched a handful of the sergeant's dark hair and wrenched his head back. Arnar choked, his Adam's apple rolling with the effort to draw a breath. Desperate now, he jerked upward with the sword still clutched in his right hand, but screamed when Silvano rammed his foot onto his wrist, pinning it to the ice.

Minna swallowed, her breath tight and quick. "Holy fucking spirits."

I agreed with her wholeheartedly, my entire world fixated on the Golden Warrior leaning forward to whisper something into Arnar's upturned ear.

Arnar roared, heaving himself upward, but Silvano was already gone, spinning on a knee in the slush, his curved sword brandished across his chest. Pride and longing roared in my head as Silvano smiled with wild abandon, then he turned his head and looked up at me.

The rest of the world filtered away, like smoke on a summer wind, Silvano's gaze pinning me in place. A patient, silent question rested in those emerald eyes, despite Arnar bearing down on him, sword raised in a crazed, two-handed grip.

Drawing myself to my full height, hands planted on the lip of the balustrade, I gave the Ilrairian a dip of my head. Silvano smirked and spread his arms wide in a graceful bow, a knight conceding to the wishes of his lady.

Then he ducked Arnar's downward blow toward his neck, sweeping his left leg out wide to knock Arnar off his feet. The sergeant's back smacked into the ice, cutting off his battle cry and ripping the air from his lungs.

Silvano rose slowly, the wild, northern wind whipping his blonde hair across his face that was dark with sweat, grime, and blood. Shoulders thrown back in silent defiance, he sheathed his sword then gently rested his left hand on the pommel. Breathing deeply through his nose, he peered down at Arnar who gasped and heaved beside his booted feet. The whites of Arnar's eyes shone brightly, his face a mask of shock and shame as he stared up at Silvano.

The Golden Warrior bared his teeth, then stepped over Arnar as if he were no more than a mud-filled puddle. He treaded slowly forward now, closing the distance between him and the last warrior, who waited patiently, hands clasped over his abdomen.

Rekorious quirked an eyebrow, as if Silvano's battle wins were of no surprise to him at all. The two men faced each other; fate, the frozen air, and bated expectation weaving a taut thread between them.

I didn't think anyone gathered was breathing for a moment. I certainly wasn't. Amadea inched closer to me, her side fully pressing into mine and her grip became tighter over my hand. Glancing sidelong at her, I took in her anxious face, her golden gaze tumbling through emotions I couldn't place. Did she still love the warlord? Did she fear for him?

Eyes widening, I looked back down into the gauntlet. In a quick, one-handed motion, Silvano removed his sword belt, gently placing his sheathed blade on the ground. Then he straightened, chin held high and waited.

Rekorious exhaled, his breath clouding between them. Then his gloved hands rose to unbuckle the leather straps across his broad chest, *Vorna* and *Vayla* slipping free from his back a moment later. Mirroring Silvano, he placed the twin swords with a quiet reverence at his feet.

A pulse of green light radiated along my arms to wreathe my fingers, and my gaze flew from my bare hands to the now circling warriors below.

They didn't need swords to settle this.

Victory would be born from sweat, blood, and fury.

The once rival commanders circled again, tension heightening between them with every cross step.

Arnar rolled onto his abdomen, fingers scraping at the slush underneath him. "Avenge us, Rekorious," he rasped.

The warlord didn't deign his cousin a reply, his gaze not leaving Silvano's for even a heartbeat.

"You won't get the chance." I barely recognized Silvano's voice. It was something deep, dark, and edged with the promise of unforgiving violence.

Rekorious rolled his shoulders. "I'm not about to oblige you."

He charged forward, just as Silvano's back drew parallel with the keep's exterior wall. The pair slammed into the rough-hewn rock with the force of a Serebo avalanche, fists flying, fragments of rock, dust, and snow engulfing them from view.

A gust of frozen air ripped the debris away, as Silvano rammed his elbow down again and again against Rekorious' unyielding back, then he gripped the warlord's right thigh and heaved.

Air whooshed from Rekorious' chest as he hit the frozen earth, his arms outstretched to break up the force of his fall.

Beside me, Amadea flinched, her face grave.

Silvano gave Rekorious no reprieve and leaped, raining punch after punch against the warlord's face. Uttering a guttural roar, Rekorious heaved upward with hips, tossing Silvano off him, then he was rolling and on his feet. Springing to a standstill, his breath controlled but deep, Silvano ran forward, and Rekorious snatched a handful of his black tunic, twisted, and threw Silvano over a broad shoulder.

I shuddered when Silvano's body struck the ground, the light and ice power in my veins rearing upward at the threat. Yet I couldn't strike, couldn't freeze Rekorious in place, or I'd doom Silvano to certain death. The two men were masters of the art of combat, equally matched for size and strength. The utter silence of the gathered crowd paid homage to the prowess on display.

But the *morean* would only grant one man as victor.

Silvano and Rekorious landed blow after blow, cuts and bruises blooming on their faces, necks and fists, the ground trembling each time one of them was slammed to the earth. Unleashing a thundering growl, Silvano locked Rekorious within his grasp and swung.

Amadea gasped, her lips parting to form a silent. "*No.*"

The warlord staggered toward Silvano's deadly uppercut, and the air froze over, time slowing. Rekorious' gaze slid to mine then, and realization struck me through the chest, slicing over my heart. The two warring sides of his soul, Aalto Thorra and Rekorious Niemi, platoon Commander and warlord, one I had called my friend, the other a traitor, constricted an invisible force around my throat. Tears welled behind my eyes, and I welcomed the burning sensation.

It was imperceptible to everyone else gathered, the tiny, understanding nod from Rekorious, his gaze not leaving mine. For saving his life from the wild ward and the avalanche on Serebo, this would be his debt repaid.

Cries rang out amongst the crowd, as Silvano's fist connected with Rekorious' jaw, sending the warlord stumbling to his knees.

Amadea snatched her hand away from mine and fully leaned over the lip of the balcony, panting, her gaze as desperate as mine had been. Lael swept both of his hands down his face.

Rekorious remained on all fours, spitting blood into the snow, Silvano a conquering force over him, and my gaze slid to Minna's. Glancing down at the two warriors, then back up to me, her features turned shrewd, and I wondered if she suspected exactly what Rekorious had done.

He had yielded, for me. It certainly hadn't been for Silvano's benefit.

The crowds began whispering when Silvano moved closer to the fallen warlord. They broke into open exclamations as he then extended his right hand.

Rekorious turned his head, his hair loose and bedraggled around his bruised face, to look at that hand. Silvano simply waited, his expression one of cool calculation and respect.

Panting, Rekorious wiped the back of his hand across his mouth, blood staining the brown leather of his glove. Slowly, he twisted on his knees and reached out to grasp Silvano's forearm. The two men gazed at each other for a heartbeat, a silent agreement thrumming between them. Silvano released a tight breath and nodded before hauling Rekorious to his feet.

Shep, Salo, Koski, Virtanen, and Arnar limped forward to take up positions at their backs. Crossing their right arms over their chests, fists clenched, they were the first to bow, Arnar a beat behind the rest.

Throwing Silvano a crooked smile, Rekorious bowed low and waited. Like a rippling wave, my fellow countrymen followed suit, until every person assembled was folded, staring at the snow-covered ground at their feet. Even Amadea, her entire body trembling, dipped her head.

Over a sea of silent Petish men and women, Silvano and I stood tall. I released my light, fully bright green now, not a hint of purple to be seen, and it plumed from my hands to wrap itself in a cool embrace around Silvano. He closed his eyes, face tilted toward the cloud-covered heavens, and let my light caress the exposed skin of his throat and collarbone.

Rekorious lifted his head, eyes wide at the waves of dancing green light encircling Silvano, then his gaze slowly drifted to me, and it was filled with dread.

CHAPTER
TWENTY-TWO

ASHER

The breath that filled my lungs was panicked, ghost-like, akin to that of a man brought back from the brink of drowning. It shuddered through my chest cavity, my blood suddenly roaring in my head with the force of a tidal wave. Adrenaline and vertigo held me in a viselike grip for several, horrendous heartbeats, then I began to feel the chill of the earth beneath my back and the light of the sky beyond my closed eyes.

It was that light that fully careened my sense of self back to my body. I jerked upright, my abdominal muscles quivering in protest, the blanket Calliope had tucked around me, crumpling around my waist.

My shadows whipped all around the campsite, lifting my dark hair in their wake. *I'm fine*, I thought. I wasn't, but it soothed the shadows enough that they slowed, curling in on themselves. I frowned, quickly assessing the position of the sun and my shadows that pulsed with something I hadn't felt since being granted them.

Their inward spiraling conveyed only one emotion: *Worry*.

Slowly, like a leopard standing from a too-long slumber, I got to my feet and tracked the sun once more. It still hung low on the eastern horizon, washing the sky a watercolor pink. I had been out of it all night, which meant Calliope, despite her slow walk and injured shoulder, was a long, long way from here.

Half of me snarled at the fact that she had poisoned me, while the other half was impressed. She was cunning, but she had been scared too, her hands shaking from the fear of discovery, not the cold. I didn't blame her for escaping, but my resolve had been on a knife-edge. If she had waited one more night ... would I have set her free? Or was I too afraid to let her go now?

The Night Pegasus had said that she needed me, and by the way my shadows circled closer, nudging my shoulders and arms, Calliope needed me *now*. Hastily, I threw my things into my pack, noting that the medical kit was missing. She had the foresight to try and tend to her shoulder without me, yet she'd never reach it to treat it properly. Stubborn owling.

I would worry about the Night Pegasus' words later. Right now, I needed to find my Truth Keeper.

And slaughter anyone who had tried to hurt her.

Thanking Merevis for the lack of snowfall, I quickly found her tracks heading due east, as if she prayed that the dawn would whisk her away to safety. Yet safety was an illusion out here, between the wilderness and the soldiers that prowled it. A magical being limited to their injured human form, made for easy pickings, especially when those soldiers realized exactly what kind of magical being she really was. She had headed in the complete opposite direction to Fort Garobear, but that didn't mean units didn't patrol out there, like Aron Isark and his ilk.

Shadows tugged at my coat sleeves, and I ran over her stilted, uneven tracks, desperate to make up the ground I had lost while the visions had held me under.

Hurry, my shadows silently pleaded. *Hurry*. Calliope had stuck to the cover of the forest, steering clear of open spaces and crossing creeks where she could, yet she hadn't thought to cover her tracks with something, *anything*. Which meant if I could track her down, then other people could too.

Fuck, if someone got to her before I did. I pushed my body harder through the snow, my thighs and calves burning with the effort. Not for the first time, I wished Pherox were here to help me make up the miles. The forest was eerily quiet, the little creatures I had grown so accustomed to hearing were silent within their burrows, nests, and dens. Only my shadows' repetitive whispers caressed my ears: run, run, *run*.

My lungs were on fire, the freezing air burning against the delicate membranes. I didn't dare slow, my shadows yanking me upright when I tripped over hidden roots or stumbled over loose rocks.

Up ahead, the terrain dropped away sharply to reveal a small, frozen river, and I slid to a halt within the shroud of the remaining trees. Her tracks suggested she had climbed down the short cliff face to the sliver of beach by the riverbed.

On a silent order, my shadows whirled away, detecting any threat in the forest beyond. Some peeled off, showing me where Calliope's tracks started up again amongst the boulders across the river. Still, all was quiet.

No breeze, no forest animals. Which meant something had come before me to force them to either flee or hide. The hairs on the back of my neck stood on end. Moving quickly, I slid down the riverbank, sprinted over the solid ice and scrambled up the other side, ducking low into a cluster of frozen ferns. Willing my blood to calm, to focus, I listened hard over the oh-so-faint sighing of dead grass and distant whisper of shadows.

There, just to the north, the low, rumbling sound of male laughter.

I broke into a full sprint, my shadows racing alongside me, my apprehension morphing into deadly intent. The laughter grew louder, and I slowed to a silent prowl to skirt a tiny clearing and the small campsite within it. Five small canvas tents circled a central campfire, and beyond them, their pelts darkened with dried sweat, and sharing a slice of hay between them were five Pegasi.

There were no flags to be seen, no sigils on any of the saddlecloths or pieces of dark gray uniform, hung out to dry on low-lying tree branches. Inhaling deeply, I recognized the scent of distant seas, steel, and boot polish.

An Ilrairian scouting party, likely ordered forward from Aarine to find how far south Colladon's defenses ran. Jaryn's soldiers. I snarled, remembering the silent promise between Pherox and me to end the southern King's life, for what he had done to a member of the kin swarm. I made to creep around the nearest tent and—

I heard her scream.

The darkness that riled in my veins, that had called my body home even before Iltavorn lay claim to me, roared in response, tunneling to a night-filled fury that left a heady song in my blood. Every movement was instinctual, honed, like my body had been carved for exactly this purpose.

To protect her.

I ran through the campsite. The Pegasi threw up their heads in alarm, wings flaring and pulling on their ropes as I flew past them, back into the snow-drenched trees. My shadows arced from me, and for the first time, I felt utterly in control, my body, mind, and shadows pliant to my every command.

Four male soldiers stood jeering and laughing amongst each other, as they looked down at two struggling figures on the ground. My vision turned monochromatic as I closed in on those final few yards. A wiry, dark-haired cavalryman had Calliope on her back, grappling for purchase on her forearms, as she raked at him with her nails.

My shadows turned fully corporeal, razor sharp and lethal. The sound of shouting and laughter was cut short, as those shimmering onyx knives struck like asps, running across the soldiers' throats in perfect unison. I was on my knees beside Calliope a heartbeat later, shoving her attacker's falling body to the side.

Eyes screwed shut, lips parted in a silent sob, she lashed out blindly at my chest and arms. Gently, but firmly, I snatched her wrists in my right hand.

"Calliope. Calliope, look at me." My left hand reached down to cup the nape of her neck, my thumb pressing into her jaw to try and stop her thrashing.

"Calliope, look at me," I ordered.

She bucked and kicked, utterly lost to her panic.

"*Callie*. Look. At. Me."

She froze, eyes snapping open, pupils wide, yet they were unseeing for a moment, completely out of focus, the gold in them banked and buried. Fragments of broken twigs were caught in her hair, and a bruise bloomed over her right cheek.

"It's me," I whispered softly while I held her gaze, my thumb grazing her cheek. "You're free."

Slowly, I released her wrists, bracing myself on the snow by her shoulder. Her chest heaved with shallow breaths, and she slowly turned her head in my hand, taking in the corpses around us. A small whimper escaped her mouth.

"Keep your eyes on me," I commanded, as I willed my shadows to curtain around us like smoke, shielding us from those who tried to harm her.

Those panicked eyes flitted back to mine, and she softened a fraction into my touch. I released a taut breath, relieved to see a flicker of fire in her gaze once more. I searched her face, my thumb gently tracing the curve of her cheek.

My voice was hoarse as I whispered again, "You're free."

A wave of understanding washed over her features, and her chest racked with a sob of relief. Sitting back in the snow, I hauled her upright, and she needed no encouragement, before her head found my chest, and she wrapped her arms around my torso, hanging on tight.

Swallowing, I hesitated for a moment, then I held her close, my right hand running up and down her shuddering spine. Second by second, cocooned by wreathing shadows, I felt her shaking subside and her breath even out.

"I'm ... I'm so sorry," she rasped.

Aghast, I pulled back, but she refused to look at me. Shaking my head, I gently clasped her chin, turning her head so that those golden eyes found my own. They were red rimmed, her cheeks tear-stained, and seeing the exhaustion in her face made me want to slaughter the soldiers all over again.

"You have nothing to apologize for, do you understand?"

"I shouldn't have—"

A small, shaky laugh scraped the back of my throat. "Poisoned me? Don't worry, owling, I forgive you."

I ran a critical gaze over her bruised face, her tattered and torn dress, the dirt in the tendrils of hair that framed her face. She needed to feel safe, warm, and protected, and we certainly wouldn't find that here.

"You're free. I'm not going to take you to Garobear." My hand moved from her chin to tuck a lock of hair behind her ear. "You can go where you wish, but just ... just let me take care of you first. Please?"

She swallowed, color incrementally returning to her pale face. "Okay."

Moving deliberately slowly, I inched backward, and my shadows pressed in closer around us. "Wait here a moment, nothing else is going to hurt you."

Shivering, Calliope hugged her knees, and a shadow brushed against her clasped hands.

"I'll be right back."

Working quickly, I raided the soldiers' camp, content to let their bodies rot where they had fallen. Their deaths would not haunt me, would not coil within my arteries and veins and thrum in my body as guilt with every beat of my heart. They had been monsters of a different kind, and the world was better off without them. It would serve as a warning to Jaryn that these were just the first, and I was coming for him.

I pilfered as many of their supplies as I could fit into my pack, finding the medical kit beside the campfire, which I hastily put out with snow. Turning the Pegasi loose, they bounded into the sky, instinctively turning south on the wing to head home to Ilrair.

Settling the heavy pack over my shoulders, I turned on my heel but stalled. Crouching down beside a half-open tent, I picked up the small, crumpled square of dark gray cloth. It had a deep V cut into one side, and on its front, an embroidered, twisting eel. A pennant from House Moray. Frowning, I scanned the campsite, double-checking for any other heraldry, but there was nothing. Glancing down at the pennant once more, a sense of foreboding flitted down the vertebrae of my spine, a shadow whispering in my ear in response.

The Lord of Moray was a recluse, content to be holed up in his lands north of Aarine, but I'd heard rumors of his power-hungry son, Narve. Over the treetops, the Ilrairian Pegasi disappeared from view, and I tucked the creased and stained pennant into my coat pocket. Readjusting my pack, I walked over to my cove of shadows, brushed them aside, and held out my hand to Calliope. She didn't hesitate as she rose and placed her palm in mine. Urging the shadows to shield us as we walked, Calliope squeezed my fingers as she willingly followed me into the dark.

CHAPTER
TWENTY-THREE

EBREL

Hestian stayed close as we flew, instinctively knowing that the best way to comfort me was through physical touch. Would the stranger's family miss him? Would his master spiral into a rage once they discovered his death? How far had his betrayal gone? Questions hounded me as we cut through the night sky.

Distant wolf howls rose to us from the scattered, unnamed forests that crisscrossed the landscape. The sound made my skin crawl, as memories of the wild ward and the branding slithered down my spine. I shook my head to clear it, not missing the worried glance Hestian threw my way. Mount Serebo loomed ahead, her jagged, crown-like peak clearly outlined by the light of a half-moon.

The clear night sky had made the temperature plummet. Having lived in the north all my life, I was accustomed to it, my shaggy winter coat kept me warm easily. Yet Hestian, who was used to warmer climates, who had likely worn blankets during the chillier nights and groomed until his golden pelt shone, had a shorter coat. He didn't complain, but I knew the cold bothered him.

Serebo inched closer, and the air around us grew charged, our feathers bristling in response as we flew deeper into the mountain spirit's aura. From far below, a giant glacier glinted in the moonlight, its sinuous path carving deep, treacherous valleys around the mountain.

"There." I pointed my muzzle to where a slim pillar of white light shot upward from beside the origins of the glacier. *"Does that feel like a summons to you?"*

Hestian tensed. *"Only one way to find out. That's not a light that nature can make or a soldier's fire."*

"Magic?" I murmured.

We lowered, circling apprehensively around the shimmering column. As we drew closer, it reduced in height, growing smaller and smaller, until we landed on a wide ledge that overlooked the glacier far below. I took a deep lungful of air, letting the more oxygen-thick atmosphere coat my lungs. Blinking, our eyes adjusted the fading glow of the light, until it narrowed to a mere pinprick from its source.

Hestian subtly shifted to stand just in front of me, as I stared wide-eyed at the creature who had summoned us. A female Unicorn. An ancient one, from the archaic, ice-like scent of her. She stood silently as she appraised us in turn. Unlike Olwen, who had been near opalescent with searing blue eyes, this Unicorn had aged to a faint silver, thick strands of it weaving through her mane and tail. Even her eyes had flecks of whirling gray that matched the slender horn on her head.

Slowly, her magical gaze drifted between Hestian and me. Her power felt like a frigid, gossamer breeze as it shifted over our pelts, and I sensed it hover over the brand on my haunch.

"You've been waiting for us?" I murmured.

She bobbed her head in affirmation. Her voice, old yet elegant, echoed in our minds as if she spoke from far, far away. *"Serebo has asked me to show you the way. Follow me, young ones."*

Like her body might betray her at any moment, the Unicorn turned cautiously on the ledge and began to sedately walk away. I made to move after her, only to note Hestian's utter stillness beside me.

"Are you okay?"

"Her scent," he whispered, aghast. *"She is hundreds of years old."*

The Unicorn halted and slowly turned her head back to pierce Hestian with a withering glare. *"Did your dam not teach you that it is rude to discuss a lady's age?"*

Ears flicking back, the stallion had the decency to look abashed. *"Forgive me, I never would have guessed otherwise. You don't look a day older than twenty."*

She looked unimpressed, and I smiled in my mind. *"Your charm doesn't work on me, stallion, despite how pretty you are."*

Hestian nudged my cheek as we followed her. *"See, she thinks I'm pretty too."*

"I never said you were pretty."

"But you've thought it," he whispered, his deep voice sending a shiver down my spine.

"You're a hopeless flirt."

His hip nudged into mine. *"Only for you."*

I rolled my eyes, but secretly, I couldn't help feeling a wave of happiness. Hestian scented the air, like he was trying to detect exactly what I was feeling, but I lashed him with my tail to get him to focus.

"What's your name?" I asked, as I trotted a few strides to catch up to the Unicorn. *"Do you help guard Serebo?"*

"My name is Eirlys," she murmured, keeping her focus straight ahead. *"I'm Serebo's chief guard."*

"How long have you been her guard?"

She threw me a sidelong glance that, honestly, only a mare could give. *"Three hundred years."*

I blinked. *"Did ... did your dam see the fall of the Trinitors?"*

"She did, alongside my granddam. We've sheltered within Serebo ever since. The mountain protects us, and we, in return, alongside the snow sirens and varki deer, protect her."

Hestian cleared his throat. Eirlys glanced at him over her shoulder, her expression cool once more. *"Is it the magic in your blood that lets you live such long lives?"*

The ledge took a sharp right turn, and we carefully navigated it, the freezing wind whispering far below. Eirlys slowed even further, each step cautiously thought out, as she picked her path through the scattered boulders and snow.

"It is, we stick to a Trinitor's natural life span. Although, as you already know, our magic doesn't grow with us. Once our reservoir of power is gone, it's truly gone. It does not replenish over the years." The Unicorn scrambled up a rocky climb, righted herself with a shake of her head, then turned to face Hestian and me below her. *"This is the cave Serebo wants you to see. So that you may remember."*

She stepped back, allowing us space to leap up and join her. I peered to my left to where the sheer cliff face loomed over us, icicles and stag moss clinging to its jagged edges. At its base, just wide enough for a Pegasus stallion to fit through, was the serrated maw of a cave.

I blanched, and Hestian tested the air before it with an aura of deep suspicion. Eirlys looked between us both, the horn on her head glowing a faint silver. She tossed her head, and a plume of bright sparks whirled from her horn. They flew rhythmically past us into the cave.

"My magic will show you the way, will help you see. Once you have found the truth, fly far from here and fly fast." Eirlys stepped back, her eyes soft. *"If you come across my daughter again, tell her I miss her."*

"Olwen is your daughter?" I breathed.

Eirlys released a low, barely audible nicker. *"She's an adventurous spirit compared to me. She's gone to track down the shadow wielder who freed you from the wild ward, to thank him.* "Her gaze drifted to take in the glacier and the formidable mountain at its back. "*Serebo misses her too.*"

"*I'll keep an eye out for her. I promise.*"

Eirlys gestured toward the cave. "*Now go, time is not on our side. History will repeat itself if we do not act.*"

CHAPTER
TWENTY-FOUR

DESTRY

"I really don't think I need flowers in my hair," I whispered, my hands wringing together over my abdomen.

Minna arched a perfect, dark brow. "You're sure?"

I nodded, a little too quickly. "The dress will be fine on its own, but thank you." I tried to placate, in the hope I hadn't offended her or any Petish customs by refusing the crown of dainty white flowers Minna set back on my bedroom dresser.

Behind me, Amadea hummed to herself, as she dragged a pale wood comb through my long hair. A thick curtain of shallow waves, I'd scrubbed it clean within an inch of its life, and my hair now smelled faintly of citrus, and not sweat, blood, and dirt for once. I winced, as she yanked a knot free near my shoulder, then placed the comb down beside the flower crown.

Peeking over my shoulder, I looked back at Amadea. She has been quiet since the *morean*, but insisted she help Minna get me ready for the ceremony. Minna was less talkative than usual too. There was an undercurrent of tension in the room, and I knew in my bones it was because neither woman trusted each other.

Dressed in a pair of soft cream lace briefs, a bandage still taut over my upper thigh and hip, I pulled the simple gray linen shift I had worn after bathing up and over my head, letting it fall to the floor.

Instinctively, I covered my arms over my bare chest, but my eyebrows shot upward at the hand Minna clamped down on my left forearm.

"Holy spirits, Destry," she said hoarsely, her gaze fixed on my scarred bicep.

I cringed, biting down on my lower lip while I let Minna draw my arm toward her, those dark brown eyes fierce as she looked at the wound.

"What is it?" murmured Amadea, stepping around me to stand beside Minna. Her eyes widened as she saw the angry, proud flesh.

"Has a medic seen to this?" asked Minna, her voice wholly that of a commander.

"No," I whispered.

Amadea inched closer. "What happened? You didn't have that in Ilrair."

I gently pulled my arm out of Minna's grasp, and she let me go, her face a mask of stone-cold violence. "The Heir Lord of Moray. He and his guardsman, Lonan, caught Rekorious and I on our way to Serebo. I fought Lonan trying to get to Rekorious, but I lost, and he left this cut. Narve then used the open wound to ..." I swallowed, releasing a shaky breath. "He used it to administer one of his poisons. The Royant medic cleaned and stitched it before Aalt-Rekorious and I set off for Serebo, but it hasn't healed properly since."

I couldn't look at either of them, my gaze fixed on the skirts of their elegant gowns, my arms wrapped around myself. Amadea shuffled on her feet, and I could sense she wanted to ask more about what happened, but it was Minna who spoke first.

"We have a Colladonian medic here, one of the finest on this side of the border. We'll have him look at it when you and Silvano return from your little honeymoon."

Amadea stepped forward, placing a hand on my elbow. I looked across at her, hoping my eyes conveyed everything I couldn't say, not yet anyway. That beautiful face, graceful, golden, and wise, gave me a small, heartbreaking smile, her thumb brushing over my tan skin.

We both shared scars.

"Promise me, you'll see the medic when you and Silvano get back from your romantic gallivanting?" Minna arched a delicate brow at me, her voice light despite the laden atmosphere in my room.

I huffed, a crooked smile on my lips. "Gallivanting?"

She turned to pick up my dress. "You know what I mean, *Koski-varri*. There isn't a woman, and probably a few men, who didn't wish they were in your shoes tonight."

Amadea huffed a laugh as I blushed. I'd had a hard time *not* thinking about what lay ahead of me after this evening. Minna stepped back toward me, the dress draped over her arms. My heart thundered at the sight of it, and my head spun with nerves and trepidation. Handling the deep blue fabric with utmost care, Minna held it aloft for me as I stepped into it. The cool, silken-soft dress hugged my figure, and I slid my arms into the full-length sleeves. Amadea's hands were warm against my chilled back, as she expertly did up the long column of pearl buttons that ran up my spine. The floor-length skirt whispered over the flagstones as I shifted my weight over my feet. I had never worn anything so luxurious, and I couldn't even begin to think how much a gown like this would have cost to make.

The white corded neckline was where the modesty ended, the dress cut just below my shoulders, emphasizing my bare collarbone and neck. I looked down at myself, and for a brief moment, I felt feminine, hell, pretty even.

Minna let out a low whistle. "I'll be damned, *Koskivarri*."

Amadea stepped around me, a soft smile on her full lips. "You look beautiful, Destry, truly."

"Will it do?" I asked, my hands playing with the folds of the skirt.

"Will it do? Ha!" Minna scoffed playfully.

I sensed Amadea relax a fraction, incrementally warming toward the Petish warrior. Surveying them in turn, I nodded at the finery they're both wearing tonight. "I didn't know Rekorious had such a good seamstress."

Cutting me a sly grin, Minna gave me a small bow. "It's not all fur, leather, and armor up here in the wilds."

Amadea chuckled, and she looked radiant in her dark navy and gold gown, her hair braided back from her face and coiled at the crown of her head. Despite it being a wedding, Minna was dressed in her usual black, although she replaced her cavalry attire for a form-fitting dress that revealed just how strong she was. The bodice was covered in intricate lacework, with silver thread highlights that trailed up and over one of her toned shoulders. A silken dark cape hung to just below her waist. Like mine, her hair was loose, and the candlelight shone softly on it, bringing out the lighter shades of brown framing her face.

Stepping into my matching blue felt shoes, I took a deep, settling breath, smoothing down the front of my dress. A knock on the door sounded, and Amadea jumped. Reaching forward, I gently clasped her hand while Minna stalked forward to reveal Rekorious in the doorway.

Leaning against the doorframe, arms crossed over his broad chest, the warlord's gaze flicked to me for a moment, before landing on Amadea. She grew still under my touch, eyes wide, and I could understand why she no longer noticed my presence at her side.

Rekorious looked wildly handsome, even despite his bruised and cut-up face. It anything, it added to his charm. Hair somewhat tamed and tied back, he wore a short, more ornamental green cloak wrapped over a dark gray shirt, black trousers, and calf-high boots.

"Have you men finished your fussing yet?" quipped Minna, jabbing Rekorious in his muscled stomach.

He didn't even flinch, his gaze never leaving Amadea's. "We've been waiting for you for the past twenty minutes, we're not the ones who've been fussing."

"Oh, please, I know for a fact you and Virtanen would have been hogging the mirror for the past hour."

My soft, scraping laugh seemed to break the spell on Amadea, her chest rising and falling quickly. Breaking away from me, she squeezed my hand and whispered, "Let's go find Silvano."

I hadn't seen Silvano since his victory at the *morean* that morning. He had been ushered under guard back into the keep, and everyone in attendance had been abuzz with how the events had unfolded. I couldn't help but feel like a portion of my light had gone with him, settled into the necklace around his neck. Preparations for the handfasting had begun almost instantly, Rekorious' council members scrambling to organize food, wine, and clothing. Lael and Rekorious had settled on a short, three-day honeymoon after the ceremony, although where that would take place, I had no idea. I fantasized about whispering away with Silvano far from the crowds who had wished for a different outcome at the *morean*.

Threading her elegant, long brown fingers in mine, I let Amadea lead me from the room as we followed Rekorious, Minna a graceful shadow at our backs. My dress sighed as we walked, and wearing something so beautiful had me lifting my chin higher, shoulders thrown back. Despite the council meetings, despite the inescapable *morean* and being wed to Silvano, I felt somewhat in control of my fate for once. The feeling made a giddy sensation run up and down my spine, my heart skittering in its wake.

Rekorious led our little party past the council room to a large, hexagonal gathering space before a huge set of closed, double doors. Black iron torches fixed on the walls illuminated the worn stone. Similar to Silvano's jail cell last night, the gathering area felt ancient, the flagstones aged and scuffed, names and symbols engraved at random into huge mortar stones. Beyond the doors, the sound of talking and laughter filtered to us. Nervousness gripped me suddenly, and I slowed my walking, hanging back behind Amadea.

"Can I have a word, Rekorious?" I asked, the warrior turning just before he reached the door handle.

"Bit late for cold feet now, *Koskivarri*," murmured Minna with a comforting smile.

"It's not that." I glanced from her to the warlord, who pulled back from the door to stand before me. "I ... I just need to talk to Rekorious for a moment ... in private."

He pursed his lips, curiosity glinting in those dark eyes. Asking Minna and Amadea to stay put for a moment, he took my chilled hand in his huge, calloused one and led me down a narrow, dark corridor off the central area. Reaching for the first door we came to, he yanked it open and pulled me inside.

I blinked at the dim, candlelit room, and I swiftly realized that this was his office. A large Niemi sigil tapestry hung behind his modest pine wood desk, and another set of aged short swords adorned the wall to my right. Holding onto the lip of his desk, Rekorious leaned back against it and tilted his head at me.

"Having second thoughts, bride-to-be?" His dark murmur filled the shadowed space between us.

I huffed a soft laugh, trailing my hand down another beautiful tapestry of grazing reindeer. "No, Niemi, I'm not. I need a favor."

"And that is?"

"I need to see Silvano before the ceremony."

His eyebrows quirked upward, and he ran a hand over his trimmed beard. "Is that so?"

"Please."

"You know it's bad luck for a bride to see her intended before the ceremony? But since you asked so nicely." He pushed himself away from the desk to stand before me.

I didn't pull back from him, content now that he wouldn't dare to hurt me again. Our relationship was a complicated one, we had endured horrors together, but I hoped I could now count him as a friend. My gaze naturally fell on his scar that peeked through the V of his shirt. Slowly, he reached for my right hand and held it in both of his. Swallowing, I looked up from our joined hands and into those bronze eyes. His gaze was filled with such heart-wrenching sadness that it made me take a sharp breath.

"Is everything alright?" I whispered.

He nodded, and his right hand rose to cup my cheek. "I'll go fetch him now for you ... but Destry ... I ... I want you to treasure every moment. Do you understand? You and Silvano. Treasure it."

I swallowed, tears burning hot behind my eyes. "Of course."

His answering smile was placating. "And I'll be sure to remind the bastard just how lucky he is to have you."

"I'm sure he'll love that, you two being best friends and all." I lifted my left hand to lay it over his, in the hope I could comfort him and lighten the forlornness that clung to his body. "I wanted to thank you for what you did in the *morean* for Silvano ... what you did for me."

He held my gaze, his lips quirking upward in a faint smile. "We both know I would have won if I hadn't."

"Keep telling yourself that, Niemi." I smiled in return.

Leaning forward, he pressed a whisper-soft kiss to my forehead, then he was moving, exiting his office without looking back. I stared at the closed door, trying to comprehend why my heart ached for the warlord and why his words felt like a warning.

Several minutes later, I was surveying the displayed short swords, a small notecard beneath them explaining that they were Rekorious' grandfather's, when I heard the office door open and shut. I didn't turn to face him, but I felt my body alight with awareness. The hairs on the back of my neck stood on end as I sensed him approaching. Silvano halted close enough to my back that I felt his breath on the exposed skin of my shoulders.

"Quite the rule breaker, aren't we?" he whispered.

"Only for you, it seems." I glanced back at him, moving to turn and face him fully, but his arm reached forward, looping around my waist, hand splaying over my stomach, to pull my back flush with his torso.

I gasped softly while his other hand gently gripped my hip to steady me. My nerve endings caught fire at his touch, and I melted against him, head tilting to the side as those sensuous lips pressed a delicate kiss on my shoulder.

"You look exquisite, wild one." Silvano trailed his pointer finger down my neck and over the curve of my shoulder, my eyes closing in response, heat coiling in my core. His mouth was so close to the shell of my ear that I shuddered as he said, "You wanted to see me?"

"I did," I breathed.

"So, my bride, what can I do for you?"

I had been so sure about this, I hadn't given myself a second to doubt it, until now. Would he want to? "There are a lot of strangers in that altar room."

He hummed in agreement, his breath caressing the nape of my neck as he twirled a tendril of my hair between his fingers. "There are, does that worry you?"

"Not for the ceremony itself, no, but ..." My thoughts addled with the strength and heat of him at my back.

"Then what worries you?" he asked gently, his hand dipping again to give my hip a reassuring squeeze.

I plunged ahead, keeping my eyes closed. "I don't want our first kiss to be in front of a room full of strangers, Silvano."

I sensed his smile against my skin, then he placed his other hand on my right hip and gently turned me to face him. His gaze dipped, his eyes darkening, as he took in my loose hair and dress. Blinking, I surveyed him in turn, breathless at the sight of him. Silvano looked devastating, the candlelight bronzing his swept-back hair and golden skin. He smelled faintly of cedarwood and amber, his black shirt and tunic snug against his warrior body. His burgundy cloak was twisted to drape across his chest and down over his shoulders.

The cut on his lower lip was scabbed over, and I raised my right hand to delicately trace it with my thumb. Catching my hand with his, he placed a tender kiss on the pad, and my entire being focused on where his lips connected to my skin.

"I want our first kiss to be exactly that, just ours," I whispered.

I wanted him to burn any thoughts of Narve from my head, to reduce them to nothing but ash that I could walk over. The scar on my arm could serve not as a reminder of what I had endured, but as a warning to anyone who tried to hurt me like that again, that they could maim my flesh, but they would never, ever break me.

Silvano's dark green gaze flicked up to meet mine, and the hand he still had placed on my hip, shifted to rest against the small of my back, pulling me closer until our bodies were flush against one another. He towered over me, the muscles of his abdomen and chest a solid wall against my own. Letting my hand go, he cupped the base of my neck, drawing me toward him, our lips millimeters apart.

I couldn't hear myself think, had to remind myself to breathe as he whispered, "I cannot wait to make you mine, Destry."

My eyes closed, drunk on the scent and heat of him, and his lips gently brushed against mine, sure but soft, as if we had all the time in the world and there wasn't a whole room full of people waiting for us to make an appearance. It felt so right to be this close to him, to thread my hands through his hair and deepen the kiss. I wanted this, wanted him.

Hand against my spine, Silvano angled my head to grant him better access, a low moan at the back of his throat that had me pressing fully against him. I wanted this forever, his hands on me and a kiss that seared into my soul. He pulled back to look at me, the gold flecks in his eyes burning bright with need. "You're everything I've dreamed of."

He kissed me again, deeper this time, and any tentativeness I had felt melted away with how confidently we moved against one another, as if our souls were being woven together by this kiss alone. Desire gilded my bones, and I felt my core tighten with need, desperate for more of him.

He broke off again, panting, and trailed kisses along my jaw.

"Silvano," I breathed.

"I know, wild one," he murmured against my bare throat, his hand clutching the back of my head. "I know."

My hands dipped to grasp his shirt, his mouth finding mine once more, both of us becoming lost in each other, exploring, our kiss turning thorough and feverish.

A loud knocking echoed through the office, and a low snarl rumbled in Silvano's chest at the intrusion. Flushed, aching, and suddenly feeling unbearably warm, I placed one last kiss to his cheek, the muscle in his jaw twitching with restraint.

Eyes closed, he pressed his forehead to mine. "How am I meant to say our vows when I can barely form a coherent thought right now?" He pulled back, placing his calloused hands on either side of my face. "This isn't over."

I smirked, feeling playful and weightless for the first time in years. "Is that so?"

Silvano stepped back, my right hand held in his, and he led the way to the door. Glancing back over his shoulder, he winked. "This is just the beginning."

Rekorious took one look at Silvano's messy hair and leveled me with a small smirk. I rolled my eyes at him, noting that the tension between the two men was gone, but they were still wary around one another, like two rival wolves feeling each other out. Their history went far back to their apprenticeship days in Irair, yet after Rekorious revealed his true identity and Silvano's dissension, I sensed the pair didn't actually know each other as well as they thought.

Walking back to the main gathering area, Lael walked out of the shadows to join Minna and Amadea, two swords in his grasp. Drawing up beside him, the Hearan smiled warmly at me, as he proffered the swords, fitted snugly into their leather scabbards, toward us.

Could the others feel *Kathkar's* arctic, half-frozen song? It hummed along the marrow of my bones, as I reverently picked it up, the lambent stones glinting as I wrapped my hand around the hilt.

"No handfasting ceremony is complete without weapons," said Lael, a hint of humor in his voice.

I buckled the sword belt around my waist, the weight of *Kathkar* familiar and reassuring against my left thigh. Lael cleared his throat, and I looked down at the second sword that he proffered toward Silvano. Its scabbard was plain, roughened leather so that whoever beheld the mighty, Colladonian blade wasn't distracted from the glowing, oval-cut ruby set into the pommel. Its multiple facets caught and refracted the flickering torchlight.

Silvano shook his head. "It's Destry's by right, she earned it."

"I need to learn how to wield *Kathkar* properly, before I even think about adding a second sword. Take it, please." I glanced up at him, my expression earnest.

"I'll be its keeper until you're ready, then I'll pass it back to its rightful owner." He threw me a shrewd glance, but his smile was soft, sincere, as if he remembered what it cost me to earn the sword in Lael's hands.

Thanking the Hearan, Silvano donned the blade, and he suddenly looked even more like a wild, unbound warrior. For a heartbeat, I wished we weren't surrounded by so many people, so that I could finish what we started in the office.

Silvano glanced sidelong at me, a silent promise dancing in his gaze, like he knew exactly what I was thinking. My attention turned to Rekorious, who had drifted apart from our group and was having a heated but hushed discussion with the spirit walker who would be conducting the ceremony. A stout woman in her forties, her mahogany hair half braided back from her heavily freckled face, she wrung her hands while Rekorious nodded along to her words.

Leaving Silvano with Lael, I gathered up the skirt of my dress in one hand and walked stiffly over to the pair, the ache in my hip now a dull thrum. Head tilted to the side, I caught the tail end of their conversation.

"... it has to be the true name, my lord, or it will be frowned upon, not just by the spirits but by some of those in attendance. I don't need to give you any clues as to who they will be," said the spirit walker.

"You're absolutely certain, Maire? It can't be the name the duchess gave her?"

"I'm sorry, my lord, but no. If we'd had more time to prepare, I might have been able to sway the inner council, but I can't. There are some who are saying we should be addressing her by her true name anyway, not her adopted one."

"Is everything alright?" I said softly to the pair, drawing up beside Rekorious, apprehension making my skin shudder.

The warlord chewed his lower lip and crossed his arms over his chest, his fingers drumming rhythmically over his biceps. "We have a small problem."

"There's something wrong with my name?" I glanced at Maire, and the woman nodded solemnly as she ran her hands over her pale gray robes.

"Destry is the name Damara, the Duchess of Aarine, gave you, is that right?" she asked.

I nodded slowly. "Yes," I said, drawing out the word.

"For a ceremony as important as this, with the spirits watching on, it's critical that we use your true name for the vows, the one your mother and father gave you."

I blinked, stunned. From across the room, I felt Silvano look up at me from his conversation with Lael.

"I don't know my true name," I whispered.

Maire winced, throwing a pleading glance at her lord. Following her gaze, I watched Rekorious carefully. He sighed and rubbed the back of his neck. "I do."

Of course, he did, the man who had been betrothed to me since my birth. He had known it this whole time, yet had used Destry as a courtesy.

"What is it?" My voice was hushed, as I waited for the inevitable.

Sliding his hands into his trouser pockets, Rekorious threw a pleading look up at the shadowed ceiling, then he looked at me, his entire body laced with caution. The light in my veins stirred, sending tiny tendrils from my fingertips to wreathe over my palms, sensing Silvano drawing up beside me. He placed his right palm on my lower back, and I leaned into the warm touch.

"Eira," murmured Rekorious. "Your true name is Eira."

The ceremony had been simple, honoring time-worn tradition, the words handed down from one generation to the next, binding our lives together until our dying breath. Vows to cherish and protect one another, to be each other's greatest ally. Words of love came next, and I stumbled over them, like I was treading through a boulder field. Was

I ready to give him my heart for safekeeping? Was I ready to treasure his?

What I felt for Silvano in the altar room, the hallowed, rough-hewn walls arching around us, ran deeper than anything I could truly comprehend. I had yearned for him, my soul broken and bleeding under Narve, had wished for his touch and words of solace. After I had abandoned him in Saltfen, I didn't think myself worthy of him. But he had come for me, having found Ebrel on his way.

My true name didn't faze him, even though it had rattled me. I had gone so long without knowing it, satisfied to use my adopted one, yet a tiny splinter of apprehension had always been lodged in my heart because of it. Over the years, it would nick my blood, and I would push it back until it felt more comfortable, but it never went away.

Silvano's hand was bound over mine with a banner of embroidered white cloth, and I looked across to find him already gazing at me, his expression filled with raw emotion. He looked so settled within himself, as if a piece of him, long lost during his time in Ilrair, had finally clicked into place with him being here in the north, with me.

Maire stepped back, murmuring woven words that only the spirits could hear, and nodded at the pair of us. Silvano and I shared a secret smile, my gaze taking in his mussed hair that had been my doing. Drawing me close to him, the knuckles of his right hand caressed my cheek as we kissed, sealing our vows, our hearts, and our fates.

"This is the key to my *tallora*." Minna pulled out a long brass key from one of the hidden pockets in her dress. She dangled it in front of me for a moment, before pressing it into my palm. "It's about an hour's ride from here, and we've loaned you two Lake Horses."

She stepped to the side and toed two sets of large saddlebags at her feet. We stood in the gathering space once more, which was now a cacophony of noise as the people of the keep spilled out of the altar room and celebrated, swiftly becoming inebriated as they toasted to us: the *Koskivarri* and her Ilrairian husband. Poor Rekorious was taking the clout of many stories and jokes about his loss in the gauntlet, but he knew how much it meant to me.

Silvano was somewhere amongst the crowds, he didn't make it far towards me, before another warrior stopped him to compliment on his prowess that morning. Arnar was nowhere to be seen.

"I had Sade, the maid who's been tending to you, pack up some of your things for you, enough to tide you over until you get back. There's a tonic in there too, unless you and Silvano intend on having little—"

"Spirits, no, not yet," I said, shaking my head as Minna cackled.

She leaned in conspiratorially, her voice a fake whisper. "Although I'm certain there is nothing little about your Ilrairian. In fact—"

"*Minna*," I hissed, lightly hitting her upper arm.

Laughing again, she wiggled her forefinger at me. "Do not break my bed, do you understand?"

My scalp prickled as Silvano drew up alongside me, a crooked smile on his face that set my heart thundering.

"I'm not making any promises, dark cloak," he murmured.

I smirked at the blush that bloomed on Minna's face at Silvano's words, although she quickly composed herself and grabbed my hand. "Come on, you don't want to be stuck with a bunch of cranky, old councilors. Let's get you two out of here."

Gently leading us through the throng of people, I caught Amadea's eye as we walked by. Breaking off from Minna, I walked over to my friend and pulled her into a bone-crushing hug. She hugged me tightly back before pulling away, her golden eyes solemn. "When you return, we'll find the time to talk."

"I promise," I said, giving her hand a squeeze. I looked around for Rekorious, only to find him already watching Amadea. Just like he had been all evening.

Following my gaze, Amadea let out a deep breath as her gaze connected with the warlord's.

"Will you be alright?" I asked as I searched her face.

Her guard was well and truly up, as she gave me a small, yet sad smile. "I'll be fine. Go, spend some quality time with Silvano."

"Do you trust him now?"

Amadea bit her lower lip, finally looking away from Rekorious to find Silvano laughing and smiling at what I'm sure was a dirty joke that Minna just told him. "I've never seen him so happy, Destry."

"But do you trust him?" I murmured.

"I think the important question is, do you trust him? Has he truly left everything behind in Ilrair?" Her hand rose and gripped my shoulder gently.

I looked to find Silvano already watching me. The pull to walk toward him felt like incessant tugging in my chest. Everything we had talked about last night, how raw and earnest his words had been, bubbled in my mind, my light weaving between it all. Ice magic hummed in my veins at the silent question put to it. Every word Silvano had spoken was true. "I trust him with my life. He's saved mine more than once."

Whispering my goodbyes, leaving Amadea to discuss the *morean* with Lael, I walked back to Silvano and Minna, but my attention snagged on a tall, lean form in the shadows, his back braced against a column of mortar stones. I slowed to a halt in the sea of people around me, the gathering space full of the sound of laughter and drinks being poured. Hands in his pockets, lips set in a mutinous, grim line, Arnar stared directly at me, the bruises on his face appearing purple in the low light.

Light wreathed my hands at the challenge in his gaze, and my spine stiffened. I bared my teeth at him, my fingers turning into claws at my sides. Arnar set a booted foot against the wall behind him, a sullen sneer on his otherwise handsome face.

He was still a threat, the magic in my veins sensed it. What had Silvano uttered to him when he'd pinned him to the ground with his knee? Arnar made to push off the stones, his hands balling into tight fists at his side. I mirrored him, anchoring myself, *Kathkar* humming a low whine of warning along my bones. Ice cracked over my nails.

His face paled as he made all of two steps away from the wall, before Virtanen and Salo barreled past me, the muscles of their backs taught beneath their dark gray shirts. Huge hand outstretched, Virtanen collared Arnar around the back of his neck, and yanked him down to the hallway toward Rekorious' office, Salo a force of silent fury behind them. Aghast, adrenaline thumping through my body, I stared after the trio. I jumped when Rekorious placed a hand on my shoulder, and I turned to face him.

"Now, now, Destry, no brawls at a wedding, especially if the bride is the one fighting," he drawled, although his face was serious as he peered down the darkened corridor. "Although I would pay to see that ice magic of yours. I'm sure it would work wonders on my cousin."

"I don't trust him, Rekorious, and you shouldn't either."

His throat worked. "I know."

"Any sign of Elias?" I whispered.

That handsome face hardened, and I could sense the countless pressures that were weighing down on his shoulders. "Nothing. I have my people scouring the land between here and the Anduns, and we haven't heard a damn thing. He's either dead or someone is hiding him." The warlord sighed and shook his head. Gazing down at me, he smiled softly. "I'm sorry I can't grace you with more than three days away. I'll need you and Coen back here and training, and we need to get you ready for the blood rider vows next week."

Threading my hands together over my abdomen, I returned his smile. "Thank you, Rekorious." Taking a short breath, I rushed through my next words. "Aalto had been my friend, I hope you can be too. It'll be my honor to serve you and Petowin."

His smile grew wider, and he suddenly appeared younger for a heartbeat, the deadly warlord softening as his shoulders relaxed a fraction. He glanced over my shoulder, and his grin turned into a knowing smirk. "Your husband is waiting for you, *Koskivarri*."

"That word is going to take some getting used to."

Rekorious laughed, and several people turned toward the sound, Amadea amongst them. "He truly left everything he has ever known for you, and I would demand nothing less from him. Now go, or you'll keep missing your chance to leave this place."

Steadily, heart thudding in my chest, I walked back to Silvano's side and was rewarded with a crooked smile that made my core clench in anticipation. Threading his long, calloused fingers through my own, he brought my hand up to his lips, his gaze never leaving mine, and placed a tender kiss on my knuckles.

Husband.

Light danced around our joined hands as he and Minna led me toward the stables.

CHAPTER
TWENTY-FIVE

CALLIOPE

We had walked for several hours, Asher's calloused hand never leaving mine, a compass in the dark, leading me onward to some unknown destination, but one I knew not to fear. His shadows had hidden us from view as we moved slowly through the pine forests. Occasionally, a wisp would caress my cheek, my ear, my wrist, and I could sense their desperation to soothe and comfort.

I gazed at Asher's broad, muscled back, completely unhindered by the pack he bore, noting how his dark hair curled at the ends to brush the collar of his coat. Twice now, he had pulled me from despair, leading me from a darkness filled with fear and pain, to one filled with gossamer-light touches and a sense of safety. Even when I had unwillingly followed him towards Garobear, I knew nothing would harm me when I was in his presence.

Trust was something I rarely felt now, which was why I had given him the wicken berry tea, my power unable to detect whether he would truly release me from his deal to Aron Isark. Yet whatever the visions had shown him last night had led him to run after me and kill the soldiers who tracked me down. I had stumbled across the soldiers while they collected ice from the river, and I didn't get away quickly enough. My owl form had been out of reach, no matter how many times I had tried calling for it while they had pinned me down. Until my shoulder healed, the solace and silence of my owl form were lost to me.

"Hey." Asher's soft, low voice brought me back to my body, my eyes blinking as I refocused on his handsome face, to his dark brown gaze that was filled with concern. He let my hand go slowly, and I instantly missed his touch, my breath catching as he stepped back. I glanced down at my hand like I would see a brand there, unable to remember when someone had last held it so tenderly.

"We'll stay here for a little while." He stepped aside to reveal a tiny hunter's shack. Consisting of coarse wood planks and a patched, slate and moss-ridden roof, it looked squat and rough against the backdrop of pristine alpine forest. "I'd heard of these little places, but didn't think I'd ever find one." He looked at the shack with the same sadness-filled gaze I had seen plague him countless times, as if guilt was consuming him from the inside out, slicing through bone and sinew. His voice was rough when he spoke again. "The shadows have checked, there's no threat around here, but they'll tell me the moment they detect anything. You're safe."

A warm, sunlight-filled power flitted through my blood. I *was* safe here ... with him.

Asher's movements were lithe and powerful as he walked up the cracked little staircase to the shack's door, which hung precariously on its slightly rusted hinges. Like a moth to a flame, I followed him over the threshold. The place smelled of must and old woodsmoke, but the single-room shack was dry. It sheltered a rough-sawn table, a tiny potbelly stove, and a narrow bed made from wide, planed wood. There was no bedding, but the wool-filled mattress looked clean enough.

I noted Asher's gaze snag on the bed, before he swiftly set his pack down on the table. Drifting slightly away from him, yet constantly aware of where he was in relation to me, I toed two empty storage crates that rested beside the stove.

"You hunters are a glamorous bunch, aren't you?" I joked softly, keen to say anything to break the tension-filled silence between us and keep the fright from this morning at bay. Asher released a deep, rasping laugh that rolled along my bones. I half turned toward him, the faintest of smiles on my lips, while I watched him play with the straps on his pack.

"Nicer than the hovel I found you in though?" He winked, a roguish smile on his face.

I arched an eyebrow at him, refusing to note how my body reacted to that smile. "*Anything* was nicer than that."

He huffed another short laugh and shucked off his coat, then, leaving the pack on the table, he brushed past me to kneel before the stove, delicately checking it with his long, calloused fingers. I blinked, feeling detached from my own skin, as I watched those hands expertly light the dry kindling that had been left behind.

Happy the little fire was holding, he partially closed the stove's door, then turned on his knees, to stare up at me. The flickering orange light shone on his stubbled jaw and the muscles of his shoulders, just visible before they disappeared under his shirt. My breath caught as I realized I was staring with complete abandon into those dark eyes that wielded unending shadows.

"Calliope." His voice was raw as he looked up at me. "What do you need?"

I shook my head clear of the thoughts that my mind began to conjure, thoughts that had me yielding to those dark eyes and straightened my shoulders instead. "I ... before we do any of that, I just ... I'm sorry, for the tea, I just didn't think you would—"

He rose slowly, strength and power rippling from him, and he took a small step toward me. "I told you earlier, you have nothing to be sorry for."

I looked down at the dusty, splintered floorboards, realizing just how tattered and dirty my clothes were.

"And yet ..." He took another step closer, our hands within touching distance. Glancing back up at him, he tilted his head, amusement dancing in his gaze. "If you had waited maybe one more night ... I don't think my resolve would have held."

"You've broken your bargain with Aron?"

"I have."

"Why?" I breathed.

"I'm still figuring that out," he murmured, his gaze searching my face.

I inched closer, as a shadow brushed a warm tendril down my forearm. "What did the visions show you?"

His jaw tightened. "I'll tell you later, I promise. Right now, let's get you cleaned up. Have a seat, I'll take care of everything."

It surprised me how pliant I was to his words, like how I had been at the campsite. I had been drowning in panic, consumed and shredded apart by it, begging my owl form to appear so I could fly free, but there was just a stranger's weight crushing me. Then there had been Asher's voice, his touch, commanding and direct, pulling me back to myself, anchoring me to the one thing that had shown me any kindness. Him.

I drifted to the bed to perch on its edge, tucking my hands under my thighs, and I was content to watch him. Whether he noted my silent gaze, I wasn't sure, but he moved around the shack like he had been born there, a man of mountains and harsh, howling weather. All the while, tucked into the upper corners of the shack, his shadows wreathed. With the fire holding steadily, he set out food, spare clothes, and blankets on the table.

We shared a bowl of cavalry rations between us, which was bland but tasted mildly like chicken. After boiling a pot of water, he passed me a clean rag, then ducked out of the shack to collect firewood and give me some privacy. It was awkward with my arm still stiff and sore, but I was able to ditch my ragged, ripped dress and bandages before washing. I longed for a full bath, but the red-hot, damp cloth would have to do. Cleaning up as best as I could, my hair utterly untamable, I pulled on the clean briefs, socks, and wool-lined trousers Asher had pilfered from the soldiers.

I swallowed harshly at the thought of them, how close I had been to being raped if Asher hadn't gotten there when he did. Taking a deep, settling breath, hands shaking slightly, I folded up a cream shirt beside me on the bed, and held a thick, dark green knitted sweater over my bare chest. My arrow wound was tender from being slammed to the frozen ground, and I knew Asher wanted to rebandage it before I dressed properly.

His boots thudded on the rickety staircase, and he shouldered the door open, his arms filled with firewood. My bare back skin stippled at the sudden draft of cold air, and his steps faltered slightly as he appraised me over the large bundle of birch branches in his arms.

Eyes meeting mine for a moment, his jaw clenched, then he stacked the wood beside the stove. Shifting to the table, he pulled off his gambeson, folding it neatly beside his coat. Half turning toward me, he rolled up his shirt sleeves, and my gaze fell on the corded strength and veins that ran up the tan length of his forearms.

After cleaning his hands, he picked up the medical kit, and the mattress dipped as he sat behind me. My head bowed, as I swept my hair from my back to let it fall over a shoulder. I wondered if his shadows could detect the thundering of my heart in my chest, or that my tremble wasn't from the cold, but anticipation.

"My hands are freezing," he murmured, blowing a breath into his palms to warm them.

I peeked at him over my shoulder. "I don't mind."

When did my voice get so husken?

He arched a dark brow. "You resenting my touch is the *last* thing I want."

My mouth was paper dry as my lips parted. *Holy spirits.*

His small, playful smile turned serious as he glanced at my injury. "May I?"

Nodding, I looked forward, trying to harness every ounce of frayed self-control I had left, as those adept hands gently grazed against my skin. His touch was gentle, yet it seared deep, and I wanted those hands everywhere, roving over my ribs to caress my—

"How's the pain?"

I snapped my eyes open, my back tensing as I cleared my throat. "It's tender, but not from the arrow, I think. Just from this morning."

Silence hung between us, laden with the unspoken knowledge that things would not have ended well for me if he hadn't intervened. I winced as he applied the alcohol, then tenderly patted the entry wound dry with a fresh piece of linen.

I craned my neck to look back at him. His lips were pursed with concentration, a deep furrow between his brows as he tended to me, like this was the only thing that mattered. Like *I* mattered to him. People had laid claim to me before, placing me on a pedestal that then became a cage. Yet none of them looked at me like he did now. Not Gren, not the Commander at Garobear, or the King of Colladon.

My body was acutely aware of every brush of Asher's fingers and the feeling of his breaths against my exposed back.

"What did the visions show you?" I whispered.

His dark gaze flitted across to me, then back down to his hands as he applied a smear of honey. I sensed the shadows woven about the room tense. "I saw Raiden, a Pegasus my father had killed when I failed to pull the trigger. I saw Gracien ... a Mountain Horse who used to rule the forest beyond Mount Ghel. He ... I ... I killed him under orders from the wild ward."

A feather-light sensation washed over me, golden and sparkling. He spoke the truth. I had never crossed a wild ward, but I'd heard tales of them whispered between bored market stall holders and disgruntled, wary hunters. Asher unrolled a clean bandage from his medical kit, and my gaze fell on the jagged, angry scar that slashed across his right palm. She had given that to him, the wretched creature, binding him to her with her abhorrent, unjust magic. I felt sick at the thought of him succumbing to her. Surely, he hadn't done so willingly? He was lean but muscular, he would have put up a fight, yet she had overpowered him anyway.

I held out my arm so he could wrap the bandage around my shoulder, pulling it snugly against my skin. My breath turned uneven, catching in my chest as his hand brushed along the nape of my neck to sweep my hair over my shoulder, letting it fall down my back.

Half twisting where I sat, I looked at him wide-eyed, heat reddening my face, while he threw me a smirk.

"You have half a forest in your hair, owling."

"Then why don't you use those talented hands of yours and fix it?"

His smirk turned into an alluring smile that had my thighs pressing together in response. Leaning forward slightly, his exhale brushing the shell of my ear, he whispered, "As you wish, my lady."

Looking forward again, so that I wouldn't lean toward him, I surrendered to pure sensation, as those hands wove into my hair, pulling out fragments of leaf litter and sprigs of moss. Just when I thought he'd finished, his hands threaded deeper into my hair until they found my scalp.

Every thought eddied away on a whisper-soft sigh, as he began to massage my head, his long fingers applying *just* the right amount of pressure. Deep, unwavering pleasure rolled down my spine, and I panted in response, leaning into his touch. A soft moan escaped my lips before I could snatch it away, and I felt Asher tense behind me. I silently begged those hands not to stop, and I almost sagged with relief as he trailed those hands down toward the base of my skull.

My eyes fluttered closed, all I could sense was his touch on me, the thunder of my blood in my head, and the muted roaring of the fire in the stove. Nothing else mattered, not my shoulder and what would happen to us once it had healed.

Keeping one hand against my scalp, Asher wrapped my hair around his other fist and gently pulled on it. Another moan slipped from my lips as I yielded, exposing my throat to him. A shadow rose upward from the floor like smoke, curling to run a featherlight touch along my bare collarbone.

"You know," Asher whispered against the thrumming pulse in my neck, his voice deep and rolling. "The rest of me is pretty damn talented too."

Keeping my eyes closed, I breathed, "I don't doubt it, huntsman."

What the hell was I doing? Spirits, I wanted to revel in his touch, to wash away the fear and hurt from my mind with his shadows and whispered words. He no longer wanted to take me to Garobear, had saved me from death and rape, but in the wilds, alone, was where I was most safe. Anyone else who got close either ended up dead or as a handsomely paid traitor.

My power knew that Asher wouldn't hurt me, but that didn't mean something might hurt him because of me. I had lost enough, and my heart would shatter if it had to hold another ounce of grief.

I barely knew Asher. He had killed five people in cold blood today, and instinct alone told me that they hadn't been the first. My mind struggled to comprehend how someone so lethal could then, in turn, make me want to turn around and kiss him until dawn. *Because he has done nothing but care for you since he found you,* my mind whispered. Olwen's words, repeated over and over in my head, yet it couldn't be real, none of it, no matter how much my power rang with the truth of it.

My resolve nearly buckled entirely, as Asher trailed his nose along my neck and jaw, his lips hovering over the delicate spot below my ear. "You should get some sleep."

In this one bed? How on earth was I—

"But first," he said softly, leaning back. I turned to face him, my nails digging into my thighs with restraint, to watch Asher pick up a scrap of linen and rip it in half with his teeth. He draped the ribbon of fabric over his powerful thigh, then twirled his finger at me to turn around. Arching an eyebrow, I did as he asked, biting my lower lip in confusion, but then his hands were in my hair again. I couldn't help but sigh softly, as he swiftly began to braid it, knotting the end with the linen.

Stunned, I pulled the end of the braid over my shoulder, marveling at it.

Asher raised a hand to rub the back of his neck, his gaze soft, earnest. "It's not my finest work, I'm afraid."

"It's perfect," I whispered, looking back at him. "Thank you."

I was rewarded with a genuine, crooked smile. "You're welcome, owling."

He stood, turning his back to me, and I used the chance to pull on the shirt and sweater, my body suddenly freezing without his heat at my back.

"I'll use my bedroll on the floor. You take the bed."

I blinked. Of course, he would be a gentleman about it. I couldn't stop feeling a slice of disappointment, but it was for the best. If all it took was his hands in my hair and his breath on my neck to feel undone by him, I couldn't begin to imagine what sharing a bed with him would do to me.

Ruin me, most likely. His was a darkness I wanted to step into, to let it caress every pore, reforging and alighting my soul.

There was only a faint glow from the stove now, the rest of the shack pitched into darkness, as Asher handed me a dark leather, wool-lined cavalry rider's coat and a spare blanket. Silently, I donned the coat and ducked outside to relieve myself, then did the best I could at making up the bed.

Asher edged into his bedroll and laid down, a comfortable silence settling over us. Tucking the blanket around me, I pulled it up to my shoulders and looked across at Asher's long, dark form on the floor.

"Asher," I whispered.

"Yes?"

"What happens now? To us?"

The seconds trickled by like melting ice, as I waited for his reply.

"Well ... your shoulder will have healed in another three or four days. I can help you treat it in the meantime. After that, owling ... I don't know. The King's Guard will begin hunting for us when we don't show up at Garobear in two days." His voice was rough, then he shifted, propping himself up on an elbow.

I did the same, and we stared at each other in the semi-darkness. "I ... I'll be safer in my owl form. In the wilds. Alone."

"I know," he murmured. Was that ... resignation in his tone?

There was a beat of silence, my heart quickening in my chest. "What will you do?"

"Right now, Calliope, I'm content to be anything you need me to be."

My breath rushed out of my lungs while I gazed at him. I didn't deserve him and his kindness. He had gone back on his bargain for the Nijinxes to secure my freedom, and a bitter, unwelcome feeling twisted in my gut. I wasn't worth it. He would be hunted for going back on his word.

"Calliope."

Instantly, he pulled me from my thoughts, back to my body. "Asher?"

"Get some sleep, sweetheart."

CHAPTER
TWENTY-SIX

DESTRY

Twilight had fallen by the time Silvano and I reached Minna's *tallora*. We had followed the Niemi River toward the southeast, the Lake Horses we had been loaned were sure-footed through the deep snowdrifts. Broad-chested and barrel-like, the stockily built, ochre work horses appeared barely winded after our hour-long ride along the river's edge, snowflakes catching in their black manes and tails.

My gloved hands clenched the thick, black mane in front me in anticipation, as we rounded the final, small bend of the river and I caught sight of the residence Minna often called home. Conical in structure, the wooden planked building stood half buried amongst the snow, its position in a summertime glen giving it outstanding views across the landscape from its front door. The sky now a deep violet, and a half-moon low on the horizon, Silvano and I closed the distance to the stone-built stable building that adjoined the *tallora*.

Feet half-frozen in the fur-lined boots I had swapped into, I winced as I dismounted and my legs connected with the frozen ground. Pain lanced up my calves, and I vowed to take riding lessons alongside sword fighting, noting the throbbing in my left hip.

The mare I had ridden, Fern, nosed my arm as I steadied myself beside her. Peering over the worn saddle, I watched Silvano dismount gracefully, and I swallowed in an attempt to quell the knot of nerves in my chest. It didn't work.

Working in companionable silence, we settled Fern and Silvano's mare, Kerrti, into the stables with fresh hay, water, and steaming feeds of soaked lupins. As lovely as the horses were, I missed Ebrel terribly. I felt like a piece of my soul had fluttered away in the wind, and I could make no sense of where she had gone, or why she hadn't returned yet. Silvano had reassured me that they would be safe together. Hestian and Ebrel appeared to have bonded during their travels north to Erskine.

I stood back, wrapped up warm in my rider's coat, and watched contentedly as Silvano checked the mares over. His skill around the horses was mesmerizing in its simplicity, how confidently yet calmly he spoke to them, as he checked their hooves for stones and brushed the dried sweat from their backs.

Glancing up at me as he dusted the dirt from his hands, Silvano smiled. "You're staring, wild one."

Feeling a sudden slice of confidence, I quirked an eyebrow. "I'm not apologizing for that."

Huffing a soft laugh, he marched straight toward me, and I yelped as he swept me off my feet and into his arms. "What are you—"

"You can stare as much as you want, Destry. I'll never get tired of it." I lost all train of thought as his nose brushed the shell of my ear, then I fell silent, as he opened the interior door from the stables to the *tallora* and stepped inside, carrying me over the threshold.

I shook my head, unable to stop my grin. "There was no need for that."

Glancing down, his smile was heart-stopping and alluring. Setting me down gently, Silvano took each of my hands in turn and removed my gloves, setting them down on a small table at his right. Then he was moving, quickly finding everything he needed to light and heat the little cabin. Half in a daze of desire, I set about lighting the many candles in the circle-shaped, one-room building.

As the glow from the small fireplace grew stronger, the rest of the small cabin was slowly illuminated, golden light gilding the edges of a kitchen bench, a patched fabric couch and a surprisingly spacious bed, draped in a thick cream quilted coverlet.

My gaze held on the bed, heat and trepidation suddenly at war within my body. The soft thudding of Silvano setting down our packs sounded behind me, but I couldn't turn away.

"I'll take the couch." Silvano's voice was a gentle whisper in the half-light.

I half turned toward him then, taking in the strong planes of his face, flushed from the cold we'd ridden through.

"No." I could barely hear my voice.

He arched an eyebrow, shrugging off his red cloak and coat, draping them over the back of the couch. "No?"

Heart hammering in my chest, I turned to face him fully, fingers knotted over my abdomen. "I ... I don't want you to sleep on the couch."

Rolling his lower lip through his teeth, Silvano stepped slowly forward, gently closing in on my personal space, giving me time to back away if I needed it. With a sure and steady hand, he reached forward and pried my fingers apart, till he held my right hand in his. Like he had done that night in the medic quarter, his thumb traced a reassuring caress over my still-chilled knuckles. "The stables will be a little chilly, but I'll take it, if that's what you want."

A laugh escaped my chest, and shock at the noise bounced around my ribcage a heartbeat later. I squeezed his hand. "I don't want you in the barn either."

"Then where, Destry, do you want me?"

Holy spirits, his voice. I desperately wanted to hear more of those gravelly, low words whispered closer.

"In the bed." I looked up at him, swallowing harshly. Spirits above, could a person really be so nervous and attracted at the same time? "I ... I'm not sure if I'm ready for—"

"Destry, you're in control here, okay? Whatever you need from me, just say the word." He stepped closer and pulled up our joined hands, laying them over his heart. The steady, settling beat resonating in his chest pulsed against my palm. "I will happily hold you until the sun rises."

My gaze dipped from his dark green eyes to his full lips and stubbled jaw. I gave a small nod, my breath shaky. I was no virgin, none of this was new to me, but to be here, with him, alone. The heat and strength of him was power I wanted to lean into. He was a heady song that called deeply to my soul.

With his free hand, he swept a tendril of hair from my face, then trailed his fingers down the line of my jaw in a whisper of touch. "To just be with you is such a gift, Destry."

It felt utterly natural to lean into his caress. Eyes closing, the sound of his breathing, the crackling of the fire, and the beat of his heart under my hand, grounded me solely to the here and now. Everything I had endured and lived through, I would take again, if it led me here, to a snow-capped night with this man.

The memory of our kiss from earlier that evening hounded me, and as if reading my mind, Silvano clasped my neck with his free hand and drew me gently closer, until our foreheads rested against one another.

Eyes closed, I breathed in the intoxicating scent of him: earth, cedar, and amber. With my hand trapped against his chest, I closed the last whisper of distance between us and pressed a kiss to his lips. It was a slow, tantalizing kiss compared to our first, yet I leaned closer into his heat when his fingers threaded through my hair. Pulling away, Silvano kissed my forehead then untangled himself from me, leaving me wanting and reeling in the absence of his muscle-clad body against mine.

"Wait here," he murmured, then he was gone, slipping through a second door I had barely registered earlier. Trying to calm my racing heart, the bed looming at my back, I placed my hands into my coat pockets and yelped in shock.

Scrambling, I opened the deep pocket by my right hip wider and peered inside. Bright black button eyes stared back at me.

"Spirits above," I hissed. "Are you trying to give me a heart attack?"

A short, high-pitched squeak was the only reply, as the little stoat stuck its head out of my pocket and peered around the now toasty warm space. Whiskers twitching, it scrambled up the leather of my coat to jump onto my palm.

"Is everything alright?" asked Silvano as he strode back inside.

Arching a brow, I smiled and held up my hand toward him. "*This* is the little jailbreaker you should be thanking for last night."

The stoat rose on its hind legs, sniffing in Silvano's direction, then it whipped its tail in glee at the sight of him. Huffing in disbelief, Silvano treaded closer and peered down at the little mammal, extending a forefinger toward it.

"Seems we have a hitchhiker."

Tilting my palm back toward me, I grinned down at my new friend, who I realized was a female. "It would appear so."

Any nerves I had felt melted away as the stoat stretched out her long spine and flopped down onto her stomach with a wide yawn. Silvano blinked in admiration at her razor-sharp teeth.

"Brave little thing, aren't you?" whispered Silvano tenderly.

My heart swelled at the gentle stroke of his finger down the stoat's tiny nose. Rolling my eyes, my heart light in ways it hadn't been in years, I set my new friend down on a little folded cloth napkin beside the stove. Curling into a tight ball, the stoat yawned once more and fell asleep. Rocking back on my heels, I leaned into the hand Silvano grazed down my cheek.

"Come with me," he whispered, and I yielded utterly to the dominance in his voice.

Pulling me to my feet, I followed as he led me through the second door and into the small, stone-walled bathroom attached to the main cabin. Water heated from the stove, filled a waist-high, wide wooden barrel for bathing. Lit by long tapering candles placed on the irregular ledges of the walls, Silvano had set out clean towels, underwear, and my sleep shift from our saddlebags.

"Thank you," I whispered. Cutting him a sidelong glance, I pulled off my coat and hung it on the back of the door. Silvano stepped back, arms crossed over his chest. His gaze ran hungrily down my body as I slipped off my boots and stood before him in my wedding gown.

"I know you can't be fully submerged with the dagger wound to your hip, but I thought you'd like to get cleaned up after the ride here."

"But you can," I blurted. "Get in the tub, I mean." Chest rising and falling as my breathing quickened, I closed the distance between us, and I swept a loose tendril of dark blonde hair from his devastating face.

"Do you want me to?" he murmured.

"Yes," I said, my voice low with desire. My forefinger traced a faint, old scar that slashed over his left cheekbone. I wanted to map all of him with my touch, explore every scar, every indentation of muscle. I'd never tire of it. "Let me look after you, please, after everything you endured this morning and before that ... just ... let me do this."

The muscle in his jaw twitched at my touch, and his next words were rough. "It will be torture." His gaze captured mine, and I trailed my hand down his jaw to his throat, sweeping it along the bare section of his chest above the opening of his shirt. "Pure torture," he ground out.

I looked up and threw him a cunning smile.

"Destry Kivisto Coen *Koskivarri*, you are a cruel beauty."

"Spirits, that's a mouthful, isn't it?" I groaned inwardly. That was an unholy number of vowels. Yet the way my new surname rolled off his tongue ... heat pooled low in my abdomen.

He leaned forward, his stubble brushing against my cheek, a soft chuckle sounding in his throat. "It means you're mine, wild one."

My eyes closed at his words, and I sucked down a sharp breath. Silvano leaned back, a look of pure male satisfaction on his face. Then he reached up for the collar of his black shirt and shucked it off, folding it neatly on top of the three-legged stool beside the steaming, water-filled barrel.

Holy spirits. Holy *fucking* spirits. I'd seen him like this before, during my training and even more of him beside the frozen lake in Saltfen, yet I'd been on death's door and so had he, and I hadn't been anywhere near coherent enough to appreciate the man who now stood before me.

Arms loose at his sides, Silvano remained quiet, an eyebrow arched in silent question and a hint of challenge. Pressing my lips between my teeth. I took a subtle step forward, the thin slice of air between us becoming taut and electric. The low light shone on the golden tan of his skin, defining every muscle over his chest and abdomen. My traitorous gaze slid down, tracking the V between his hips before it disappeared under his black trousers.

Blinking, a bit dazed, I half turned and trailed a forefinger around the rim of the wooden tub. I flicked my gaze from him to where my hand rested, and Silvano silently obeyed. Eyes never leaving mine, he shed his boots, trousers, and briefs, utterly confident and at home in his powerful body. Bracing his arms on either side of the barrel, he climbed in, the water sluicing around his neck and shoulders as he submerged, knees folded to his chest.

Honed arms resting around the rim, I fought the urge to drag him back out, as his low, throaty moan echoed around the small room, the moment I laid my hands on his shoulders and neck.

Taking a seat on the small stool, I sat just to the side of him. Dunking a small, soft, white cloth, I washed the fine layer of dust from his face and arms. Silvano's eyes were closed, his face a picture of deep contentment, happy to surrender to my tending. Lips parted in concentration, I kept my movements slow, achingly deliberate, trying to commit every second of this to memory.

Water beaded over the two necklaces he wore, the lambent stone that I had gifted him, and the simple, twisted leather one I had noted in Saltfen. Having cleaned up his upper torso, I gently swiped my thumb over his right bicep and the black ink flames that wrapped around his entire upper arm. Resting his head back against the wooden lip, exposing the tan column of his throat, Silvano's gaze slid to mine.

"I got it done after I became bonded to Hestian. Although my superiors were not pleased about it, especially when I became a commander. Tattoos are forbidden. Jaryn overruled them though."

My hand stilled on his skin. "Did you always want to be a commander?"

He thought silently for a moment, choosing his words carefully. "I just wanted my own Pegasus and vowed to be the top of every class to be able to get there. My superior officers took notice of me and bookmarked me for small leadership roles. I loved being a unit leader the most, you're in a small team of five Pegasus riders. Yet Jaryn and my extended family continually pushed me to do more, to *be* more. Being just a unit leader was never going to cut it. I fought, argued with them all. Being a unit leader is so intimate, you become brothers and sisters in arms, your Pegasi too." His soaking wet hand enveloped mine over his arm. "Jaryn talked me down at every turn, silencing every argument I gave him. I was desperate to keep Hestian, so I moved on up to the next role, then the next, until before I knew it, I was a commander, in charge of a whole damn platoon, with no real memory of how I got there."

His gaze ran over the dark, twisting ink of the tattoo. "It wasn't until after I brought you back to Ilrair that it hit me what Jaryn had been orchestrating all these years. He had created a friend, who was also the perfect soldier, who'd blindly follow his orders, no matter how depraved, how forceful toward our people, how brutal to our perceived enemies."

Water dripped down my neck and onto my chest when he raised his hand to cup my face, his touch exquisitely gentle. "It took *you*, all that wild energy and rage, to snap me out of Jaryn's hold. To wake me up." The golden flecks in his eyes glinted. "I should have followed you when you fled Saltfen, and Destry, there isn't a day that goes by when I don't think about it."

"You were right ... about Rekorious. I shouldn't have trusted him, but Silvano, it was my decision to leave. You're not responsible for that."

"Last night, in my cell, you mentioned torture ... did something happen on your way to Serebo? Jaryn said in one of his war tent meetings that he had someone hunting you both."

Lips set in a grim line, I inched backward, as an assault of memories stabbed into my heart. Silvano's hand on my face was unyielding, but his fingers dipped to lift my chin, his gaze meeting mine. Earnest, caring, and beneath that, a deep, unending rage at what I knew he suspected from the look on my face alone.

"I need to show you something," I whispered.

He nodded, his hand slowly falling away, disappearing under the dark surface of the water. Our gazes held, rooting me to the here and now, silently commanding me to think of him and only him. We were here together, alone, the only sound: our breath and beating hearts. There was no poison, no endless screaming, just this ... peace, a sanctuary of silence in which Silvano was my anchor.

Turning my back to him, Silvano rose to his knees in the water, his large hands deftly undoing the long column of pearl buttons down my spine. Pressing a tender kiss to my shoulder when he was finished, I stood.

And let the dress fall in a dark pool at my feet.

Silently, my breath sawing from my chest, heart trying to claw its way up my throat and out into the world, I knelt. I couldn't take it, the excruciating and suffocating thoughts of shame and pain, and I looked down at the darkened ground.

My skin stippled. Water sloshed and shifted next to me, then I was enveloped in a hard, warm, yet soaking wet body. One arm looped around my back, gently hauling me to my feet, the other collaring the back of my neck.

I kept my eyes screwed shut, knowing full well by the tilt of his cheek against mine that he was taking in the horrendous scar down my left bicep. A cruel, mocking twin to the tattoo on his arm. Both place markers in time, one celebratory, the other vicious and ragged.

"Who?" he asked in a voice that was a guttural whisper. "Who did that to you?"

"Lonan made the cut." My throat was scratchy, like daggers had lodged themselves inside my vocal cords. I burrowed my head under his chin. "But it was Narve ... Narve who ..."

I had managed to keep it together with Minna and Amadea, glossing over the facts as if we had been talking about a bad snowfall that night. But being here with Silvano, there was something about him that slitted me bare, that reassured my soul that I could feel vulnerable, and he would take every fractured piece of me and weather it, then help me rebuild, piece by jagged piece.

He held me tighter against him, my brain short-circuiting the fact he was utterly naked, and I nearly was too. Tears fell unbidden down my cheeks, saltwater coalescing with the beads of freshwater on his skin.

"I ... I cut off his hands with *Kathkar* the next morning," I choked out, my teeth grinding together at the memory of steel cleaving through flesh and bone. "Yet my nightmares never remember that part."

Hand pressing coaxingly against my neck, Silvano tilted my head back so that I could lose myself in those green eyes. I could sense his restraint, how at any moment he could snap, stalk out of this cabin, track down Narve, and slice him from scrotum to sternum in one swift motion.

"Why his hands, wild one?"

I swallowed, looking away once more. Silvano shook with rage against me.

"I'll fucking kill him, but I won't."

My gaze flitted back to him, confusion written on my face.

"Because you're going to kill that fucker for what he did to you, and I'm going to watch and enjoy every minute of it." Faintly, in a ghost-like touch, he followed the edges of the scar with a forefinger. "I can't erase what he did to you, wild one. But I sure as hell can help you heal from it. Whatever you need from me, take it, it's yours. My body, my very breath, my heart, all of it … it's yours." Lifting my hands to his mouth, he pressed a tender kiss to my knuckles, then with a roughened thumb, he swiped the tears away from my face. "No one and nothing is ever going to hurt you like that again."

My mind was a haze after that, falling into a stunned silence, as Silvano washed me, wrapping us in thick cotton towels. Body pliant to his every motion, I let him dress me, then he was carrying me and laying me down with heartbreaking gentleness on the bed. A bed that no longer felt foreboding.

I fell asleep wrapped up in his arms, my spine snug against his chest, his breath a warm serenade against my neck, our legs tangled together, and at last, my nightmares stopped.

CHAPTER
TWENTY-SEVEN

EBREL

T ime felt like it didn't exist here. Within the still, cool, and unending dark of the cave, the seconds seemed to drag by, like the
scrape of a nail across stone. Hestian led the way, the small, silver flecks
of light of Eirlys' magic pulling us onward. Slowly, acutely aware of
every sound we made, we treaded deeper into the cliffside, descending
into the very fibers of Serebo's land.

I inhaled delicately, barely able to catch the faint scent that still
clung to the walls after all these years. *"People have been here, Hestian."*

"I know, I can smell them too," he said, his voice low.

"Lowlanders?"

"Most likely, or Colladonians on their travels south to Aarine."

We rounded a curve in the tunnel, the specks of light fanning
outward to reveal a huge cavern, one large enough to house two dozen
Pegasi. Hestian and I halted on the threshold, our breath disturbing
small plumes of fine dust that had been long settled into the pick marks
on the walls.

"Holy spirits," I whispered in awe, casting my gaze upward. Hestian
mirrored me, wings half spread in wonder at the intricate mural that
spanned not only the walls, but the entirety of the ceiling. Eirlys' magic
spun slowly in place at the corners of the cavern, perfectly illuminating
the time-worn finger paintings.

I took a hesitant step forward, then another, my hoofbeats thudding into the packed earth.

"Ebrel," murmured Hestian roughly. *"The center of the ceiling."*

Walking to the very heart of the cavern, I peered up at the main piece of art that commanded the roof. Perfectly replicated, with tender care in every brush of paint, was the Night Pegasus, wings spread to their utmost extent, light lashing in violent curtains of emerald in every direction. My breath quickened, as I tracked the largest plume of light as it arced down the curve of the roughened wall. It spiraled, growing brighter, until it pooled around the outline of a man lying sprawled on the ground.

Hestian stalked forward, staring intently at the painting of the man. Green fire consumed him wholly, yet it was the figure to the right, on their knees, arms raised, that drew out a shuddering, low gasp from my throat. A woman, her dark hair whipped back from her face with the force of the fire, looked poised to engulf the man in the ice magic that coated her hands.

My gaze snapped to Hestian, then back at the huge mural, not believing what I was seeing. Above the two humans, flying in every direction, were Trinitors, their horns glowing with unspent power. I looked down, taking in the semicircle of black that was painted underneath the burning man. A black so deep, it consumed the faint particles of light that shone in the cavern.

"Eirlys warned of history repeating itself," Hestian ground out.

Turning in place, I followed the artwork as the scene changed. A huge depiction of a Trinitor stallion spanned the height of the wall. He was rearing, wings curled over his back and around his neck, a bronze collar. The humans had even gone so far as to paint old battle scars across the black stallion's withers, backs, and knees. Even I could sense the power and feeling of royalty that covered the painting.

"It's Colbass," I whispered. *"King of the Trinitors."*

"The one who doomed them all?" replied Hestian, stepping up beside me, ears pricked.

"King of the Cursed."

From his horn, ice particles and snowflakes plumed, encircling his ears in a frozen crown. His head was turned to look over his shoulder, taking in the next piece of art that sent a shiver down my spine. Again, the dark-haired woman was painted, ice magic flowing from her hands once more, arcing in a beautiful spiral to join with the fragments Colbass had cast.

Hestian shook his head in frustration. *"None of this is linear. It doesn't make sense."*

"It does, follow the light." My gaze flicked back to the Night Pegasus, and I tracked another painted beam. This one arced in the opposite direction of the first, where it connected with the woman again, filtering light into her palms. *"In the folktales, an ancient Kivisto woman frees the Night Pegasus from a cave he was trapped in. In return, he gifted her with a portion of his light."* My eyes narrowed as I followed a faint thread of emerald that slid down the wall to the floor. I stepped back, fanning my wings to remove the fine layer of dust that covered the painting beneath our hooves. *"She falls in love with a mortal man, who is favored by Tavaris,"* I choked, eyes scanning over the two humans entwined in a loving embrace, green and orange flames encircling them. *"And imbues him with her power."* My breath turned tight and uneven. *"He dies for her, becoming the Night Pegasus."*

Even Hestian's breath was ragged. *"And the cycle continues, over and over."*

"No," I begged. *"This can't be their fate. It's like a snake eating its tail, it won't stop."*

"If Destry breaks the curse on the Trinitors, can we use their power to stop ... to stop the man's death?" asked Hestian, his golden gaze desperately searching mine.

"We have to break the curse to stop Jaryn, but Hestian, what if freeing the Trinitors causes the death?" My voice was hoarse, my mind reeling with the facts the painting had laid bare.

"No," he growled. *"I won't let it. It won't come to that."*

"We don't know—"

"Jaryn has to be stopped."

"We risk both Destry and Silvano," I whispered, shaking my head. *"Hestian, we can't lose them."*

"Serebo showed us this cave as a warning, to prepare us. Now we have to fight it, we have to break the cycle. If saving the Trinitors is our only hope, we have to risk it."

I looked away from him, lifting my head back up to take in the Night Pegasus once more. His hooves raked the night air, his gaze cast downward toward the mortal body he had left. Trembling, I leaned into Hestian's warmth, wings brushing against one another in reassurance.

"I need to get a message to a southbound Ilrairian unit." Hestian looked at the burning man once more, nostrils flaring wide, eyes white rimmed. *"Then we need to find our riders."*

"How do we tell them? This is too intricate to try and communicate via intention. They don't possess telepathy like Asher the huntsman does."

"Then we find him first, get him to act as a translator."

"He could be anywhere, Hestian, and he could still be with the Ni-jinxes."

The stallion arched his neck, purpose pulsing through him, a true commander's mount. *"We'll find him. We have to."*

CHAPTER
TWENTY-EIGHT

ASHER

I awoke to find Calliope's bed empty. Bolting upright, I quickly reached out to my shadows, but they were relaxed, wholly content, both inside and beyond the small hunter's shack. Silently, I edged out of my bedroll and walked to the lopsided and drafty door. Inching it open a fraction, I peered beyond to see heavy snowfall carpeting the little glade in front of the shack, and at its center, stood Calliope. Her pale hair, still in its braid but mussed from sleep, was stark against the dark leather of the stolen rider's coat. Face looking to the sky, eyes closed, bare palms uptilted, she looked to be receiving a winter blessing from Merevis, as snowflakes clung to her lashes.

The door groaned with the force of my grip on it, while I reined in the urge to march over the snowdrifts and pull her body close to mine. Last night ... last night had been ... my tether had been fraying second by second the longer I had my hands on her. And the way she had responded, like she wanted my touch, did little to quell the heady need in my body.

Yet seeing her amongst the elements, her golden skin glowing against the stark white of the snowfall, I knew she was worth more than being penned to my side. She wanted to return to her owl form and find peace in the deep, remote forests of the wild north. It was bad enough I had dragged her this close to Garobear, I was not about to ask her to remain grounded because of me.

I would make the most of these next few days, treasuring every moment I spent in her presence until her shoulder fully healed, then I would let her go. She deserved her peace, just as much as the Nijinxes did, and I was awful for saying otherwise.

I had to let her go.

The task the Night Pegasus had set for me lingered in the back of my head. The spirits were engineering an outcome that I had probably been woven into since before I was born. Removing my right hand from the sill of the doorway, I stared down at the angry scar on my palm, hating the feel of it whenever it brushed against the calluses of my fist. Were the spirits the reason I didn't pull the trigger on Raiden that day?

Were my father and uncle always destined to be killed by Pegasi?

Panting, I dragged my hand through my hair, my gaze drinking in Calliope once more. If not for the wild ward, I would never have hunted the Truth Keeper down, and slowly, it dawned on me.

I would happily tear myself apart with knives of shadow, if it meant she flew free. Deep in my heart, I knew Pherox would do the same for Vesperum, and our Nijinx lore rang like a cymbal over and over in my head.

Defend and death.

"We'll start heading towards the Scarp tonight, it'll be safer traveling in the dark, so get some rest here over the next few hours. We need to cover as much ground as we can." I doled out two mugs of stew with dried meat and root vegetables and handed one to Calliope.

Sitting on the bed, bundled up in her green sweater, she clasped her hands around the warm mug and gave me a nod of thanks. "I'll be glad to move at night. This is the most awake I've been during daylight hours in years."

"I look forward to keeping you up at night then." I hid my smirk behind my mug, secretly relishing the eye roll she gave me in return, although it did little to hide the blush that bloomed over her face.

"Yes, your snoring is quite extraordinary."

I scoffed. "I do not snore."

"Oh, your shadows never told you? That's sweet of them."

I leaned against the closed door, taking a quick sip of the stew. "My shadows tell me plenty."

"Is that so?"

"The little tune that you hum to yourself when you're alone, hmm? Is—" I stopped talking as I saw her walls snap down behind those golden eyes, her shoulders bowing inward at my words. Her gaze dipped to the floor, refusing to meet mine. *Fuck.*

"That's none of your business."

"I'm sorry, I didn't mean to overstep. I ..."

"It's fine," she murmured flatly. Her gaze was vacant, haunted, like she wasn't in the room with me.

Setting my mug down on the table, I crouched in front of her and peered across at her like I had done that first night in the cave.

"It's clearly not fine," I said gently. She swallowed and gave me a tiny nod, those ghost-like eyes sending tendrils of worry over my mind. I sighed and slowly reached out with my hand to lift her chin with my pointer finger, she didn't resist, as I turned her head to look back up at me. "We clearly both have moments in our past that we're not ready to discuss. Moments that we might not ever be able to talk about. I'm sorry for prying."

"It's a lullaby," she whispered after a few heartbeats, gripping her mug tightly.

I blinked. "Oh. It's beautiful, the parts that I've heard."

"It's one my mother sang to me too."

I brushed a tendril of hair from her face, desperately trying to think of anything to lift the sorrow that clung to her. "I promise I won't subject you to my singing."

She arched a perfect brow. "Is it that bad?"

"Worse," I countered, trying not to let the flood of relief show on my face. "I've been kicked out of taverns for my magical voice."

A tiny, fragile laugh escaped her lips, and my eyes closed at the sound. *Thank the spirits*.

"Well, now I'm curious."

Throwing her a roguish grin, I tapped her nose. "I'm sorry, you're never going to hear it."

"Even if I say please?"

Instantly, my resolve wavered. "Nope, sorry. No can do."

Calliope smiled, rolled her eyes, and took a deep drink of her stew. She swirled the contents of her mug, throwing me a cunning glance as I stood again and leaned back against the table.

"I'll find a way to break you."

"Oh, I don't doubt it." My gaze narrowed with amusement, returning her smile. Settling my mug between my hands, I ran my thumbs over the cracked rim, as I debated how to ask the question that had been needling me since yesterday. I took a breath, and Calliope tilted her head. "In my visions, the Night Pegasus said that his mortal form was destined to die."

Almost instantly, Calliope's eyes glowed brightly in confirmation. *Holy shit.* "What else?" she whispered.

"He said you would be able to tell me his human name. That I need to be there when the time comes when ... when his human body dies."

She swallowed, her features turning vulnerable. "This will take a few moments," she said softly.

"Take as long as you need."

The Truth Keeper set down her mug on the floor, rubbed her palms over her thighs, then sat cross-legged on the mattress. I stilled, my breath hesitant, as Calliope ran a hand down her braid, rolled her lower lip through her teeth, then closed her eyes.

Her breathing turned deep and intentional, an aura of complete calm settling over the shack. My shadows curled silently in on themselves, unsure what to make of the creeping, cold power that slowly filtered through the air. Calliope's skin seemed to glow faintly from within, eyes flickering under her closed lids. Her hands twitched in her lap, and I fought the urge to go to her and hold her. A small furrow appeared between her brows, and her beautiful, rosebud lips pursed in concentration.

A moment later, her glow dimmed, no longer stark against the smattering of freckles on her face and neck. She released a long, shaking exhale and opened her eyes. My gaze flicked straight to her, and the golden fire that lay there nearly sent me to my knees. How many other mortals had seen this display of power? How many people had she trusted enough to delve within herself like that? Willingly?

She scanned my face intently, like she could read every part of my history on my weathered skin. "You've met him."

"What?"

"You've fought beside him."

Slowly, unfolding her elegant limbs, she rose and walked over to me, her gaze pinning me in place against the table. I knew the Night Pegasus as a human? It was impossible. I held still as she reached up on her toes and leaned in close, her breath warm against my neck. Her sensuous lips brushed my ear, and a man's name tumbled from her mouth.

It was an effort to stay standing.

Fuck. Holy *fuck*.

Calliope settled back on her feet, her gaze solemn as she read my reaction.

I shook my head. "It *can't* be."

"But it is," she whispered softly. Gently, her right hand inched closer to mine, and she brushed her forefinger against the back of my fist. It took all of my willpower not to lean into her warmth, my jaw clenching as I registered the first comforting touch she had ever given me, offered in genuine reassurance.

"Do you know where he is?" I asked, my voice hoarse from the knowledge I'd just learned and from where my skin still burned from her touch.

"Yes." She looked from my eyes to my mouth and swallowed. "To the west, beyond the forests, amongst the Petish glens but close to Colladon's border."

I ground my teeth. It would take me off course to go to him, pulling me away from the Nijinxes and the protection of the Scarp. The glens could be merciless, bar the few forests that were scattered amongst them, there was no cover out there. Nowhere to hide until you reached a long mountainous ridgeline.

I had studied enough hunters' maps to know this land like the back of my hand, but even I would struggle to navigate the glens with stealth, even with my shadows. We would have to stick to our plan of traveling only at night, finding hiding places during the day.

Then my mind stumbled. *We.* Would there even be a "we"? It would take us several days to reach the glens, by then Calliope's shoulder would be healed, and she could fly free. I dragged a hand through my hair, then down my face, the stubble there now thickening into a short beard.

"Your shoulder will be healed soon, let me protect you until then. By the time we reach the border, you'll be free of me and can stay in the forests where you'll be safe ... in your owl form." I glanced down, then back up at her to find her watching me closely. I waited, hands clenching the tabletop at my back.

She blew out a breath, then gave a shallow nod. "Okay. Until we reach the glens."

"Okay."

Calliope's breath quickened like she might say more, like she wanted to weave more into our deal, but that was just my false hope, as she turned away and stoked the fire with shaking hands. The Night Pegasus had called her mine. She didn't know it, but she held my heart in those elegant, freckled hands, and I just prayed to whatever was listening that maybe ... she would trust me enough to let me guard hers.

***

I had kept watch by the fire while Calliope had slept, curled up under her coat and blanket on the bed. My shadows came and went, flickering back with whispered messages of what lay beyond in the forest: a red squirrel digging up its secret cache of food, a ptarmigan stalking the undergrowth, and two young, hungry bucks nibbling on tree bark. Just before sundown, I roused Calliope, our supplies packed and ready to go.

With a hand at the small of her back, I ushered her out of the tiny shack, having restocked it with firewood ready for the next traveler in need of shelter. Keeping a stride behind me, Calliope followed me as we became enveloped by the trees, the low dusk light reflecting on the snow at our feet. I had to remind myself not to constantly look back and check on her, but seeing the setting sun shine on the hair framing her face, and the gold glow of her eyes, I couldn't help myself.

Shadows trailed all around us, weaving seamlessly through the trees as I followed the setting sun. I would see out this demand from the Night Pegasus, then I would retreat back to the Scarp, rejoin with the Nijinxes, and tear myself apart over letting Calliope go. She deserved her freedom just as much as the kin swarm did.

I would protect her, honor her, then I would let her go.

The shadows around my torso constricted in a whispered embrace, but the feeling of comfort wouldn't come.

CHAPTER TWENTY-NINE

DESTRY

The first thing I realized was just how warm I was, almost to the point of overheating. It took several moments for my body to check in with my mind, to register the powerful thigh that rested between my own. With every ratcheting beat of my heart, I became aware of more and more, the strong arm wrapped around my torso, long, calloused fingers interlaced with my own, tucked close against my throat.

My sleep shift had risen in the night, bunching around my waist, and I reveled in the sensation of Silvano's bare legs against mine.

More, my body sang like a finely tuned instrument. *More*.

Tilting my head upward ever so slightly, I peeked the rounded muscles of Silvano's shoulder curling over my back and felt his breath against my neck.

The second thing I noticed was how relaxed I felt. Despite my climbing desire, my body felt totally at ease, my mind calm. I realized the last time I had felt so peaceful was when the Night Pegasus had held me in Ilrair. Anxiety didn't gnaw at my bones the moment my eyes opened, apprehension didn't choke me for a few heartbeats when I looked around the room. The little stoat was completely stretched out along the back of the sofa, her little legs dangling on either side of the cushioned back.

Smiling to myself, I reveled in the feeling of being safe, warm, and protected. I was also *starving*. I had eaten just before we had ridden out of the Niemi keep to get here, but had passed out before dinner, and I was pretty sure Silvano hadn't eaten anything either before wrapping himself around me.

Making to extricate myself, albeit a bit unwillingly, from Silvano's arms, I stalled as his thigh notched itself a little higher, causing heart-shuddering friction between my legs. Stilling at the touch, I rolled my lower lip through my teeth and squeezed my eyes shut in an attempt to focus. *Food, water, brush teeth, and—*

"Going somewhere?" whispered Silvano against my ear, his voice husky from sleep. Every thought of food went silent in my head when Silvano gently caught my ear lobe between his teeth. I couldn't stop the small moan that escaped, back arching instinctively, giving him better access to my neck, heat building and building in my core.

His right arm, tucked into the hollow between my neck and the pillow, curled over my chest. He inhaled deeply, as he dragged his nose down the plane of my neck, his fingers dancing lazily against my left palm where our hands had been entwined.

"Breakfast," I panted, my voice low and reedy. "We didn't eat—"

Gently, he bit down on the soft skin between my neck and shoulder, followed by a string of kisses back to the delicate spot right behind my ear. I could think of nothing else, only focus on where his lips brushed tantalizingly against me. Languidly, he trailed his left hand up my arm, over the curve of my waist and the indentation of my hip, stopping right on the hem of my shift.

"I'll never get tired of this, waking up next to you." A small tender kiss on my cheek, his fingers pressing into my hips just a little. His little finger extended over the hem and brushed the soft skin of my thigh.

Neither will I, I wanted to say, but words were beyond me right now. I was just a vessel of sensation, only able to perceive his touch and nothing else. Slowly, his hand caressed my throat and collarbone.

His voice dropped an octave, becoming the most gentle I'd ever heard. "Is this okay?" I nodded, panting, and he placed a delicate kiss behind my ear. "You're sure?"

"Yes," I whispered.

"I have dreamed of touching you." He squeezed my hip. "Tasting you." Another, open-mouthed kiss on my neck. "For weeks, wild one. But do you know what I have thought of the most? What's taken me over the edge, again and again?"

I whimpered, writhing against him, desperate for more friction, more of him. I could feel just how hard he was against me. How long had it been for me? Too long, I knew, my body was touch starved and burning with an unspoken need. Clarity sparked up my spine, and despite my thundering heart and panting lungs, I was ready. I wanted this.

Maybe all this time, I had been waiting for him.

Silvano moved, towering over me, his arms barricading my head. Planting a kiss to my collarbone, I gasped as he shifted off the edge of the bed, wrapped his hands over my thighs, and yanked me to its edge.

Propping myself on my elbows, my throat rasping, I gazed down at him.

"Do you want me to stop?" he uttered from where he knelt on the floor, palms resting on my inner thighs, the coarseness of his stubble rubbing on the inside of my knee.

"Don't stop," I said hoarsely. "Please."

I didn't dare look away, as he inched closer to the apex of my thighs, his gaze never leaving mine. "All I thought about, Destry, was doing this."

With the broad pad of his thumb, he hooked my underwear to the side, then his tongue was on my hot, wet center. The sound that left my throat was utterly primal, as he swept his tongue up expertly, circling my clit tortuously slowly. My hips bucked, begging for more, but then his right hand cupped the back of my left knee, spreading me wider, while his other hand pinned my hip to the mattress.

"Fuck, the sounds you make," he groaned against me. "So wet for me already, Destry?"

My back arched, my arms quivering with the effort to keep me up. His tongue was the sweetest pleasure and utter torment wrapped in one. Head rolling back, my hair grazing the duvet, I whimpered, heat building and building at the base of my spine.

Calluses scraping, he ran his right hand over the soft rise of my stomach, dipping down until his middle finger gently teased me. I let out a strangled cry, and Silvano pulled me closer against his tongue, a hum of approval sounding deep in his throat.

His pointer finger joined the first, nudging into wetness that was all for him. My elbows gave out, and my hand snaked down as soon as my back connected with the mattress, curling my hand tightly in his hair. A silent demand that he did not heed.

"*Silvano,*" I pleaded.

"That's it, wild one," he whispered against my too sensitive skin. "Come undone for me."

I had never felt so present, so alive and aware of my body. I pulled on his hair again, and he simply huffed a soft laugh, then he was pulling his mouth away. Hips bucking in a desperate attempt to get him back, he simply pinned me in place once more with his free hand. His fingers slid up and down, thumb teasing my clit over and over and over.

I shuddered beneath his touch, gasping and saying his name like a prayer. "*Silvano.*"

"Eyes here, Destry," he ordered.

Breath ragged, I looked down, my hand lost in his hair, and as our gazes collided, he sank those two fingers in deep. Back bowing, I fisted the sheets, I would never get enough of this, of him. Slowly, he withdrew, then plunged in again, edging me closer and closer to the brink. I lifted my hips to every stroke of those fingers. This liminal space on the brink of all-consuming pleasure, I wanted to burrow into this fraction of time forever, forging my blood with it.

"Fuck, *Destry*," Silvano groaned, his teeth scraping along my inner thigh.

It was that small bite of pain that had my release barreling up my spine. Wrung out and limp, Silvano coaxed me through the waves of my orgasm, and I shuddered against his hand. I couldn't take any more, was past the edge—

His mouth was on me again, sucking and licking. Holy spirits, this was my *husband*? I sensed him shift and felt him groan against me a moment later, as he gripped himself rhythmically.

"Let go, Destry, come for me," he ordered, his voice coarse and low.

Light sparked in my blood and around my heaving torso, my second orgasm rippling over me in a tidal wave of all-consuming pleasure. Silvano groaned my name as he found his release, then he pulled back, breathing hard, and I looked across at him.

A smile of wicked delight spread across his face, as he wiped the back of his hand over his mouth, then he shifted up the bed. Pausing to pull my shift down over my thighs, he collapsed onto the coverlet beside me, his face flushed. Then he pulled me into his chest, wrapping his arms tightly around my back, tucking my head under his chin. Both breathless, we lay in silence while I tried to gather my scattered brain.

I swallowed as an emotion, one that was raw, visceral, and had me grasping on what on earth it *was*, clawed at my chest, pricking tears behind my ears. Inhaling deeply, soaking my lungs with his scent that now held the faintest drop of sweat and my arousal, I spoke into his panting chest.

"No one ... I've never ... no one has ever ..." Unable to find the words, my hands gently traced faint, obscure patterns on the bare skin of his chest.

He pressed a fervent kiss against my hair. "No one has ever made you come before?"

I shook my head. No, they hadn't. I had been finding my own release for years now, and I was no virgin, but the handful of men who I had taken to my bed, or had hurried encounters with in darkened corridors of Reckforton Castle, had never been able to make me climax. Part of me wondered if I should have faked it, to show them I was enjoying it just as much as they were, yet I couldn't bring myself to. Not that the men I'd slept with had even cared, rolling off me or stepping away as soon as they had found their release, hastily saying their goodbyes a moment later.

None of the men had done what Silvano just accomplished. A few had the foresight to at least try and get me ready with their fingers, but their touch had been rough, careless, sparking none of the gravity-altering pleasure like he had.

Silvano curled around me, his voice husken in my ear. "They won't be the last orgasms I give you, Destry, I promise."

That quickly, I was ready for him again, my touch turning braver as I ran my hands down the muscles of his abdomen. I froze when my stomach tried to imitate the call of a humpback whale. My body refused to let me forget that, despite being high on the ecstasy of two orgasms, I hadn't eaten yet.

Silvano's warm laughter filled the cozy cabin, and spirits, I wanted to hear that sound until my dying breath.

After a hearty breakfast of porridge, bacon, and eggs, we took care of the horses, feeding and cleaning their stables. Our little stoat companion had scurried about our feet, diving into hay bales and poking its tiny head amongst the cracks in the walls, happily hunting down a meal. I caved after a few minutes and laid out a small cut of raw beef on a large dessert spoon.

The creature had squeaked, then dove into its breakfast with glee. Silvano had chuckled, leaning on his pitchfork while he watched the little predator.

"She needs a name," he said softly.

"She does." I ran a forefinger down her neck after she finished eating, and she wove her flexible little white body over my hand, licking my thumb in thanks. "Minna had said a little *tyvare* had stolen a pair of her mittens." I chuckled as the stoat scrambled up my wrist to curl up in the crook of my arm. "Behold, a little thief."

"Hmmm, it suits her. She's mischief in a cute, but could bite your finger off, bundle."

Indeed, her razor-sharp teeth, so similar to those of a cat's but in miniature, had made quick work of her breakfast. Having settled her in the cabin, with a word to behave herself, we left Tyvare to her own, nefarious devices.

I was practically drunk on the notion that the entire day was ours alone. For now, there were no responsibilities, so we saddled up the two mares and rode out into the early morning light. Making our way through the snow, tainted a blush pink and dusky blue by the low-hanging sun, we carefully navigated toward one of the gently rising hills that skirted around the glen on which the *tallora* sat.

Fern was the most patient horse I'd ever met, and when we approached the base of the mild incline, Silvano urged Kirrtu into a canter, and I followed suit. The mare's canter was like being sat in the world's most comfortable rocking chair, but I was rusty, and she instinctively slowed her stride, allowing me to find the right balance in the saddle. Remembering to grip with my thighs and not my knees, I took up handfuls of her beautiful thick mane, let out the reins a fraction and let the mare fly.

The two Lake Horses bounded up the hill, and despite the ache in my heart where my love for Ebrel sat, I could still feel the joy of being free on the back of a horse. The powerful feeling of a half-ton beast moving fluidly beneath you, their billowing breath and churning hooves, made me feel like my soul, my very spirit, was free of the mortal constraints placed upon it.

An exhilarated smile lit up my face as I drew level with Silvano, and he matched me, the pair of us urging the mares up to the crest of the hill. Fit despite their size, the two horses raced one another, snow and stag moss flying in our wake. Slowing to a walk as we reached the top, the mares' breaths clouding around us, Silvano and I simply looked at one another, our faces flushed with happiness.

He looked so at home in the saddle, perfectly poised so that despite his height and brawn, he was in no way cumbersome for the horse that carried him. The breeze had tousled his hair off his devastating face, and *spirits*, it made me want him, the need in my core building to the point of being unbearable.

Drawing Fern to a halt, I dismounted and looped the reins over her head. A small frown on his face, Silvano did the same and walked to stand in front me, sweeping back a strand of hair that had pulled free of my braid. I felt enraptured by him and by the landscape that felt like home, freedom, and magic rolled into one.

Desire rippled through my blood, and I didn't care that we were utterly exposed on this hill. We were the only souls for miles around. My body felt as light as air, carefree and euphoric. Emerald green light wove about my head, the threads undulating with every beat of my wild heart.

I inched closer to Silvano, my gaze dipping from his eyes to his mouth, then I sank to my knees in the snow and removed my gloves. Surprise lit up Silvano's features, before turning to wanton desire, as I freed his hardening length from his trousers. Gripping the base of him, I let out a soft moan as I took him in my mouth. Silvano jerked against me, looping my braid over his gloved fist to hold me in place.

"Fucking *hell*, Destry," he hissed gutturally through gritted teeth.

He was perfect, his size bringing deep whines of need from my throat as I worked him with my hand, mouth, and tongue. I felt self-conscious, wondering if this was how he liked it. Was I going too fast? Too slow? But with every sound I wrung from him, every groan, whimper, and whispered "*fuck*," my confidence grew, his hand wrapped in my hair pulling tighter, which only increased my desire to do this for him. I wanted him as undone as he had made me earlier, wanted to claim his release.

Silvano panted hard, thrusting into my mouth. "I'm going to come, holy fuck, Destry, you're exquisite."

Wrapping my free hand behind his right thigh, I pulled him closer to me, and I felt the hard muscle there tense. He was close.

It was an addiction, I realized, being intimate with Silvano. It emptied my head of every worry and thought, forcing me to be present in my body, becoming sensitive and attuned to every movement and sound that he made.

With an aching groan, he came, and I enticed every last ounce from him, until he stepped back from me, breathless, his features wrecked from his pleasure as he readjusted his trousers. Hastily swallowing what he had spilled and wiping my mouth dry, Silvano hauled me to my feet and crushed my body against his. Claiming my mouth with his own, he gave me a punishing kiss, lips and teeth colliding, hands in each other's hair as we clung to one another.

Breath ragged, I pulled back, stepping up on my toes to press a tender kiss to his forehead. "I can't get enough of you, and I don't think I ever will," I whispered.

Gently taking my hand, he led me back to Fern. "I'm counting on it, wild one."

Grinning, I stepped up onto his outstretched joined hands and let him leg me up into the saddle. Passing me my discarded gloves, he placed a soft kiss to my knuckles, his gaze not leaving mine. My light wreathed around my fingers, caressing the plane of his jaw. He gave me a shrewd wink then mounted up onto Kirrtu. Walking steadily, side by side, we made our way down the hill, content and thankful to share each other's company, shielded from the world by the snow-capped glen.

Exhilarated, unable to wipe the slightly smug smile from my face, we settled the horses back into the stables. We had ended our ride through the small birch forest that cloaked the southern end of the glen, the branches gilded by ice that sparkled in the sun's rays as the horses walked past. Silvano had told me of his time in the Ilrairian cavalry, mostly stories of when he was a unit leader, and the missions he had been sent on. He appeared younger as he spoke, his face animated and happy as he regaled me with his tales.

The thought of Jaryn, of Ilrair inching closer to the north, was on the distant fringes of my mind, yet as I brushed down Fern and gently pulled the bridle from her head, the usual fear and despair didn't punch me in the gut. Watching Silvano deftly shake out the saddlecloths, looking so at home here, I had the sense that I could face anything, be anything, with him at my side. We had saved one another, fought for one another, and I would not let that ruthless snake take anything from me again. Not Silvano, not Amadea, or my freedom.

All that I was missing was Ebrel. I knew that she and Hestian would protect one another, that Ebrel would be more than comfortable surviving this far north. She was built for this wild sky and rugged terrain. I had certainly found freedom and solace on the back of a horse, but riding Ebrel was a whole world apart.

Storing the brushes away, I plucked the loose strands of hay from my riding skirt and stood by the back door, waiting for Silvano to finish giving Kirrtu her hay. It had just gone midday, and the sky had clouded over, bringing the promise of fresh snow. Despite being exposed in the heart of the glen, the wind remained calm, Ilmari content to give us a day's respite from bitter winter weather. Although the thought of being snowed in here, we had plentiful supplies of food for us and the horses, was extremely tempting.

Having set down his pitchfork, Silvano rolled up his shirtsleeves and washed his hands in the dented metal sink along the back wall. I couldn't help but watch the tendons in his forearms flex as he scrubbed his nails clean. After drying his hands, he looked up and across at me. I stilled at the expression on his face, lips parting as his gaze darkened. We stood for a moment, drinking each other in, then he was stalking toward me, his hips pinning mine to the rough stone wall at my back, his hand snatching out to brace the back of my head from the impact. His touch was sensuous, as his large hand clasped my chin, angling it up so he could press heated kisses along my exposed throat.

My fingers dug into the iron strength of his biceps while he whispered, "You consume me, wild one. I'll be content if we never leave this cabin."

Please, please, let there be a snowstorm, I prayed, my hands drifting to his shoulders when his mouth captured mine.

"But right now," he murmured against my flushed cheek. "I have a promise to keep."

Placing one last searing kiss on my lips, he dropped to one knee on the packed dirt floor. My mind reeling, he lifted up my riding skirt and yanked down my fleece-lined leggings and underwear. Hefting my right boot onto an empty storage crate, my balance became unsteady from my leggings around my ankles. Silvano rose slowly, his eyes on mine, until he towered over me, his left hand placed on the wall by my head.

I couldn't tear my gaze from him, as his right hand ran up the soft skin of my spread inner thigh, until those masterful fingers found my slick center that begged for him. Mouths millimeters apart, I panted against him, hand braced on his pectoral muscles as he circled my clit slowly. Tilting my head against the stone, I moaned, and Silvano leaned forward, consuming the sound as his mouth met mine. I tried to grind myself against those fingers, but he would always whisper away, a carnal taunt that left me whimpering.

Biting my lower lip, back bowed, my fingers dug into his shirt, clenching the soft material in desperation.

"So wet for me again, wild one, such a good girl," he whispered against my ear, his fingers sliding into me just a fraction.

I gasped at the sweet sensation. "*Please*, Silvano."

His soft chuckle scraped down my neck. "Begging already, my love?" He slid those fingers in further and edged out. "You don't know how happy it makes me, to know that I'm the first one to make you feel like this." Torturously, he picked up the pace, claiming me even deeper until his hand palmed me entirely, his thumb circling my clit. "The sound of my name on your lips, fuck, Destry, it will never be enough."

My entire world narrowed to his voice and his hands, his words coaxing levels of desire from me that I didn't know existed, like I was the only thing that mattered to him. His free hand drifted from the wall to the side of my head, his thumb caressing my cheek. I moaned, my entire core trembling while his fingers glided in and out.

When I whimpered, his forehead dropped to mine. "I know, I know," he soothed. "I've got you, wild one. Always."

His thumb applied more pressure, flicking back and forth until he had me sobbing in his arms, yielding fully to him. Sensing I was close, his free arm wrapped around my lower back, keeping me upright when my climax rocked through my body in an all-consuming wave. Hands trembling, I clung to him, gasping his name over and over.

Gently, he withdrew his hand, then lifted me, placing a tender kiss to my forehead as I curled into him. Carrying me into the cabin once more, he took me into the bathroom, and with the utmost care, helped me clean up. Lightheaded, I gazed at him in wonder, as snow began to gently fall beyond the small thick glass window.

CHAPTER THIRTY

DESTRY

S ilvano, apparently, loved to cook. Leaning my hip against the narrow kitchen counter, steaming mug of strong tea in my hands, I watched on, as he efficiently chopped an onion, garlic, then dried rosemary. The ground beef we had brought with us was added to a scalding hot pan. Tyvare nosed the air from where she sat on a pile of books by the sofa. Minna, it turned out, was a book hoarder, collecting a plethora of mythical, heated romances in teetering stacks all around the cabin.

"Who taught you to cook?" I asked, taking a sip of my tea.

"My mother taught me the basics before I enlisted. Turns out knowing how to make a half decent meal makes nearly everyone want to be your friend when you're out on deployment." He quirked me a small smile as he stirred the contents in the pan.

"Is she still alive?" I said tentatively.

His shoulders tightened under his black shirt. "She is, my father too. They live on an estate on the outskirts of Orman."

I clenched the handle of my mug and bit my lower lip. "Do ... do you miss them? What will they think when they discover"—I gestured to the *tallora*—"your dissension?"

He shifted the pan off the central heat of the wood stove and let it simmer gently. With his back turned to me, he cleaned away the skin of the onion. "I missed them when I was younger, but not in recent years. I've been away so much that they got used to me never being there, at the estate." Turning, he cleaned his hands in the small sink, then braced his lower back against the counter, facing me with an expression that I couldn't read. "News will get back to them, eventually, about what I have done. My lie about hunting down other dissenters will fall apart at some point, all it did was buy me some time."

I placed my mug down on the counter as he strode purposefully over to me, tucking a strand of hair behind my ear. The nauseating feeling that we were on borrowed time washed over my skin, and I swallowed harshly.

"Jaryn will be furious," I whispered.

His eyes were shadowed. "I've betrayed him, his pride will not be able to take it. Rekorious is right, he will come for me, you ... Amadea." Gently, he cupped my face between his hands. My light wreathed thread-thin strands around his fingers. "But I'll be ready, and we will fight. He has to be stopped."

I placed my right palm over his left. "Together, Silvano. We'll fight him together. But ... I'm sure it's not too late, if you wanted to go back." My voice cracked. "If you regret what's happened. Ilrair is your country, your family is there." I paused and took a deep breath. "When the time comes, will you fight your former comrades?"

He stiffened, his features laced with pain. "I have already fought Ilrairian soldiers, wild one, and I don't regret it."

"That was Knock Platoon, there has always been animosity between you. But what about Bromtide? There will come a time when you have to go against them, against your former unit members."

His hands lowered, then he leaned against the wall, gazing down at the worn stone floor at our feet. "I know," he murmured. Resignation making his muscled shoulders fall. "I want them to fight alongside us. A good number of them can see the injustices Jaryn has caused."

"They will get a new Commander, right? When they find out what happened to you?" I whispered, inching closer to him to cup his stubbled cheek.

Guilt gnawed at me, despite everything he confessed in his jail cell, words that I knew in my bones and by my ice magic to be true, I couldn't help but feel his entire life was on the precipice of being torn apart. Lael had confessed that the Royant Platoon had laid the groundwork for Ilrair to be governed solely by the senate should Jaryn fall, but we had a long, perilous way to go before then.

Then there was the matter of the lead jewelry Jaryn had in his arsenal. If Amadea or I were caught by them, our lives would likely be forfeited if we tried to escape them. I shuddered at the thought, and the memory of the ancient, carved door in the palace with the Trinitor upon it, sealed shut for centuries by lead.

A muscle in Silvano's jaw ticked, but he leaned into my touch. "It's likely they have installed a new Commander already. I've been gone for too long. Rekorious will have come to the same conclusion." He grasped my hand in his and kissed my uptilted palm. "But the loss of the Royant Platoon and Amadea will have weakened Jaryn. With the sea ice still intact, he can't sail for Petowin or Colladon. He'd barely make it past the coast of the moorlands with his ships intact."

"So he's waiting for late spring?"

Silvano nodded, his gaze searching mine.

"That's a good three months away, at least. Which gives him time to shore up his front line north of the Anduns ... what if ... what if we take the fight to him? Take care of Jaryn before he can press any further north?"

"I'm not risking you getting anywhere near that palace, Destry. Not a chance."

I ploughed ahead. "You, me, Rekorious, and Amadea. All four of us can take care of that monster."

"We most definitely could, if given the chance. But that's a massive risk. Even if we did infiltrate his personal quarters, if things go wrong, Jaryn will have us all served on a platter." He pulled back and gazed down at me, those emerald eyes dark. "The council that Rekorious answers to will not let their lord venture into enemy territory, and they do not trust me enough to sneak you and Amadea in and back out, with our lives intact." I rolled my lower lip through my teeth, noting how Silvano tracked the movement. "If I suspect Rekorious and Amadea still feel what they did for each other, there is no chance in hell he's letting her near Jaryn either."

I leaned forward, pressing my head to his muscled chest, and wrapped my arms around his waist. Those strong arms pulled me in closer, his chin dropping to rest on my hair.

We were silent for a moment, and I let the sound of his steady heart echo in my body. "You pulled Amadea out, after Jaryn had her whipped?"

He swallowed, but his voice was still rough. "I did."

Keeping my arms locked around him, I pulled back and looked up at him while his hand ran up and down my spine. "Why did you save him, Silvano?"

Closing his eyes, he breathed deeply. "It was my last act as his friend. I hoped ... in some twisted way, that if it ever came down to it, he would owe me a life debt in return."

His eyes opened, and they watched me carefully, waiting for my judgement. "You let him go, in the hope that if your life was on the line later, he would let you live?"

The muscles of his back shifted against my palms. "Not my life, wild one."

He fell silent, letting his words sink down into the depths of my soul. I stared at him, lips parting while it felt like my heart was turning over in my chest. "It won't come to that," I whispered.

"Not if I can help it," he murmured, pulling me close to his chest once more. He held me tightly while I prayed and prayed to the spirits, my gaze resting on *Kathkar* hanging on the bedpost, that he would never have to call in the debt.

After cleaning myself up that evening and having changed the bandage on my thigh, I stood just behind the bathroom door in my shift, feet bare on the chill floor, wondering if I really was as brave as I thought I was.

Maybe I was, actually, a coward for hesitating like this. The same nerves that had coiled around my body last night were back, leaving my skin prickling in their wake. I had stalled for long enough in the bathroom. I just had to walk back into the cabin before my toes froze.

It was ridiculous. I had seen him naked, and I had pretty much bared everything to him. He had given me three leg-shaking orgasms. Why did tonight feel different? Maybe because I had fallen asleep on our wedding night ... making *this* our actual wedding night? Surely he felt that too? The fact we hadn't consummated anything yet?

Blowing out a breath, I ran a hand through my loose hair, opened the bathroom door, and walked into the cabin's toasty warmth.

I found him reclining against the headboard of the bed, one of Minna's books propped up against his bent knees. He wore his black, soft sleep pants, but like last night, his chest was bare. He gestured to the book in his lap and arched a cunning brow at me.

"I could learn a thing or two from the men in these romance books."

I laughed but hovered by the door. "Is that so? Hoping to master some new tricks?"

Silvano set the book down beside him and pinned me with his gaze. "Only one way to master them ... practice."

My breathing turned shallow.

He quirked his head to the side, eyes narrowing. "Are you okay?"

I wrung my hands over my abdomen. "Never better."

"Destry." He swung his legs off the bed in a slow, considered motion, then braced his forearms against his thighs and steepled his fingers. "What's wrong?"

"Nothing," I rushed, heat flaming my cheeks.

He looked down at his hands and chuckled. Then he was moving, walking over to me with predatory grace. His right hand rose to brush a thumb over my reddening face. "I've never seen you flustered before."

Another laugh rose from his throat as I glared at him. "I'm not flustered."

"I like it," he whispered in my ear as he ran a knuckle over my jaw. "But ... as much as I would love to keep tormenting you right now, something is bothering you. Tell me."

His voice was a deep growl next to my ear, and my heart thundered in my chest while my thighs pressed together. Leaning back against the door, I stared up at him and watched the firelight play against the strong planes of his face.

"Does it not bother you that ... that we haven't—" My bare foot tapped the stone floor, and I quickly looked away, then back at those captivating eyes. "That we haven't consummated anything yet?"

His low laughter brushed against my collarbone. "I'm sure the council would fall into a tittering mess if they knew, but they don't matter. You, however ..." He brushed the hair off my face and inched closer, our hips nearly touching. "Are the most important thing. I wanted you to feel ready. I know tradition dictates we should have slept together last night, but I refuse to pressure you into this." I leaned into his touch as his hand cupped my jaw, his thumb gently tracing the curve of my lower lip. "I'm yours, Destry, and I'll wait for as long as I need to."

"And I'm yours," I whispered. My hands clasped together behind his neck, my fingers grazing the length of his dark blonde hair.

Those hips finally connected against me, as he pushed my back flush against the bathroom door, his lips capturing mine in a kiss so tender, it threatened to consume every part of me. He pulled away and gently gripped my chin. "When you took me in your mouth today, fuck, Destry, I've never felt anything like it. It took all my resolve not to just take you there in the snow."

Leaning forward, my breasts grazing his chest, he gently bit the lobe of my ear, the whisper of his breath sending another shudder down my spine. My head rolled back, eyes closing as he placed tantalizing kisses along my jaw and exposed neck.

"But you weren't ready for me then," he said, a throaty noise in his chest as his mouth found mine.

"I wouldn't be so sure about that now," I panted against his lips. My breasts ached, the apex of my thighs demanding attention. I parted my legs slightly, and he nestled in closer, the thickness of him nudging at my lower abdomen through the thin fabric of our clothes. The hand that had been clasping my hip drifted down my thigh, and he hiked my left leg up. Reacting on instinct, every fiber of my being needing to be closer to him, I wrapped my calf around his waist. My dress rose, baring myself to him, and he shifted, angling his hips so that the head of his cock pressed perfectly against me. I sent a silent, thankful prayer to the moments of bravery I had felt before leaving the bathroom, when I had forgone my underwear in the hope that this would happen. That he would have me hot, wet, and aching for him. And by the spirits, he did.

My world stilled as he nudged at me through his pants, his free hand splaying along my lower back to steady me.

His voice was a torturous purr. "No, my love, you're not ready for me yet."

I whimpered, hips bucking in an attempt to grind against him, but he edged back, a wicked smile on his face.

"Please."

He thrust against me, the sudden, sweet friction tearing a gasp from my throat.

"As much as I love to hear that word on your lips, I won't make you beg, Destry. Not yet." Slowly, as if it pained him to let go, he released my leg and stepped back. The sudden draft of cooler air against my skin was agonizing. Holding my gaze, he said roughly, "Take off your dress, let me see you."

I didn't feel an ounce of shame or fear, only red-hot desire that coaxed me to burn even brighter. The light in my veins felt electrified, like a storm gathering momentum. My hands clasped the hem of my shift, and I slowly, because, hell, I wanted to torture him a little too, lifted it up and over my head. I discarded it in a heap by my feet and took a deep, quivering breath.

Silvano's gaze darkened, his Adam's apple sliding up and down his throat as he ran his gaze all over my bare body. My neck arched, and I leaned back against the door once more, the cold bite of the wood making my nipples peak. With the way he looked at me, I didn't care about the scar on my arm.

"You're perfect, in every damn way." He shook his head in disbelief. "I'll never get tired of seeing you like this." Raising his right hand, he grazed his pointer finger down my throat, between my breasts and over my abdomen. "So fucking beautiful," he said hoarsely.

I closed my eyes, my body utterly focused on that single point of contact. Then he sank to his knees. Breath rushing from my lungs, eyes snapping open, I had a second to orient myself before Silvano swung my left thigh over his muscled shoulder, then his mouth was on me.

A deep moan wrung itself from my throat, as Silvano licked and sucked at my clit. My hands dove for his hair, threading my fingers through the thick strands of it while my nails gently dug into his scalp in desperation. He groaned in appreciation, as he slid two fingers along my soaked center. I was ready now, more than ready, but he didn't stop. Those fingers teased over my throbbing skin, denying me over and over.

My hips bucked and back arched, whispered pleas tumbling from my mouth. Silvano just rubbed his fingers back and forth slowly, his tongue never leaving the bundle of nerves between my legs.

I cried out to the spirits, my chest heaving for breath at the exquisite sensations barreling through my body. Then, finally, just as I started to contemplate mutiny, he slowly slid those two fingers in. The cabin was a hazy blur as I glanced down at the man kneeling before me, his head buried between my legs. I nearly climaxed just at the sight of it. Sensing me move, Silvano tipped back his head, not stopping his fingers that leisurely pumped into me, and looked up, a pure male smirk on his face.

Eyes locked on mine, he gently nipped my thigh that was strewn over his shoulder. "Tell me, Destry, do you think you're ready for me yet?"

My hands tugged at his hair. "*Yes.*"

He hummed in thought, his fingers curling against that delicious spot inside me, and I quivered against him, not able to look away. I could feel my release slowly building, it was just out of reach, and my fucking husband knew it.

"Hmmm, I think I have to disagree with you, wild one." His thumb circled against my clit, and I bucked at the pressure. It was world-moving for me, to let him take control like this. I had never trusted anyone enough to hand over the reins, to let someone orchestrate the sensations coursing through my body. It shattered and reforged my soul with how freeing it felt.

"Silvano," I breathed. My eyes fluttered closed as his thumb flicked against my clit once, twice, three times, my back bowing in response. I was going—holy *fuck*, I—

Then he withdrew his hand. My soft whimper of protest was muffled as he claimed my mouth with his. He invaded my every sense with his heat and strength, those talented hands exploring and caressing every inch of bare body.

I was done being teased. My hand moved down the slim space between our bodies, and his throaty moan alighted my core when I delved into his pants and fisted his rigid length. His arms barricaded my head as he placed his palms against the door. Burying his head against my neck, he thrust into my grip as I slowly fisted it up and down, smearing my thumb over the broad head.

His moans sunk into my skin as he released a drawn out, tortured, "*Fuck*."

My free hand moved to his lower back, marveling at the bunching of the muscles there as he moved against me.

"I don't think *you're* ready yet," I crooned into his ear, and he twitched in my grasp.

"I'm always fucking ready for you, you're all I think about." He tried to quicken the pace, but I kept it slow. Then I felt him smile against my neck. "The thought of sinking my cock into you, having you scream my name, has driven me crazy for weeks."

And despite how my hand worked him, it weakened my knees to know that he was still in control. He was able to make me desperate for him without even touching me.

"Have you thought about it too, my beautiful wife? Have you thought about what it would feel like, to have me fuck you?" His teeth grazed the hammering pulse in my neck.

I was becoming undone at his words. Of course, I had thought about it. I had daydreamed about how he would feel moving inside me. His back shifted, and he gently bit down on the sweet spot between my neck and shoulder. I arched into him, my head tilting to the side to grant him better access. We moaned in unison as I squeezed the base of his cock, then dragged my hand back up.

"Is that what you want?" he panted, his mouth hovering over mine. "Is it what you *need*?"

I nodded, eyes closed. His fingers found my chin, tilting my head back so that I looked directly into his eyes. "I need to hear you say it, Destry."

"Yes," I said, my voice breathy. "I want you, Silvano."

Whatever control he had placed on himself, snapped. His gentle grip on my wrist had me releasing him, then he lifted me, his arms banding against my back as my legs wrapped around his waist. He turned us and took the three steps to the bed. With the utmost care, he settled me down on the covers, his dark gaze filled with desire as I lay under him. He stood, stripped off his pants, his cock finally springing free.

My lungs clawed for breath at the sight of him. Shifting onto my elbows, I moved back further onto the bed, and he followed me, his gaze locked onto mine as he sank to his knees between my legs. He leaned down, stretching out his glorious body, bearing his weight on his forearms on either side of my head. Bracing his powerful right thigh against my knee, he spread my legs wider and inched closer.

His cock nudged against me, and I lifted my hips in response. My hands trailed down his back, caressing the intricate expanse of muscles that flexed under my touch. He brought his right hand closer to cup my cheek, then he kissed me, a sweet, heartfelt kiss that nearly brought me to tears.

"I can't believe you're mine," he whispered, his gaze searching my face.

I smiled up at him, my palm resting on the back of his neck. "And I'm yours, Silvano. I have always been yours." My back arched, and his cock slid against my soaking wet center. He shuddered, his jaw clenching. "I want you to claim me," I whispered. "With every inch of you."

Gritting his teeth, Silvano gently rested his forehead against mine and re-angled his hips. His hand clasped my own, fingers twining, and he lifted it above my head, right as the tip of his cock pushed inside me. We moaned together. I swallowed, eyes closing as he edged in even deeper, then stilled.

My right leg lifted, hooking around his waist in an effort to draw him in, and with a guttural groan, he obliged. He squeezed my hand, the muscles of his arms bunching as he thrust again. He was perfect, my body feeling like it was burning for him. He whispered my name as he slid in that last inch, the girth of him feeling so exquisite, I knew I would never get enough of this, us.

Silvano pulled back to look down at me, then to where our bodies were joined in the most intimate of ways. Slowly, he edged out, then sunk back in, and I gasped, my chest tightening at the pleasure that rolled up my spine.

"You take me so fucking well, Destry," he growled against my mouth, gently biting my lower lip. He kept the pace slow, letting my body adjust to him. His cocked gleamed as he pulled out halfway, then thrust again.

My right hand threaded into his hair. I started to meet his thrusts, hips lifting, I needed more, my body near trembling. Releasing my hand, he gripped my thigh, spreading me wider. We kissed, and it was no longer tender. Our tongues clashed, teeth clinking together as that final thread of restraint between us shattered.

"There's no one around for miles, wild one," Silvano murmured as he palmed my breast. "So let go for me."

I arched into him, gasping his name, my body compliant to his every word, to every plunge of his cock into me. He quickened the pace, every stroke of him hitting that perfect spot that had my release building. I clung to his body, my hands braced around his neck and bicep.

"You feel amazing," I whimpered against his throat, a light sheen of sweat covering our bodies. The sensation of his bare skin against mine made my heart swell. He was claiming not just my body, but my heart and soul as well. The feeling was overwhelming, and tears pricked at the back of my eyes with just how perfect he felt.

Yet I knew it wasn't just that. I was safe, protected, cherished. Silvano had me. He understood the deepest parts of my soul. Had saved me when no one else had. A tear rolled down the side of my face, and Silvano slowed with a torturous roll of his hips.

"Are you okay?" he uttered, wiping the tear away with his thumb. "Do you need me to stop?"

I shook my head, words beyond me for a moment.

"Destry, look at me."

Blinking back tears, I looked up at him, our faces inches apart. "Please don't stop," I said, my voice hoarse. "This, us ... I—Silvano. What I feel ..." I swallowed, my throat burning. "It's all-consuming."

A perfect smile lit up his handsome face, and he lowered his mouth to press a kiss to my forehead. "I know, I feel it too," he murmured as he ran a hand over my hair, his gaze searching my face. "I've got you, okay?"

I nodded, trusting him wholly. "Don't stop," I said softly.

He shifted inside me, carefully watching my reaction. I moaned and lifted my hips to meet him. "I meant it when I said let go, Destry. I want you undone. I want to know what it feels like to be buried inside you when you come."

And so I did. Perfectly in sync, our bodies moved together, our gasping breaths mingling as we held onto one another. My cries and Silvano's deep moans echoed through the cabin, then became lost in the thick snowfall of the night beyond. The sweet fullness of him stoked my pleasure higher and higher, then he reached down between our bodies and worked my clit.

My climax rushed up my spine, my toes curling with the buck of my hips. Silvano buried himself deep inside me, groaning against my neck as I clenched around his rigid cock. I trembled with the aftershocks while my lungs heaved for breath. *Holy fucking spirits.*

Legs quaking, I had just enough coherence to register Silvano slowly pulling out of me.

"What," was all I managed to choke out, before his hands gripped my hips and he flipped me onto my front. Bracing himself on his hands, he arched low over me and grasped the curve of my upturned ear between his teeth.

"You," he whispered, as he spread my thighs apart with his knees. "Are so fucking perfect." His right hand dipped to firmly grasp my hip, lifting me to meet him as he plunged back in. I moaned into the covers in response. After running his free hand through my hair, he followed the curve of my spine, and I couldn't help but push back against him, the angle of his cock deeper than before.

He leaned down against me, his muscled abdomen brushing against my arched back. "Do you want me to come inside you?"

"Yes," I pleaded. My hands fisted the sheets in desperation. He straightened and gripped my hips with both hands. His thrusts were faster now, possessing every inch of me, and I yielded to it, another release was so fucking close.

"Are you going to come for me again?" he uttered, edging me closer and closer to the peak. Releasing a hand from my hip, he reached down and hauled me back against his chest. Angling my head, he captured my mouth with his and thrust upward.

I writhed against him, and he held me in place, his grip firm but gentle on my body.

"Come for me, Destry," he coaxed, his hand splayed over my stomach.

With my name on his lips, my second orgasm rippled through my body, and my head fell back against his chest. Palming my breast, teeth grazing my shoulder, Silvano drove into me. With my core pulsing around him, he shuddered, the muscles of his abdomen tensing against my lower back as he found his own release.

I would never get enough of the sounds he made, the low, throaty moans of pleasure that mixed with every twitch of his cock as he spilled himself inside me. Panting hard, Silvano held me close, placing tender kisses along my throat.

"That was ..." he said between deep breaths.

My legs were trembling hard, and I knew I wouldn't be upright if it wasn't for Silvano holding onto me.

"Everything I've ever dreamed of," I whispered, my voice wrecked.

He kissed my shoulder then slowly pulled out of me, leaving a sweet, addictive ache in his wake. Lowering myself to the mattress, I half collapsed onto my side, trying to regain control of my breathing as I lay down in a haze of sated bliss. Silvano smiled down at me, seeming to know exactly what I needed, as he lay down beside me, one arm curled under his head, the other looping around my lower back to draw me in close.

Dazed and completely spent, we gazed at each other in the half-light of the cabin. Seeing the goose bumps on my skin, Silvano reached down and pulled the coverlet over us. I nestled into his chest, basking in the heat that radiated off him.

He pressed a kiss to my hair. "My wife," he murmured. "My heart belongs to you."

Joy sparked deep in my chest. I brushed a chaste kiss to his throat. "And mine to you."

CHAPTER
THIRTY-ONE

EBREL

Shrouded by pine trees topped by heavy snow, Hestian and I clung to the faint shadows cast by the half-moon. It was somewhere close to midnight, and a million stars flickered in the sky above Fort Vervelli. The stone and wood structure sat atop a huge mound of earth, a deep, dry moat surrounding it on all sides. Another, wider rough square formed an extra continuous hill several meters out from the fort, the perfect trap for the archers stationed at each wooden turret.

I inhaled deeply, my gaze running over the strange formations made from the ground. My feathers bristled with the knowledge that this place, beyond Mount Ghel, had been something else, something important, long before a fort was built atop it.

The last small unit of Bromtide Pegasi and their riders had landed an hour ago, and the next watch had just taken up their shift on the palisades. The Ilrair flag hung limp and lifeless from the post above the northern turret, the storm cloud of Bromtide beneath it.

"Any minute now," whispered Hestian, his gaze focused on the wall closest to us.

Inching nearer to him, shoulders brushing, I watched as intently as he did.

There was the sound of hoofbeats, leather shifting over furs and the rustle of papers, then a dark gray, almost black, Pegasus stallion and his rider took flight from the central square. Wingbeats steady and strong, the pair rose over the walls spiked with iron and turned to head south.

Staying hidden within the trees, Hestian called out, *"Nimbus!"*

The gray stallion halted midair, nearly sending his neck colliding with his rider's face. Wings pummeling, he looked down at the trees beneath him. *"Hestian? Where the hell are you, brother?"*

"Hidden. I can't afford to reveal myself to Tamara."

His rider was now also looking around, gently squeezing with her calves to get her mount to fly on. "Come on, Nimbus, we don't have time for this," she said softly.

"And why is that?" purred the gray. *"Does it have anything to do with the fact you and your rider have simply vanished? There's rumors you've dissented, although nothing has been formally announced."*

Hestian bristled, his gold and brown eyes wholly focused on the pair. *"I need you to send a message to all the Pegasi, everyone that you see."*

"Lucky for you, sending messages is my job." Nimbus swooped, ignoring the tugging on his reins and began to circle wide around the trees. His voice deepened, brushing against my mind like velvet. *"What's wrong?"*

"Nimbus, for the lady's sake, quit messing around," pleaded Tamara from the saddle.

"The curse will be broken. I need the Pegasi to resist when it does, to become warriors in their own right."

Nimbus snarled as he shot overhead, flying directly over our hiding place. *"They are dangerous words, even for you, Hestian. You were always one to push the boundaries, but this goes too far. You know what happens to Pegasi that break the rules."*

Hestian ploughed ahead. *"I'll need help infiltrating the palace when the time comes. Can I rely on you?"*

Shaking his bridled head, Nimbus circled again. Tamara, her dark blonde hair streaming behind her from beneath her felt hat, suddenly turned her attention from her mount, down to the trees. "What's out there, Nimbus? Do you see something?"

"You can always rely on me, brother, but I warn you. If this all goes to hell, you'll be the first one to pay the price for it."

"I'll let you know when we're ready, then meet me at the usual spot."

"No longer in charge but still giving orders, huh, Hestian?"

"Speaking of being in charge, who's in command now?" Hestian lashed his tail, the only sign of annoyance he let show, as his voice remained calm and collected.

"You haven't heard yet? My, my, you have immersed yourself into the wilds, haven't you?"

"Tell. Me. Nimbus."

The stallion turned off his looping circle and straightened to head south. Tamara ran a hand down his neck, throwing the trees one last quizzical look.

"Taneli Farrow commands Bromtide now, and have a guess at what or should I say who he's hunting for?"

Hestian went rigid beside me, maw opening in silent rage.

"Better fly far and fly fast, Hestian, and take that pretty little roan with you." Nimbus cast one last look over his shoulder, then dove into the starlit night.

I blinked, then stepped back to look at Hestian, shocked by the animosity that roiled in every inch of him. His gaze was still cast skyward, muzzle tight and wings half arched.

"Who is Taneli Farrow?"

Taking a deep breath, Hestian closed his eyes. *"He was a spy in Bromtide for years, a sergeant, secretly feeding Rekorious information while he commanded the Royants. Farrow is the reason Destry was nearly killed in Ilrair. Seems like he's switched sides entirely in an effort to save his worthless hide."*

Concern lit his gaze, and I nosed his muzzle gently. *"He's hunting for you and Silvano?"*

"Ebrel, he knows exactly *where the keep is. He told Silvano how to find it."*

Dread coiled its icy grip around my heart. *"We need to leave, now."*

CHAPTER
THIRTY-TWO

ASHER

The dark sheltered us as we walked through the still forest. Creatures of the night knew to give me and my shadows a wide berth, and we came across no trouble. We kept our voices to a hushed whisper and only spoke when we absolutely needed to. The constant motion kept us warm at least.

Calliope moved differently in the dark, her stride purposeful, eyes wide and alert as she kept pace with me. She seemed ... alive. Like she was built and honed to be weaving through the dark, a golden shadow in her own right.

I halted and waited for her to draw up alongside me. "Do you miss it?" I whispered. "Your owl form?"

She gave me a small, sad smile. "Every minute of every day." Then she cast her gaze around the trees circling us, lingering on the shadows that drifted close and far. "But being up at this hour helps."

We walked on, staying side by side now as she mirrored my path through the forest.

"It's funny how quiet it is when you're around," she murmured with a soft chuckle.

"What do you mean?"

"Normally, the creatures in the forest make such a racket whether it's night or day, but with you here, everything is too scared to come out."

"They know when there is a monster around. I'm sorry."

"Don't be, I'm quite enjoying the peace and quiet for once."

It was my turn to laugh, and I instinctively reached for her hand. My brain caught up with my body the moment before my fingers touched hers, and I froze. Curling my hand into a fist and grinding my teeth, I pulled away. Calliope tracked me as I put some distance between us, taking in the fraught air that now surrounded me. Had she noticed I had nearly tried to hold her hand? I had led her out of that scout camp with her hand tightly in mine, clinging to her as much as she had clung to me, but that had been different. Hadn't it? Her in a daze of spent adrenaline and panic, me in a trembling rage at what the soldiers had tried to do to her.

But this? The pair of us at ease, hell, *laughing*. What did I think gave me the right, that it was okay to touch her?

Her gaze locked with mine, an unspoken question on her shadowed face. *Fuck*, she had noticed. Calling myself a fool, I started to walk again, wishing I had snowshoes with me to make this trek easier. Or even better, Pherox to just whisk me away.

"Wait," she said softly.

Closing my eyes, I halted, then looked over my shoulder, eyebrow arched.

She stepped after me, until I could feel her heat against my side. "You're not a monster, Asher."

Silently, I willed a shadow to arch upward and gently brushed her cheek. Those golden eyes burned into me, and I wished, *I wished*, it was my hand touching her, not my shadows. "I am."

Calliope shook her head. "I've seen true monsters, and you are not one of them." She glanced around at my shadows that pressed in closer, hanging onto her every word. Slowly, she bridged the gap between us and gently took my hand in hers, threading our fingers together. "Lead the way, huntsman."

I blinked, savoring the feeling over her skin against mine. Giving her a conspiratory smile, I gave her fingers a soft squeeze, reveling in every second I had with her. Knowing that, all too soon, she would fly free from me forever.

The sky had begun to take on the muted, pale pink of a nearing dawn, and I tasked my shadows to find somewhere to spend the day. They returned a few moments later, showing me another squat cave that would be impossible to stand in, but would do well to shelter us. Maybe even risk a fire.

Starting to climb several large, moss and snow-ridden boulders, I hoisted Calliope up onto them, my grip firm but gentle around her waist. She reached down for me, hand outspread to help me up, not that I needed it, but I froze, gaze distant as another group of shadows whirled back to me and orbited frantically around my head.

Calliope stilled, her hand still reaching for me. "What's wrong?"

Another scouts' camp lay two miles to the north of us, its soldiers and Pegasi nowhere in sight. Strewn inside one tent, as if the unit had left in a hurry, were maps. My jaw clenched, I was too far away to turn my shadows corporeal and fetch the maps. I'd need to get closer.

I relayed the information to Calliope. She slid down the frozen boulder to join me on the forest floor, my hand reaching out to grasp her elbow and steady her.

"I'm coming with you."

It wasn't a request, and I couldn't help but give her a smile. "Is that right?" The glare she threw me was one that was so unimpressed, she couldn't have looked more owl-like if she tried. "Of course you're coming with me, I can't protect you at that distance."

She nodded, her features softening, and we half ran through the snow to the camp. Breathing hard, Calliope slunk after me as we circled the perimeter, noting the still smouldering fire.

"They've not been gone long," I whispered, my body taut with tension as I walked into the camp, my gaze drifting from tent to tent. There were five again, like the last unit.

Calliope drifted away from me, brushing back the first tent's opening. The canvas crinkled loudly as she took in the mussed bedroll and spare clothes. "For soldiers, they're messy."

"You can afford to be when your superiors aren't watching," I muttered as I searched the next tent.

"Asher," whispered Calliope, as she dropped to one knee in the slush, keeping the tent open for me to peer inside.

A large map lay spread over a neat bedroll. The entirety of the northern Boreals was depicted, including all three coasts and the outlying islands. My gaze snapped to our location within the western Colladonian forests, then trailed left to take in the widespread glens and fells of Petowin. Marked in blue ink and scattered at random throughout were small triangular shapes. Most sat next to the banks of streams and rivers, others in the heart of a few forests.

"What are they?" said Calliope, tilting her head to take in the map.

My hand whispered over the parchment, noting the long line of mountains beyond the glens that cut across the map from north to south. "They're *talloras*. Little cone-shaped cabins." Several red crosses had been inked next to the majority of the triangles. "They're looking for someone. Each red cross means they came up empty."

"Do the Petish even use them anymore?"

My gaze narrowed, reading the name of the keep tucked atop the ridgeline. "Since the Nijinxes left, I assume so." I tapped the keep with a forefinger. "Does the name *Krakanarr* mean anything to you?"

Calliope froze. "My power knows that place. That's where we ... you need to go." My shoulders tensed, her words cutting deep. Avoiding my gaze, Calliope stared at one of the *talloras*, her eyes widening. "We'll be too late."

"What?"

She pointed to a bend in the Niemi River and the *tallora* not far from it. "He's there, they're both there."

"*Both*?"

"The scion, she's there too."

CHAPTER THIRTY-THREE

DESTRY

Something clamped down my nose, *hard*, with four tiny pricks of sharp pain. My eyes snapped open, but they were hazy with sleep, and all I could see was a blur of white. Hand snatching out, my fingers connected with a soft little body that would not let go of my nose.

"*Tyvare*," I hissed, the tiny stoat finally coming into focus. Gripping her body gently, I sat up in bed, and she finally let go. Blinking, I cupped her with both hands and frowned. She was trembling.

Slowly, I cast my gaze around the near-dark cabin, what little light there was coming through the small, diamond-shaped window in the front door. The skin on the back of my neck prickled, and Tyvare nosed my palms, her fur standing on end.

"*Silvano*." I doubted he would have heard me, but instinct told me to be as quiet as possible. My light banked into the depths of my soul, safely hidden away, but the ice magic stirred, cracking and groaning in my mind.

The muscles on Silvano's bare back shifted, he blinked once up at me, twice, then he slowly, carefully, sat up, instantly reading every nook of the cabin like I had done. His dark gaze took in Tyvare's shaking, then it slid to the front door.

"Something's wrong," I said in a hushed voice, and Tyvare gave a tiny squeak of agreement.

Through the door to the stables came the sounds of the two Lake Horses shifting through the straw, a low whicker shared between them.

"Someone's here, and I don't think they're friendly." Silvano moved from the bed and yanked on his clothing, then his rider's coat, throwing mine to me a moment later. I quickly got dressed then slipped into my boots. Tucking Tyvare under the downy covers, I gave her head a reassuring pat, before creeping on silent feet to where our swords hung on the bedpost. Silvano was beside me in an instant, and we donned our blades.

Gesturing for me to stay put beside the door to the stables, Silvano ducked along the curved wall to peer carefully out of the diamond window. Its lower half was dusted with snow, but it gave a fairly clear view outdoors. With the cabin pitched in near darkness, and the sun rising outside, it allowed Silvano to see whatever was out there far more easily than anyone trying to look in.

Watching him carefully, I tensed as his features turned into a livid glare, a hushed curse on his breath. "An Ilrairian scouting party just landed. Five Pegasi and their riders," he whispered. He swallowed harshly, and his left hand rested on the hilt of his curved sword. "Adonitus Unit, they're a part of Bromtide."

"*Bromtide*?" I half choked on the word.

Silvano's voice had turned into a snarl. "And I can't make out their faces. If it's a unit I know well, I may be able to talk them down, but I won't risk just walking out the front door."

Both the front door and the door to the stables were locked, but it left the Lake Horses defenseless and a chance for us to be trapped and possibly roasted alive if they decided to torch the *tallora*. "The stables."

Silvano didn't doubt me for a second. He scooped up his daggers, tucking one into my sword belt, plucked Tyvare from the bed, then heaved on his boots. As silently as we could, we unlocked the door to the stables and ducked inside, neatly closing the door behind us.

I quickly haltered Fern and Kirrtu and threw the lead ropes over their necks, knotting them into loops to form makeshift reins. We wouldn't have time to saddle them properly if this all went to hell. Silvano tucked Tyvare onto a straw bale, and the stoat dove between the strands to hide. Tiny drops of blood dripped off my nose, and I brushed them away with the sleeve of my coat. If we survived this, I made a mental note to serve her a steak in thanks.

"They don't know that I'm with you, but they may guess it when they see the two horses. Stay hidden till then." Silvano ducked behind the stable door.

I mirrored him, hiding behind a stack of storage crates on the other side of the doorframe. Then, not wanting to give them any advantage whatsoever, I grabbed the pitchfork and leaned it against the wall behind me.

I closed my eyes and dove into myself, running a careful, tentative hand down the well of ice in my chest. I hadn't dared to touch it or use it after nearly killing myself with it. It had slumbered contentedly, only the occasional pop or snap of fresh tendrils growing sounding in my head. But here, now, outnumbered and possibly trapped, I would risk it again. Releasing a cool breath, frost coated my fingernails.

We sipped for air as we waited. The seconds slid by, then came the earth-shattering crash of the front door being caved in. Tyvare had bought us the fragile minutes we had needed to get the hell out of bed. I winced, we hadn't broken Minna's bed, but we owed her a new door at least. Muffled female and male voices filtered to us, and Fern shifted in her stable, her black ears pricked toward the commotion.

"... sure you saw smoke?"

"Not fucking blind ..."

"The stove is still hot," said a rich, male voice.

"... be anyone ..." replied a female cautiously.

Silvano caught my eye and pointed to his chest. *Me first*. Then he proffered his hand in a sweeping gesture. *Then your turn, my lady*. I couldn't help but throw him a feral grin. Spirits help whoever was trying to find us. They had scared Tyvare and *ruined my honeymoon*.

Kathkar keened softly as I withdrew it from its scabbard, the blade feeling so utterly right in my two-handed grasp. The ice on my hands joined with the power slumbering in the sword, and I suddenly felt like a missing piece of me was finally home, forging with my very blood, bone, and breath. One day, I would do this sword justice, but for now, I would have to rely on every ounce of training Silvano and Rekorious had taught me.

The lock on the stable door scraped back, and I tensed, adjusting my stance. I let my power seep down my legs, through my feet and into the chilled floor. My light thrummed against my body, pacing back and forth like a mountain lion waiting to be unleashed.

Slowly, the door opened, and the soft shine of a sword appeared in the doorway, followed by the male unit leader who held it. Peering through the gap between two crates, I noted how he wasn't much younger than me, maybe early twenties? Was that what Silvano had been like? Keen to seek out the danger and going in first? With close cropped, light brown hair and matching stubble, his light green gaze quickly took in the room, his body stilling within the protection of the doorway. Eyes lingering on the two haltered horses, he didn't look away as he whispered over his shoulder, "Beretta, Martelli, go outside and guard the outer stable door."

Muted footsteps sounded in the cabin, then sifted through fresh snow, leaving us with three soldiers inside. His swords still in their scabbards, Silvano stepped slowly out from the shadows and into the clear space before the stables. He ignored me wholly as he calmly took in the young Ilrairian cavalryman.

"Ademar Augustine," uttered Silvano. He clasped his hands over his abdomen and cocked his head. "Looking for someone?"

The unit leader didn't look surprised, he simply smirked and lowered his sword. "I was beginning to think we'd never find you."

Silvano spread his hands and shrugged. "Yet here I am, how long have you been searching?"

"Two weeks," said Augustine, his cultured voice was coarse and deep, like he had drunk only whisky his whole life.

I quickly did the maths. Bromtide had been searching for Silvano soon after he said he was off hunting dissenters, which meant his ruse had fallen through within a day or so of leaving, which meant ...

"Who's your new commander?" he asked.

Augustine's sword lowered even further, but he took one small step into the stone building. "Farrow."

Silvano's jaw tightened, his shoulders stiffening. It took all my control not to unleash my light and ice. That *conniving* bastard.

Another step forward. "He's made his intentions quite clear to the King, he gets Bromtide in exchange for handing over you and Thorra. He also mentioned a light wielder who is now considered a traitor to the crown, oh, and the small matter that *the Queen was kidnapped*."

My breath stuttered, and I leashed my snarl. The ice in my veins clicked, like an orca in the deep, poised to strike at any moment.

Silvano gave Augustine a dangerous smile laced with warning. "Kidnapped? Is that the story the King and Farrow are spinning you? Is that their just cause for encroaching further north? Tell me, Augie, did it ever cross your mind that the Queen wanted to leave? That Jaryn might have placed her at Erskine as bait?"

A muscle in Augustine's jaw jumped. "We have you trapped and now you're twisting the truth to suit you. I never took you for a lying weasel, but then I guess you're full of surprises."

"Amadea has been Jaryn's prisoner for years, sending her to Erskine was meant to lure Thorra out of hiding, which it did. Thorra loves her, has always loved her, and she loves him. Jaryn, the fucking fool, never considered the possibility that he would actually get her out to freedom." Silvano's hands twitched like he considered reaching for his swords, but then stilled. "And now Farrow has sent you to track me down? Let me guess, he never told you how he knows Thorra and I are up here?"

Augustine's jaw clenched, and he held Silvano's gaze, hurt and anger flashing over his features.

A woman's voice from behind him uttered, "Let's just get this over with, Augie, we know they're both here."

Silvano inched forward within sword-striking distance. "Farrow was a spy in Bromtide for years, secretly feeding Royant Platoon all our secrets. He helped Thorra hide his identity as a Petish warlord. Now he's turned on Thorra, turned on me, and is using all of that power for himself to get Jaryn's favor." His gaze flicked to the two soldiers standing behind Augustine, his features devastatingly grave. "I taught you all better than this."

Augustine's eyes narrowed, his entire body tensing. "We have our orders."

"I know you do."

"We will not betray the crown, not like the Royants and not like *you*," Augustine snarled. "The respect you earned as our Commander vanished the moment you high-tailed it out of Saltfen."

"Is that what you all think? That I *ran away*?"

My eyes widened, shocked at the whispered outrage coming from Silvano. Farrow, it seemed, was telling his platoon half-truths and lies.

"Farrow said you couldn't take it anymore, after the fire siege of Aarine. That you lied when you said you were hunting down dissenters, when in actual fact, you were broken mentally and fled."

To risk everything to save someone you cared about, that was redeemable, honorable even, to some. Yet to paint the picture that Silvano had fled out of fear, that he was no longer capable of being a commander, to get those that were once under leadership to resent him, what better way to discredit your enemy?

Silvano stared at Augustine, animosity and incredulity rippling from him. Then those dark eyes flicked to my hiding spot, and I knew my time had come. Keeping my grip on *Kathkar* steady, I finally unleashed my light in well-controlled banners that wove through the air, orbiting in rough circles over our heads. Stepping out silently, I kept my gaze locked on Augustine and the two soldiers at his back that finally came into view.

Wrapped up warm in their dark green winter uniforms and waxed leather coats, their wary gazes tracked my every move as I stopped at Silvano's side. Augustine stared at me intently, and I sensed Silvano grow in height, his left hand finally resting on the hilt of his sword.

"The fact you would fall for such lies after I've trained you for the past ten years," Silvano snapped.

The two soldiers behind Augustine, one young woman and man, flinched. Their tanned, heavily freckled faces and light green eyes were so similar that they could be related. Augustine didn't react to Silvano's scathing tone, but his gaze bounced between the two of us, realization flickering in his eyes.

"The light wielder?" he said.

"Destry Kivisto *Coen*," Silvano uttered, not taking his eyes off the threat before him, but I felt him shift a fraction closer to me.

"You married her?" gasped the soldier behind Augustine's left shoulder, "Caulderon" stitched into the left lapel of his rider's coat.

"He did," I replied, my voice soft but laced with steel.

All three of them eyed the faintly glowing sword in my grasp and the sage green light hovering over us. The young woman was quick to hide the hurt on her face, before it was replaced with a sneer of disgust. I bared my teeth at her, and she replied in kind.

"*Enough*, Pendrosa," ordered Augustine over his shoulder, and the woman slunk back a step. The unit leader turned back to face his former Commander. "You left Bromtide, for her?"

"I left a great many things for her, and I would do it all again in a heartbeat if I had to."

My heart cracked at his words, but the ice in my chest rumbled with the truth of it. Caulderon looked down then, finally noticing the thin layer of ice that coated the ground, and followed the intricate pattern until it traced back to me. His eyes lit up with surprise, but he stayed silent, like he knew better than to provoke me.

"Technically," said Silvano charmingly. "You're ruining my honeymoon."

Augustine released a short laugh, and Pendrosa glanced at him in alarm.

"We have to take them back," she hissed.

Just then, a pounding on the exterior stable door sounded. "Everything alright in there?" called another male voice. "It's fucking freezing."

"It's fine, Beretta," Augustine replied, not taking his eyes off me. "We're alright."

"Then what's taking so long?" complained a different, deeper voice. "Are they in there or not?"

"You can't be serious?" hissed Pendrosa, as Augustine slowly sheathed his sword. I mirrored him and slipped *Kathkar* back into its scabbard in one smooth motion.

"Come in, you two. You need to see this," the unit leader uttered, his gaze finally flicking back to Silvano. My ice retreated a fraction in response.

"Augie," warned Caulderon softly. "If Farrow finds out."

We looked over the cavalry riders' heads as two hulking young men appeared behind them, their faces flushed with the cold and fresh snow covering their hats and shoulders.

"Oh shit," whispered Martelli, registering Silvano and me.

"We found them?" said Beretta, his broad body blocking the rest of the cabin from view. "Commander, why on earth—"

"He's not our Commander," spat Pendrosa.

"I said, *enough*," snapped Augustine, and his unit fell deathly quiet. "Tell us what we should do."

Silvano's face softened at the resignation in Augustine's voice. "I know the cost of what I am asking you. The fact you have found me and survived out here as a unit is a credit to everything you have learned. I could not be prouder."

My heart broke for them, this unit who was bound to one another for their survival, who had trained just like Silvano had. Their attention was focused wholly on their former Commander, hanging onto his every word.

"Jaryn must fall."

PART THREE

The Dawn

CHAPTER
THIRTY-FOUR

EBREL

I wanted to lie down for a week, wanted to curl up in a patch of late spring grass and let the longer daylight hours warm my pelt. The thought of endless grazing tormented me, as did the image of strong updrafts that were a dream to soar on. My body was exhausted, my mane and tail bedraggled and knotted in places.

The muscles over my back, shoulders and neck, normally so strong and unbreakable, were beginning to tire, becoming slower to recover each morning. Even my right wing, which I had damaged when Spearian had sent me tumbling from the skies, but had healed perfectly, was beginning to protest at the relentless pace of flight I was putting upon it.

I knew Hestian felt the same, but he still found the energy to curl around me whenever we found a place to rest for the day. Still had the energy to watch out for predators, despite his body trembling as much as mine each time we landed. I prayed for clear skies and calm winds, the thought of battling another snowstorm almost making me break down.

We had to find them. We had to.

Orrin and Murrkill never understood the compulsion, the complexity of connection Hestian and I both shared for our riders. Although we had bonded in different ways with Silvano and Destry, it was a thread still bound by respect, love, and something that was intangible, that called directly to our souls. The will of the spirits perhaps, if the maneuverings of the Night Pegasus was anything to go by. A spirit who we now knew the true identity of.

After our night staked out by Fort Vervelli, then our punishing flight north, the best hiding place we could find was a shallow, dry dip in the earth beside two small fells. The vast expanse of the glens lay before us, undulating but ruthless. The light was bleak and gray-washed from the snow clouds overhead, the normally vibrant landscape appearing sullen and brooding.

Hestian half staggered as he made it to the small patch of dry earth, his pelt now permanently dark with dried sweat. His lush, white mane and tail were no longer, now they were muddied and gorse-ridden. I lay down first, knowing all too well that I hadn't eaten or drank enough. Hestian, his voice silent in my head and breathing hard, folded his body beside mine, his wings twitching with tiredness.

"We'll find them," I said hoarsely, then I mumbled again, half-asleep as darkness tugged at the corners of my mind. *"We'll find them."*

"I know, love, I know," Hestian whispered in return, his breath warming my cheek as he rested his head beside mine.

Love. Despite being half-frozen and tired beyond anything I had ever felt before, I let the small endearment warm my soul.

I knew from the heaviness of my body that I hadn't had enough sleep as I threw my head up. Blinking, disoriented, I gazed across at Hestian whose ears were pricked toward the northern horizon. He tested the chilled air, the fragile, meek light of dawn just peeking over the eastern fell on our right. Slowly, limbs stiff and aching, he stood. By his quietness I knew not to speak, so I stilled and waited.

Gait steady, he crossed the dip and climbed up the northern fell and casting his head about warily, he scented the air again, wings tucked in tight. As he crested the rise, a shaft of sunlight broke through the snow clouds, shining directly against him, highlighting the few golden sections of his coat that weren't muddied.

I gazed up at him, unable to tear away. He stood proud and alert, head held high as he assessed the breeze that swept over the undulating land. Every ounce of domesticity had been stripped from him, and he looked utterly rugged, weather-worn, and above all … free. A Pegasus who had thrown himself at this unforgiving, harsh land and survived.

"There's a group of Ilrairian Pegasi to the north," he said, closing his eyes as he inhaled deeply. *"I know them."*

Muscles aching, I lurched to my hooves and walked up beside him, my limbs protesting with every step. *"They're a long way from home."*

"A scouting party, no doubt," he muttered, his gaze roving over the rolling land.

"How far away?" I asked, unable to keep the pain from my voice.

He winced. *"If they stay where they are, two hours at least, possibly more."*

The bitter wind picked up, hurling scraps of dead heather, grass stalks and snow flurries with it. It cut across our pelts, and I flinched at the bite of it. Then I froze and angled my gaze slightly to the northeast.

"Destry," I whispered, hardly believing what I could sense. The taunting scent of amber was laced with hers, masculine and strong, *Silvano.*

Hestian stilled as he caught it, too, a low whicker in his throat. I looked down at my forelimbs then across at the stallion once more. Could we risk injuring ourselves to go to them? The wind was against us, the air freezing. It would be a torturous flight. Yet the pull to go to them was near overwhelming.

Nosing my neck and cheek, Hestian spoke softly. *"We can do it, we are brave, wild Pegasi after all."*

"We?" I croaked.

"Do I not look the part at least?" he chuckled.

I whickered a low laugh and nuzzled his neck in return, the first tender touch I'd ever given him. Hestian seemed to realize it, too, and he curled his neck toward me, his breath twining with mine. This stallion ... I had never felt more safe than with him. Slowly, I could sense him rebuilding my scarred and shattered heart, knowing that if I let him, he would never let me fall.

"Yes, you most definitely do."

"I'll take that as a compliment."

"Careful now, if your ego gets any bigger, you won't be able to fly."

He playfully nipped me. *"You love my ego as much as the rest of me."*

I rolled my eyes at him, then tentatively stepped forward and half spread my wings, testing them. The wind buffeted them, the speckled brown feathers rippling across the huge expanse of bone and muscle. Then I eased into a slow canter, spreading my wings further, the ability to launch myself straight upward was beyond me now. I needed momentum to get airborne. Hestian followed suit and then broke into a smooth gallop beside me, the pair of us launching into the air as the fellside lurched away and we dove into the wind.

Beyond the low-lying mountains of Niemi's keep and past the river it was named after, was a wooden, cone-shaped building, smoke filtering high into the sky before being tugged away by the wind. Yet I barely registered the little cabin and the two stone buildings next to it.

Every ounce of my energy was being funneled into keeping my wings aloft, but my wingbeats were becoming irregular, not the sinuous flow I was used to, something I barely had to think about under normal circumstances. My body was a finely tuned instrument, capable of feats of strength and power that had awed mortals for centuries.

But not now.

Hestian roared at me to keep going, his neigh laced with worry despite the demand in it. I was freezing, my pelt sweat-ridden. I knew Hestian's was the same, and he brushed his wing against mine, a silent plea to keep flying.

From below, five different whinnies rose up to us, their voices snatched and half-frozen by the snow that began to fall again. My blood felt sluggish, and my neck lowered in effort. Hestian roared again, the ear-splitting sound booming over the land, and it jerked me fully awake. I had never heard him sound like that, his voice full of dominating command.

The other calls of the Pegasi sounded in answer, but I was too far gone to decipher them. My descent was fast, too fast, the white ground rising to meet me. Destry was down there, her scent so much stronger now. Beyond the point of exhaustion, my energy reserves completely spent, I attempted to circle before landing.

"Ebrel!" yelled Hestian from above me.

Several feet above the ground, a stone's throw from the cabin, my wings gave out, and I half crashed into snow, legs buckling on impact. I rolled onto my side, wings draped over the white drifts, legs curled beneath me as I gasped for breath. The gray sky morphed with the uneven ground, and I blinked in an attempt to focus, but everything remained hazy. There was a flurry of movement by the front door, and there came the sound of people yelling at each other.

The earth shook as Hestian slammed to the ground over me. Wings fully brandished despite how they trembled, ears flat back against his skull, he opened his mouth, and his cry thundered into the air. The five Pegasi waiting outside the cabin trotted over, but I was unable to make out one from the next, their voices all rolling into one.

"... Hestian!"

"... thought we'd never see you again ..."

"Is that a wild Pegasus?"

With an aching groan, the stable door blew open, sending fragments of wood and ice particles everywhere. The soldiers' Pegasi shied away but settled quickly, turning their bridled heads to take in the chaos.

"Get the *fuck* out of my way," snarled Destry at the Ilrairians that spilled out from the stables, and green light lashed over the ground.

"Lay a hand on my wife, Augustine, and I won't hesitate to end you," came Silvano's rumbling voice.

They were both here. My head slumped against the snow in relief. We'd found them. Thank the spirits. Destry's scent was a balm against my lungs, and I let out an exhausted whicker.

"Threaten our unit leader one more time, Coen, and I swear—"

Silvano growled. "You'd dead before you got the chance, Caul-deron."

"Ebrel!" cried Destry as she ran over the snow.

"Holy shit ... is that *Hestian?*" remarked the tallest soldier, Beretta, his dark eyes wide.

The soldier in the center of the group, Augustine, the scent of nobility clinging to his strong body, uttered, "He's bonded to the roan."

"You don't say," murmured Beretta.

Hestian called out again, softer this time, then he dropped his head and nosed my upturned cheek. Destry sank to her knees beside my neck, her warm hand sweeping my forelock back from my eyes. "Oh, sweetheart, you're okay, you're going to be okay."

Silvano stormed over and threw his arms around Hestian's neck, burrowing his face into the stallion's now light brown mane. Hestian released a string of short, helpless-sounding whickers, then nosed my cheek once more.

"*Cold ...*" I said.

"*We need to get you into the stables, Ebrel,*" said Hestian, his voice strained.

"*Can't.*"

"*Please, sweetheart.*"

Another of the soldiers, his near-black hair and dark tan skin setting him apart from the others, stepped forward.

Hestian snapped up his head, a warning squeal sounding deep in his chest.

The soldier froze, then spread his hands wide. "Let me look at her, Commander."

"*Again* ... he is not our Commander anymore," said the female soldier.

Silvano laid a broad hand on Hestian's neck. "Steady, Hestian. Martelli is the animal medic of the group, let him look at Ebrel."

Relaxing the barest fraction but remaining towering over me, Hestian gave a tiny nod of his head. The animal medic crept forward and knelt opposite Destry, who eyed him warily.

"The last thing I would ever do, would be to harm someone's Pegasus, light wielder, your mount is safe with me." His dark hazel eyes were sincere as he gently laid a hand on my neck. My pelt twitched at the stranger's touch, but I sensed no threat in him. My legs trembled from the cold and the fact that I was completely at their mercy.

Destry swallowed, her gaze bouncing between Martelli, Silvano, and me. Then she sat back in the snow, her light wreathing a twisting crown against her head.

Martelli took that as his signal to examine me. His large hands were deft and knowledgeable as he took my pulse, then checked my eyes and gums. He softly pinched my pelt, watching as it slowly retracted back against the muscle of my shoulder.

"She's dehydrated, cold, and I worry her blood sugar is too low. I can't tell what injuries she might have with her recumbent like this." The medic's voice was like smooth velvet, and I wanted to wrap myself up in his calm, assured words. "We need to get her into the stables or make a windbreak here if we can't move her. Do you have molasses?"

Destry nodded. "We do."

"Make her up a warm feed and bring out warmed water too. Any hay you can spare from the Lake Horses would be best."

"I'll bring out some blankets," said Destry. She looked across at the medic, her eyes soft. "Thank you."

Martelli gave her a small but tight smile. "Let's get to work." He and Destry rose, and he towered over her. The medic glanced at Augustine, a silent conversation passing between them. Hestian tensed, nostrils flaring, but he calmed when Silvano ran a hand down his neck.

"Caulderon, Beretta, start building a windbreak in the snow. Our Pegasi could use one as well. Pendrosa and I will fly back to camp and grab our supplies." Augustine leveled a warning glare at Pendrosa, who tried to speak. "We'll move our camp here."

Silvano nodded in agreement, and a flicker of pride washed over Augustine's handsome face. Hastily, shovels digging deep into the snow, a wind break was built on my right, blocking out some of the brutal cold. Destry rushed into the cabin, then came back out with her arms full to the brim. Setting down a steaming bucket of water, she threw a spare blanket over me, tucking it around my wings to cover my back, then lifted my head to help me drink.

The warm water soothed my ravaged throat, and the air trapped by the blanket slowly began to warm me. She did the same for Hestian, who still stood protectively over me. A quiet, uneasy truce had settled over the humans as they set about caring for the Pegasi, Silvano disappearing into the cabin to make food for the soldiers.

After a feed of soaked sugar beet pulp and molasses, I was able to raise my head and nuzzle Hestian, who sighed with relief.

"You scared the hell out of me, roan one."

"I'm sorry."

"Don't be, I shouldn't have made you come up here."

"You didn't make me do anything, Hestian. I wanted to come. We needed to find them."

His warm exhale brushed over my forelock. *"You know, you look quite impressive when you're trying to be big and scary."*

"If your method of flirting is just insulting me, then I'm all here for it."

He huffed gently at my tired laugh, then I cast my head around, the scene before me finally coming into sharp focus. It was close to midday now and snow was falling thickly. Three Ilrairian Pegasi mares, one black the other two a deep, burnt red, huddled close together by the stable wall, sharing hay between them. Dark green blankets covered their backs, their saddles and bridles sitting in neat piles by the blown-apart stable door.

Their riders were putting the finishing touches to an extended wind break, firming the sides down with the flat edges of their folding shovels. The animal medic laughed at something the absolute giant, Beretta, whispered to him.

Destry and Silvano stepped out from the stables, slices of hay in their gloved hands, and carried them over to Hestian and me. The three soldiers stopped their work and watched them carefully as they approached. A tiny white stoat bounded after Destry, leaping between the whispers of light that curled in her wake.

Beretta folded up his shovel and set it down as he tracked the stoat. "What in the name of fairy tales is going on?"

Caulderon laughed, giving the windbreak one final pat with his shovel. "It's crazy, huh?"

"Seriously, though, is someone going to start singing? Because that would just set this whole thing off," said Beretta, placing his hands in his coat pockets as he followed Destry over.

"I mean, I can, if you want. I've been told I have a lovely singing voice," chimed Martelli.

Caulderon scoffed. "By the lady, please don't. I'm still scarred from the last time I heard you singing in the barrack showers."

Martelli threw a hand over his chest. "You wound me."

Silvano threw them a smirk, but his gaze remained wary. "At least your unit leader isn't here to listen to your theatrics."

"Augie *loves* our theatrics, Commander. The prince just doesn't have an ear for musical talent like I do." The animal medic grinned as he stood beside his fellow soldiers, all three of them looking like they could get up to all sorts of trouble if left unsupervised.

Silvano dropped to one knee in the snow and ran a finger through my reddish mane. I turned to nose his hand and huffed into Destry's face as she spread out the hay. Gingerly, I heaved myself upward, my legs no longer shaking under my weight. Hestian grumbled while Martelli approached once more, removing his gloves.

"He sure is protective, isn't he?" quipped the medic as he crouched in the snow and began examining my legs, feeling for any undue heat or cuts.

"He's not the only one." Silvano eyed each of the soldiers, the warning in his voice clear. Neither Destry nor I were to be harmed, even though we could take care of ourselves.

"I know that look on your face," whispered Hestian.

"What look?"

"It means, try and cross me, I dare you. *It's one of my favorites."*

I nuzzled Destry's loose hair, inhaling deeply. *"You have more than one?"*

"Of course I do."

"Considering how she landed, her legs are fine. The cold probably helped bring any inflammation down, but we need to keep her fluids up in order to lower the risk of colicking at bay." Martelli rose and stepped back, giving Hestian and me a wide berth now that his examination was over.

"Thank you for checking her," said Destry, keeping a hand on my neck. I glanced between her and Silvano, noting how they were constantly aware of each other's presence, how Destry's light would subconsciously caress Silvano's arm or cheek, the green of her light matching the sage flecks of his irises.

The ice in her veins was quiet again, but I could sense it, a frigid, lethal layer in her blood, biding its time, and a thread of fear beat in my heart. She had nearly killed herself using that power in Erskine. Would she use it again, to bring Jaryn down? Would she wholly succumb to it, if the man at her side was put in danger, like the cave painting foretold?

The unit leader and female soldier returned, their mounts carrying the rest of their supplies. Destry promised she would keep an eye on me, then the humans warily grouped together and headed into the *tallora*, the scent of trepidation on the air.

Augustine was the last to enter, slinging his pack over his muscled shoulder, he threw Hestian and me one last glance, his eyes narrowing as if he focused hard enough, he might read our minds.

My ears pricked, head tilting, as I read him in turn, sensing the turmoil in his soul, how duty and honor ravaged each other like feral wolves. The prince's jaw tensed, before he disappeared from sight.

CHAPTER
THIRTY-FIVE

ASHER

We did not linger in the camp, my instincts snapping at me to get Calliope as far away from there as I could. I let their supplies be, content with the amount I had on me. There was enough to tide us both over until her shoulder healed, and after that ... well, I shoved that thought down, down until it gnawed at my bones instead.

My shadows led the way to a steep, narrow but dry ravine, and we carefully climbed down into it, cautious to cover our tracks with a fallen branch of fir. The Colladonian soldiers would have no qualms about hunting us now, and I wasn't about to lead them straight to our hiding spot.

"Do we risk a fire?" said Calliope quietly, her breath clouding between us as we settled into a rough undercut in the ravine wall.

Content there were no signs of hibernating bears or any other creatures that used the wide but low-hanging space, I crouched on the bare dirt floor, dragging my heavy pack after me. The sun was well up now, but snow fell beyond the cave's mouth, and I could just make out Calliope's features in the semi-darkness. Her owl-like eyes glowed slightly in the dimness, an otherworldly fire all their own.

I clenched my jaw. "I'm afraid not, this cave isn't really suited to one, it would smoke us out within minutes. That, and we're too close to that scout camp to risk it."

She nodded, her brain clearly mulling over the fact that we'd have to resort to something else to stay warm.

"Is body heat okay with you?" I asked, staring at the pack in my hands, before slowly looking across at her.

She met my gaze fearlessly, and she gave a nonchalant shrug that I knew was anything but. "It's fine with me."

I cleared my throat. "Okay then. Any updates on Silvano and Destry?"

She chewed her lower lip as she closed her eyes. "It's undecided, there's no imminent threat, but I can't read the intentions of the others. It's impossible to say. One of the soldiers, he …" Her brows furrowed slightly, and she ran a hand over the back of her neck. "He's royal. He's the one clouding everything."

"Related to Jaryn?" I asked, unable to keep the bite out of my tone.

Calliope dipped her chin. "His only nephew. Sent out into the wilds in the hope that he stays there, or that it kills him, sparing Jaryn the trouble." She opened her eyes and studied the anger on my face. "What did Jaryn do to you?"

"He killed a member of the Nijinx kin swarm when I … when I belonged to the wild ward. Pherox, the male Nijinx I'm bonded to, we swore to end Jaryn in retribution. No one attacks the kin swarm and gets away with it." I glanced down at the scar on my palm, then curled my fingers over it, blocking it from sight. Shaking my head, I pulled out our bedrolls, buttoning them together, then brought out the medical kit.

Turning her back to me, the wild creature in me so content with the fact she didn't show any fear now, Calliope shrugged off her coat, then her jumper and shirt.

"I'll make this quick, I promise," I whispered as I shifted to sit behind her, thoughts of last night hounding me. My hands in her hair, my mouth so close to tasting her perfect skin. I hastily warmed my hands, it was freezing, and I couldn't bear the thought of her being cold, despite how much I wanted to trace every freckle on her back.

Calliope tilted her head to the side, eyes closed as I stripped away the bandage and took in her arrow wound. It was looking perfect, healing exactly as it should, and a small, immature part of me hated the fact. I wanted to drag this process out, wanted it to take longer than the few more days it actually needed.

Her trust in me felt as fragile as a blossom before a frost, so precious and easy to break. I took in her closed eyes and how she no longer flinched at my touch, grinding my teeth with the effort of sticking to the task at hand.

"You're rushing," she breathed.

"I don't want you catching a chill."

So softly I almost didn't catch it, she murmured, "Pretty sure I'm not at risk of that."

I leaned slightly to the left to look at her face, taking in how her golden lashes brushed against her cheeks that held a delicate pink blush. Her lips were parted ever so slightly, and I clenched my fists, my nails cutting half-moons into my palms. Yet it wasn't enough to stop me, as I dragged the knuckle of my pointer finger slowly down her back, just beside the groove of her spine. Her breath caught, and her back bowed as she arched into the taunting touch.

So responsive. Shadows pressed in around us, and with half a thought, they swept gentle caresses over her exposed collarbone and down, over her ribs. She shivered, and her grip on her shirt faltered, the swell of her breasts pebbling with the cold. My right hand unfurled to follow the path my shadows had taken, and I swept my hand up her side, following the dip of her waist then the rise of her chest that panted for breath.

Swallowing harshly, my control on a knife-edge, my thumb glided over the sensitive skin on the underside of her breast.

"*Asher.*" Her voice was a whispered plea, and I—

No.

She was cold, she was injured, probably starving and exhausted after our trek, and I ... *fuck.* I pulled back. "Get dressed," I said roughly. "We need to eat."

She whipped her head to look at me, clutching her shirt to her torso again. I busied myself with stowing the medical kit and bringing out our food rations and skins of water. With fire not an option, dried meat, bread, and cheese would have to do. I could feel Calliope's gaze burning into me, but I couldn't look at her.

Because if I did, I knew it wouldn't stop there, that my hands would find her skin again, and I would see just what other kinds of sounds I could wring from her. Would she whimper my name under my touch? Would she—

My shoulders curved inward, and the muscles across my back strained as I focused on cutting up the slab of dried reindeer meat. From the corner of my eye, Calliope shifted and threw her layers back on, her golden skin flushed, and I knew it wasn't from the cold. I silently slid her food to her, and she took it from me. Was she aware of how I felt? Could she sense how badly I wanted her?

Tucking her sheaf of birch bark onto her lap, we wordlessly ate our food and watched the snow fall beyond the mouth of the cave. It was coming down thickly, and I contemplated having to make snowshoes or skis if we were going to have any success in traversing through it tonight. Our boots were well worn and waterproof, but the snow would be knee-deep in places and would soak our trousers in minutes.

Our breathing the only sound, we cleaned up and washed as best we could, brushed our teeth and removed our boots and coats. Calliope tucked herself into the joined bedrolls first, and I followed suit, tucking my hands behind my head to stare up at the dark ceiling.

She leaned back, her weight propped on her elbow. Not looking at me, she uttered, "Does it ever trouble you? The loneliness?"

Slowly, carefully, I looked up at her, and she refused to meet my gaze, those golden eyes tracking the snowflakes instead, but her breathing quickened, and her delicate pulse jumped as I watched her.

Did it trouble me? Between the kin swarm, my shadows, and her, no, I hadn't felt alone. Yet sometimes, despite being in close proximity with a living, breathing, sentient creature, it didn't stop me from becoming trapped inside my own head. I could reach out and place my hand on Pherox's neck, but still feel a million miles away, my mind content on trying to devour itself with thoughts of what I had done.

"Yes. There are days when I just want to let the darkness consume me, to experience some peace."

She dipped her chin and looked down, interlacing her long fingers. "It's why I miss my owl form. The memories ... they're less sharp, less painful, like I let a piece of my humanity go." She dragged a forefinger over the padded fabric beneath us, tracing what looked like a name into it, before wiping it away with the palm of her hand. "But then I'm in danger of forgetting what it means to *be* human. In my owl form ... I'm surviving day to day, where there's no future or past. But ... Asher ..." Calliope looked across at me then, our gazes meeting, and I nearly crumpled at the vulnerability on her face. "When you touch me, hold me, I remember what it's like to feel alive, to feel present ... I'm human, when I'm with you."

Her words struck me like a dagger through the chest, twisting against my heart and slicing through my resolve. Mirroring her, I propped myself up on my elbow and reached across to tuck a stray piece of hair back behind her ear. Her eyes closed, and my hand stilled as she leaned into my palm.

"I would become every monster imaginable to keep you safe, Callie." My voice was low and coarse, as I ran my thumb over her cheek. "I'm yours. I will be whatever you need me to be." I leaned down, pressing my forehead to hers. "Even if that means being the man that lets you go."

She inhaled a deep, shuddering breath. "You'll be safe when I'm in my owl form. You can whisper away into the wilds with the Nijinxes. You can help save the Night Pegasus and his scion. I'm a danger to you, like this." She gestured to her prone body.

I shifted closer, our lips millimeters apart. "You're anything but dangerous to me," I whispered. Angling her head with my thumb, I pressed a featherlight kiss to her cheek. "You are a light I cannot ignore, a fire that cuts straight through my darkness. I would do anything for you, Calliope."

My hand fell away as she moved, her gaze locked on mine, and her eyes glowed gold in the half-light. Lying back, my body burning with need, I looked up at her in wonder. Tendrils of white-blonde hair framed her face as she sat up, then braced her arms on either side of my biceps. With a gentle hand, she swept her palm from my brow, down my cheek to swipe her thumb over my lips, just like she had done the night she had poisoned me. My hips jerked at the touch, every muscle and instinct straining to claim her.

Heart thundering in my chest, my right hand rose to thread through her hair to cup the back of her head, drawing her closer, the image burned into my brain of exactly what I wanted to do to her that night. Now it was here, her beautiful body arched over mine once more. Her leg swung over my thighs until she straddled me, and I was barely able to leash the aching groan in my throat.

I clasped the dip of her waist with my free hand, her body hovering over mine, her gaze noting every feature of my face as she gently dragged her nails through my now short beard. Turning my head, I nipped at her exposed palm, her soft gasp a balm to my soul as I kissed the small hurt.

Her shirt and jumper were too big for her, and the fabric draped against my chest, exposing the smooth skin of her lower back. Venturing slowly, watching her carefully, I slid my hand from her waist to the small of her back, pulling her hips flush against me. Her eyes flared wide, back arching at my touch, and she leaned closer.

We gazed at each other for a moment, our heartbeats galloping, then her mouth was on mine, and I finally experienced what it felt like to know heaven. My fingers tightened in her hair, hauling her closer, and she yielded, a soft moan on her lips that set my blood on fire. Shadows whirling above our heads, I twisted us onto our sides, gripping her thigh over mine while I deepened the kiss. Her hands shot to my hair, and I ran my fingers up her spine, hips grinding against one another as we finally let go. She felt perfect against me, so right in my arms with a kiss that felt like I was dying and being reborn.

She would be free, I wanted her to be free, but for this very moment, I needed to know what it felt like for her to be mine.

CHAPTER
THIRTY-SIX

CALLIOPE

H e was a seductive darkness and a scorching fire, every touch branding me wherever his hands caressed my bare body. His calluses scraped along the sensitive skin of my back and ribs, and by the spirits, I never wanted it to end.

His hand tightened in my hair, and my core heated with the pull of it, the unspoken need it communicated to me. I wreathed against him, my thigh draped over his, angling me perfectly over his rigid length. Hands seeking, I pushed them under his shirt and groaned at the corded muscle of his back and abdomen. Exploring with abandon, lost in his punishing kiss, I mapped every indentation, marveling at the power that lay there.

Asher broke away, panting deeply, planting molten kisses down my throat. "You have no idea what you do to me, Callie," he murmured against my too hot skin. "You haunt my every waking moment."

His hand skimmed up my side and paused just under my aching breast. I was desperate for more of him. I had never felt so perfectly safe as the strength of his body pressed into mine. His hooded, dark gaze tore a low whimper from my throat. Tauntingly, he ran his thumb over the curve of my breast.

"Is this okay?"

"Yes," I panted, arching my back to press my nipple against his broad palm.

The muscle in his jaw jumped, and he leaned across to nuzzle my neck. I buried my head into his solid chest, clutching at his shirt and back. I sucked down a sharp breath as he bunched up my clothes, then brought his mouth to my nipple. My lower leg pulled him closer to me, and I shifted my hips back and forth, desperate for any friction. I needed him, all of him. My body felt electrified, and it thrummed with desire. Thoughts, worries, and fears vanished with his hands and mouth on me, the muscles of his back shifting under my touch, leaving me awestruck.

A shadow pulled away from up above, curling to brush up against my exposed stomach in a ghost-like touch that had me bucking my hips. Asher rolled his tongue over my nipple, sucking deep, and he released a low moan at the nails I dragged down his spine in response. I ached for him, the white-hot need coursing through my blood, leaving me breathless.

Palming my breast once more, he followed the contours of my waist and hip, his straining length thrusting against the apex of my thighs. Then his fingers grazed the waistband of my trousers, and I froze. My mind whined in desperation for him to keep going, to strip me bare and let me come undone beneath him. But he would see it. If we went any further, he would understand what haunted me. Why the call of my owl form was so devastatingly strong.

Sensing me tense under him, Asher stilled and pulled back, moving onto his elbow to look down at me. His gaze narrowed in concern while his broad chest racked for breath. "What's wrong? Are you okay?"

I couldn't lie to him. But the words to explain were like molten tar in my throat. My lower lip trembled. "I ..."

"Hey, shhh, it's okay." Pressing a kiss to my forehead, he straightened my clothes and lowered me onto my back on the bedroll. Tucking me into his side, he wiped away a stray tear that fell down my cheek. Propping his chin in his hand, his knuckles drifted up and down my right arm. "I'm sorry. If I rushed you. I ... we don't have to do anything you're not ready for."

I dragged my hands down my face in a mix of desperation and shame. "I want you, Asher, holy spirits, I *want you* ... there's just—" My voice cracked, and my throat burned with the effort to stop crying.

With his fingers wrapped around my wrist, he pulled my hand away from my face. His expression was so open, so earnest, I wanted to bury my face into his chest and sob.

"Oh, Callie, you're okay, you're safe with me," he said softly against my hair. Threading his arms around me, he pulled me close, and my body trembled with the effort to keep my tears at bay. His heart rate began to slow against my cheek. His heat enveloped me, changing from the charged, wild thing it had been moments ago, to one of comfort. "You don't have to tell me, Callie. I can die happy knowing what it was like to simply kiss you."

I pressed closer to him, my hands curling together in the tight space between our chests. His strength was a sanctuary and one I never wanted to leave.

CHAPTER
THIRTY-SEVEN

DESTRY

If I thought the cabin was cozy with just Silvano and me, it was downright cramped and stiflingly warm with us plus five warriors crammed between the slanted walls. Fresh cup of coffee in hand, I sat cross-legged on the bed and took in the soldiers practically inhaling the food Silvano had prepared for them.

"Forgive our lack of table manners," said Beretta between bites of bacon. "But this is sheer luxury after the wilds we've been camping in."

"Considering there is no dining table, I forgive you," I said, a lone eyebrow arching in amusement.

Silvano chuckled as he sat down on the bed beside me. His thumb traced circles against my lower back, and I couldn't help but lean into the touch. Gaze analytical, he let the soldiers eat in peace before trying to form a plan about what the hell we were going to do next. Augustine, from the distant, worried look on his face, seemed to be doing the same. He and Pendrosa, her back straight and eyes darting everywhere, shared the couch. Caulderon had perched his muscled body on a tiny, three-legged stool dragged from the kitchen space, while Beretta and Martelli, their broad frames too big for the couch or the bed, sat on the fleece rugs covering the floor.

My body had relaxed a fraction, knowing that Ebrel and Hestian were recovering from their journey to spirits knows where. From how haggard they looked, it seemed they had flown the breadth of the Boreals and back, traveling through a string of storms along the way.

Caulderon, clearly the caretaker of the unit, picked up everyone's empty plates and took them to the kitchen. The poor stool creaked as he sat down again, and I hoped we wouldn't owe Minna any more new furniture. I winced at the thought of the stable door. My control had shredded apart when we had heard Hestian's deafening whinny, and the soldiers had been side eyeing me warily since my ice display.

Dragging a hand through his short hair, Augustine straightened, and his unit followed suit, their gazes flicking from their leader to Silvano. My husband's jaw tightened, but his hand remained against my lower back, like he needed that physical connection to get through this conversation. And to be honest, I needed it too.

"We have few options here," he uttered, looking at each soldier in turn. "You follow your orders and take Destry and I with you to Fort Vervelli, but I warn you. We will not go willingly, and you may pay for that choice with your lives."

Augustine stiffened but nodded, not arguing with the fact that Silvano and I could, and would, end them if it came to that. As much as we would hate ourselves for it in the aftermath.

"You lie about having encountered us, reporting to Farrow that you saw nothing out here. Now I know you've been combing this terrain for weeks, and to go back empty-handed will not broker you a warm welcome." Silvano's gaze lingered on Augustine. "The third option …"

He looked at me, and my chest tightened with foreboding. Clearing my throat, I looked around the members of the Adonitus Unit, my gaze lingering on the storm cloud sigils stitched onto their worn uniforms.

"The third option is you return to the keep with us. Fight alongside us." It was an effort to keep my voice steady as their eyes widened at my words.

Augustine leaned forward, arms braced against his powerful thighs. "And give my uncle another reason to have me slaughtered?"

Silvano didn't hesitate. "You know as well as I do that to station you up here was a suicide mission. He hoped the north, be it the environment, the Petish, or the Colladonians, would kill you and your unit, sparing him the effort of doing it himself."

"He's right, Augie," whispered Martelli, his dark features serious. The taper of ice in my chest hummed and clicked. I realized then, that despite how kind and tender he had been with Ebrel, he posed the greatest threat if a fight were to come. The brawn of Beretta was a mere distraction, while it would be Martelli who slit your throat.

"So what, we become dissenters too?" snapped Pendrosa. "Everything we've worked for, our careers, just gone like that?"

"Those who wish to join us are welcome to, but we won't force you. If you want to return to Fort Vervelli, then be my guest," said Silvano.

Augustine rose to his full height and began to pace the slim section of bare floor before the wood stove. Eyes wary, Caulderon watched his every move.

"If you disappear, Jaryn will assume his plan worked and the wilds claimed you. Yet if members of your unit wish to return to Fort Vervelli, they'll need to concoct a foolproof lie about what happened to the other members of their unit."

Hands on his hips, Augustine dragged his lower lip through his teeth. The low light brought out the faint strands of gold in his hair and highlighted the way his shirt clung to his lean but honed body. Despite bearing no crown, no sign at all of his nobility, the way he carried himself clearly stated he was someone of importance. Not just a soldier, but someone worth listening to.

"Could we spy for you? Gather intelligence on Farrow?" the prince uttered, his gaze fixed on the pointed ceiling.

A sly smile cracked over Beretta's handsome face. Well, he had at least one supporter.

"We still can't go back empty-handed though." Caulderon twined his fingers together, his right knee bouncing.

"Farrow would likely redeploy you as soon as you returned, Augie. Jaryn will have told him to keep you far away." Silvano tracked the prince's every move.

I inched closer to him, my coffee suddenly tasting bitter against my tongue. "Not if he goes back with intelligence that will make him indispensable," I whispered.

Silvano tensed, his expression guarded as he looked at me. "Such as?"

Ignoring his gaze, I looked across at Augustine. "Are there any other scouting parties on this side of the keep?"

"There was a unit stationed to the east of us, not far from Fort Garobear. But they missed their last rendezvous. We don't know where the hell they are or what happened to them," cut Pendrosa.

I eyed her warily, noting the hurt on her face, then I turned to Augustine once more. "Return to Vervelli and tell Farrow that Rekorious is gathering a large force along the Colladonian border."

"Destry," murmured Silvano.

"What would Farrow do if he had that information?" I asked him, clutching my chipped mug between my hands.

"Likely pool his resources to the eastern front. He knows Niemi well, better than any of us. The warlord is a gifted fighter, and any army under his leadership will be a very real threat."

"Would Farrow be likely to call up reinforcements from Ilrair?" I turned to look at the prince.

Augustine nodded. "Murmur Platoon were awaiting orders to advance north when the scouting parties returned with their reports."

"Who would be left to defend Ilrair?" I watched Silvano carefully, waiting for him to understand.

"You want to assassinate the King?" gasped Beretta, catching on quickly.

"After we break the curse on the Trinitors, yes, we assassinate the King," I said through gritted teeth.

"Fucking hell," beseeched Caulderon, leveling me with a cold stare.

"You can't break the curse. The old throne room is sealed shut." Augustine was a tall, tense shadow behind the unit's tracker and medic. "Besides, you'd need royal blood to break apart the wards if you managed to get in."

The fact nobody had immediately shut down my proposal gave me a small flicker of hope. Silvano leaned in, planting a tender kiss to my shoulder.

I placed a hand on top of his, then looked at Beretta. "Do you have any lead on you? Cuffs or torcs?"

Beretta wiggled his eyebrows. "Cuffs you say?"

Silvano shot him a glare that promised a slow death, and the tracker had the decency to look a little sheepish.

"Here." Augustine reached for the collar of his shirt, revealing a slice of sculpted chest and the lead torc that sat snugly against him. Pulling it free, he pinched it between two fingers and handed it to me.

Silvano gently grabbed my wrist, his eyes pleading. "You're sure?"

I dipped my chin and hoped to reassure him later. Then I flipped the torc in my hands. Its weight was solid in my grasp, and I closed my eyes. Ice magic waited for me, encroaching on my every sense with cold, fragile tendrils. To free the Trinitors and help slay Jaryn, I would risk using this power. My fingers grew numb. A faint blue glow flared, and my eyes blinked open.

Gazing down at the torc, the entire cabin fell silent as everyone watched it become marbled white in color, then it began to crack. Breaking this torc felt easier than the one that had been around Lonan's throat, probably because I had already been wounded and cold by the time I tried to fracture it apart. I wasn't in mortal danger here, and I had Silvano by my side. Given the circumstances, I was as safe as I could be at this moment.

My power ground down against the lead, spearing deeper through the finger-thick torc. Beretta swore as it began to cleave apart, then disintegrated, leaving a mess of white, gray, and black shards in my lap.

"The door to the old throne room is lined in lead," I said, looking at the maelstrom of ice in my cupped hands.

Augustine crossed his arms over his chest. "That's impressive."

Silvano cupped my cheek. "But is it worth the cost?"

Averting my eyes, I glanced up at the prince. "We could break the curse on the Trinitors and have the aerial cavalry fight alongside us. With my power combined with theirs, we could put a stop to Jaryn."

A loud bang sounded against the front door, and we all jumped. Beretta moved first, sidling along the wall and loosening a dagger from the sheath at his hip. In a burst of movement, he unlocked the door then stepped back, slack-jawed. Hestian filled the entire doorway, and he shoved his head, neck, and shoulders as far into the cabin as he could. He huffed into Beretta's face, a low rumble in his throat at the dagger in the tracker's hand, then the stallion turned to survey us all.

Those brown and gold eyes fixed on me. He whickered and bobbed his head. Beretta put away his dagger, blinking and mumbling about fairy tales again.

I swung my legs off the bed, dumping the ice and lead shards onto a piece of blank paper on the kitchen counter. "Is Ebrel okay?"

Hestian nodded, and by how calm he looked, I knew she was fine. He just kept staring. Silvano glanced between us.

"Is this about the Trinitors?" he asked.

The stallion whickered again, and it was my turn to feel dumbfounded. "You can ... help us? Will the Pegasi fight when the time comes?"

Another low whicker, and from outside, their whinnies created a cacophony of noise, the other Pegasi sounded their agreement. I didn't need to be able to speak to them directly to understand. They would fight alongside us.

"I think that's where they disappeared to, Destry. Hestian and Ebrel have been helping us," murmured Silvano in awe.

Instinct told me there was more at play here, that the Pegasi didn't just wake up one day and decide to push back against the system that had captured their all-powerful ancestors. Green light curled delicately in my upturned palm. The Night Pegasus brought Ebrel and I together. Was he orchestrating all of this too?

"Thank you, Hestian," I whispered, and the palomino tossed his head, threw Beretta one last judgmental look, then backed out of the doorway.

Dazed, the tracker politely closed the door behind him.

Pendrosa waved a too casual hand, gold rings glinting on her elegant fingers. "Say we kill Jaryn, who, by the way, was your best friend." She pointed accusingly at Silvano. "A King we are sworn to protect. He dies, what then? Who does all that power fall to?"

As one, we looked up at Augustine, who began pacing again like a caged, golden lion, all sinuous motion and barely leashed strength.

"I don't want it. I have never wanted it," he growled.

"The Queen?" ventured Caulderon.

I shook my head. "I doubt she'll want to leave Rekorious."

Did we trust them enough to share the maneuverings of the Royant Platoon and the groundwork they had put in place for the senate to take control? I glanced at Silvano, and he gave the tiniest shake of his head.

Martelli ran a hand over his short, dark beard. "We should vote."

"All those in favor of taking in these two, raise your hand," ordered Augustine.

Silvano and I tensed, but the soldiers remained still, their eyes locked onto their unit leader.

Augustine sighed. "All those in favor of returning to Vervelli as is, raise your hand."

Dragging a hand over her face, Pendrosa slumped against the back of the couch.

"And all those in favor of lying to our current Commander, spying on our own platoon, and preparing a plan to kill our King, raise your hand."

My heart stuttered as five calloused hands rose into the air.

CHAPTER
THIRTY-EIGHT

ASHER

Calliope had fallen asleep against me sometime after midday. Exhaustion had tugged her under, and with my shadows keeping watch, I was content to hold her close, finding sleep not long after she did. My dreams were hazy, not the crystal clear nightmares I was used to. They were filled with crisp white, gold-tipped feathers, orange flames, and orbiting darkness that hid any other details from view.

A shadow gently brushed against my ear just before sundown, stirring me awake. Calliope's head was tucked perfectly under my chin, her body pressed seamlessly to mine, and she gripped my shirt even as she slept. I didn't want to move, content to just be for as long as possible. Her upper torso rose and fell under my hands with her steady breaths.

Had I moved too quickly last night, in my desperation to claim her? I had stopped as soon as I sensed she was uncomfortable, and by her words, she sounded as torn as I felt. She stirred, burrowing her face closer against my chest, and my heart squeezed in response. Another shadow curled around my ear, whispering what it had found further down the ravine.

Moving carefully, I swept the strands of loose hair back from her face, mapping the scattering of freckles across her cheek with my thumb. She blinked, her sharp gaze swiftly coming into focus as she looked at me.

"I want to show you something," I whispered, the edge of sleep still clinging to my voice.

She nodded, and my chest tightened at the complete trust in her gaze.

After constructing crude skis with my folding saw and spare rope, we carefully navigated over the deep snow down the narrow ravine. The steep walls were pitched in darkness, but so like that fateful day many weeks ago, golden light brushed the crests of the steep rock faces. Above us, the sky was a deep magenta. The snow clouds had cleared, leaving a biting cold sky above us. We had about half an hour of daylight left.

The ravine jackknifed, and I slowed, letting Calliope catch up with me so I could see her face when she saw what my shadows had found. Completely ungraceful on her skis, the scowl of concentration on her face brought a deep chuckle from my throat.

She huffed, sliding forward to draw level with me. Blowing back the hair from her face, she finally looked up and gasped. Carved by the elements at varying depths into the earth and buttressed by large boulders, were three hot springs.

I looked across at Calliope and watched her shoulders slump with the mere thought of plunging into warm water. It was a feeling I shared. "Shall we?"

She clutched the thin birch branches that were her ski poles, a look of steely determination on her face. "Yes." Turning to look at me, she cleared her throat. "Can ... can you go first? I'll follow you."

I arched a brow. "Okay." Then set down my poles and pack on a dry boulder.

Calliope pulled at the rope on her boots and took off her skis, then she straightened, wringing her hands over her abdomen.

I made to pull off my coat but halted. "We don't have to go in, Callie. It's—"

She shook her head. "No, it's okay, please. After you."

"You're sure?"

Her gold gaze was defiant. "Yes."

Knowing she was watching, I undressed slowly, the cold nipping at my skin the moment I pulled off my layers. Now I really was stripping for her benefit, and from the rosy blush on her face and how her gaze didn't leave me, she was enjoying the view.

Stepping onto my downturned coat, I removed the rest of my clothes and slowly climbed down into the hot spring. I moaned as the perfectly warm water hit my body. Muscles that had been tense from the cold and carrying our supplies, instantly eased, the aches soothed from every limb. Sinking down until my torso was submerged, I turned in the water and looked up at Calliope.

She followed my lead and slowly undressed, her gaze unwavering from mine and removed first her trousers and underwear, then her jumper. Her cream shirt hung over her curves, the hem grazing the middle of her luscious thighs. Then she stopped, shoulders thrown back, her hands clenched at her sides.

Taking a quick breath, she pulled her shirt up and overhead, letting it drop beside her in a crumpled heap. The white of the bandage was stark against her, and I made a mental note to redress her wound after this.

My vision ebbed for a moment, as I drank in the simple elegance of her. Her gaze locked onto mine again, unashamed and without an ounce of fear. I would remember this day until my lungs no longer drew breath, yet it wasn't her outstanding beauty that had me dropping to my knees before her.

She stood on the lip of the hot spring, her bare body towering over me, steam wreathing her golden skin. Her nostrils flared, and I sensed her resolve waver, then she looked at the snow-capped horizon, and a breath later, she closed her eyes.

A brutal scar slashed across her lower abdomen, the work of skilled yet urgent hands. Whoever had caused it, had not been neat in their efforts to sew her back up. Women only got that scar from one thing, and it was a miracle if they survived the surgery. Usually it was their life, or their baby's that swung in the balance, yet fate often stole both.

"*Something very precious was taken from me,*" she had whispered.

Holy spirits. *Holy fucking spirits.* I opened my mouth, yet no words came out. Instead, I inched closer, my hands reaching upward to gently clasp her hips, and I pressed my forehead to her bare abdomen in unconditional reverence.

Gently, she pushed her fingers through my hair, a deep yet shaky breath sifting from her chest.

This woman was a gift from the spirits, who had known true horror and loss, yet still shone like a dawn sky, who put the safety of others before her own. I would crumble at her feet for eternity in absolution. If anyone tried to harm her, my shadows would tear them apart. I would do *anything* to prevent that kind of torture from finding her again.

My voice cracked. "How ... how can you ever forgive me?"

Her right hand slid from my hair to my chin, and she tipped my head back so that I looked up at her. "I knew from the first moment I met you, Asher Fields. I knew you would never hurt me."

My entire body shuddered, and I rose shakily to my feet so I was eye level with her. Her gaze was resolute, the truth of her, not her magic, but the truth of the life she had lived and the love she had lost, lying bare before me.

I reached forward and cupped her cheek, my fingers grazing the back of her neck. She released a soft sigh, and she nuzzled into my touch. My left hand twined with hers, and I squeezed her fingers gently. "If you're not ready to tell me what happened, I understand. If you can never find the words, that's okay too. Just know that I'm here, I will always be here. You ..." I ran my thumb over her cheekbone, and tears shone in those stunning eyes. "You are the bravest woman I have ever met, Calliope."

Her lower lip trembled, as she shifted forward and pressed her forehead to mine. She shivered under my touch and not entirely from the cold. I glided my hands down her sides and moved them to the backs of her knees, sweeping her off her feet and into my arms. The weight and warmth of her felt so utterly *right* against me that I let out another low groan as I eased us both into the steaming water.

Calliope interlaced her fingers behind my neck, and she shifted to kneel over my thighs, as I sat down in the hot spring. Silently, she burrowed her face into my neck, and I traced long strokes up and down the groove of her spine in the water. I desperately wanted to explore every part of her, but I would wait until she was ready, wholly content to hold her like this for as long as she needed.

I nestled my chin atop her crown of white-blonde hair and inhaled deeply until my lungs were fully coated with her scent. My right hand grazed up her back to the nape of her neck, where my fingers traced small circles under her thick mane.

Shadows wreathed around us, filtering the reddish light like a smoke shield. Undulating, they sheltered us from view, from life beyond the hot spring. Iltavorn had told me that my shadows would not lead me astray, and he was right, for they had led me to her, to this very moment.

Calliope eased back upright, and I moved my hands to interlace with hers under the water. I waited silently, my left thumb caressing her knuckles. Her throat bobbed, and she took another shaky breath.

"You don't have to tell me if you're not ready, sweetheart."

She swallowed again, but whispered, "I rarely used my owl form back then."

I wasn't even sure I was breathing, but I continued to listen and hold her.

"Five years ago, I was living on the outskirts of a village north of here, close to the forest if I needed an escape route. I kept to myself, making and mending quilts to earn some money, not that the villagers had much in the way of coin. But once a month, a traveling market would come through, and I'd sell quilts there too." Calliope blew out a sharp breath, her face cast skyward for a moment, then she looked back down at our joined hands, and she squeezed my fingers.

"I'm here, Callie," I whispered, as she met my gaze again, which was so full of trust that it tore my heart open. Yet I guessed what was coming, and I let the wave of jealousy slide over and past me.

"I met a trader there. My mother warned me not to trust anyone with my gifts, to keep that secret locked away. But he was sweet and kind, we would meet up at every market. I knew he suspected what I was, but I was foolish enough to believe he wouldn't act on it. Then ..."

She took several deep breaths, and I reached up to cup her face, water slicking down my wrist. "Then I discovered I was pregnant. Truth Keepers can't use their owl form once we're with child, it risks the pregnancy. We made plans that he would move to the village when he came back up with the next market. He did come back, but he came with Colladonian soldiers."

I went wholly still, and my heart racketed in my chest. "What were their names?"

She shook her head. "I can't remember all of them, but the Commander was called Lonan. His second-in-command was Aron."

My palm tightened around Callie's hand, and rage made my shadows flurry around us.

"I tried to run, would have flown far, far away if I could have. They caught me, threw me in a wagon, and we made our way to Fort Garobear."

"The trader?" I gritted out.

Her voice was like ice. "Living in an estate north of Moray now, surrounded by riches." She moved off her knees to sit beside me, and I wrapped a protective arm around her, tucking her close beside me. I never wanted to let her go. "The King visited me once but didn't make me use my powers while I was pregnant. They wanted both of us to survive, if I had a girl, he would have two Truth Keepers at his disposal. I tried to escape so many times. They ended up barricading me in a windowless room for months."

Instinctively, her hand grazed the scar that was forever etched onto her skin. "There was a snowstorm when my labor started. They moved me to the fort's medical suite. It went on for hours. I knew before the medics and midwives did, that my little one was stuck." Her voice cracked, and my arm tightened around her. "In a way, I was grateful I was at the fort, if I had been at the village, neither of us would have made it. The medics tried to get me to take the sedative, but I wanted to be awake. I wanted ... *I wanted* ..." Her tears fell then, and my own jaw clenched at the agony in her voice. I could do nothing but hold this space for her. I couldn't undo the trauma that she had suffered through.

But I would make damn fucking sure she would never go through something like this again.

Her back shuddered, and her words were laced with agony. "They gave me something for the pain, and they got her out, but ... but she wouldn't ... couldn't breathe. They tried for what felt like forever, but eventually they wrapped her up in one of the quilts I'd made and passed her to me."

It had been a girl. A precious little girl. Callie was shaking, and I pressed a gentle kiss to her forehead. Her breath came in racking sobs then, and I scooped her into my arms and across my lap once more. It was a flood, a release, and I weathered it, my arms wrapped around her like a shield.

"What was her name?" I whispered into her hair.

"Helena. I named her Helena." Exhaustion coated her words, and she slowly regained control of her breathing.

"That's a beautiful name," I said softly.

I felt her smile against my collarbone. "She was beautiful, perfect."

"How did you escape Garobear?"

She sat up straighter, one of her hands drifting through the warm water. "I didn't want to bury her. I begged the fort's Commander for a pyre, I wanted her ashes to filter into the sky, so that if I ever took flight again, she would be with me. The Commander obliged. The entire staff and soldiers were rattled by what had happened, some said it was a bad omen, others called me a witch."

I stiffened at the thought of anyone accusing her of being anything but the magnificent woman she was.

"I could barely walk after the birth, and I wouldn't let my baby go. They took the risk of carrying me out on a pallet to the drill square, where they had set up the pyre. I didn't want any of them to touch her, so I dragged myself off the pallet and laid her to rest." Her voice was gravelly again, her gaze vacant as she relived those heartbreaking moments.

"As the fire began to dim, some of the soldiers walked away, leaving me on the cobblestones to mourn. There was nothing wrong with my arms, and I decided to take the one chance I had to escape, for me, and my baby." She sucked down a harried breath, and I curled myself around her, lending her my warmth and the protection of my body. Calliope rested her head against my broad shoulder. "I sent out a prayer to Varranar to give me strength and to Ilmari to give me strong currents to fly on. I don't know if they heard me, or maybe I was half-frozen from the cold which helped numb the pain further, but I was able to stand. Then I shifted.

"It was agony, those first few wingbeats, but then I was clear of the walls and over the forests. I picked up a fierce westerly wind and flew as far as I could. I stayed in my owl form for years. I healed more quickly from the surgery that way. It was easier to let the predator take over."

I buried my head into her neck, taking in another deep lungful of her scent. "I don't have the words, Callie, what you've been through ... I can't believe I tried to take you back there."

"How could you have known?"

"I know what it feels like to be trapped against your will. I should have freed you from the very beginning."

She turned to face me, cupping my face between her wet hands. "You had your reasons, huntsman."

"They—" I started.

Tilting back my head, she kissed me softly, conveying everything she couldn't say, and I kissed her deeply in return. Words couldn't express the emotions that thundered through my body. They threatened to shatter my heart.

I pulled back and gently clasped her hand, chuckling at the pruning of her fingers. "Come on, owling, let's get you dry."

"Asher," she murmured, her palm against my cheek. "I want to find Silvano with you."

My jaw clenched. "I don't know what kind of people are going to be around him. There could be more Colladonians just like Aron, and I can't risk you, Callie."

"And I can't risk being alone for the rest of my life, fearing anyone who treads through the forests. Take me with you, let me protect you too."

The thought of the pair of us taking on the world together, having each other's backs, shielding each other from harm, equals in every way ... My teeth gritted together as I tried to control the sheer need in my body for that future.

"One day at a time," I said, pressing another kiss to her perfect mouth. "One day at a time. You and me."

She smiled, and it was the most perfect fucking thing I'd ever seen. The spirits had brought me the most precious gift, and I would treasure her for the rest of my life.

CHAPTER
THIRTY-NINE

DESTRY

The faint crimson of the early evening sky washed the *tallora* in a fiery glow, the snow piled against its wooden sides shifting from white to gold. I leaned my body back against Silvano's broad chest. His heat radiated into me and memories of last night had me releasing a contented, sated sigh. We stood in the sheltered front doorway and watched as the Lake Horses, Hestian and Ebrel, looked for grass under the drifts. Tyvare dove for mice buried deep within the snow, her tiny body scampering between the equines, who were completely unbothered by her presence.

Adonitus Unit busied themselves with saddling their Pegasi. Meticulously completing final checks over their gear and supplies.

"Will they stay true to their word?" I asked, my voice low.

Silvano banded his arms around my chest, and I rested my chin on his forearm.

"I feel for Augie. He wants to do what's right by his unit, and he's not a monster like his uncle. If anything, Jaryn did him a favor by keeping him away from the palace and deploying him on far-flung missions. It means the venom of the court hasn't sunk into his blood," he murmured against my ear.

"Hopefully, Rekorious doesn't kill me for this," I mumbled, praying I hadn't made the wrong choice. Adonitus would hand over their fake intelligence report, and we would watch and wait to see if Farrow would take the bait.

"Rekorious would have to get through me first, wild one."

"What if it doesn't work? What if Farrow doesn't fall for it, or Jaryn stops him from moving his forces?"

Silvano nuzzled my neck. "We'll plan for the best but prepare for the worst. Rekorious is an experienced commander, as am I. Between us all, we'll bring Jaryn down."

I looked down at my right palm, and the small tendril of sage light that convulsed there. "Could you do it? Deliver that killing blow?"

He was silent for a moment and held me closer. "I would. Tradition dictates Augie should be the one to end Jaryn, even if he doesn't want the crown, but if no one else was able, then yes, my love, I'd drive my sword through his chest and not lose sleep over it."

"If anything, Amadea should have the honor."

Stubble grazing my cheek, he murmured, "Yes, she should."

Augustine threw the reins over the head of his light gray Pegasus mare and led her over to us. Letting me go, Silvano and I stepped closer, and the prince looked between us, like he could see the invisible threads that bound my soul to my husband's. Then he looked down at the thin strand of light that wove around our boots. Behind him, his unit mounted and waited quietly, the Pegasi tossing their heads and arching their wings in preparation to take flight.

"I don't believe in the spirits, but I know there is something I can't explain at work here," said Augustine. The low sun illuminated the side of his tanned face, sparking the flecks of gold in his olive-colored eyes.

"What gave it away? The stoat?"

Augustine's lips quirked into a hint of a smile at me, and even I could appreciate how regal he looked. Then his gaze slid to Silvano standing at my side.

"You taught me everything I know. I trust you, Silvano, don't make me regret it."

"Jaryn will fall, Augie. It's up to you whether you want to be a part of that, in changing history."

The prince straightened, nodding at his former Commander. The pair clasped forearms, then Augustine turned to me. I looked up and took in the calculating gaze on his face. Ice clicked along my bones, but I was unable to get a read on him, for better or for worse, like his true soul was a well-guarded secret that he never let anyone see.

"I look forward to seeing you again, light wielder. We all knew that whoever our Commander married, would have to be spectacular indeed." He reached forward and gently gripped my hand with his, placing a kiss to my knuckles.

"Did Silvano teach you that too?" I quipped, unable to keep the surprise from my voice.

Augustine chuckled. Letting my hand go, he stepped back. "A man has to have his secrets, Destry."

"Of course, he learned it from me." Silvano looked down at me with a wicked grin.

My expression wary, I threw Augustine a smile in return. "Safe travels."

"I'll send word when Farrow makes his decision." Turning on his heel, Augustine strode away and mounted up. In quick succession, the unit took to the skies, and we watched them fly until they were five dark forms on the southern horizon.

Twilight descended around us. Stars began to glow faintly in the deep lavender sky, and I tilted my head back and breathed in deeply.

Wrapping an arm around my waist, Silvano tucked me into his side and followed my gaze. Tomorrow, we would head back to the keep, and I wanted to luxuriate in these last few hours of what felt like freedom.

The cold nip of the air made me feel alive, the half-frozen air in my lungs setting fire to my blood in a heady touch. I tilted my head, resting it on Silvano's shoulder, and despite our surprise visitors today, contentment seeped warm tendrils over my skin. Ice clicked in my head, and I let it be. It had been terrifying, using it on the torc today, with how close to death I had felt the last time I had wielded it. But tonight, it slumbered quietly alongside my light. The two powers in my body shifted alongside one another, twining, the potential for them to be lethal was a faint purr along my bones.

Silvano squeezed my waist gently. "Let's get you inside."

"Are your toes getting cold?" I smiled.

"That, and we have an entire day of our honeymoon to make up for."

Heat coursed up my chest and neck at the dark, whispered promise in his voice. I turned to face him, our bodies pressed together, and gripped the lapels of his riding coat. With a hand at the small of my back, Silvano pushed closer, his already hard cock grinding against me. His other hand cupped the nape of my neck, and he hauled my mouth to his.

"I don't think a lifetime is long enough for all the plans I have for you, Destry."

I huffed a laugh. "You'll still want me even when I'm wrinkled and gray?"

His gaze was soft as he looked down at me and whispered, "I'll never stop wanting you, wild one."

CHAPTER FORTY

SILVANO

I wanted her to know just how much she meant to me, but words alone weren't enough. So I would worship her body with my own. As if each day was my last, she would know exactly what her mind and her body did to me. This woman, my *wife*, was my salvation, and I would treasure every moment spent in her presence.

I knew some of the horrors she had survived, and I would do everything within my power to help her heal. Yet I didn't want to fix her or change who she was, because she was perfect. But if she wanted to become undone in order to reforge herself, if she wanted to surrender to the fire in my veins, then I'd show her what it felt like to be loved and revered. She was the only kind of altar I would kneel to.

Last night, she had placed her complete trust in me and had let me lead the way, letting herself enjoy the freedom and wild abandon I could give her. Tonight, however, I wanted to let her take that control back for herself.

With darkness cloaking the cabin, Tyvare tucked into a tight ball atop two romance novels. The wood stove crackled faintly. I sat down on the bed and pulled Destry down with me. We had rushed through dinner, then had taken our time washing each other, hands and mouths roaming tantalizingly slowly. With our bodies bare, Destry swung a leg over my thighs, kneeling on the bed to sit on my lap.

Her hands clasped together against the back of my neck, and I gripped the top of her bare thighs, steadying her. Anticipation pulsed between us. I was so fucking hard for her already, but not yet, *not yet*.

I searched her flushed face, her brown eyes dark with desire. "What is it you want, wild one?"

Destry rolled her hips, and she was already soaking wet as she moved against my cock. My hips jerked, jaw clenching in an effort not to pin her to the bed and fuck her until she couldn't remember her own name.

"You," she murmured, leaning forward to kiss my neck.

"Use your words, my love, what is it you want?"

She rubbed against me again, but I fought to hold still.

"I want to ride you, Silvano."

"Then go ahead. I'm all yours." I nuzzled her neck, inhaling her addictive scent. "It's your turn to claim me."

"I've not been in this position before, I—"

"Just move with what feels good for you, because no matter what you do, it's going to feel amazing for me." I reached up and gently gripped her left hand, then I guided her down and moaned as she wrapped her hand around my cock.

She rose on her knees, and my left hand shifted to her lower back, keeping her close while she positioned herself above me. The tip brushed against her, and my chest tightened with how soaked she was. A low, throaty moan escaped her mouth as she slowly sank onto me. My hand tightened on her hip as she took the full length of my cock.

Both of us panting hard, Destry stilled, letting her body adjust to this new, deeper sensation. Unable to help myself, I leaned forward and took one of her nipples into my mouth. She arched into me, her right hand pulling my hair tight as I sucked lightly. Her spine curved, and she tilted my head back and away from her breast so she could claim my mouth.

Tongues dancing, Destry began to move. Holy *fuck*. I craved her and the slow, sensuous movements of her hips. I captured her whimpers with my mouth, content to devour them as she rocked up and down on my throbbing cock.

She was a storm cloud before the lightning struck, an untamable force that I desperately wanted to unleash. I wanted to bite her neck and shoulder in an instinctual, primitive way, so that the world understood that she was mine. Burying her head into my neck, Destry's cries grew louder, her body riding me with deeper, faster strokes.

"You're doing so fucking well, Destry," I said roughly. "You feel incredible."

It was a near-religious experience, watching her take me at her own pace. I could sense her slowly surrendering to what her body craved. Her whimpers grew more desperate, and I moved my hands to run them up and down her spine. She was trembling, breathless, and she was mine, our bodies moving against one another in a language all our own.

I kissed her shoulder, my right hand rising to fist in her loose, dark hair.

"Silvano," she breathed.

"Keep going, you can take it. I want to see you come like this."

Her hands clenched tighter in my hair, and damn me, I couldn't hold back any longer. I rolled my hips against hers, and her desperate cry filled the cabin.

"Right there, huh?" I said, my teeth grazing her ear.

"*Yes.*"

I held her close, and she kept the pace, meeting my upward thrusts. I could feel her getting tighter around me, her release slowly building.

Holy spirits, this woman, I would be content if we never left this cabin. Nothing else mattered, only this very moment, her warm body taking me perfectly. Faint green light circled around her head like an ethereal crown.

"I'm ... Silvano, I—" she gasped.

Wrapping my arms around her, she slumped against my torso as her climax rolled over her. I continued to move, wringing every ounce of pleasure from her release as I could.

"Fuck, Destry," I groaned against her shoulder. My cock twitched with need while she pulsed around it. "Are you okay?"

Arms draped over my shoulders, she nodded against my neck, and said faintly, "Give me a minute."

I released a low laugh and traced a hand down her spine. "Take all the time you need, my love."

"I am beyond any form of coherence right now," she whispered.

"Do you want to stop?"

"Spirits, no."

"Then I'll take it from here."

CHAPTER
FORTY-ONE

ASHER

Feet strapped to our skis, Calliope and I steadily traversed over the snow, the trees around us slowly becoming sparser and smaller. The cold had officially sunk beneath my skin, pressing a constant ache along the broad width of my shoulders and chest. What I wouldn't do for a warm, comfortable room and bed, with Calliope tucked into my side like she had been yesterday.

She skied beside me, her face grim with concentration for every step she took. My shadows flanked us like a pack of loyal outriders, sifting through the night and weaving amongst the trees. In the distance, an owl screeched, and Calliope lifted her head to the sound, a faint smile on her lips.

"Friend of yours?" I asked.

"They all are, the owls I mean."

"Can you understand them?"

She nodded, halting to tuck loose strands of hair behind her ears. "They're the only animal I can communicate with, naturally."

"That's amazing."

A faint blush spread over her cheeks. "It's the same with you and the Nijinxes, though, right?"

"Yeah. Pherox and I ... we're like brothers. As strange as that sounds."

She walked over to me, her gaze soft. "I don't think that's strange. I consider the other owls my wing sisters and brothers too. They're like ... family."

The smile I gave her was genuine, and it was like a small weight on my chest was lifted a fraction. "That's exactly what it feels like."

I gazed at her, my shadows curling inward to brush against her face. She closed her eyes and sighed, content to let them caress her.

"It feels so right when your shadows touch me," she breathed. "It feels—"

A dark, archaic roar filled with warning slammed into my body, but it was too late, as an arrow slammed into my right bicep a heartbeat later.

"*Asher!*"

I made to move toward her, shadows leaping away from me to viscerate the threat, then a second arrow buried itself into my right thigh. I half collapsed to the snow, snarling in pain. *Men, trees, weapons, horses,* my shadows stuttered.

Calliope stripped off her skis and dove for me, then she looked to her left, bared her teeth and hissed. My shadows pulled in close, veiling us, but they trembled, no longer moving in cohesion to my thoughts as excruciating pain hammered through my body.

"They—I can't, they're changing their minds too quickly," Callie half sobbed, as she wrapped her arms under mine and heaved, her body trembled with the effort, but I barely moved an inch. I was too heavy.

Pain threatened to blind me, but I knew better than to yank out the arrows. Sucking air through my gritted teeth, my gaze snapped to hers. "You need to shift, Callie. Get out of here."

"I'm not leaving you."

"You have to shift, Callie, right fucking now. They took me out first, knowing I'd go down trying to protect you. They're not here for me."

"Oh, I wouldn't be too sure about that." A calm, deep voice sounded from beyond my fracturing shadows.

Calliope went wholly still beside me, the gold in her eyes taking on a cold, predatory edge. She angled her head toward the voice and rose to her full height. Taking a small half-step in front of me, she whispered, "Call back your shadows, Asher."

I could barely form the command, but I didn't need to, my shadows compiled instantly to her voice, and they lowered to the snow like a dark curtain. Then they weaved back to me, spooling into my body, helping me hold myself together as I took in the ten horsemen across from us.

I had been so fucking distracted with Calliope that I hadn't detected them until it was too late. From his saddle, Aron smirked down at us. Calliope hissed again, her fingers curling into claws at her sides. There was a flash of brilliant golden light, and I shielded my eyes as the glow faded.

The woman I had fallen for was gone. No, she was still there, but transformed, ascended. Gold-tipped wings outstretched, feathers piercing the meek light of the dawn that struck through the forest, Calliope turned to look over her shoulder to face me. Her eyes were a molten, gilded fire that burned with an intensity that held me transfixed.

If magic had a form, it was her.

Her yellow beak parted, a faint, low cry sounding in her chest, then she turned back to face the soldiers, and her cry turned into an ear-splitting, enraged shriek.

"Thought you could have her all to yourself, huntsman? Thought you could slaughter Ilrairian soldiers and disappear?" said Aron.

Calliope hissed again, her wings shifting to keep me shielded from view. Panting through the pain, I looked down at the blood darkening my trousers, watching it seep into the snow beneath my injured leg.

Aron's horse stepped forward then halted again. "We found them, the skin was black where you had slit their throats." He cocked his head, peering over Callie's wing to fix me with another smirk. "You broke your bargain with me, huntsman, now I have no qualms in taking the pair of you to my King."

"Over my dead fucking body," I snarled.

The Colladonian shook his head. "As much as it would satisfy me to put my sword through your chest, my King has requested we take you alive."

The fierce snap of Calliope's beak closing echoed over the trees, and Aron's gaze snapped to hers.

"And as for *you*—" he started, his voice filled with loathing.

Using the last of my strength, I raised my left arm and slammed my fist into the snow. Shadows erupted from me, vortexing and whipping around Calliope and I in a tornado of darkness that tugged at her feathers and nearly tore the arrows from my skin. Calliope's cry was wrenched away, and she laid a wing over me, my shadows climbing higher and higher, cresting over the treetops to pierce the dawn sky. Some would mistake it for smoke, but to someone, with magic akin to my own, I hoped they saw it for what it was.

A distress signal. A ragged, desperate plea.

A third arrow was fired into the darkness, grazing the side of my face just below my eye, to skid into the snow behind me. My shadows trembled, and I roared, shoving everything I had behind my power.

Soldiers ran for us. Calliope pummeled her wings, gaining just enough height to rake her talons across the sternum of the soldier who neared us first.

Releasing the dagger from my hip, I staggered to my feet, my weight braced on my good leg. Ducking Callie's wing, I stepped around her owl form, fury like I had never felt before coursing through my body with every tortured beat of my heart.

Aron was shouting, hurling orders at his men as they attacked. I did not falter, my dagger striking deep and true.

CHAPTER FORTY-TWO

DESTRY

I slammed open the front door, Ebrel and Hestian's shrill whinnies washing over me as the freezing cold of daybreak slammed into my chest. Silvano was a step behind me, as we ran from the *tallora* and skidded to a halt beside our Pegasi, turning our heads to where they kept looking out over the glens. The western lands still clung onto a shred of night, but there, at the edge of the horizon, darkness plumed into the sky, whirling violently in on itself. It ebbed and flowed, slowly growing smaller ... weaker.

"That isn't smoke." Silvano strapped his swords to his waist, and I followed suit.

"Shadows," I uttered.

"There's only one man I know that has that kind of power, I fought beside him at Aarine. He helped free Orrin, Ebrel, and Olwen."

"Asher?" Ebrel cantered over to me, nosing my hand, my arm, my shoulder. Hestian did the same to Silvano, low, urgent whickers in his throat. "The huntsman who tried to shoot me at Saltfen?"

"The very one and same." Silvano pinned me with a wary look. "We have no idea what we'll be flying into."

"He's in trouble," I said, turning back to look at the plume of dark magic steadily receding on the horizon. "It's like the flare I sent up at Erskine."

Silvano's hand cupped my cheek. "And thank the spirits that you did."

Gripping Ebrel's mane, I heaved myself onto her back, her wings settling on either side of my thighs. "Are you sure you're up for this? Your wing?"

The mare tossed her head, pawing at the snow in eagerness to take flight. Hestian called out to Silvano, who ran back to the stables. A moment later, Kirrtu and Fern cantered out into the snow, tossing their heads, then the pair of them turned, heading northwest back toward Niemi's keep.

Taking a running sprint, Silvano jumped onto Hestian's back, curling his hands into the stallion's dusty mane. "Asher might be wounded, in which case we need to fly straight back to the keep. The mares can find their way home."

I peeked open my jacket pocket to see two black button eyes staring up at me. "Hold on, little one, this might get a bit bumpy."

Tyvare squeaked and burrowed deeper into my pocket, curling into a tight ball. Silvano rode up alongside me and gripped my hand. I looked up to meet his gaze, my heart squeezing just to look at him, the words I wanted to say sticking in my throat. Later, when we had time, I would say them later.

"Together," he said softly. "We do this together."

I squeezed his fingers, light and ice magic rumbling awake in my body. "Together."

CHAPTER
FORTY-THREE

CALLIOPE

B efore, pain would have been dull. Before, I would have flown away and left a man to die. Before, I would have not used my talons to shred a soldier apart.

Yet now, with the sight of Asher on his knees in the snow, blood dripping from him, arrows protruding from his body, it felt like my heart was slowly being torn from my chest. I was stronger, more deadly, in my owl form, but I desperately wanted to shift back, so I could wrap my arms around him and tell him we were going to be okay, that everything was going to be okay. Even if those words were lies.

We were not okay. Not even close.

My shoulder would not hold out much longer, having not been granted the day or more healing it needed to fully recover. Throbbing pain ripped over my back with every wingbeat. Six men remained now and four of them had arrows trained on us. After I had eviscerated two, and Asher had gutted another pair, Aron had pulled back the rest of his unit and waited.

"You know he needs a medic, Calliope," snapped Aron. "Come with us willingly, and we can heal him."

Walking jarringly on my taloned feet, I hovered over Asher, my head hunkered low as I gently wrapped my talons over his uninjured leg. He slumped against my thigh, his shadows turning from midnight black to weary gray.

"Don't even fucking think about it," snapped the head archer, his hands primed to drawback the string of his longbow. "Don't you fucking dare."

My screech echoed over them, and I dipped lower, preparing my body for one last final test. I'd get us out of here. I had to.

"Callie," Asher groaned weakly.

I trilled in response, my gaze never leaving the soldiers. Could I clear the trees before they fired?

"*Don't*," growled Aron as he finally drew his sword.

As carefully as I could, I snared the back of Asher's coat. I could do this, I could get us away from here, I just had to—

Pain seared through my extended right wing, an arrow slicing through tendons and sinew. The haunting screech of my owl turned into a ravaged scream as I shifted back to my human form. I clung to Asher, my left arm clutching his back while I tried and failed to comprehend the arrow that was stuck in my forearm.

Aron stalked forward. "You didn't have to make us do that, this could have all been far easier. If you hadn't fought, then your lover may not bleed out before he can get help."

Asher lifted his head, a viscous, inhuman snarl ripping from his throat. "Touch her, and I will kill you."

"You're in no position to be making threats, huntsman." Aron struck and slammed the pommel of his sword against the side of Asher's head.

I screamed again, as Asher slumped unconscious to the snow. Curling my body over his, I glared up at Aron, who smiled faintly down at me.

"Did you really think you would ever be free? Did your stupid bird brain believe for one moment that the pair of you would live happily ever after?"

"I will fight you with every fiber of my being," I gritted out. "*We* will fight."

Aron tutted and sheathed his sword. "Oh, Calliope, I'm going to enjoy every min—"

I threw my head back at the huge dark forms that slammed down between the trees and skidded to a halt on the snow beside us. Before Aron could yell a command, a tall, dark-haired woman threw a leg over the neck of her Pegasus and ran for us.

An arrow fired, and she dropped, sliding effortlessly on her feet. As soon as her fist connected with the deep snow, ice erupted. Men screamed, their horses whinnied and bolted at the arctic magic spearing from under the snow like a multi-headed leviathan lunging from the deep. Rising slowly, her proud face calm and collected, she scanned the scene in a heartbeat with piercing dark eyes.

Her gaze locked onto me, assessing how I cradled Asher against my body, the arrows lodged in the pair of us. Understanding rippled over her wise face. A beautiful, golden-haired man stepped up beside her, a sword in each hand, and they both looked at Aron with a glare that promised death. Their Pegasi stepped up behind them, their huge wingspans blocking any escape.

"If any of you," said the woman sharply to the soldiers, her steady voice laced with violence, "try to move an inch, I will gut you where you stand."

I blinked, pain making the edges of my vision blurry, and I stiffly turned my neck to look at Aron, unable to figure out why they weren't attacking the strangers. Thick ice held them firmly in place, enameling their bodies to just below their collarbones, allowing their chests just enough space to suck down sips of air.

"You have no business here, light wielder," spat Aron.

Her eyes narrowed. "Oh, I think we disagree on that." She stalked forward, and the lambent stone embedded in the hilt of her sheathed sword glimmered faintly. Wisps of pale green light curled in her wake as she moved, so similar to Asher's shadows.

The golden-haired man kept a step back, content to let her take the lead with the soldiers. He shifted, keeping a wary eye on Aron, he moved toward Asher and me. His dark green gaze met mine, and my power suddenly thrummed in my blood. *Silvano.*

The Night Pegasus and his scion.

"They're our prisoners," said Aron quickly as he strained against the ice that held him.

"And why is that?" snarled Destry, her left hand resting on the pommel of her sword.

"For crimes against the crown."

In one sinuous motion, Destry drew her blade, and the steel glowed a faint blue in the low light. I gripped Asher's gasping body tightly, hardly believing what I was seeing. It was like a song calling to my very blood and bone. Truth magic lay in Destry's sword.

Destry stared Aron down, her lips pulled back over her teeth. "*Liar.*"

Silvano dropped to his knees by my side, quickly assessing my wound, then Asher's.

"You came for us," I croaked.

The smile he threw at me was warm, tender. He didn't appear worried at all for the woman behind him, who looked like she was going to tear into Aron with her bare hands.

"We saw Asher's shadows," he said softly, as if that was all the explanation I needed, but it just left me with more questions.

"They're coming with us," said Destry, her face mere inches away from Aron's.

"A Petish woman and an Ilrairian?" Aron spat on the ground. "Fucking disgrace, I should—"

Destry's left fist snapped upward, striking so hard, Aron's head cracked to the side. Blood sprayed as his nose shattered. Shaking out her hand, Destry turned to face the other soldiers, who gaped at their unconscious Commander.

"They're coming with us," Destry repeated again. Turning her back to them, she called over her shoulder, "The ice will melt in a little while."

Sheathing her sword, Destry knelt beside Silvano, her features instantly warming as she appraised me, then the man in my arms.

"We need to stop the bleeding," said Silvano. "They fucking peppered him, enough to keep him down but not kill him instantly."

Rage flitted over Destry's face, but then she was moving, her fingertips reaching forward to brace against the muscle of Asher's thigh.

Asher groaned, his eyelids flickering as he drifted in and out of consciousness. "Don't ... hurt ... her."

I couldn't stop the tears from falling then, and I leaned him back against me with my good arm. His head rested against my chest, his breath coming in shallow sips.

"*Callie*," he murmured.

"I'm here, Asher, I'm here," I pleaded into his hair. "Hold on for me."

Destry's fingers dug into Asher's leg, ice coating her nails in an intricate web, then it filtered down through his blood-soaked clothing.

"This should be enough to slow the blood down, but we need to get him back to the keep as soon as possible."

"Do ... not ... trap ... her," Asher panted.

Silvano leaned forward and gripped Asher's face between his gloved palms in a firm grip. "I swear it, huntsman. Neither of you will come to any harm."

Asher swallowed harshly, a broken curse on his tongue as Destry carefully manipulated his shoulder to plunge her ice deep into the muscle. Then she turned on her knees and gently took my hand in hers. I stared at her, she was around my age, and an aura of wild energy clung to her body.

Light wreathed her fingertips, and it curled around my wrist in a comforting caress. "May I?" she whispered, eyeing the arrow in my forearm warily.

I gave a sharp nod. "Do it."

"I'm sorry." Cold like I had never felt plunged into my skin around the wound. Ice so cold, it burned for several heartbeats, then receded, leaving a hollow numbness in its wake.

"Can I take Asher now, sweetheart?" asked Silvano, his vivid gaze holding mine. "He's going to fly with me, you'll fly with Destry. We're going to a keep owned by the local warlord, but we swear as soon as you're both healed, you can leave. Do you understand? You will walk into that keep and walk back out again with Asher at your side, but we need to hurry."

I nodded again, words beyond me, and Silvano reached forward and picked Asher up, carefully placing him over a broad shoulder so as not to disturb the arrows protruding from him. His beautiful golden Pegasus cantered up to us, breath billowing in the air, and knelt on a foreleg in the snow, allowing Silvano to drape Asher over his back.

Destry looped an arm under mine and hauled me to my feet. The roan Pegasus mare nudged her rider's back and knelt, wings stretching along the snow in an elegant sweep. She appeared as wild as Destry, her long mane knotted and windblown. Large brown eyes tracked me as Destry half dragged me to the large beast's side. I gazed at the mare, one winged creature recognizing another, and the Pegasus relaxed, a low whicker in her throat that seemed to say, *hello, wing sister.*

Tucking me carefully in front of her, Destry banded her iron-strong arms around my sides to grip the mare's mane. Together, the Pegasi took to the air, snow clouding in their wake, drowning out the shivering cries of the soldiers now far below us.

To the east, the sun broke free of the horizon, a dawn sky rising over the snow-capped land. The Pegasi raced through the frozen air, their riders urging them on with pleas whipped away by the wind. My gaze remained pinned on Asher as I prayed and prayed and prayed.

Stay with me. Please, please, stay with me.

THE TRINITOR CHRONICLES: INDEX

Elemental Spirits

Darkness: **Iltavorn.** Mortal scions can wield shadows, Nijinxes are also his scions.

Fire: **Tavaris.** Mortals can wield truth magic with his power. No current bloodline has this gift.

Water: **Merevis.** Scions are Orca.

Land: **Perama**

Forest: **Tellervo.** (Son of Perama). Scions are Mountain Horses.

Ice: **Varranar.** (Son of Merevis) Mortals can wield truth magic with his power. Truth Keepers and one female bloodline currently have this gift.

Air: **Ilmari.** Scions are Pegasi.

Night: **Vorna.** (Son of Iltavorn)

Day: **Vayla.** (Daughter of Tavaris)

Northern Lights: **Night Pegasus.** *Fire Prince/Wings of Fire* (Son of Tavaris). Only one female bloodline currently acts as his scion and they can wield his light.

Southern Lights: **Corapesi.** *Painter of Light*, (Daughter of Tavaris)

Mountain Spirits

Serebo: Scions are Unicorns. Her peak is protected by varki deer, ibex, and snow sirens.

Ghel: Serebo's younger sister.

Bronzo: Serebo's younger sister.

Nychta: Not yet discovered by mortals.

Eira: Nychta's younger sister (Consort to the Night Pegasus, when she flies with him, her form is that of a falling star.)

Sister Moons

Amarhi: The Moon

Aurin: The Sun (Claimed by Tavaris)

Ullko: The North Star

Earth

Creatures

- Nokken - Found in Colladonian lakes and streams. Eel-like body and equine shaped head. Opportunistic hunter.

- Truth Keepers - Human women blessed by the ice spirit, Varranar. Gifted with the power to shapeshift into a very large owl. They can answer any question truthfully. Incredibly rare. Their owl form features snowy white feathers, gold eyes and gold tipped wings.

- Mountain Horses - aka 'Mounties', scions of Tellervo, the forest spirit. Chocolate brown pelts with blond manes and tails. They are significantly faster than an average horse. Known to reside in Glentay Forest. They are a faction of the Trinitor curse.

- Nijinx - Scions of Iltavorn, the spirit of darkness. Visually an equine with black bat wings, silver fangs and clawed feet.

They have no eyes and they speak/see via echolocation. They are a faction of the Trinitor curse.

- Pegasi - Scions or Ilmari, the air spirit. A faction of the Trinitor curse, southern Pegasi are more refined and willing towards humans, whereas northern Pegasi are rugged and utterly wild. They are an equine with the gift of flight, with large feathered wings.

- Unicorns - Scions and protectors of Serebo, the mountain spirit. They are a faction of the Trinitor curse. Their magic, cast from the horn atop their head, does not grow as they age. Can live extended lifespans of a hundred years or more.

- Lake Horses - A draft breed of horse indigenous to the glens and forests of Petowin and western Colladon. Typically black or dark brown in colour.

- Wild Ward - A type of witch that uses the power of nature to fuel their magic practices. Descended from royal mages, they distort the balance of the wild in their attempt to control it. Brindle stone, in the form of shards or stone circles, heighten their power even further.

Characters: Human
Petish

- Destry Kivisto *Koskivarri* - Scion to the Night Pegasus. Last of her bloodline. Eira is her true name.

- Ariadne Kivisto (nee Rovesi) - Destry's birth mother. (dec.)

Killed by Nijinx's.

- Rekorious Niemi - Warlord and leader of the Niemi clan. Former Commander of the Royant Platoon, Ilrairian Aerial Cavalary under the alias "Aalto Thorra."

- Heara Marte Thorra/Niemi - Mother to Rekorious

- Meredith - Wild ward (dec.)

- Minna Turunin - Commander in Niemi's land cavalry.

- Salo - Minna's second in command.

- Hearan Lael - Councilman, former warrior.

- Heara Helmi - Councilwoman.

- Koski - Councilman, former warrior.

- Virtanen - Sergeant in the land cavalry.

- Grier - Niemi's ghost spy.

- Arnar - Niemi's eldest cousin. Unit leader in Niemi's aerial cavalry.

- Elias - Niemi's youngest cousin, younger brother to Arnar. Wisp spy in Arnar's unit.

- Sade - Maid within the Niemi keep.

Colladonian

- Oban Fields - Asher's father. Pegasus hunter (dec.) Killed by Pegasi.

- Edgar Fields - Pegasus hunter, younger brother to Oban (dec.) Killed by Pegasi.

- Lonan Donaghue - Sword for hire, previously a guard for the Heir Lord of Moray.

- Lord of Moray

- Narve - Heir Lord of Moray, once betrothed to Destry.

- Wylmar - Narve's personal medic, specialising in poisons.

- Elmar Hild - Blacksmith and sword master, works for Niemi.

- Aron Isark - Commander of the Colladon King's Guard.

- Calliope Hallador - Truth Keeper.

Ilrairian

- Damara Orcatain - Duchess of Aarine. Destry's adopted mother. (dec.) Killed by Wylmar.

- King Jaryn Adacus - Ruler of Ilrair. Married to Amadea.

- Silvano Coen - Bromtide Platoon Commander in the Ilrair aerial cavalry.

- Taneli Farrow - Bromtide Platoon sergeant. Spies for Niemi.

- Kramer - Bromtide Platoon flight medic.

- Ademar Augustine - Prince of Ilrair. Jaryn's only nephew. Adonitus Unit Commander, Bromtide Platoon.

- Monroe Martelli - Adonitus Unit animal medic, Bromtide Platoon

- Dionne Pendrosa - Adonitus Unit, Bromtide Platoon

- Leo Beretta - Adonitus Unit tracker, Bromtide Platoon

- Artorius Caulderon - Adonitus Unit, Bromtide Platoon

- Tamara Ludovici - Bromtide Platoon messenger.

- Halle - Commander of Knock Platoon.

Aarinian

- Cormac - Duke of Aarine. Destry's adopted father. Presumed dead after the Aarine fire siege.

Omivarrian

- Amadea Machimaja - Queen of Ilrair. Water wielder.

Characters: Animals

Pegasi

- Ebrel - Strawberry roan mare. Branded as a wild loner by the wild ward. Former mate to Fintan. Destry is her rider.

- Hestian - Palomino stallion. Cavalry mount. Silvano Coen is his rider.

- Kalana - Dapple gray mare. Cavalry mount. Rekorious Niemi is her rider.

- Spearian - Dapple gray stallion. Wild. Band leader (dec.) Killed by Carter.

- Hex - Light gray mare. Wild. Spearian's lead mare.

- Carter - Black stallion. Wild. Orrin's half-brother. Son of Nessa.

- Murrkill - Blood bay mare. Wild. Carter's lead mare.

- Nessa - Light bay mare. Wild. Gracien's mate. (dec.) Killed by Spearian.

- Nimbus - Dark gray stallion. Cavalry mount. Tamara Ludocvici is his rider.

Unicorns

- Olwen - Light gray, almost white, mare. Blue eyes.

- Eirlys - Silver gray mare. Silver eyes. Olwen's mother.

Mountain Horses

- Gracien - Silver bay stallion. Former King of the Forest. (dec.) Killed by Asher.

- Fintan - Silver bay stallion. Gracien's eldest son. Ebrel's former mate. (dec.) Killed by Spearian.

- Orrin - Silver bay stallion. King of the Forest. Gracien and Nessa's youngest son.

Nijinxes

- Vesperum - Black female. Queen of her kin swarm.

- Pherox. Black male. Vesperum's mate.

Horses

- Fern - Black Lake Horse mare.

- Kerrti - Black Lake Horse mare.

Other:

- Tyvare - Stoat. Messenger between the mortal and spirit world.

Petish Translation Guide

- *Kathkar* - Soul Keeper. Destry's sword. Imbued with truth magic by Varranar, the ice spirit.

- *Koskivarri* - Light Wielder

- *Crevatarn* - King

- *Vorna and Vayla* - Night and Day. (Niemi's swords but also spirits in their own right.)

- *Tyvare* - Little Thief

- *Morean* - Bride Trial

- *Tallora* - Cabin. Conical in shape.

- *Tarva* - Morning.

PLAYLIST

Sanctuary by PRAANA, Ed Graves

Inner Solitude by PRAANA

You & Me - Rivo Remix by Disclosure, Eliza Doolittle, Rivo

Release by Keith Merrill

Hrimfaxi – Extended by Kalandra

I'll be Around – Chill Mix by Elderbrook, Amtrac

The Singing Ice of Storsjon by Jonna Jinton

I'll Wait For You by Harry Gresgon-Williams

Acknowledgments

It's always a magical feeling to step back into the world of the Boreals, but after Night Sky Burning was released and I discovered I was pregnant with our youngest daughter, it felt like all my creativity had gone thanks to horrendous morning sickness and tiredness. Thankfully, after our little B was born, the writer's block vanished and the story of Dawn Sky Rising demanded to be told.

None of it would have been possible without my incredible husband, Rob, who has supported me through everything. DSR was a sanctuary in the postpartum haze, and Rob held the gates open for me.

A massive thank you to my alpha reader, RG Hurley, who was incredible to work with. Your unhinged comments in my Google doc always brightened my day. To my brilliant beta team; Jade, Justine, Dani, Bambi, Melissa and Brianna, your feedback was instrumental in making DSR what it is today.

To my wonderful editor, Melissa Smith, who worked her magic once again and to David Gardias, who brought my paperback cover dreams to reality, just like he did with NSB.

A special mention to Emiliya, whose stunning artwork graces the hardback special edition again. It is a joy to see these pieces of art brought to life.

To my mum, who has never stopped believing in me. I love you so much.

And finally, to my girls. I'll always be there to protect that little spark that makes you both shine.

About the Author

Hayley is a Western Australia based indie author with a passion for horses. An experienced veterinary nurse, Hayley focuses on writing fantasy and romance. She lives in a little country town with her husband, two young daughters, a cheeky Labrador and probably to many chickens. She loves to curl up with a strong cup of tea and a good book. Some of her favourite authors include Ali Hazelwood, Sarah J Maas, A L Rojo and Claire Butler.

If you loved this book, please consider leaving a review on Amazon or Goodreads. Reviews are incredibly important, especially to us indie authors, and we appreciate them so much. Thank you!

If you wish to connect, you can find me on IG and Threads @h.a.walkerwrites